A LITERARY LIAISON

The Daring Damsels
Book 2

Mihwa Lee

Dragonblade Publishing, Inc. is an imprint of Kathryn Le Veque Novels, Inc.
P.O. Box 23
Moreno Valley, CA 92556
ceo@dragonbladepublishing.com

Produced in the United States of America

First Edition November 2025
Trade Paperback Edition

ARE YOU SIGNED UP FOR DRAGONBLADE'S BLOG?

You'll get the latest news and information on exclusive giveaways, exclusive excerpts, coming releases, sales, free books, cover reveals and more.

Check out our complete list of authors, too!

No spam, no junk. That's a promise!

Sign Up Here

www.dragonbladepublishing.com

Dearest Reader;

Thank you for your support of a small press. At Dragonblade Publishing, we strive to bring you the highest quality Historical Romance from some of the best authors in the business. Without your support, there is no 'us', so we sincerely hope you adore these stories and find some new favorite authors along the way.

Happy Reading!

CEO, Dragonblade Publishing

**Additional Dragonblade books by
Author Mihwa Lee**

The Daring Damsels
Touched by a Traitor (Book 1)
A Literary Liaison (Book 2)

THE REVIEW

Metropolitan Review, *8 January 1840*
A Review of Whispers of the Heart *by Aengus Steele*

Dear Esteemed Reader,

In the course of one's earthly life, it is a rare privilege to encounter a literary work of such profound magnificence that it transcends the mere arrangement of words on a page. Such a work, through some indefinable transformation, may reach into the very depths of one's being, soothing the small child within with whispered consolations and gentle caresses of the soul. Rarer still is the opus that, through its seemingly unpretentious narrative, renders even life's darkest moments resplendent with an unexpected beauty.

Whispers of the Heart, *penned by one Aengus Steele, is utterly devoid of such qualities.*

E. Lovelace

Edgar Marshal Albury, the Duke of Lancaster, squinted at the broadsheet with his bloodshot eyes, which had been rendered thus by the arduous labor of excavating a subterranean passage from his wine cellar to the outhouse.

He read the review again, his jaw tightening with each word until a muscle twitched beneath his skin. The chair toppled backward as he shot to his feet, fury driving him to pace his study.

"The sheer audacity!" The empty room absorbed his thunderous voice. "Who is this E. Lovelace to dismiss months of labor with such… such casual cruelty?" The broadsheet crumpled in his grip, edges cutting into his palm. "A single paragraph to deliver her barb. At least have the courage to critique the work properly, you cowardly scribbler!"

His desk drawer rattled as he yanked it open with savage force, the inkwell jumping. "So you wish to engage in literary warfare, do you?" His voice dropped to a dangerous purr as he extracted fresh parchment. "Very well, let us cross quills, you pompous, self-important hack."

The pen dipped into the ink with savage satisfaction, droplets spattering across the pristine page. A predatory smile curved his lips as he began his letter to Miss Lovelace. Each word was carefully chosen, dripping with honeyed venom.

My Most Esteemed Miss Lovelace,

Your recent critique of my humble offering has prompted me to express my deepest admiration…

Edgar set down his pen and savored each poisoned compliment. The final paragraph was particularly satisfying—let the mysterious critic try to wriggle out of that challenge without revealing herself as either a fraud or a hypocrite.

His rage demanded immediate action. Without hesitation, he folded the letter with deliberate care and sealed it with red wax. He'd be damned if he'd let some pompous scribbler's condescension go unanswered.

"Anderson!" The secretary appeared within moments.

"Your Grace?"

"See that this is delivered to the *Metropolitan Review* offices immediately." Edgar thrust the letter forward with grim satisfaction. "And ensure they understand it requires urgent attention."

"Of course, Your Grace."

As Anderson departed with his literary ammunition, the fury began to ebb, leaving behind a restless energy that clawed at

Edgar's chest. He needed air, movement, distraction from the taste of wounded pride that lingered in his mouth.

Hatchard's would clear his head. He needed books anyway—something to occupy his mind now that he'd fired his opening salvo in this literary war.

THE BELL ABOVE Hatchard's Book Shop tinkled softly as Edgar entered, leather and paper scenting the air around him. Morning sun slanted through tall windows, catching dust motes that danced between towering shelves. The satisfaction of having dispatched his letter had cooled during the walk, leaving a vague unease about his impulsive action.

No matter. What was done was done, and E. Lovelace richly deserved whatever discomfort his missive might cause.

Poetry would restore his equilibrium. Byron, perhaps. But as Edgar made his way toward that section, a woman reaching for the *Metropolitan Review* shelf caught his attention. Something about her purposeful movements—she moved like someone with a mission rather than a casual browser.

"Pardon me," he murmured, stepping closer without moving aside. Curiosity drove him to see what had drawn her to that particular shelf.

She looked up—and Edgar's breath caught. Her eyes were the most extraordinary shade of green, like sunlight through forest leaves, sparking with intelligence. Chestnut hair was pinned back severely, but rebellious curls had escaped to frame her face. Beautiful, certainly, but it was the quick intelligence in her gaze that held his attention.

"Not at all," she managed, trying to step around him.

Edgar shifted slightly, trapping her between the shelf and a reading table. His gaze fell to the papers clutched in her hand—today's Metropolitan. The same issue that contained that damnable review. "Ah, a fellow devotee of literature?"

"Indeed." Her chin lifted, refusing to be intimidated by his looming presence.

That defiant tilt sent something warm through Edgar's chest. He pulled a copy of the Metropolitan from the shelf, opening it deliberately to the review that had driven him from his house in a fury. "And what do you make of this?" He gestured to the page. "Rather harsh, wouldn't you say?"

"On the contrary," she replied, her voice taking on a lighter, more conversational tone. "I thought the review quite sensible, though perhaps a touch severe."

Edgar's carefully restored calm evaporated. Here was someone defending his tormentor, speaking as if literary assassination were merely good sense. "Sensible? She practically destroyed the poor author."

"Well, I shouldn't go quite that far." Her head tilted consideringly. "Though I confess the novel did seem rather... earnest in its emotional appeals."

The diplomatic phrasing stung worse than if she'd simply echoed Lovelace's brutal assessment. "I see. I gather you've read the work in question?"

"Oh yes, I make it a point to read what everyone's discussing."

"And you consider yourself equipped to judge such matters?" His voice carried a sharper edge than he'd intended.

"I hardly think one needs special credentials to recognize when a story rings true versus when it..." She paused delicately. "...perhaps tries rather too hard to wring feeling from its readers."

Heat rose in Edgar's collar. Her measured tone somehow made the criticism worse than outright condemnation. "How enlightening. Tell me, what qualifies you to distinguish between genuine emotion and mere literary artifice? What profound experiences have shaped your understanding of human passion?"

Color flooded her cheeks, and Edgar felt a twist of satisfaction at having finally penetrated her composed facade. "Sir, that is hardly an appropriate question to pose to a lady you've only just met." Her voice remained steady, but he caught the slight tremor of indignation. "My personal experiences are neither your concern nor relevant to the matter at hand."

"Of course not." Edgar stepped back with exaggerated courtesy. "Forgive my impertinence, Miss…?"

She gathered her things without supplying her name. "Good day, sir."

She swept past him, her head high, but Edgar caught the slight quickening of her step as she made her escape. He watched her retreat—the proud set of her shoulders, the way she clutched her books like armor against further interrogation.

Damn impertinent woman. Who did she think she was, dismissing his questions and walking away from him? A duke, no less. The audacity was…

Actually rather impressive.

Edgar's irritation began to shift as he replayed the encounter. She hadn't simpered or apologized when he'd challenged her. Hadn't backed down when he'd loomed over her or used his superior height to intimidate. Instead, she'd met his provocations with dignity and intelligence, refusing to be cowed even when he'd pushed too far with his personal questions.

Most women of his acquaintance would have either fled in tears or dissolved into fluttering apologies. This one had simply gathered her composure around her like a cloak and walked away with her head held high.

His heart was racing—not from anger, he realized, but from something else entirely. The woman was magnificent when challenged—all flashing eyes and dignified outrage. Her spirited defense of her opinions, her refusal to be intimidated by his rank… when was the last time he'd encountered someone with such backbone?

Byron would have to wait. Perhaps by evening he'd have his answer from the mysterious E. Lovelace. The thought brought back his earlier satisfaction. Let the cowardly critic chew on his challenge for a while.

He didn't even know the intriguing woman's name.

ELISHA SMOOTHED THE silk of her borrowed dove-gray gown, grateful that Amelia Thornton, her best friend and editor, had insisted on lending it for the evening. Amelia stood beside her at the mirror in Elisha's modest lodgings, adjusting the lace at her own collar.

"Remember," Amelia said, pinning an errant curl back into Elisha's chignon, "half these literary lions were nobodies themselves once. Your words matter more than your wardrobe."

Both their gowns were modest compared to what they'd encounter at the salon, but there was strength in entering together. They were, after all, two women who had fought their way into London's male-dominated press.

"I still can't believe we secured an invitation," Elisha murmured, checking her reflection one final time. "Wordsworth rarely grants interviews, and never to women correspondents."

"Which is precisely why this matters so much." Amelia's expression grew serious. "My brother's patience with the Metropolitan's finances grows thinner by the month. We need this interview, Elisha. Something substantial enough to boost our circulation."

The weight of responsibility settled on Elisha's shoulders. She'd built her reputation as E. Lovelace through sharp, uncompromising criticism, but tonight she needed to be diplomatic. Charming, even. The skills required for drawing out a reluctant poet were entirely different from those needed to eviscerate a poorly written novel.

"What if he refuses to speak with me?" The doubt she'd been suppressing all day finally surfaced. "What if he takes one look at us and decides we're not worth his time?"

"Then we'll make ourselves worth his time." Amelia squeezed her hand. "You have a gift for seeing through pretense to truth, Elisha. Use that tonight."

The hackney wound through London's evening streets, and Elisha's thoughts drifted to her encounter at Hatchard's that morning. That insufferable man with his mocking bow and personal questions... All day she'd been telling herself she was glad she'd never see him again, yet something about the encounter continued to nettle her.

It wasn't just his arrogance, though that had been infuriating enough. It was the way he'd looked at her—as if he could see straight through her careful composure to something underneath. And those eyes... She shook her head firmly. She had no business thinking about any man's eyes, especially not tonight.

"You're frowning," Amelia observed. "Having second thoughts?"

"No, just... woolgathering." Elisha straightened her shoulders as their carriage drew up before Lord Hardwick's imposing townhouse. "Shall we go charm a poet?"

CRYSTAL CHANDELIERS CAST warm light over mahogany panels and gilt-framed portraits at Lord Hardwick's literary salon. The carefully modulated voices of power hummed around them, past Prime Ministers watching the evening's proceedings with painted gravity.

Elisha stood near the refreshment table with Amelia, acutely aware of the weight of her borrowed pearl comb against her carefully arranged hair. Although elegant, the accessory stood in stark contrast to the diamond-encrusted splendor of the ladies around her.

"There," Amelia murmured, nodding toward a corner where

a gray-haired man stood looking like he'd rather be anywhere else. "Wordsworth. He looks as approachable as a wounded bear."

Elisha studied their quarry. The poet's reputation for avoiding social interaction was clearly well-earned—he clutched his wine glass like a sword and his eyes darted toward the exits with trapped-animal frequency.

"The Wordsworth situation is becoming desperate," Amelia continued, keeping her voice low. "If we don't secure that interview soon, my brother will—"

"His Grace, the Duke of Lancaster!"

The announcement cut through the general murmur of conversation. Elisha's head snapped up to see the duke, famous for his good looks and infamous for his rakish reputation, being greeted effusively by their host.

Her heart plummeted straight through the floor.

It was him. The insufferable man from the bookshop, now resplendent in formal evening wear that emphasized every aristocratic line of his breeding. Of course. Of course the arrogant stranger would turn out to be a duke. Her cheeks burned with the memory of how she'd spoken to him—the casual dismissal, the way she'd challenged his opinions without the slightest deference to his rank.

"Elisha?" Amelia touched her arm. "You've gone quite pale."

"I had a rather… memorable encounter with His Grace at Hatchard's this morning. Before I knew he was His Grace."

"What sort of encounter?"

"The sort involving a heated debate about literature and proper conduct."

Amelia's eyes widened. "Oh dear. And was he very critical?"

Elisha didn't have a chance to respond. As if sensing her gaze, the duke turned, those impossibly blue eyes finding her instantly across the crowded room. Recognition flickered in their depths, followed by something that might have been amused satisfaction. The corners of his mouth curved up in that same mocking smile she remembered from the bookshop.

Her first instinct was to flee. Her second was to hide behind the nearest potted plant. Instead, she forced herself to straighten her spine and meet his gaze directly. She was E. Lovelace, feared critic of the *Metropolitan Review*. She would not be cowed by a duke, no matter how unsettling his attention or how her pulse insisted on racing whenever he looked at her.

She curtsied slightly, pasting on a polite smile. To her horror, he said something to Lord Hardwick and they began making their way toward her and Amelia. Escape was impossible without causing a scene.

"Breathe," Amelia murmured. "You look like you're facing a firing squad."

"I feel like I am," Elisha whispered back, watching Lancaster's approach with the same fascination one might reserve for an approaching storm. There was something predatory in his smile, something that suggested he was very much looking forward to their reunion.

"YOUR GRACE," HARDWICK performed the introductions with practiced ease. "Allow me to present Miss Linde, correspondent for the *Metropolitan Review*, and Miss Thornton, editor for the same gazette."

Of course—she worked for the *Metropolitan Review*. That explained her passionate defense of E. Lovelace's criticism this morning. She'd been defending a colleague, showing loyalty to her publication.

The realization cast her bookshop spiritedness in an entirely new light.

"Miss Thornton." He bowed politely, then turned his full attention on Miss Linde, savoring the way her composure wavered. Christ, she was even lovelier when flustered. "Miss

Linde and I've had the pleasure, though I believe I failed to properly introduce myself at Hatchard's. Miss Linde and I had quite the spirited debate about literature and proper discourse."

"Did you indeed?" Hardwick's eyebrows rose with interest.

"Oh yes." Edgar's smile widened as heat crept up her neck. All day he'd been thinking about her—the way her eyes had flashed fire, that proud tilt of her chin when he'd challenged her. He wanted to see it again. Needed to see it again.

"Tell me, Miss Linde, have you given any more thought to our discussion about literary criticism?"

The question was a deliberate trap, and he watched her recognize it. But instead of retreating, she lifted her chin in that delicious way that had been tormenting him since morning.

"I maintain that thoughtful analysis serves literature well, Your Grace, though I confess I prefer a more… diplomatic approach in polite company."

Her subtle barb hit its mark, and Edgar's pulse hammered in response. God, she was magnificent when she fought back. "Diplomacy? How refreshing." He affected surprise, knowing it would needle her. "And here I thought you favored direct confrontation."

There—fire building behind those extraordinary green eyes. Her fingers tightened on her reticule, and Edgar could practically feel the spirited woman from the bookshop straining against the bonds of proper decorum. The temptation to push her further was almost overwhelming.

She opened her mouth—undoubtedly for some scathing retort—but something behind him caught her attention. Wordsworth, approaching with his usual trapped-animal expression.

Edgar watched her entire demeanor shift from wary defiance to focused determination as she stepped forward, extending her hand. "Mr. Wordsworth, what an honor. I'm Miss Linde, correspondent from the *Metropolitan Review*. I've been hoping for the chance to discuss your recent work."

The poet was her target, he realized.

Wordsworth's polite interest was already glazing over at the mention of "correspondent". It was a masterful performance—Wordsworth speaking at length about the weather, his garden, anything but the penetrating questions Miss Linde tried to pose about his work. "The roses this year have been particularly vibrant," Wordsworth mused, addressing his remarks primarily to Lancaster rather than the women before him. "Though nothing quite compares to the wild beauty of the Lake District."

Edgar caught the flash of desperation beneath her professional composure. This mattered to her. More than casual journalistic interest would warrant.

"I couldn't help but notice," Edgar heard himself interrupting Wordsworth's rambling commentary about sheep grazing, "the parallels between your latest work and Burke's reflections on the revolution. Miss Linde made an astute observation about your use of natural imagery as political metaphor."

He hadn't the faintest idea if she'd made any such observation, but the surprised gratitude in her eyes was worth the small deception. Even Wordsworth, caught off guard by the intellectual direction, had to acknowledge the point.

Edgar watched with pride as Miss Linde seized the opening he'd provided—not with obvious triumph, but with subtle skill that drew the reluctant poet into real discourse. Her questions revealed considerable understanding of both literature and politics, and she managed Wordsworth's prickly temperament with impressive diplomatic finesse.

She was remarkable. Not just beautiful, but genuinely clever. The kind of woman who could match wits with anyone in this room and emerge victorious.

By the time Wordsworth took his leave—having clearly provided what Edgar could tell was a successful interview—Edgar's respect for Miss Linde had crystallized into something deeper. She closed her notebook with quiet satisfaction, the tension finally leaving her shoulders.

She looked up and caught him watching, color rising in her cheeks.

"Thank you for your intervention," she said quietly, her earlier wariness replaced by genuine gratitude. "You didn't have to."

"Perhaps not," Edgar replied, moving closer. "But I confess I was curious to see how you'd handle him."

"And your verdict?"

Edgar smiled. "Most impressive, Miss Linde. Most impressive indeed."

As he watched her retreat to rejoin Miss Thornton, Edgar's mind churned with questions about what other surprises the intriguing Miss Linde might be hiding beneath her professional exterior.

THE PROVOCATION

Metropolitan Review, *15 January 1840*

My Most Esteemed Miss E. Lovelace,

Your recent critique of my humble offering has prompted me to express my deepest admiration for your extraordinary literary perception. Rarely have I encountered such economy of language in service of such devastating insight. To reduce an entire novel to a mere paragraph while simultaneously revealing its every flaw demonstrates a talent that must surely be the envy of your colleagues.

I confess myself curious about the extensive body of work that has qualified you to judge matters of the heart with such authority. Your confident dismissal of "overwrought sentiment" suggests intimate familiarity with genuine passion. I'm positively quivering with anticipation that you may direct me to your published works on this subject, that I might benefit from studying a master's approach to romantic expression.

I remain, with the utmost respect for your superior judgment,
Your most humble and obedient servant, Aengus Steele

Elisha shot up from her seat and paced the length of her study, Steele's letter clutched in her fist. "I say, I've never heard such twaddle in all my days!" Her voice rose with indignation, causing Amelia to look up from her desk with raised brows.

Smoothing the now-crumpled letter, she read it aloud to her friend, her tone growing increasingly sour with each line. "'Positively quivering with anticipation'? Heavens, the man writes as though he's penning a letter to his mistress rather than engaging in literary discourse."

Amelia's lips twitched as she said, "He does have a certain charm."

"Charm?" Elisha scoffed, tossing the letter onto her desk. "The only thing more inflated than his prose is his ego." She dropped into her chair and yanked a fresh sheet of paper toward her. "Very well, Mr. Steele, if you wish to dance…"

Her quill flew across the page with practiced efficiency. Once she signed her name with a flourish, Elisha sat back, a satisfied smile playing at her lips. "There. Let him chew on that for a while."

Amelia limped more than usual across their shared office, her injury acting up as it often did after long days at work and peered over her shoulder at the response. "Oh dear. I don't suppose there's any chance of this ending peacefully?"

"Ending peacefully?" Elisha's lips thinned with determination. "My dear, I do believe this is merely the opening deluge."

Amelia spoke hesitantly, glancing at her friend. "I believe I shall publish Mr. Steele's letter."

Elisha's head snapped up. "For what purpose?"

"Your critique of Mr. Steele's novel seems to have captured the public's imagination. We have experienced a marked increase in new subscriptions accompanied by praises of your review. To capitalize on this, I propose we share his response to it, and you begin, hopefully, a regular correspondence with him."

"Are you suggesting we manufacture drama to gain notoriety?"

"It need not reflect poorly on us. It could be viewed as a friendly exchange of wit."

"Amelia, you are well aware of my position on this matter. I steadfastly refuse to engage with authors, lest I find myself inundated with missives from writers who take issue with my critiques."

"Indeed, I am cognizant of your stance. However, we have

not generated such interest in some time. And…" Amelia fidgeted with the ribbon adorning her gown, winding and unwinding it about her finger.

"Amelia, what troubles you?" Elisha rose and approached her friend. "What has transpired?"

Large brown eyes met hers, and Elisha was relieved to find them free of tears.

"Steven has altered the terms of our remuneration to a percentage based on the net profit. At our current rate, we lack sufficient funds to sustain ourselves. I may be compelled to return to lodgings here with you."

Elisha clasped her friend's hands, roughened from years of handling parchment.

"I am most grieved to learn of your half-brother's unconscionable behavior. I can well imagine how greatly this must distress you. When did this transpire?"

"He called on me at my residence yesterday," Amelia replied, raising her eyes. "He declared our publishing house insufficiently profitable. Should we fail to increase our profits by ten percent each month, he threatens to shutter the establishment."

"Surely he cannot do such a thing!"

"I fear he can, and indeed he shall. He is, after all, the proprietor," Amelia said, her voice quavering. "Oh, Elisha, I am ashamed to admit it, but at times I find myself positively… disliking him. He is a kind brother but a ruthless businessman."

"Any person of sound mind would be averse to him at least a little. I believed he was residing in India."

"He was, but he contracted malaria. He has returned to recuperate. He plans to take a more active role in the gazette." Amelia looked down at her hands, fidgeting with a kerchief.

Elisha's stomach sank at the possible implications but dared not show it. "Do not despair, Amelia. We shall devise a means to increase our profits. In the interim, do you truly intend to return to lodgings here in the attic?"

Amelia shook her head. "Not immediately, but perhaps if our

circumstances do not improve by next month."

"I shall not allow that to come to pass. You have only just secured your own house. We shall manage, I assure you. I shall compose a new, most scandalous letter to Mr. Steele."

Amelia looked up then, her countenance displaying sorrow and relief.

"I am deeply sorry, Elisha. I know how greatly you value your literary freedom and integrity."

Elisha smiled for her friend's sake. "It is but a small sacrifice. I only pray that it shall not transform our esteemed publication into a mere scandal sheet. We must strive to maintain the hard-earned respect we have garnered in literary circles. However, we must eat before we can fight a battle as big as that."

THE GUTTERING CANDLELIGHT cast long shadows across the stone walls of Edgar's secret chamber, concealed deep within his estate. He stood bent over a makeshift escritoire, crushing the review page of the Metropolitan with his fist.

"'Immerse yourself in works of genuine literary merit?'" he snarled at the offending paper. "The presumption! The sheer, unmitigated gall!" He began to pace the confined space, his boots echoing against the stone floor. "To lecture me on the sublimity of a sunset, as though I were some untutored schoolboy who has never lifted his eyes to the heavens. And that condescending tone—'this counsel I offer not in malice.' Ha!"

He slammed the crumpled paper onto his desk, disturbing the neat piles of salacious literature he had been sorting for distribution. "Well, Miss Lovelace, if you believe your lofty philosophical musings will cow me into silence, you are gravely mistaken. I shall—"

A coded rap interrupted his tirade. The distinctive pattern heralded the arrival of Patrick Adams—son of an exiled nobleman of Warsaw, a trusted friend, erstwhile military officer, and current protection officer for hire.

Adams entered the chamber through a concealed ingress, cleverly disguised as a humble outhouse. His mien, as ever, was one of grave solemnity and reserve. Attired in the garb of a common laborer, he had been tasked by Edgar to investigate the true identity of Miss Lovelace.

Adams' eyes widened as he surveyed the workspace. "What is this cave? This is what you've been digging all this time? You have acquitted yourself admirably, Lancaster. Most admirably indeed."

"Your approval is much appreciated. The toil was most arduous, but it shall prove worthwhile. We can now hide hundreds of erotic literatures and illicit tomes in here, ready to be distributed at a moment's notice," Edgar replied.

Adams nodded, fingering through the Metropolitan newssheets.

"Have you gathered any intelligence regarding the woman?" Edgar asked.

"The pressmen are a taciturn lot. None will disclose any particulars. She is rumored to reside in the Borough and has not been seen at the Metropolitan office. She could be someone in the office, however. Perhaps Miss Elisha Linde or Miss Amelia Thornton. It might prove most efficacious to blackmail the proprietor."

"Nay to blackmail or any unlawful activities, Adams. I shall attend literary functions and attempt to uncover information about her."

"How would identifying her benefit you?" Adams asked, leaning his broad frame against the wall. He was practically as wide as he was tall, like a bulldog, an intimidating presence for anyone.

Edgar folded his arms. "It would satisfy my curiosity. I'd also feel better knowing she is an aged spinster, perhaps adorned with a bushy mole on her nose. One look from her will likely freeze the sun."

"Not very Christian of you," Adams mused. "Have I not been counseling you to make better use of your life before it's too late? But you paid no heed to my advice, choosing instead to pursue fleeting pleasures like selling erotic literature. Do you never awaken the following day feeling hollow and disgusted with yourself?"

Edgar regarded his friend with an impassive countenance, though the tension in his muscles betrayed a suppressed urge to deliver a sound thrashing. "Pray, why should I heed the words of a man whose father was exiled from his own country? I have half a mind to ship you back forthwith to face the guillotine."

"My father's circumstance was the result of history beyond his control. You, on the other hand, could be taking a more active role as a member of Parliament."

Edgar glowered at his friend, whose silent glare was more rebuking than any words he could have uttered.

"I am forging my own history," Edgar spat.

Adams scoffed. "By selling tales of love and erotica?"

Edgar let his quill hover over Adams' name on the member list. "I presume you are not partaking in the next release of 'The Forbidden Diaries of Lady X'."

"Don't be ridiculous. Of course I am. If it's to transpire regardless of my opinion, I might as well partake in the enjoyment."

Still glaring, Edgar extended his hand. "Did you bring the fee?"

"I did." Adams retrieved his wallet. "How fares the profit?"

"I cleared three hundred pounds last week."

Adams whistled. "Not inconsiderable." He shook his head in mild exasperation. "How do you contrive to find the time, given your propensity for brothel visitations, bouts of inebriation, and general tomfoolery?"

Edgar's lips curved in a roguish grin. "I've been telling you. One needs to be born with the skills to live the life of a wastrel. Now, lend your assistance in mailing these stories. I must remain anonymous."

"And I mustn't? People recognize this handsome face, you know."

"You have two dozen men at your command. None of them would dare peek inside the envelope, whereas my servants will have the seal melted before I have turned my back."

"Very well. If I'm incriminating myself by helping you, I want to be a partner in your venture."

"What happened to doing more with your life, Adams?"

"A profitable business is a respectable endeavor for a gentleman as far as I'm concerned."

Edgar dipped his quill in ink, a wicked smile playing at his lips as he contemplated his next literary salvo. Miss Lovelace thought herself so superior, so untouchable in her ivory tower of criticism. Well, he would see about that. If she wanted to question his understanding of genuine emotion, he would give her something to truly consider.

GAS LAMPS CAST a warm glow over the *Metropolitan Review's* small classroom, where a dozen students hunched over dog-eared primers and worn slates. Elisha moved among them, pausing to praise a young chimney sweep's lettering while Amelia quietly distributed tea and modest suppers of tripe and bread.

"Now," Elisha said softly, drawing their attention, "who would like to begin our passage from *Oliver Twist*?"

A factory girl raised her hand, swallowing her last bite of bread. As the girl's halting voice filled the room, others followed along, their tired eyes fighting to stay open after long days of labor.

A gentle knock interrupted their lesson. Elisha looked over as Amelia opened the door to reveal Mrs. Cobbs holding out a sealed envelope, her knowing smile visible through the doorway before she departed.

The sender's identity was obvious from Amelia's grin. Elisha rolled her eyes and continued teaching, wondering what literary challenge Mr. Steele had devised now. Though strangely, she was minding these exchanges less and less—perhaps because their literary feud had increased subscriptions by thirty percent. Each new subscriber meant another student could join their literacy program.

An hour later, when the last student had gone and the classroom was tidied, Amelia and Elisha settled into the editorial office downstairs. The letter lay between them, Mr. Steele's bold handwriting stark against the cream envelope.

"What do you suppose he has written now?" Amelia mused, pouring them each a fresh cup of tea. "Perhaps he's conceded defeat in your literary duel?"

Elisha snorted delicately. "Unlikely. The man's ego is as robust as his plots are flimsy." She sliced open the envelope and unfolded the letter within.

Metropolitan Review, *25 January 1840*

My Most Esteemed Miss Lovelace,

While I may not have plumbed the depths of theological discourse or fully comprehended the intricacies of fatherly devotion, I remain entirely capable of unwavering faith and boundless love for a child, should such a blessed occasion arise.

For you see, I possess the innate capacity to love with fervent passion. I have, in truth, loved most ardently, Miss Lovelace. I find myself wondering, with all due respect, whether you can claim the same?

I await your missive with bated breath,
A. Steele

"Blast and damnation! The gall of this pompous popinjay! Who does this A. Steele think he is, spouting such arrant nonsense? By Jove, I've never read such twaddle in all my days!" Elisha turned to Amelia, her face flushed with indignation.

Amelia stared wide-eyed at her friend after that outburst. Elisha paced the room, her skirts swishing furiously as she continued her tirade.

"Blast it, Amelia! This addlebrained nincompoop dares to question my capacity for love? The nerve of the man! He's nothing but a blithering idiot with the wits of a turnip!"

Pausing to catch her breath, Elisha fanned herself vigorously with Steele's letter before resuming.

"Confound it all! This letter is pure codswallop! I swear, if I ever lay eyes on this A. Steele, I'll give him a piece of my mind that'll make his ears ring! The insufferable pillock!"

Amelia's hands flew to her mouth upon Elisha's reference to the male member. In that moment, the office door swung open, drawing Elisha's attention and revealing a striking gentleman. The sudden intrusion caused both women to start, their eyes widening in surprise.

"I beg your pardon, ladies. I couldn't help but overhear the tirade. I thought I better rescue the poor man receiving this verbal assault." The man's lips curved into a pleasant smile.

Elisha was momentarily speechless as she studied the newcomer. He cut an imposing figure in his meticulously tailored suit, the cut of the garment emphasizing his lean frame. His tanned face was striking rather than classically handsome—black hair neatly cropped, straight brows arching over dark, intense eyes that seemed to pierce whatever they gazed upon. Though his eyes were small, giving him a perpetually scrutinizing look, there was something magnetic about his sharp features that drew and held one's attention. He appeared to be perhaps three or four years their senior, old enough to lend him an air of worldly confidence but not so much as to place him in an entirely different sphere from Elisha and Amelia. The maturity sat well on his features, adding gravitas to his already commanding presence.

Amelia, quick to recover her composure, stepped forward. "Steven! What an unexpected pleasure. Please, allow me to introduce my dear friend, Miss Elisha Linde." Lowering her voice, she added, "Also known as Miss Lovelace."

The man nodded approvingly. Amelia turned to Elisha, who was still flushed from her outburst. "Elisha, this is Mr. Steven Thornton, my half-brother and our esteemed proprietor."

Elisha curtsied hastily, her cheeks burning with embarrassment. "Mr. Thornton, I do beg your pardon for my unseemly behavior."

Mr. Thornton waved off her apology with a good-natured smile. "Not at all, Miss Linde. I daresay it's refreshing to hear such spirited discourse in these halls." Holding her gaze and grinning with amusement, he continued, "I must apologize for my late arrival. I've just come from meeting with the solicitor for the company and thought I'd pop in to introduce myself."

Amelia nodded, her countenance apprehensive but smiling nonetheless. "You are very welcome. Would you like a tour?"

"Thank you, but no," he said. "I'll be attending to my duties as proprietor starting tomorrow. Perhaps you could do me the favor then."

"Yes, of course," Amelia said.

Mr. Thornton looked around the office, his eyes pausing on the stacks of boxes lining every wall. "I was wondering if there might be a room available for my use?"

Amelia's face lit up. "As a matter of fact, we've just cleared out the old storage room. It's quite spacious and has lovely windows overlooking the street."

Thornton looked pleased. "Excellent! That sounds perfect. But I must ask, what became of all the items that were stored there?"

With a slightly sheepish smile, Amelia gestured to the numerous boxes in their office. "We've temporarily relocated them here."

"Ah, I am sorry to have caused this clutter," he said.

"We don't mind. Do we, Elisha?"

"It isn't ideal, but you are the proprietor…"

Thornton chuckled, looking directly at her with his piercing eyes. "I admire your candor, Miss Linde. And your resourcefulness, Amelia." He bowed politely. "Well, ladies, I look forward to working with you both. Until tomorrow, then."

As Mr. Thornton took his leave, Elisha and Amelia exchanged glances, trepidation in their eyes.

"Well," Amelia ventured, her tone carefully neutral, "my brother seems quite taken with you."

Elisha snorted delicately as she gathered the used teacups. "Your brother seems quite taken with the notion of turning his gazette into a profitable venture, which is perfectly sensible."

"Oh, come now, Elisha. He gazed at you with such admiration—"

"He admires the promise of increased subscriptions," Elisha corrected, though her cheeks colored slightly. "A man like your brother, who has worked so diligently to elevate his station, would hardly seek a match with someone of my background. No, he would wish for a wife with connections to the *ton*, someone who can open doors that would otherwise remain firmly closed to him."

Amelia's brow furrowed. "You do him an injustice. Steven values intelligence and capability far more than social standing."

"Perhaps," Elisha conceded, shuffling papers on her desk to avoid her friend's knowing look. "But I have observed enough ambitious men to recognize one when I see him. Your brother is determined to claim his place among London's elite. A wife from the workhouse would hardly advance that aim."

"And yet here you are, dining with lords and ladies, critiquing the novels of the most renowned authors…"

"That's different. My connection to their world extends only as far as the printed page."

Amelia opened her mouth to protest, but Elisha held up a hand. "Now, shall we return to these submissions? They won't review themselves, you know."

But even as she spoke, Elisha's gaze drifted to Steele's letter still lying crumpled on her desk. The man's audacity in questioning her capacity for love had struck deeper than she cared to admit. What did he know of love? What did any of them know of the careful walls she'd built around her heart, or the reasons she'd chosen the safety of literary criticism over the dangerous vulnerability of genuine emotion?

She picked up her quill, already composing her response in her mind. Mr. Steele wanted to know about love? Very well. She would give him a lesson in the subject he wouldn't soon forget.

PARRIES AND THRUSTS

Metropolitan Review, *5 February 1840*

Dear Mr. Steele,

How wonderful that you believe yourself to have loved ardently. However, upon careful examination of the rather shallow emotional depths plumbed in your literary offering, I am obliged to inform you, with no small measure of regret, your claim may be somewhat erroneous.

I beseech you not to be disheartened by my assessment, for I am certain you are not to blame. Since I have your attention, I believe it to be my duty to rectify your misconception that every soul possesses the faculty for ardent affection. I assure you, sir, that your passion shall pale to mine. It is my sincere hope that an acceptance of this reality may serve to ameliorate any undue suffering you may encounter in matters of the heart.

I remain your most humble critic,
E. Lovelace

"Your passion shall pale to mine." The words slammed into Edgar's chest, making his hand tighten around the *Metropolitan Review* until the paper crackled, threatening to tear.

She had no idea. No bloody idea what she was talking about.

The memory hit him without warning—Lucia's face, radiant with laughter as she spun in the meadow behind her father's cottage. The way her hand had trembled in his when he'd first dared to kiss her. The agony in her eyes when his father had torn them apart with threats of disinheritance and ruin.

Edgar lurched to his feet, the chair scraping against the floor. He stalked to the window, his reflection ghostlike in the glass. In the years since losing her, he'd wandered through life like a man walking through fog—everything muted, distant, half-real. The eligible young ladies thrust before him seemed like pale watercolors compared to Lucia's vivid warmth.

And now this critic dared suggest he'd never loved at all.

"If only you knew, Miss Lovelace," he whispered to his reflection. The hollow ache in his chest flared—that old wound that never quite healed. "Though perhaps it's better you don't."

A knock interrupted his brooding. Hereford sauntered in without ceremony, helping himself to brandy before settling into a chair with the casual arrogance of twenty years' friendship.

"No curtsy, Hereford?"

"Go hang yourself, Your Grace." Hereford's eyes sparkled with mischief as he picked up one of the erotic pamphlets scattered across Edgar's desk. "No time for formality when there's literature of the highest standard to review."

"Perhaps I should edit them. The grammar is nearly as vulgar as the content."

"Absolutely not. The errors add authenticity—one can truly believe a courtesan scribbled this after rolling from her lover's bed." Hereford leaned forward, scanning the pamphlet with obvious relish. "This bit about the stable master's skilled hands is positively tantalizing. Though I must say, these adventures pale beside your recent exploits. Your name's been mentioned with alarming frequency in the scandal sheets. Brothels and gaming hells? You make me look positively saintly."

Edgar's jaw tightened. "Making up for lost time."

"Lost time?" Hereford's expression grew serious, his fingers drumming against the chair arm. "Does this mean you're finally ready for courtship?"

"It means I'm ready to divert myself with the fairer sex without becoming attached."

"Christ, Edgar. When will you do your ducal duty and produce an heir? You're practically ancient."

"I'm five months older than you, you ass." Edgar's voice carried an edge. "At one and thirty, I've years left to raise children. But taking only one woman to wife still feels like..." He trailed off, unable to voice the word *betrayal*.

"Like betraying Lucia's memory?" Hereford's voice gentled. "It's been five years, my friend."

"She still lives within me."

"Does she? Or does your guilt live within you?" Hereford leaned forward, his gaze piercing. "There's a difference."

Edgar turned away, facing the window. "I can no longer tell."

"Her birth to a farmer wasn't her fault. Society's rigid rules weren't yours to break at twenty-six. Lucia wouldn't want to see you torturing yourself like this."

"I know." The words came out rougher than intended. "What I truly regret is my cowardice. My failure to stand against my father."

"You were young. We all were." Hereford's voice carried the weight of shared memories. "Courage isn't about never failing— it's about what you do after you've fallen. What will you choose now?"

Silence stretched between them until Hereford brightened deliberately. "Perhaps your recent... diversions... will prepare you for your future duchess. Or at least distract you long enough to sire an heir."

Edgar's laugh held no humor. "I pray she'll be fertile so I can fulfill my duty quickly and be done with it."

"Provided there's a duchess willing to have you after you've scandalized half of London."

"Seduction should be as easy as taking a garter from a courtesan."

"Clearly you haven't met my courtesans. They guard their possessions with admirable tenacity."

"Then I'm the superior seducer."

"Your women are simply more desperate." Hereford grinned,

then grew thoughtful. "Speaking of ladies, I'm hosting a charity event for Dickens. Something more stimulating than the usual soirées. A literary contest, perhaps—men versus women to make it interesting. Lady Faulkner could organize the ladies' team."

Edgar's pulse quickened. "Now you have my attention."

"You'll attend?"

"I will. Though I make no promises about my behavior."

"I'll ask Lady Faulkner if she knows Miss Lovelace. Just try not to be discovered in a compromising position."

"I'll be as colorless as dishwater."

As Hereford departed, Edgar returned to his desk. Miss Lovelace wanted to know about passion? Very well. He would tear open old wounds if necessary to show her what real love looked like—and perhaps, in the process, discover if his heart was truly as dead as he'd believed.

Metropolitan Review, *12 February 1840*

My Most Esteemed Miss Lovelace,

I confess, your most recent retort elicited a surge of exhilaration within my breast. However, this sentiment proved ephemeral, for I quickly recalled that the tip of an iceberg cannot be set aflame no matter how fervently one believes in its possibility.

You, Miss Lovelace, possess the constitution of such an iceberg. You may affect a delicate and radiant demeanor, but the credit for such luminosity belongs solely to the sun. You remain an expansive mass of ice, immovable even as life flourishes all around you.

While you may have deemed me a shallow spring, consider that the relentless assault of life upon my riverbed has inevitably led to a broadening and deepening of my channel. My love, my passion, now possess the potential to stir the very soul.

If this fundamental truth has thus far eluded your compre-

hension, I can only surmise that you have yet to be truly sculpted by the transformative power of love. For this lamentable circumstance, I find myself filled with profound sympathy.

I remain your most humble and sympathetic servant,
A. Steele

The letter shook in Elisha's hands as she read it a second time. *An iceberg.* The audacity—the sheer, breathtaking arrogance—of this man to suggest she was cold, untouched, incapable of passion.

Her heart hammered against her ribs. He had no idea. No idea of the fire that burned beneath her careful composure, or the reasons she'd learned to bank those flames.

"Another missive from your devoted correspondent?" Amelia looked up from her desk, quill poised.

"He calls me an iceberg." Elisha's voice emerged steadier than she felt. "Suggests I've never been 'sculpted by love's transformative power'."

Amelia winced. "Rather presumptuous of him."

"What troubles me isn't his presumption—it's that he's unknowingly struck a nerve." Elisha sank into the chair opposite her friend, the letter still clutched in her fingers. "To claim I've never loved…"

"You're thinking of Mark."

The name affected her still. Elisha closed her eyes, remembering. "Do you know, I was sixteen when I realized what it meant to be seen—truly seen—by another person?"

Amelia set down her quill, attention fully focused.

"Mark had a way of appearing whenever the stones grew too heavy for me to carry. Never making a show of it, never expecting gratitude. Just… there." Elisha's voice grew soft. "I didn't understand it was love at first. It crept up like dawn— gradual, then suddenly overwhelming."

"You never told me about him."

Heat bloomed in Elisha's cheeks. "He was my first kiss. Behind the laundry shed. I thought my heart might explode from my chest." She laughed, but the sound held old pain.

"What happened to him?"

"He's done well for himself. He is a foreman at a factory not too far from here." She smiled wryly. "He's married now with three children." Elisha's fingers traced the edge of Steele's letter. "Perhaps that's why this rankles so. Mr. Steele assumes my heart is untouched simply because I don't parade my feelings for public consumption."

They sat in comfortable silence until Amelia spoke wistfully. "Do you ever wonder why we haven't attracted eligible suitors? Are professional women so frightening to men?"

"More likely we're too occupied with this enterprise to notice them noticing us." Elisha stretched, working out the kinks in her back. "Perhaps we should attend lectures where intellectual gentlemen congregate."

Amelia's eyes took on a dreamy quality. "I'd settle for any man who loves books as much as I do. Intelligence and integrity matter more than social standing."

"You want marriage."

A blush stained Amelia's cheeks. "I want a family. Children of my own to love and protect."

Something tight in Elisha's chest loosened. "I want that too. Sometimes I wonder if it's possible for women like us."

"Why wouldn't it be?"

"Perhaps because I have a talent for emasculating men?" Elisha grinned. "Remember Buck? That odious boy when we were thirteen?"

"Your first conquest!" Amelia's eyes danced. "I was so smitten with him, the way he'd swagger around the boneyard."

"You'd manufacture excuses to cross his path with alarming frequency."

"Until I stumbled and he couldn't be bothered to help me up. Just mumbled an apology and started to walk away."

"The rage I felt!" Elisha clenched her fists in mock fury. "I marched over to help you while giving him the tongue-lashing of his life."

"He said he'd act like a gentleman when I started acting like a lady."

"So I introduced my boot to his bollocks!"

They dissolved into laughter, the sound echoing through the small office. When they finally caught their breath, Amelia reached for Elisha's hand.

"Any man worthy of you would treasure that fierce loyalty, not fear it. Perhaps we haven't found our matches because we refuse to settle for anything less than souls who understand our worth."

"Then we wait together," Elisha squeezed her friend's fingers.

"Together," Amelia agreed softly.

As evening shadows lengthened across the floor, Elisha picked up her quill. Mr. Steele thought her an iceberg? She'd show him the depth of her passion—carefully controlled, elegantly expressed, but unmistakably real. Let him try to dismiss her capacity for love after her next response.

Metropolitan Review, *19 February 1840*

Dear Mr. Steele,

I perceive that your rudimentary nature fails to comprehend my professionalism. How could you fathom the expansive perspective I gain from my lofty perch atop the iceberg while you languish in your modest basin below? My affections flow as richly and deeply as a cascading waterfall, a mighty river, or the vast ocean itself. Yet I choose to nourish my beloved quietly, preserving the sanctity of my sentiments, unwilling to sully them through casual discourse with a mere stranger.

Indeed, sir, such is the totality of my devotion that I dare not speak of my beloved to a man whose entire repertoire of thoughts might be contained within a humble chamber pot. For when I love, I love with the fullness of my being, leaving no room for half-measures or shallow sentiment.

Mr. Steele, if you have truly experienced a love of such exquisite perfection as you claim, I implore you to elucidate for myself and our esteemed readers the particulars of this consummate affection. Pray, enlighten us with the depth and breadth of this grand passion you purport to have known.

I remain your most eager critic,
E. Lovelace

"'Chamber pot,'" Edgar read aloud, his voice dangerously quiet. "'Entire repertoire of thoughts might be contained within a humble chamber pot'.'"

In the underground chamber, Hereford looked up from sorting pamphlets, eyebrows raised. "Your mysterious critic has a delightfully sharp tongue."

"She wants to know about my grand passion." Edgar's fingers tightened on the newspaper. "She dares to suggest I'm incapable of deep feeling while claiming her own love is too sacred to discuss."

Edgar's jaw tightened. "She claims to love with 'the fullness of her being' while suggesting I'm incapable of the same."

"And are you? Incapable, I mean."

The question hung in the air between them. Edgar's mind drifted to Lucia—the way she'd fit perfectly in his arms, the taste of tears on her lips when they'd said goodbye for the last time.

"I was capable once," he said quietly. "Perhaps too capable."

"Then show her. This correspondence has half of London riveted—use it."

"Use it for what?"

"To remember who you were before guilt convinced you that you had died with her."

The weight of truth in those words made Edgar's chest ache. When had he stopped being a man and become merely a ghost haunting his own life?

"Your brilliant mind made Midnight Press London's most profitable underground venture," Hereford continued. "Who else but the Duke of Lancaster could distribute erotic literature under the authorities' noses? Yet you act as though you're capable of nothing but emptiness."

"Perhaps because emptiness feels safer than the alternative."

"Which is?"

"Feeling everything again." Edgar's voice dropped to barely above a whisper. "Risking that kind of loss twice."

They worked in companionable silence, plotting distribution routes across London. But Edgar's thoughts kept returning to Miss Lovelace's challenge. She wanted to know about his grand passion? Very well.

The clock struck ten, signaling their departure for the night's clandestine business. Edgar donned his darkest coat while Hereford checked his concealed pistol. They moved through gas-lit streets with practiced stealth, Edgar's pulse quickening with the familiar thrill of danger.

Their contact emerged from the shadows—a grizzled printing press operator whose discretion was bought with generous coin.

"Fresh from the press," the man said, producing a cloth-wrapped bundle.

Edgar examined the pamphlets, their pages still warm with ink. "Excellent work." He dropped payment into the man's palm, who vanished as quickly as he'd appeared.

"Distribution?" Hereford whispered as they walked toward their carriage.

"I've arranged for Royal Mail cooperation. Should expedite delivery significantly."

"Any word on those rumors of investigation?"

"Not yet. But our literary feud provides perfect cover— everyone's too distracted by Steele versus Lovelace to notice our real business."

As their carriage rolled through darkened streets, Edgar fingered Miss Lovelace's letter in his pocket. The irony wasn't lost on him—while trading barbs about love and passion, he was simultaneously profiting from London's baser desires.

Tomorrow, he would craft his response. The question was whether to use Lucia's memory as a weapon against this presumptuous critic—or as the key to unlocking the heart he'd thought permanently sealed.

Miss Lovelace demanded the particulars of his grand passion. Perhaps it was time to give them to her, consequences be damned. After all, what did a dead man have left to lose?

BLOOD SPORT

Metropolitan Review, *26 February 1840*

My Esteemed Miss Lovelace,

I am thrilled to have my thoughts compared to a chamber pot, for my chamber pot is sizable.

It was her hair that undid me—a cascade of sun-kissed silver and gold against gilded grasses. As spring breezes caressed her alabaster skin, I yearned to become the wind itself, suffusing her being, entwining with her mortal form for eternity.

Without a moment's hesitation or doubt, I found myself willing to surrender my own being, to relinquish my corporeal form, if only to become an intrinsic part of her existence.

Such, my dear Miss Lovelace, is the nature of the perfect love you bid me to describe. I lay bare before you the depths of my most intimate emotions, trusting that you will receive them with the gravity they deserve.

I remain your most humble and obedient servant,
A. Steele

The letter trembled in Elisha's gloved hands as morning mist swirled around her bench in Myddelton Square. She'd fled here after reading Mr. Steele's response, needing air, space, something to counter the unexpected intimacy of his words.

Her hair that undid me. The phrase echoed in her mind. This wasn't the pompous literary posturing she'd expected—this was raw, genuine emotion laid bare on the page.

A group of early strollers passed, tipping their hats politely, but Elisha barely noticed. Her world had narrowed to the elegant script before her, to images of sun-kissed hair and spring breezes that made her chest tight with unnamed longing.

She'd demanded proof of his grand passion, expecting flowery nonsense she could easily demolish. Instead, he'd given her something that felt like truth—the kind of devastating honesty that made her question everything she thought she knew about love.

To become the wind itself. The poetry of it struck her unexpectedly. This wasn't the shallow sentiment of his novel; this was a man describing a love so complete he'd surrender his very existence for it.

Envy pierced her heart—sharp and immediate. What would it feel like to inspire such devotion? To be loved with such intensity that a man would wish to dissolve into air just to remain close?

The rational part of her mind urged caution. This was literary warfare, nothing more. Yet as she refolded the letter with trembling fingers, she couldn't shake the image of sun-dappled fields and a love so profound it transcended flesh.

For the first time in years, Elisha wondered if perhaps there was more to romance than she'd allowed herself to believe.

THE AFTERNOON FOUND her still unsettled, pacing the Metropolitan's cramped office while Amelia worked at her desk. The letter seemed to burn through her reticule, its presence a constant reminder of feelings she'd thought safely buried.

"You're wearing a path in the floorboards," Amelia observed without looking up. "What has you so agitated?"

"Mr. Steele's latest response." Elisha stopped pacing, her hands clasped tightly. "It's... different."

"Different how?"

"Genuine." The word came out rougher than intended. "He

wrote about his beloved with such… such raw honesty. I expected pompous drivel, but instead…"

"Instead?"

"Instead, he made me envious." Elisha sank into her chair, the admission leaving her drained. "Of a woman I'll never meet, loved by a man whose name I don't even know."

Amelia's quill stilled. "Perhaps that's precisely what he intended."

"What do you mean?"

"You challenged him to prove his capacity for love. He's done so in a way that shows you what you're missing." Amelia's voice gentled. "Sometimes the heart recognizes truth even when the mind resists it."

Before Elisha could respond, a sharp knock interrupted them. Mrs. Cobbs appeared in the doorway, holding an envelope with obvious excitement.

"Begging your pardon, ladies, but this just arrived by special messenger." She bustled forward, practically vibrating with curiosity. "From Mr. Thornton himself."

Amelia rose from her chair, her foot landing with a heavier thud than usual—her injury from the textile mill acting up after their long day of work. The sight of her friend's slight wince transported Elisha momentarily to that terrible day when they'd both toiled as girls, when Amelia's skirts had caught in the machinery and her leg had been compromised for her survival.

"Elisha, we've been invited to Steven's residence for supper!" Amelia announced, her face brightening despite the obvious discomfort.

"Tonight?" Elisha's stomach dropped. The last thing she needed was navigating Mr. Thornton's increasingly obvious interest while Mr. Steele's letter had left her emotions so raw.

"This very evening!" Amelia's eyes sparkled with mischief. "And I still maintain he harbors tender feelings for you."

"Don't be absurd. He scarcely knows me."

"Since when does a gentleman require intimate knowledge

before developing affection? You're comely, intelligent, accomplished—"

"Cease such talk." Elisha busied herself gathering papers. "Perhaps it's merely dinner to better acquaint himself with his sister's dearest friend."

Amelia's knowing smile suggested otherwise.

THE HACKNEY DEPOSITED them before Mr. Thornton's Georgian house in one of London's fashionable districts. The imposing facade bore an air of austere neglect that seemed at odds with its prestigious location—like a man who'd forgotten that houses, like hearts, required tending.

A dour-faced butler admitted them into an entrance hall conspicuously bereft of warmth. No ornate mirrors, no plush carpets, no family portraits—just bare walls and the steady tick of a plain clock that emphasized the emptiness.

"Good Lord," Elisha murmured, taking in the spartan drawing room. "It's like a monastery."

"Steven has always prioritized function over comfort," Amelia sighed. "Every bare wall proclaims his need for a wife."

When Mr. Thornton appeared, his lean figure clad entirely in black, Elisha noted how different he seemed from the passionate voice in Mr. Steele's letter. Where Mr. Steele wrote of surrendering his very being for love, Mr. Thornton's sharp features and calculating gaze suggested a man who measured everything, including affection.

"Miss Linde," he said, his voice crisp as his appearance. "A pleasure to see you again."

The dining room offered simple fare—more suited to a middle-class household than one of Mr. Thornton's standing, but welcome enough to women accustomed to modest repasts.

"I've been following the *Metropolitan's* progress with great interest," Mr. Thornton began, his gaze fixed on Amelia. "You've established it as a reputable publication in a remarkably short time."

"I couldn't have managed without Elisha's invaluable assistance," Amelia replied, then turned to her friend with obvious pride. "She has such a gift for recognizing literary merit—and the rarest talent for expressing her opinions with both wit and precision."

Elisha nearly choked on her soup. "Please—"

"Oh, but it's true! Why, just last week she identified three promising manuscripts that other publications had overlooked entirely."

Mr. Thornton's attention shifted to Elisha with genuine interest. "Indeed? I intend to establish a publishing house, capitalizing on your popularity, Miss Linde. I may have need of your expertise in selecting promising authors."

Amelia beamed. "She is perfect for it."

The conversation flowed through literary matters and Mr. Thornton's business aspirations. He spoke with the precision of a man accustomed to analyzing markets and opportunities, his questions about promising authors both informed and practical.

"Elisha also has the most remarkable memory for poetry," Amelia interjected during a lull. "She can recite entire verses after reading them only once."

"Amelia…" Elisha warned.

"What? It's an extraordinary gift. Show him that sonnet you memorized from last month's submission."

"I will do no such thing," Elisha muttered, taking a rather large gulp of wine.

Mr. Thornton watched this exchange with amused interest. "And what of your literary feud, Miss Linde? One might almost think it orchestrated, so perfectly does it captivate our readers."

"I assure you, the debate with Mr. Steele is entirely genuine." Elisha met his gaze steadily, grateful for the change of subject.

"Indeed, it has been beneficial for our circulation numbers."

Mr. Thornton leaned forward slightly. "I look forward to seeing how you respond to his latest challenge."

Elisha nodded, taking a sip of her wine. "I'm still considering my approach."

"And she approaches everything with such thoughtfulness," Amelia added helpfully. "She never acts in haste. Very sensible in a lady, don't you think?"

Under the table, Elisha kicked Amelia's foot, making her flinch mildly.

"Quite sensible," Mr. Thornton agreed. "And what of your personal goals, Miss Linde? Surely a lady of your accomplishments must have plans beyond literary criticism?"

"Oh, Elisha is wonderfully independent," Amelia rushed to answer. "Though not so independent as to be unmarriageable, naturally. She simply hasn't found the right gentleman yet."

Elisha wished the floor would swallow her whole.

"I see." Mr. Thornton's lips curved in what might have been a smile. "And what qualities might the right gentleman possess?"

Another kick under the table, more pointed this time.

"Yes, tell us, Elisha," Amelia said with a grin. "What qualities do you wish for?"

"Intelligence," Elisha managed. "Integrity. A love of literature would be… agreeable."

"All qualities my brother possesses in abundance," Amelia declared with the subtlety of a charging bull. "Wouldn't you agree, Steven?"

"Amelia," Elisha hissed.

"What? I'm simply stating facts."

Mr. Thornton, to his credit, seemed more amused than offended by his sister's matchmaking attempts. "Perhaps we might continue this discussion at greater length, Miss Linde. Perhaps over tea next week?"

The invitation was delivered with businesslike directness—polite, appropriate. Elisha found herself appreciating his restraint even as Amelia practically bounced in her seat with excitement.

"I… that is very kind of you, Mr. Thornton."

"Wonderful!" Amelia exclaimed. "I'm sure you'll find much to discuss."

Elisha resisted the urge to roll her eyes. How to delicately navigate her employer's advances while avoiding crushing her friend's hopes?

"Well, that went splendidly!" Amelia declared as their hackney carried them home through London's evening streets.

Elisha gave her friend a withering look. "Amelia Thornton, you have all the subtlety of a circus parade."

"Whatever do you mean?"

"'Not so independent as to be unmarriageable'? Really?"

Amelia had the grace to blush. "I was simply… highlighting your positive qualities."

"You were serving me up like the evening's main course." Elisha shook her head, though she couldn't quite suppress a smile. "Poor Mr. Thornton probably thinks I put you up to it."

"Did you see how pleased he looked when you accepted his invitation?"

"He looked like a man conducting a business transaction. Which, knowing your brother, is probably exactly what it was."

Amelia's face fell slightly. "You don't find him agreeable?"

"He's perfectly agreeable," Elisha said gently, mindful of her friend's feelings. "Intelligent, successful, well-mannered. Any woman would be fortunate to receive his attention."

"But?"

"But he approaches personal matters with the same calculation he applies to business ventures. There's nothing wrong with that—it's simply not what draws me." Elisha paused thoughtfully. "When I think of genuine feeling, I think of spontaneity, vulnerability… the kind of honesty that takes courage to express."

She thought briefly of Mr. Steele's letter, his unexpected openness when describing his beloved.

As their carriage drew up before their lodgings, Elisha reflected that Mr. Thornton was undoubtedly a catch by any reasonable measure—the sort of practical marriage a woman in her position should be grateful to obtain. But practicality, Elisha was beginning to realize, might not be enough for her heart.

THE SOIRÉE PART 1

T HE GRAND DRAWING room of Hereford House glittered with candlelight, flames dancing in gilded mirrors and across polished marble floors. Edgar paused in the doorway, automatically scanning the assembled crowd until his gaze found a familiar figure in azure silk.

Miss Linde stood near a marble column, her bearing markedly different from the affected poses of the *ton's* ladies. There was a keen focus in her expression as she observed the gathering, though he noticed she kept glancing toward the gentlemen with what might have been professional assessment.

"Ah, Lancaster," Hereford appeared at his side, champagne in hand. "Surveying the enemy forces, are we?"

"Enemy forces?" Edgar accepted a glass, though his attention remained on Miss Linde. "Rather dramatic for a literary evening, don't you think?"

"My dear fellow, you clearly haven't witnessed Lady Faulkner's team preparations. The ladies have been meeting twice weekly, armed with more books than a lending library." Hereford gestured toward where several ladies clustered around their formidable captain. "I fear we may be outgunned."

Edgar's attention sharpened as he spotted the severe-looking gentleman now approaching Miss Linde. "And who might that be?"

"Steven Thornton. Made his fortune in India, recently returned to establish a publishing house. Sharp as a tack, though he has all the warmth of a tombstone." Hereford paused, noting Edgar's continued scrutiny. "Word has it he's rather taken with Miss Linde."

Edgar watched as Thornton's granite expression softened in Miss Linde's presence. The sight stirred something unexpectedly sharp in his chest. "Indeed? And Miss Linde's feelings?"

"Difficult to say. Though I suspect you've developed your own interest in that particular mystery."

"Don't be absurd," Edgar replied, even as Thornton leaned closer to whisper something in Miss Linde's ear. "I merely find it curious that our most formidable opponent might be distracted by romance."

"Miss Linde? Formidable?" Hereford's eyes glittered with amusement. "You've clearly read her articles in the *Metropolitan*, then."

Edgar's pulse quickened as he recalled the offensive writing. "Oh yes, quite the sharp pen when it comes to critiquing the aristocracy. 'The Frivolous Education of England's Elite'—caused quite a stir last month."

"As did her piece on the gaming hells of Mayfair." Hereford chuckled. "I believe she referred to our set as 'overgrown schoolboys with too many feathers and too little sense'."

The description stung, particularly given Edgar's own recent activities. "Charming."

Then his attention sharpened. Adams had suggested E. Lovelace could be either Miss Linde or Miss Thornton. There was something remarkably similar between Miss Linde's cutting articles about dissolute aristocrats and E. Lovelace's brutal assessment of his novel—the same sharp wit, the same unflinching judgment.

"DID YOU SEE the way His Grace was watching you?" Amelia whispered, though her tone held more concern than excitement. "Like a hawk circling its prey."

Elisha followed her friend's gaze to where the Duke of Lancaster stood with Lord Hereford, both men clearly enjoying some private conversation. "More likely he's plotting how to crush the ladies' team. Men don't take kindly to intellectual competition from women."

"Hmm." Amelia's voice carried a note of skepticism. "Though I'd wager he's more interested in you personally than in any literary contest."

"Don't be ridiculous, Amelia. He's exactly the sort of man I write about—overprivileged, undereducated, and utterly debauched."

"Perhaps. But he seems rather… focused on you specifically."

Before Elisha could respond, Mr. Thornton appeared at her side, his usual stern expression softening slightly. "Miss Linde, Amelia. I trust you're both well-prepared for the upcoming literary combat?"

"As prepared as one can be," Elisha replied. "I confess curiosity about what strategic advantages the gentlemen believe they possess."

"Confidence, perhaps?" Mr. Thornton's lips quirked in what might have been humor. "Though I suspect that may prove to be their downfall, given the ladies' evident preparation."

"You've noticed Lady Faulkner's military-style organization, then?" Amelia asked.

"Complete with diagrams and reading assignments," Elisha confirmed, unable to suppress her smile.

"Good Lord," Mr. Thornton muttered. "I am grateful my team allegiance is with the *Metropolitan Review* writers then."

"Oh," Amelia said, "I must get some cake before it's all gone. I'm grateful Steven is here to keep you company, Elisha."

"Don't you dare, Amelia Thornton!" Elisha hissed so only her traitor of a friend could hear. "I know what you're about!"

"I will be back shortly." Amelia grinned and headed toward the buffet table, her limp pronounced from the day's labor despite her effort to walk straighter.

"These affairs never fail to remind me how unsuited I am to London Society," Thornton said as he joined her, his deep voice carrying a note of self-deprecation. "Though I suspect you've already discerned as much."

"On the contrary," Elisha replied, "you navigate these waters with remarkable skill for someone who claims to be unsuited to them."

A quiet chuckle of amusement escaped him. "Necessity breeds adaptation, Miss Linde. In India, business often hinged on one's ability to endure endless social obligations. Though I confess, my ideal evening involves nothing more taxing than a book by the fire and a large dog at my feet." His lips quirked. "Which I currently do not possess."

The unexpected touch of whimsy in his admission startled a laugh from her. "No dog yet, Mr. Thornton? Or do you refer to the book?"

A gentle chuckle warmed his voice. "Both, Miss Linde. As I am certain you noticed, my home on Russell Square remains rather… austere. It needs a woman's touch, or so my sister frequently reminds me." He paused, dark eyes warming slightly. "And a dog's pawprints on the Turkish carpets."

"Do you miss India?" she asked, noting how his expression shifted at her avoidance of the subject.

"Parts of it. Though not, perhaps, what most would expect." He seemed to choose his words carefully. "I miss the children who would gather outside the mines each morning, hoping for work. Not the circumstance that brought them there—that was devastating—but the opportunity to help. We established a school instead, taught them to read and write. More valuable than any mineral we extracted, in my opinion."

Elisha studied him with new interest. This was not the cold industrialist she'd thus far believed him to be. "That must have caused quite a stir among your fellow businessmen."

"It did." Something like mischief flickered in his eyes. "Almost as much as selling to an American company that promised to maintain the school's funding. Sometimes, as you're aware, the most profitable ventures have nothing to do with money. The school continues to thrive, from what my friends report," Thornton said, a rare warmth softening his features. "Though I admit, walking away was—"

"Strategizing against your own sex, Thornton?" came a familiar voice behind them.

Elisha turned to find the Duke of Lancaster approaching, his blue eyes bright with what might have been challenge or amusement. She straightened slightly, her professional instincts sharpening.

Mr. Thornton's expression settled back into its usual granite mask. "My allegiance is with my staff at the *Metropolitan Review*, Your Grace."

"Immediate defection would be wise," His Grace replied, his lips quirking in one corner.

As if Mr. Thornton comprehended a double meaning in the duke's statement, he dipped his head to the Duke of Lancaster and addressed Elisha. "Miss Linde, please excuse me."

Upon the proprietor's retreat, the duke stepped closer and stood beside her.

"Your Grace," she said politely. "Come to assess the opposition?"

"Merely engaging in friendly reconnaissance," he replied with a roguish grin. "If Lady Faulkner's reputation for strategic planning is any indication, we gentlemen may be in for quite the battle."

"Are you so easily intimidated, Your Grace?" Elisha asked, raising an eyebrow.

"On the contrary, Miss Linde. I find worthy opponents far more interesting than easy victories." He paused, studying her face. "Based on your work in the *Metropolitan*, I imagine you'll make an impressive adversary."

Heat crept up Elisha's neck. "You read my articles? How fascinating, considering they rarely concern racing horses or gaming hells."

Rather than take offense, the duke threw back his head and laughed. "You wound me, Miss. I do occasionally read material of a more… substantial nature. 'The Frivolous Education of England's Elite' was particularly memorable. Tell me, Miss Linde, do you make a habit of keeping such thorough account of my activities?"

"Your Grace's exploits are rather difficult to ignore when they occupy half the scandal sheets in London. Some of us believe a duke's time might be better spent on his responsibilities than on perfecting his reputation as a rake."

"Ah, but I have an excellent younger brother who manages such tedious matters. Edmund positively revels in estate management and crop rotation. It would be cruel of me to deprive him of such pleasure."

"How thoughtful of you to spare him the burdens of brothels and gaming hells."

"I do try to be considerate," he said with a roguish grin. "Though I must say, your disapproval is far more entertaining than the usual fawning I encounter."

"If you seek entertainment, Your Grace, might I suggest the library? Though perhaps I should recommend something with pictures, to ease you into the experience."

The duke's eyes sparkled with genuine delight. "My, my. Sharp tongue, sharper wit. I don't suppose you'd care to join me for tea in a week?"

"I fear I must decline. I wouldn't wish to deprive London's enterprising young ladies of your attention. I hear they've started a betting pool on who will be your next conquest."

"Have they indeed? And what odds do you give yourself?"

She narrowed her eyes at his teasing inquiry—a fox with a bewildered rabbit. She kept her voice free of any emotion.

"Rather less than my chances of spontaneously becoming Queen of England, Your Grace."

"Such certainty," he murmured without seeming discouraged. He stepped closer. "And yet you're the first woman in recent memory to engage my full attention."

Elisha's heart skipped a beat at the bold query. "A dubious honor I shall try to bear with fortitude."

He threw back his head and laughed with abandon, filling the room with warmth. Elisha steadfastly ignored the small thrill it sent down her spine. After all, she had no intention of becoming another notch on the Duke of Lancaster's bedpost, no matter how engaging he might be.

He leaned closer, his voice dropping. "Perhaps I'm not quite the wastrel you imagine me to be."

"And perhaps pigs shall sprout wings."

"Such skepticism," he murmured with a barely audible chuckle. "What must I do to convince you of my hidden depths?"

"Depths? Your Grace, I'd settle for evidence of a shallow pit."

His deep baritone laugh seemed to reverberate through her bones. "You know, most people at least pretend to find me charming."

"I leave pretense to those with greater ambitions than honest journalism."

"Honest journalism? Is that what you call those scathing articles?"

"I merely offer my opinion, Your Grace. Though I'm considering reporting on the debauched lifestyle of the Mayfair Mavericks—that notorious quartet of wealth, good looks, and roguishness consisting of yourself, the Marquess of Hereford, the Earl of Carlisle, and Mr. Patrick Adams. I fear keeping up with your collective exploits may prove exhausting."

He stepped closer still, and Elisha caught the subtle scent of sandalwood and leather. "If I didn't know better, Miss Linde, I'd think you were rather fixated on my activities."

"Purely professional necessity, I assure you."

"Is it indeed?" His voice had dropped to a low rumble that sent an unwanted shiver down her spine. "Then why, my sharp-tongued lady, are you blushing?"

Elisha cursed her fair complexion. "The punch must be stronger than I realized."

"Tell me, do you believe people can change? Or are we forever bound by our reputations?"

The question felt oddly personal, though Elisha couldn't quite grasp why. "I believe people reveal their true nature through their actions, Your Grace. Words are easily spoken."

"Indeed they are. Though sometimes words can reveal more than actions—particularly when people write what they truly think rather than what society expects." His gaze grew more intense. "That correspondence between E. Lovelace and A. Steele, for instance."

Elisha's breath caught. "You've been following that exchange?"

"Rather difficult to avoid, given the attention it's garnered. Moreover, there's something almost... personal about it. As if both writers are sharing far more than they intend."

Before Elisha could respond, the conversation was interrupted by a burst of laughter from across the room. Both she and the duke turned to see what had caused the commotion.

"It seems Lady Binbrook has discovered Lord Whitmore's poetry," Elisha observed dryly. "Perhaps we should rescue his lordship before she reads it aloud."

"Ah, but that's where you're wrong, Miss Linde. Everything deserves a second chance—even terrible poetry." His eyes held hers meaningfully. "Don't you agree?"

THE SOIRÉE PART 2

EDGAR PAUSED IN the doorway of Hereford's grand salon, his gaze immediately drawn to the familiar figure in azure silk. Miss Linde stood near the front of the rearranged seating, her notebook balanced on her knee with professional efficiency, her attention focused on Charles Dickens as he prepared for the evening's contest.

Blast and damnation. Even in a room full of London's finest, she commanded his attention with effortless grace. She was everything he could want in a woman—intelligent, spirited, fearless in her convictions. Everything except the birth and station that would make such wanting anything more than folly. No lady of proper breeding would work for a living, much less in the scandalous profession of journalism. Her very presence here tonight, brilliant and beautiful though she was, marked her as utterly beyond the pale of acceptable society matches for a duke.

The memory of Lucia's tears still haunted him. His father's threats, the scandal, the way Society had crushed their love with ruthless efficiency. And yet here he stood, drawn to another woman whose circumstances made her as impossible as she was irresistible.

"Lancaster!" Hereford's voice broke through his brooding. "Stop mooning about like a lovestruck schoolboy and join us. Dickens is about to begin."

A frisson of excitement swept through the room as the celebrated author made his way to the fore, acknowledging the warm reception with a modest bow.

"Mr. Dickens," Lord Hereford intoned, "we entrust to you the task of posing the questions and arbitrating any disputes that may arise. Are you prepared to undertake this weighty responsibility?"

Dickens' eyes twinkled with good humor as he replied, "My lord, I shall attempt to discharge my duties with all the impartiality and knowledge at my command. Though I dare say, judging between such illustrious minds may prove a greater challenge than penning a three-volume novel!"

A ripple of laughter coursed through the assembly, easing the palpable tension that had begun to build.

Charles Dickens surveyed the assembled company, then began his peculiar ritual of adjusting his waistcoat and checking his pocket watch. "Ladies and gentlemen," he began, "tonight's charitable stakes are considerable. The ladies champion the *Metropolitan Review's* literacy program, while the gentlemen support the Mayfair Sailing Club for Underprivileged Youth."

Edgar's attention sharpened as he watched Elisha's face light up with genuine enthusiasm at the mention of her program. Gone was the sharp-tongued critic; for a moment, she looked almost luminous with hope.

"Let us begin," Dickens declared. "Ladies, gentlemen— 'Season of mists and mellow fruitfulness'."

"Keats!" Edgar and Elisha spoke in perfect unison, their voices blending. Edgar caught her startled glance and saw the flush that rose to her cheeks.

The questions flew rapidly. "'The curfew tolls the knell of parting day'."

"Gray's 'Elegy Written in a Country Churchyard'." Lady Faulkner called out, a split second before Lord Binbrook responded.

As the contest continued, Edgar found himself more intrigued by Elisha's responses than concerned with winning. Her knowledge was impressive, but more than that—her passion for literature shone through.

"We find ourselves at an impasse," Dickens announced after several tied rounds. "One final question shall determine the victor. 'The lady doth protest too much, methinks.' Origin and context, if you please."

Edgar stepped forward confidently. "Shakespeare's *Hamlet*, Act Three, Scene Two. Spoken by Queen Gertrude regarding the Player Queen's vows."

But before the gentlemen could celebrate, Elisha's clear voice rang out. "While His Grace is correct about Shakespeare's usage, those exact words first appeared in Sir Philip Sidney's *The Countess of Pembroke's Arcadia*, twenty years before Hamlet. Shakespeare was borrowing from Sidney."

A profound silence fell. Edgar turned to find her watching him, challenge bright in her green eyes, and despite his competitive nature, he found himself more impressed than vexed.

Dickens nodded thoughtfully. "The lady's answer demonstrates exceptional scholarship. The victory goes to the ladies!"

The room erupted in applause and congratulations. Edgar watched as Elisha was embraced by her teammates, her face radiant with triumph and something deeper—relief, perhaps, that her literacy program would receive the funding it desperately needed.

As the excitement began to settle, Edgar made his way to her side. The crowd had thinned around her, leaving them in a relatively private pocket near the windows.

"I concede defeat with grace," he murmured, close enough that only she could hear. "Though I wonder if you might be persuaded to give me a chance to reclaim my honor in a more… private contest of wits?"

She turned, and for a moment he saw something flash in her eyes—interest, perhaps, even desire—quickly masked by practiced reserve. "Your Grace," she said softly, "I rather think you'd find such a contest more challenging than you anticipate."

"On the contrary," he replied, enjoying the way her breath caught as he leaned slightly closer. "I'm counting on it."

Before she could respond, she was swept away by well-wishers, but not before casting one last glance over her shoulder—a look that sent heat coursing through his veins.

THE VICTORY FELT sweeter than Elisha had expected, not just for the triumph itself but for what it meant—funds for their literacy program, validation of her work, proof that she belonged in these intellectual circles despite her origins.

But even as she accepted congratulations from Lady Whitmore and the other ladies, the attention began to feel overwhelming. Everyone wanted to discuss her Sidney reference, to praise her knowledge, to claim acquaintance with the evening's victor. The press of bodies and voices made the room feel stifling.

"I should take some air," she murmured to Amelia when her friend appeared at her elbow. "All this excitement has left me rather warm."

"Shall I come with you?"

"No, stay and enjoy the celebration. I won't be long."

Elisha slipped away to the terrace, grateful for the cool night air and blessed quiet. The moon cast silver light across the formal gardens below, and she could hear the distant sound of laughter from the salon behind her—celebration continuing without her, exactly as she preferred.

She'd barely had a moment to collect herself when she heard footsteps. She didn't need to turn to know who had followed her.

"I trust you haven't come out here to practice a victory dance?" The duke's voice held warm amusement as he approached.

"I wouldn't dare until I had returned to the privacy of my own chambers," she replied, turning to face him.

His laugh was rich and genuine. "How considerate of you to spare the wounded pride of myself and my fellow gentlemen."

"I believe I've already wounded it sufficiently for one evening." She met his gaze directly, noting how the moonlight caught the sharp planes of his face.

He moved closer, and she caught the subtle scent of sandalwood and leather that seemed to be his signature.

"You are either very brave or very foolish to address me so boldly, Miss Linde." His voice was low with a hint of bewilderment.

"Perhaps I simply see no reason to treat you differently than any other man who values appearance over substance." The words were sharp, but her voice held a slight tremor that betrayed her awareness of him.

He braced one hand on the balustrade beside her, not quite trapping her but certainly crowding her space and forcing her to tip her head back to maintain eye contact. Her gaze dropped briefly to his mouth before snapping back to his eyes. His lips curved faintly at the tiny tell. "We've been in each other's company all evening, and I've been a perfect gentleman."

"The night is still young," she replied, though without her usual bite. "Plenty of time for you to prove me right about your character."

His laugh rumbled softly through her and heated her belly. "And if I prove you wrong instead?"

Elisha looked up, meaning to deliver another sharp retort, but the words died in her throat. His face was close to hers, his eyes dark with an emotion she dared not name. For a moment, the rest of the world seemed to fade away, leaving only the sound of their breathing and the flush of her cheeks. She moistened her lips, and His Grace tracked the movement with dangerous interest.

The spell broke at the sound of voices in the hallway. They sprang apart like guilty children.

"Thank you for your company, Your Grace," Elisha said

stiffly, smoothing her skirts.

But as she turned to flee, his voice stopped her. "Miss Linde." When she looked back, his expression was uncharacteristically serious. "You're not entirely wrong about me. But you're not entirely right either."

Elisha hesitated at the door. "Perhaps," she said softly, "we're both guilty of judging too quickly."

She hurried away before he could respond, her heart beating an unruly rhythm.

⁂

WHEN EDGAR FINALLY returned to the salon, he found the party settling into its final phase. Dickens had claimed a chair near the fire and was regaling a small group with tales of his travels, his nervous energy channeled into animated storytelling rather than button-polishing.

Edgar positioned himself beside Miss Linde, who had rejoined her friends near the piano and Dickens.

"Fascinating man, Dickens," he murmured, noticing Miss Linde glance his way. "Brilliant writer, yet prone to the most peculiar habits. Did you know he rearranges all the furniture in his rooms before he can sleep? Claims he cannot rest unless everything is positioned just so."

Miss Linde moved slightly closer, apparently drawn into the conversation despite herself. "How did you come to learn such intimate details, Your Grace?"

"He's dined at my home several times. Quite forthcoming about his idiosyncrasies, though he suffers terribly in social situations. All that fidgeting and watch-checking—pure nervousness disguised as eccentricity."

"I hadn't realized," she said softly, glancing toward where Dickens was now unconsciously straightening the items on the nearby table while he spoke.

"Most people don't. They see the celebrated author and miss the anxious man beneath." Edgar paused, studying her profile. "Rather like how people might see a sharp-tongued critic and miss the passionate advocate for education."

She turned to look at him directly, surprise flickering in her expression. "Are you suggesting I see beneath your roguish façade, Your Grace?"

"No, Miss Linde. I wouldn't expect such honor. You have more important things to tackle."

As the evening wound toward its close, Edgar found himself reluctant to let Miss Linde disappear into the London night. When the guests began making their farewells, he positioned himself near the entrance, offering his arm with practiced gallantry.

"Permit me to escort you to your carriage, Miss Linde."

She hesitated only briefly before placing her gloved hand in the crook of his elbow. The simple contact sent awareness shooting through him—the delicate weight of her touch, the subtle fragrance of lavender in her hair, the way she held herself with such careful dignity.

"Tell me," he said as they walked slowly toward the entrance, "do you not fear Society's judgment when seen with a notorious rake?"

"I rather think they'll be more interested in how thoroughly I bested you in literary combat," she replied with a hint of her earlier spirit.

"Indeed they will. Though I must admit, I find myself more intrigued by the defeat than wounded by it."

She glanced up at him, something unreadable in her expression. "That's very gracious of you, Your Grace."

"Gracious?" He paused at the top of the steps, turning to face her fully. "Miss Linde, there was nothing gracious about my thoughts during that contest. When you cited Sidney over Shakespeare, when you proved your knowledge superior to mine… I wanted nothing more than…"

The unspoken words hung between them in the cool night air. Miss Linde's eyes widened, her lips parting in surprise. Edgar was uncertain if she understood what he was about to say.

"Your Grace," she whispered, but whether in protest or invitation, he couldn't say.

"Good evening, Miss Linde," he said roughly, stepping back before he could say something even more foolish. "Congratulations on your victory."

He watched her carriage disappear into the London fog, his heart pounding with the desire to lay himself bare. Tomorrow, he would not regret his restraint. Tonight, he could only stand in the gaslight and wish he'd taken her in his arms and kissed her senseless.

DANGEROUS ENCOUNTERS

THE GAS LAMPS cast long shadows on the cobblestone streets of London's East End as Edgar emerged from the nondescript building. Dressed in the plain clothes of a merchant, he tugged his cap lower, concealing his aristocratic features. The meeting with his associates had run late, and he was eager to return to the safety of his townhouse.

A bitter wind whipped through the narrow alley as he rounded a corner, only to find his path blocked by three rough-looking men. Their leader, a burly fellow with a scar running from eye to jaw, stepped forward into the lamplight. "Well, well. If it ain't Mr. Flack. Thought you could skip town without settling your debts, did ya?"

Edgar's mind raced through his options. He couldn't reveal his true identity—that would raise far too many questions about why a duke was skulking around the East End. And without his signet ring or other identifiers, all of which were safely stored at home, he had no way to prove he wasn't this Flack character.

Just as the men began to close in, their intentions clear in their clenched fists and ugly smiles, a clear, feminine voice rang out through the darkness. "Darling! There you are!"

Edgar turned, his heart skipping when he saw Miss Linde hurrying toward him. His thoughts quickly drifted to how he would keep her safe from these blackguards. She wore an expression of relief and exasperation, presumably playing a role as his savior. He stepped toward her when one of the men caught him by the arm. He watched as the woman who had so thoroughly captured his attention approached the dangerous scene with remarkable composure.

She reached his side, linking her arm through his as naturally as if they'd been married for years. "I've been looking everywhere for you, my love."

Despite the role-playing, her words sent warmth through his chest. She turned to the group of men, her expression shifting to one of polite confusion. "Is there a problem, gentlemen?"

The scarred man frowned, his gaze shifting between them with suspicion. "This man owes us a considerable sum."

Miss Linde laughed, a sound of genuine amusement that somehow cut through the tension. "That is not possible. We've been living in France, you see." She addressed the men, her tone shifting to one of confidential friendliness that Edgar found himself admiring. "This is Mr. Edward Crook, my soon-to-be husband. We're in the East End sourcing fabrics for our new print shop."

Edgar caught her cue and patted her hand affectionately, adopting a jovial smile and thanking the stars for her quick thinking.

"Who is it you are looking for?" she asked, her tone innocent.

"Mr. Flack," the leader said, some of his earlier certainty wavering.

Miss Linde looked up at Edgar quizzically before turning back to the increasingly confused group. "We don't know anyone by that name, but then, we don't know many people in England. You see, we're expanding my father's business. In fact, we just left a meeting with Mr. Jameson about a shipment of Indian cotton. You know Jameson's Imports, of course? Just down on Brick Lane?"

The leader's aggressive stance faltered. "Jameson, yeah. We know him."

"Wonderful!" she beamed, her enthusiasm so convincing that

Edgar had to admire her skill at deception. "Then you must join us for the grand opening next month. I insist! Bring your friends. Drinks are on us."

Edgar squeezed her hand in warning—she was pushing their luck—but her confidence never wavered.

The men exchanged uncertain glances. Finally, the leader shrugged. "Right. We'll be there, Mrs. Crook, Mr. Crook. Be careful out here. These streets ain't always forgiving."

As the group shuffled away, Edgar released his breath. "Mr. Crook? Is that the first name that came to your mind when you encountered my visage?"

"No. Savage came to me first, but I didn't think you'd appreciate that very much. Nor would you have liked the other alternatives." Her eyes sparkled even as relief colored her voice.

"I cannot thank you enough for sparing me the name of Savage and the fate of Mr. Flack."

Her eyes regarded him coolly, then she turned wordlessly, walking back in the direction she came. Edgar trailed after her like a scolded puppy, his ducal dignity shrinking with every step.

"What business did you have here at this hour?" he asked, noting how confidently she navigated the treacherous streets.

"I was visiting a bookshop. I lost track of time, talking to the proprietor. And you, Your Grace? If this is your way of understanding the plights of the poor, you're going about it wrong."

Edgar ignored her question and said, "I shall escort you home."

"I don't need an escort, Your Grace. I'm a grown woman. I've been traversing these alleys since I was a little girl."

"Is there something else I can offer to repay your kindness?"

Miss Linde suddenly stopped and turned to face him. "You could tell me why the Duke of Lancaster is skulking around the East End in disguise. That would be a good start."

"I am afraid I cannot."

Shrugging, she continued on her way. "I assume your presence here is related to your salacious interests."

Edgar hurried to close the distance between them, drawn by her fearlessness.

"I am in your debt. How can I repay you?"

Miss Linde stopped to stare. "If it would help you sleep more soundly at night, there is one thing you can grant me," she said, her face serious in the dim light.

"Certainly. Let me hear it."

"These erotic pamphlets circulating through London—*The Forbidden Diaries of Lady X* and such—they're causing quite a stir. You wouldn't happen to know anything about their distribution?" Her eyes studied him intently. "They seem to originate from this area."

Edgar's expression froze for a moment before he recovered his composure. "I'm afraid I can't help you with your inquiry."

"Can't? Or won't?" She smiled, but it didn't reach her eyes. "Very well, Your Grace. I believe I have my answer. Good evening."

She turned and climbed into a waiting hackney coach. As it pulled away, Edgar watched her disappear into the darkness, cursing silently. She was far too perceptive for his comfort—and far too dangerous for his heart. Yet something about her fearless pursuit of truth stirred his blood like nothing had in years.

He had to admire her cleverness. In one brief exchange, she'd managed to confirm her suspicions about his activities while making it clear she was someone to be reckoned with. It would be wise to keep his distance from Miss Linde but somehow, he suspected that would prove impossible.

Back in his bedchamber when the night was at its darkest, Edgar reclined on his chaise longue by the hearth, a tumbler of brandy cradled in his hand. Though the hour was late and fatigue weighed heavily upon him, his mind remained in a state of turbulent contemplation, fixated on the memory of the woman who had held his gaze.

Miss Linde's countenance, etched with astonishment, her bosom heaving as he closed the distance, her warm breath caressing his jaw as he had leaned toward her. These recollections intermingled with the vivid memory of their spirited discourse, wherein they had crossed verbal swords as equal adversaries.

She had shown no deference to his ducal status, meeting him as an intellectual equal. He found himself pondering what circumstances had imbued a woman of such humble origins with such remarkable courage and self-assurance.

As he sipped the brandy, the amber liquid warming his throat, Edgar marveled at her undeniable allure which sparked a fascination within him that he found both exhilarating and disquieting. It was a sensation both foreign and oddly familiar, one that promised to occupy his thoughts for many nights to come, and one that had his member excited.

He reached down and unfastened his falls, gripping his thick girth in his hand and stroking to the remembered sound, scent, and vision of her. It would be thrilling to have her beneath him, panting and gasping, relinquishing her pride and begging him to bring her pleasure. His hand moved faster at the thought.

He knew she'd be a passionate lover, uninhibited and wholly dedicated to pleasure. The thought pushed him into his climax, her name at the tip of his tongue as he imagined sliding his member between her mounds.

The next day found Edgar at the Athenaeum Club, which pulsed with the convivial atmosphere of gentlemen at their leisure. In a secluded corner, partially shielded by a large potted palm, he sat lost in thought, barely registering Hereford's presence across from him. His mind kept returning to the soirée—to the flash of intelligence in Miss Linde's eyes, the way her sharp wit had both challenged and enthralled him.

"I say, Lancaster," Hereford drawled, swirling his brandy, "that was quite a performance you and Miss Linde put on at the soirée. I daresay you've set tongues wagging across London."

Edgar's lips quirked in a half smile. "She's… extraordinary," he admitted, surprising himself with his candor. "Unlike anyone I've encountered before. The way she stands her ground, that brilliant mind of hers…"

"Your exchange with Miss Linde reminded me rather of Steele's ongoing correspondence with Miss Lovelace," Hereford observed.

Edgar reached into his jacket and withdrew a folded paper. "Actually, before I tell you something rather significant, you should see this. It arrived this morning."

He handed over the gazette, watching as Hereford unfolded it and began to read aloud:

Metropolitan Review, *18 March 1840*

Dear Mr. Steele,

I find myself compelled to clarify that tragedy need not always manifest as a catastrophic event. Indeed, it may present itself with remarkable subtlety, such as in a gentleman's failure to truly comprehend, coupled with his unwavering conviction in the infallibility of his own opinions.

In a similar vein, true love is not merely a collection of pretty words or sensations, as you have so artfully described. Love, in its truest form, is achieved through the ultimate sacrifice of that which one holds most dear.

Your sacrifice, sir, seems no more taxing than a gentle spring zephyr. I implore you not to despair. Instead, retire your quill and search this vast land for the lady who might just love you in its truest form.

Your most steadfast critic,
E. Lovelace

Hereford looked up with raised eyebrows. "Rather cutting, isn't she?"

Edgar took a long drink of brandy, then met his friend's knowing gaze. "About that correspondence… I should tell you something."

Hereford waited, pausing amidst swirling his brandy.

"I'm Steele."

Hereford's eyebrows shot up. "You are the author of *Whispers of the Heart?*" He exhaled with an astonished mien. "Well, well, that explains rather a lot, including why you have been so preoccupied lately. Two intellectual battles at once—Miss Lovelace in print and Miss Linde in person."

"I never intended the letters to become such a sensation," Edgar admitted. "When Miss Lovelace first criticized my work, I responded as Steele on impulse. But now…" He trailed off, then pulled another letter from his pocket. "I shall mail this tomorrow." He handed it to Hereford, who read it with growing interest:

25 March 1840

My Esteemed Miss Lovelace,

Your evasive manner leads me to surmise that you have perhaps not experienced the transformative power of love. I implore you not to despair, for I have a solution…

"Good Lord," Hereford murmured, refolding the letter. "You've thrown down quite the gauntlet. I wonder what our mysterious Miss Lovelace will make of this challenge."

Edgar remembered the excitement of those written exchanges even as his mind wandered to Elisha's challenging gaze.

"Now you find yourself entangled with two fascinating women," Hereford finished. "The mysterious Miss Lovelace who matches you wit for wit in print, and the very real Miss Linde who seems to have thoroughly captured your attention in person."

"God help me, but yes." Edgar ran a hand through his hair. "Miss Lovelace's letters are brilliant—she understands literature in a way few do. But Miss Linde, there's something about her, Hereford. The way she challenges everything—my assumptions, my privilege, my behavior. I can't stop thinking about her."

"My God," Hereford breathed. "The notorious Duke of Lancaster, undone by a woman who earns her bread through journalism?"

"When I'm with her, none of that seems to matter." Edgar's voice was rough. "Her mind, her spirit, she makes me want to be better. To be worthy of her good opinion."

"And what of Miss Lovelace?"

"The letters are stimulating, but they're just words on paper. Miss Linde is…" Edgar searched for the right words. "She's real. Vibrant. When she looks at me with those eyes…"

"This is dangerous territory, old friend. Miss Linde's station alone—"

"I know. Lord knows I've suffered from loving a commoner, loving Lucia." Edgar stared into his glass. "But I find myself caring less and less about that. Though I doubt Miss Linde would have me even if I offered. She seems to thoroughly disapprove of everything I represent."

"And yet there was definite tension between you at the soirée," Hereford observed. "I wasn't the only one who noticed how you were both following each other across the room."

Edgar's fingers tightened around his glass as he recalled those moments. "Perhaps," he said softly. "But she's not like the other women I've known. She'd never settle for being a mistress no matter how much luxury she is showered with. And a marriage is… I wonder."

"Good Lord. You actually care for her."

The usual clamor of the club faded into the background as Edgar considered this. Since Lucia, he'd kept women at arm's length, allowing himself only superficial dalliances. In fact, he had lived aimlessly, fearing the pain may return should he start thinking clearly. But there was nothing superficial about his reaction to Elisha Linde.

"I think I do," he admitted finally. "God help me, but I think I do."

Hereford studied him for a long moment. "Well, my friend, it seems you have a choice to make. Pursue something potentially meaningful with Miss Linde or stop before either of you gets hurt because you will need to fight the *ton* with everything you possess if you wish to marry her."

Edgar nodded slowly, his mind filled with images of Elisha. For the first time in years, he found himself willing to risk his heart again even if it meant risking everything else in the process.

THE MORNING LIGHT streaming through the gazette's windows caught the crisp paper as Elisha unfolded Steele's latest correspondence. Her fingers trembled slightly as she read:

Metropolitan Review, *25 March 1840*

My Esteemed Miss Lovelace,

Your evasive manner leads me to surmise that you have perhaps not experienced the transformative power of love. I implore you not to despair, for I have a solution.

Rather than me retiring my pen, how about you pick up your quill and do more than smear good authors' work?

Since you profess to understand the deepest romantic love, why not show us by creating the experience? Share your passion with the world through your words. Author a short romantic tale of your own within the span of five months.

To add a measure of intrigue to our undertaking, I suggest a wager of considerable stakes. Should your short novel, published under a nom de plume of your choosing, garner more favorable reviews than my own (which shall also be published under a new pseudonym), I pledge to publicly acknowledge your superior understanding of the genre and make a substantial donation to a charitable organization of your selection.

Conversely, should your work fail to captivate the reading public, you must abstain from critiquing romantic literature for a full year. Furthermore, you shall be obliged to pen a glowing review of my next novel, to be published in your esteemed gazette. The victor of this challenge shall be revealed on New Year's Eve of this year.

What say you, Miss Lovelace? Are you prepared to subject your considerable talents to such a test? Or do you prefer the relative safety of your critic's perch, from whence you may hurl barbs at those who dare to create?

I remain your most intrigued servant,
Aengus Steele

Her mind raced with possibilities. Write a romance novel? The audacity of the man! And yet... what an opportunity to prove her understanding of true passion wasn't merely theoretical.

Lost in thought, she pushed open the gazette's office door—and stopped dead. Mr. Thornton was seated at her desk, his elegant fingers rifling through her papers with casual authority.

"Excuse me, sir," she said, her voice sharp with barely contained alarm. "Those documents are works in progress."

He looked up, and Elisha felt her breath catch. She had seen Steven Thornton before, of course, but never in the stark morning light that streamed through the windows. His eyes were a deep, rich brown, like polished mahogany in shadow, set above proud cheekbones that belied his merchant roots. But it was the intensity of his gaze that held her—the way he seemed to look straight through her carefully constructed facade.

"Miss Linde." He rose smoothly, and she noticed how he seemed to fill the small office with his presence. "Forgive my presumption. I find I learn more about people from their absence than presence."

"And what have you learned from invading my privacy, Mr. Thornton?" She moved to her desk, suppressing her ire and roughly gathering her papers.

His lips curved slightly. "Hardly private when they're the properties of the *Metropolitan*." He gestured to the letter she still held. "New correspondence?"

"From a reader," she said, tucking it away. "Nothing of consequence."

"I doubt anything you deem worth reading is inconsequential." He stepped closer, and Elisha fought the urge to retreat. "Tell me, Miss Linde, how do you find working here? Is there anything you need?"

The last word carried an undertone that made her pulse quicken—whether with warning or anticipation, she wasn't quite sure.

Schooling her features into a smile, she met his gaze directly. "Actually, Mr. Thornton, Amelia and I believe expanding our coverage to include political literature and policy changes could serve our readers well."

Delight flickered in his eyes. "Indeed? I made rather useful connections in India. Political circles that could benefit from a sharp mind and sharper pen." He paused, studying her. "Would you be interested in accompanying me to some of these gatherings? Your perspective could prove invaluable."

The offer dangled before her like a key to a locked door. But before she could respond, he added, "Of course, such expanded duties would warrant a corresponding increase in compensation."

Elisha's eyes narrowed slyly as she ventured, "What are you offering, Mr. Thornton?"

His face brightened with a startled smile. "I'm offering to double your wage, Miss Linde. Your talent is precisely what has made the *Metropolitan* a success."

Despite her shock, Elisha was emboldened by his generosity. "Then might I suggest Amelia deserves the same consideration? She works twice as hard as any of us."

A look of tender amusement crossed his features. "My sister's raise was approved this morning."

"Oh." Elisha felt her cheeks warm with embarrassment. "That is very generous of you. I hope I didn't offend you with the presumption."

"Not at all." His eyes lingered on her face with unmistakable fondness. "Your loyalty to Amelia is one of your most admirable qualities."

As he turned to leave with a graceful bow, Elisha found herself watching him go with a slight unease settling in her chest.

"I look forward to working closely with you, Miss Linde," he said from the doorway. "I think we're going to do great things together."

Later that evening, the printing presses had fallen silent, their day's work complete, but the gazette's office still hummed with nervous energy. Elisha found Amelia at her desk who was grimacing as she massaged her own shoulders. The day had been a parade of disgruntled advertisers until Thornton had swept in, wielding charm and solutions with equal measure. His facility at smoothing ruffled feathers had been almost unsettling to watch.

"He's rather good at that, isn't he?" Elisha said, gently moving Amelia's hands aside to take over the massage. "Your brother, I mean. Like watching a master fencer at work."

"Mmm. He learned a great deal in India, it seems. Though sometimes I wonder what else he learned there." Amelia leaned back, studying Elisha's face. "But something's got you practically vibrating with excitement, and I doubt it's my brother's diplomatic skills."

Elisha pulled Steele's letter from her pocket, holding it like a prize. "Mr. Steele has thrown down a rather spectacular gauntlet."

Amelia straightened her back, wincing slightly. "Do tell!"

"He wants Miss Lovelace to prove her understanding of romance by writing a novel of her own." Elisha's loose curls bounced with each eager gesture. "To be published under yet another pseudonym and judged against his own new work."

"Good Lord! The arrogance of the man!" Amelia exclaimed, though admiration flickered in her eyes. "I must admit, however, it's rather brilliant. What are the stakes?"

"If I win, he makes a charitable donation. If he wins…" Elisha's lips curved. "Miss Lovelace must write him a glowing review and cease critiquing romantic literature for a year."

"That seems rather uneven," Amelia frowned. "Your reputation—"

"What if I counter with a specific sum? Say, five hundred pounds sterling for the literacy program?"

Amelia's eyes widened. "Five hundred... Elisha, that would fund the program for years! We could expand to more workhouses, hire actual teachers instead of relying on volunteers..." She paused, her expression growing shrewd. "Though I notice you're more concerned with the program's funding than protecting Miss Lovelace's reputation."

"Perhaps Miss Lovelace could benefit from putting her theories to the test," Elisha said softly. "After all, it's one thing to critique passion and quite another to create it."

"Speaking of passion..." Amelia's tone turned sly. "I saw how the Duke of Lancaster looked at you at the soirée. And now this challenge from Mr. Steele... You seem to be attracting quite a lot of masculine attention lately."

Elisha's hands stilled on Amelia's shoulders. "The duke is a notorious rake who probably saw me as a novel challenge. And Mr. Steele..." She sighed. "Mr. Steele doesn't even know who I really am."

"Perhaps that's why this is the perfect opportunity." Amelia turned to face her friend. "You can write about love without the constraints of being Elisha Linde, feared correspondent, or Miss Lovelace, feared critic. You can be someone entirely new."

Elisha's gaze drifted to the darkening streets outside, where gas lamps were beginning to glow like earthbound stars. "A chance to prove myself as just... a writer."

"Exactly." Amelia squeezed her hand.

Elisha moved to her desk, pulling out fresh paper and dipping her pen. The challenge of the novel lay before her, but so did other, more immediate concerns. Thornton's curiosity, Lancaster's unsettling attention, and now this wager with Steele... When had her life become so complicated?

But as she began to write, she couldn't quite suppress a smile. After all, complications made for the best stories.

THE WAGER

Metropolitan Review, *1 April 1840*

Dear Mr. Steele,

I hope you were not overwhelmed with regret after issuing me a challenge, for after much deliberation, I have decided to accept. I must, however, make one exception.

Should you win, I cannot refrain from critiquing, as it would negatively impact the Metropolitan Review. *Therefore, I shall organize and host a literary salon in your honor, inviting the most influential members of London's literary society.*

May I inquire as to the amount of your charitable donation upon my victory? I'm afraid anything less than five hundred pounds sterling will not suffice. Of course, you will need to make a public acknowledgment of my superior literary prowess as well.

I must confess, your challenge has stirred within me emotions I had not felt so deeply for some time—trepidation about your inability to pay the sum and excitement about your public tribute to yours truly. I suggest you reduce the size of your bowl and chamber pot so that you may squirrel away the requisite funds.

May our pens be sharp and our minds sharper still.

Your most determined critic,
E. Lovelace

Steel sang against steel in the fencing salon, the afternoon light catching the blades with each strike. Edgar pressed forward with a combination of attacks, each thrust carrying the momentum of his racing thoughts.

"She accepted," he said, his blade meeting Hereford's with a sharp clash. "Miss Lovelace actually accepted."

"En garde!" Hereford called, barely deflecting a particularly aggressive thrust. "I sense this bout has become about more than mere practice. What's got you so fired up, man?"

Edgar advanced again, his movements reflecting his inner turmoil. "The stakes," he said between exchanges. "They're not enough. A literary salon? It's…" He broke off as Hereford nearly caught him with a clever riposte. "It's too easy."

Hereford stepped back, lowering his foil. "And what would satisfy the great Aengus Steele? Or should I say, the even greater Duke of Lancaster?"

Edgar removed his mask, his face flushed and breathless with more than just exertion. "What if… she had to serve as his personal secretary for a month?"

"Good God!" Hereford's eyebrows shot up. "Having the caustic Miss Lovelace at your beck and call? That's deliciously cruel."

"And a public reading," Edgar continued, warming to the idea even as something twisted uncomfortably in his chest. "In Hyde Park. Let her proclaim the greatness of my prose to all of London."

"Lancaster…" Hereford studied him thoughtfully. "This feels rather personal for a mere literary debate. Has Miss Lovelace struck a nerve?"

Edgar turned away, ostensibly to retrieve his water flask. "Perhaps." His mind drifted to Elisha again—her fierce intelligence, her proud bearing. Would she show the same fire as Miss Lovelace if she knew his author identity? "Though lately I find myself more intrigued by another lady."

"Ah, yes, the writer." Hereford's tone was knowing. "How does it feel, pursuing one woman while plotting the humiliation of another?"

Edgar's hand tightened on his foil. "When you put it that way, it sounds rather ungentlemanly."

"And yet you persist." Hereford raised his blade again. "So what name will you publish under? Since Steele must remain anonymous in this challenge."

Edgar parried Hereford's attack, his movements almost distracted. "I was thinking… Edmund C. A."

"Your brother's name?" Hereford's blade faltered in surprise. "He'll be furious."

"Perhaps." Edgar executed a perfect lunge, scoring a hit. "But there's something fitting about it. Edmund always was the better man—more honorable, more genuine. Everything I pretend to be as Steele."

"And everything Miss Linde seems to inspire you to want to be?" Hereford's observation struck as precisely as any blade.

Edgar lowered his foil, suddenly weary. "God help me, Hereford. What am I doing? Playing at being Steele, coveting Miss Linde's good opinion, plotting to humiliate Miss Lovelace…"

"You're playing a dangerous game," Hereford agreed, removing his mask. "The question is, what matters more: winning the game or becoming the man worthy of Miss Linde's heart?"

Edgar stared at his reflection in the polished blade of his foil, seeing the duke, the author, and somewhere beneath it all, the man he might yet become. "The truly damning thing is… I'm no longer certain."

"Then perhaps," Hereford said quietly, "this challenge is about more than just literary prowess."

Edgar raised his blade once more, falling into position. "Again," he commanded, needing the physical exertion to quiet his troubled thoughts. As their blades met once more, he couldn't help but wonder if this battle with steel could ever resolve the one waging in his heart.

Metropolitan Review, *4 April 1840*

My Most Esteemed Miss Lovelace,

I am delighted that you have accepted my challenge. Your trepidation is noted, and I assure you, I will employ a part-time valet who only irons the visible portions of my shirts. If you would be so good as to raise a carrier pigeon, I could save on Penny Blacks as well.

While I find your suggestion of a literary salon charming, it may not fully capture the spirit of our wager. Therefore, I propose the following amendments to our agreement:

In the event of your defeat, you shall serve as my personal secretary for one month and read passages from my winning tale aloud at Hyde Park, one day a week for a month.

Should you emerge victorious, I shall indeed make a public acknowledgment of your superior understanding of romantic literature. Furthermore, I shall give a charitable donation of 1000 pounds sterling to an organization of your choosing.

I believe these terms more accurately reflect the magnitude of our challenge and the stakes at hand. After all, if we are to engage in this literary duel, should we not commit ourselves fully to the fray?

Your most determined servant,
Aengus Steele

"The utter gall of that insufferable man!" She thrust the letter toward Amelia, rising from her chair in a rustle of modest brown muslin. "Read for yourself what he proposes as our wager!"

As Amelia read, Elisha began to pace the confines of her small office, her skirts swishing against the worn carpet. The man's arrogance was breathtaking. To suggest she become his secretary—her, a woman who had worked her way up from cleaning hallways to become one of London's most respected literary critics! And the public reading in Hyde Park... her mind conjured the mortifying scene of being forced to recite his florid prose before a crowd of sneering onlookers.

"He has doubled the charitable donation," Amelia noted carefully. "One thousand pounds sterling is no small sum, Elisha. Think of what we could do for the literacy program with such funds."

Elisha paused in her pacing, her fingers worrying at the cameo brooch at her throat. "You cannot possibly suggest I accept these terms? To be paraded about like some... some trained monkey for his amusement?"

"Perhaps," Amelia said slowly, smoothing the crumpled letter on the desk, "we might consider what lies beneath his apparent provocations. Mr. Steele has doubled his own stakes, after all. And his suggestion of public readings..." She trailed off meaningfully.

Before Elisha could formulate a response, another knock at the door interrupted their conversation. The office boy's nervous voice carried through the wooden panel: "Miss Linde, Miss Thornton, the Duke of Lancaster requests your presence."

Elisha and Amelia exchanged startled glances, their earlier discussion forgotten. The Duke of Lancaster? Here, in their modest offices above Fleet Street?

The duke's entrance transformed their small office, making it seem suddenly cramped and shabby by comparison. He filled the doorframe with his impressive height, his dark blue coat tailored to perfection across broad shoulders. Yet it was his eyes that captured Elisha's attention—keen and observant, with an intensity that seemed to peer straight through her carefully maintained facade.

"Your Grace," they said as they curtsied in unison, though with mortification, Elisha noticed a spot of ink on her sleeve as she did so.

"Ladies." His voice was deep and cultured. "I must beg your pardon for this unannounced intrusion. I had hoped to make the acquaintance of Miss Lovelace, but I'm told she conducts her affairs from a remote location."

Elisha forced her features to remain neutral as she replied,

"Indeed, Your Grace. Miss Lovelace values her privacy most highly."

"So I've gathered. Though I find myself equally intrigued by her representatives. I understand you handle her correspondence with Mr. Steele?"

Amelia chose that moment to make her excuse about refreshments, abandoning Elisha to face the duke's penetrating gaze alone.

"Please, be seated, Your Grace," Elisha managed, gesturing to the chair recently vacated by Amelia. As he settled his impressive frame into the modest furniture, she couldn't help but notice how his presence seemed to fill not just the space, but her awareness.

"I trust you'll forgive my curiosity, Miss Linde," he said. "I've found great entertainment in following this literary debate between Miss Lovelace and Mr. Steele. In fact, I've just come from his club where he was composing his latest novel with particular enthusiasm."

Elisha's hand strayed to Steele's letter, still lying crumpled on her desk. "I fear Mr. Steele's enthusiasm has led him to make some rather presumptuous demands."

"May I?" He held out his hand for the letter, and Elisha found herself surrendering it before she could think better of the action. She watched as he smoothed the paper with long, elegant fingers, his expression thoughtful as he read.

"You find these terms offensive?" he asked finally, looking up to meet her gaze.

"I find them…" Elisha paused, choosing her words carefully. "I believe Mr. Steele intends to humble Miss Lovelace through public spectacle."

The duke leaned forward slightly, his expression intent. "An interesting interpretation. Might I offer another?"

Something in his tone made Elisha's breath catch. "Please do, Your Grace."

"Consider that Mr. Steele, having engaged in this battle of wits from a distance, now seeks closer acquaintance through the only means available to him. The position of secretary, while perhaps lacking in delicacy, would provide daily interaction. And the public readings…" He paused, his blue eyes holding hers. "What better way to gauge an audience's true reaction to one's work?"

Elisha felt her cheeks warm under his steady gaze. "You suggest his motivation is professional rather than punitive?"

"I suggest, Miss Linde, that sometimes we see what we expect to see, rather than what truly lies before us." He gestured to their surroundings. "For instance, I came here expecting to find mere employees of an absent authoress. Instead, I've discovered something far more… intriguing."

The weight of his words hung in the air between them. Before she could formulate a response, he changed tack with expert precision.

"Tell me about your literacy program, Miss Linde. I understand it's the intended beneficiary of Miss Lovelace's potential winnings?"

Grateful for the safer topic, Elisha found herself describing their evening classes, the challenges of teaching adults who'd never held a pen, the joy of watching them write their names for the first time. As she spoke, she noticed the duke's attention never wavered—he asked intelligent questions about their methods, their costs, their dreams for expansion.

"And what inspired such a noble endeavor?" he asked, his tone genuine.

Elisha hesitated, then decided to offer him the same honesty he'd shown her. "I learned to read by watching through schoolroom windows while cleaning halls, Your Grace. Every child peering through those same windows today deserves better."

Something shifted in his expression—not pity, but a deeper understanding. "Indeed they do, Miss Linde."

As he prepared to leave, he paused at the door, turning back to meet Elisha's gaze. For a moment, she thought he might say something more, something that would shatter the careful balance they'd maintained throughout his visit. Instead, he merely tipped his hat and departed, leaving Elisha to wonder if she'd imagined the look of admiration—and something more—in his eyes.

"Well," Amelia said, once they were alone again. "That was…"

"Indeed," Elisha replied softly, her mind already composing her response to Mr. Steele's letter. Perhaps it was time to view this challenge from a different perspective entirely.

DANGEROUS ATTRACTIONS

T HE FIRE CRACKLED softly in Edgar's bedchamber as he stood by the window, Miss Lovelace's latest letter still clutched in his hand. Hawkins moved about the room, preparing His Grace for bed, but Edgar's thoughts were elsewhere entirely.

Metropolitan Review, *15 April 1840*

Dear Mr. Steele,

I must say, your latest missive has left me in a state of bemused exasperation. It seems you are determined to push the boundaries of our little wager to the utmost limits. Very well, sir. I accept your amended terms except for one. Should you lose, you shall read excerpts from my book at Hyde Park and serve as my assistant as well.

Let us submit our tales on the same day on 15 August 1840 with the results being announced on New Year's Eve.

Your generosity in doubling the charitable donation is noted and appreciated. It seems that, win or lose, some good shall come of our arrangement.

I look forward to our little duel. May it prove as enlightening as it is challenging.

Your most determined adversary,
E. Lovelace

"I went to gain better understanding of their literacy program since I am pledging a thousand pounds sterling should I lose," Edgar murmured, his eyes fixed on the London skyline. "You should have seen her radiant smile when discussing the charity students. She has such spirit, Hawkins."

Hawkins glanced up from turning down the bed. "Indeed, Your Grace? That's most intriguing."

Edgar turned, a boyish excitement lighting up his features. "It was extraordinary, Hawkins. The way her eyes were like flames of green and amber catching the sunlight even during quiet contemplation. And her hands… have you ever noticed how a person's hands can be so expressive? Hers dance when she speaks, emphasizing each point with a grace that's almost hypnotizing. Even her scars are beautiful."

Hawkins hid a smile as he laid out Edgar's nightshirt. "It seems Miss Linde has made quite an impression."

"More than an impression," Edgar continued, pacing the room. "Did you know she has a habit of biting her lower lip when she's deep in thought? It's oddly endearing. And when she smiles—truly smiles, mind you—there's this tiny dimple that appears on her left cheek. You'd miss it if you weren't paying attention."

"Which you clearly were, Your Grace," his valet observed dryly.

Edgar paused, running a hand through his hair. "I was, wasn't I? Good God, what am I to do? I am entangling myself with a commoner. Even if she has achieved some success, she grew up in an orphanage, then a workhouse, for Heaven's sake! Why am I repeating history? Was once not enough?"

"It is not too late to step away, Your Grace," the older servant said, holding out the duke's robe.

"Blazes, that is unthinkable…" Edgar said, shrugging into the garment.

"Why is that?" Hawkins asked.

"I find myself utterly captivated by her intellect and spirit. To step away now would be akin to turning my back on a rare and precious bloom."

"A rare bloom that might suffocate you into oblivion, perhaps," Hawkins intoned with practiced indifference.

"Yes, well…" Edgar trailed off, unable to refute the point.

"Pray tell, when was the last occasion Your Grace attended a proper Society function and engaged in discourse with young ladies of suitable breeding?"

Edgar exhaled heavily, raking his fingers through his hair in a gesture of frustration. "I confess, I cannot recall with any certainty."

Hawkins cleared his throat delicately. "In that case, might I suggest that Your Grace seek out the acquaintance of young ladies of your own station? Perhaps there exist other extraordinary women of whom you are as yet unacquainted, given your propensity for… less salubrious establishments these past six years."

"Perhaps…" Edgar conceded reluctantly.

"It would do no harm to temper your sentiments toward Miss Linde while you search for an even rarer jewel, as it were."

"I suppose not," Edgar acquiesced, his tone tinged with resignation.

"Does this signify that Your Grace is at last prepared to contemplate the prospect of matrimony?"

Edgar's head snapped up, his eyes wide with alarm. "Good God, Hawkins! Let us not be hasty. I merely agreed to widen my social circle, not throw myself headlong into the parson's mousetrap."

Hawkins' lips twitched in a suppressed smile. "As you say, Your Grace. However, might I remind you that your position and the expectations of Society do necessitate certain… considerations for the future?"

Edgar sighed, sinking into a nearby chair. "I am well aware of my duties, Hawkins. But surely there must be a middle ground between my current… indiscretions and shackling myself to a vapid debutante for the sake of producing an heir?"

"Indeed, Your Grace. Which is precisely why I suggest broadening your acquaintance among the *ton*. You may yet find a lady who stimulates both your intellect and your heart, while also satisfying the demands of your station."

As Edgar pondered this, he found himself comparing every lady of his acquaintance to the vivacious Miss Linde. Would any of them possess her quick wit, her passion for knowledge, her dedication to improving the lives of others? He shook his head, attempting to dispel these thoughts.

"Very well, Hawkins. You may begin the odious task of accepting invitations to the upcoming social events. But I warn you, if I am forced to endure one more insipid conversation about the weather or the latest fashions from Paris, I shall hold you personally responsible."

Hawkins bowed, a glimmer of amusement in his eyes. "Duly noted, Your Grace. I shall recruit Mr. Anderson to select gatherings where the discourse might prove more… stimulating."

As Hawkins took his leave, Edgar found himself staring out the window, his thoughts a tumultuous combination of duty, desire, and the lingering image of a certain lady with a penchant for biting her lower lip when deep in thought.

The next morning, Edgar sat at his escritoire, composing what he hoped would be his most provocative letter yet to Miss Lovelace. If she wanted to play games with terms and conditions, he would show her exactly what kind of adversary she was dealing with.

ELISHA SMOOTHED HER gray wool dress, wishing she'd chosen something less severe as she waited in the *Metropolitan's* proprietor's office. The unexpected summons from Mr. Thornton had set her nerves jangling, though she couldn't say why.

The morning sun slanted through the office window, illuminating yet another missive from Steele in Elisha's hands. Her fingers traced the simple wax pattern before breaking it with more force than necessary, a small act of defiance against the man who seemed determined to upend her carefully ordered world. As she unfolded the expensive vellum, a faint scent of sandalwood wafted up. Of course the insufferable man would perfume his correspondence.

Metropolitan Review, *19 April 1840*

My most esteemed Miss Lovelace,

I find myself practically levitating with joy at your acceptance of our amended terms. I confess I'm uncertain which prospect thrills me more—you bringing my morning tea or the sound of my prose falling from your lips in Hyde Park. Indeed, it seems dreadfully unfair that one man should contain such boundless delight in his breast.

As my future secretary, you shall need to be acquainted with certain peculiarities of my domestic arrangements. I take my tea with milk and precisely two nips of sugar—though I suspect you'll master that particular detail swiftly enough. My study windows must remain exactly halfway open at all times, regardless of London's capricious weather. I find it aids the circulation of both air and ideas.

But perhaps most crucial is the matter of my morning exercise. My current assistant, Mr. Anderson, has the unenviable task of engaging me in physical combat to reinvigorate my mental faculties. As my secretary, this duty shall naturally fall to you. I strongly advise beginning your training posthaste, lest I render you unconscious within the first few seconds of our inaugural bout.

I remain, with barely contained anticipation,

Your most devoted servant,
Aengus Steele

"The absolute audacity!" Elisha muttered, crumpling the

letter before immediately smoothing it out again. Physical combat? The man was clearly mad. And yet… there was something almost playful about his tone that made her lips twitch despite her indignation.

"Miss Linde." Thornton's deep voice preceded him into the room. Elisha folded the letter and slid it between the pages of a notebook she carried. The proprietor appeared in a perfectly tailored navy suit, looking as authoritative as his voice. "I find myself in need of your expertise. Sotheby's is auctioning several rare volumes today, and I confess my knowledge of literary value is limited."

"Surely Amelia would be better suited—"

"My sister's leg is troubling her," he said quietly. "And I trust your judgment equally."

She hesitated, wanting to avoid any misconception about their relationship on his part. "Mr. Thornton—"

"It would be a purely professional engagement," he said, as if reading her mind.

Which was how she found herself that same afternoon on Steven Thornton's arm, entering Sotheby's elegant auction room. They had barely crossed the threshold when a familiar laugh made her stomach clench.

"Oh!" A silk-clad figure collided with her as they rounded a display. "How clumsy of me."

Elisha steadied herself as Thornton's arm wrapped tightly around her waist. She then came face to face with a stunning blonde whose diamonds probably cost more than the *Metropolitan's* yearly revenue. But it was the man beside her that made Elisha's breath catch.

"Lady Stanton, may I present Miss Elisha Linde and Mr. Steven Thornton of the *Metropolitan Review*," Lancaster said stiffly.

Elisha managed a precise curtsy, acutely aware of her plain wool dress. Even before Lord Stanton's untimely passing, Lady Stanton had been the toast of London Society, her salons drawing nobility and artists alike. Now, standing before the woman herself in her practical walking dress, Elisha felt every thread of her own modest attire.

"Charmed," Lady Stanton said, her smile sharp as she pressed closer to Lancaster. "His Grace speaks of you so often, I feel we're already acquainted."

"You're too kind, my lady."

"How… practical you look today," Lady Stanton purred. "Surely there are more amusing ways to spend a morning than being a spectator?"

Elisha felt Thornton's arm tense beneath her hand and patted his arm soothingly. "Miss Linde is assisting me with some acquisitions today," he supplied smoothly.

Lancaster's gaze flew to her hand then back to Thornton's eyes, but his tone remained light. "I believe you mistake the purpose of Miss Linde's 'practical' attire, Lady Stanton. Miss Linde has an extraordinary eye for rare manuscripts. One can hardly go crawling through dusty archives in silk. I would watch Mr. Thornton very carefully. He shall prove to be your strongest rival with an expert by his side."

Warmth bloomed in Elisha's chest at Lancaster's defense, even as her eyes caught on the way Lady Stanton's perfectly manicured fingers curled possessively around his arm.

"You're too kind, Your Grace," she said softly, the words tasting bittersweet on her tongue. "I'm afraid my scholarly pursuits pale compared to the excitement of your… social engagements." Before he could respond, she turned away, tugging Thornton gently toward the auction room where the first lots were being arranged for viewing.

She'd been a fool to think… but no. Better to focus on the task at hand than dwell on what could never be.

Elisha forced herself to focus on the leatherbound volume before her, though her awareness of Lancaster and Lady Stanton lingered like a thorn in her side. Thornton's presence beside her did nothing to steady her nerves. When he leaned closer to examine a page she indicated, she caught the subtle scent of pine and leather—masculine, but not overwhelming.

"Your thoughts seem elsewhere," he murmured, his penetrating gaze studying her face with concern. The tenderness in his expression would have set most ladies' hearts aflutter.

"Forgive me. I was considering the annotation styles." It was a half-truth at best.

From across the room came Lady Stanton's musical laugh followed by Lancaster's deeper tones. Thornton's hand brushed her elbow as he steadied her, and she realized she had tensed.

"Interesting how some books," he said quietly, "no matter how beautifully bound, fail to capture our hearts the way simpler volumes do."

The knowing look in his eyes made her cheeks warm.

"Some might say the same of people," he added, then mercifully returned to discussing print dates and paper quality.

Later, when Lancaster found her standing alone by a window as Thornton conversed with another gentleman, she steeled herself for another polite exchange.

"Miss Linde," he said softly. "Might I request the pleasure of your company for tea tomorrow? Hyde Park has a particularly fine selection this season."

"I'm afraid I must decline, Your Grace." Her voice was cool and professional. "My schedule is quite full, and I have no wish to provide fodder for gossip about Mayfair Mavericks and their… companions."

"My interest in you is genuine, Elisha."

Her eyebrow arched. "I didn't give you permission to use my Christian name, Your Grace. I find your claim to be most insincere and can't help wonder how Lady Stanton feels…"

"Lady Stanton is a friend, nothing more." He stepped closer, lowering his voice. "I suspect it would interest you to know Wordsworth has agreed to attend a gathering at the *Metropolitan Review*."

She stilled. "Wordsworth?"

"He has expressed curiosity about your charitable works. A

more comfortable arena for him than politics, I should think."

Her eyes narrowed. "And this gathering would take place…?"

"After our tea tomorrow." His lips curved. "Unless you are still too busy?"

She hesitated, clearly weighing professional opportunity against personal risk. The man was insufferable—using her professional interests to manipulate her into a social engagement. And yet, Wordsworth…

"Three o'clock," she finally said. "Don't be late, Your Grace."

"I wouldn't dare," he murmured, but she had already turned away, leaving only the ghost of her lavender scent behind.

EDGAR GRIPPED HIS glass too tightly as he watched Thornton lean close to Elisha throughout the afternoon, ostensibly to examine manuscripts she was pointing to. The man's hand hadn't left her elbow since their initial exchange, and the intimacy of the gesture made his cravat feel impossibly tight.

"Darling," Lady Stanton whined beside him, "you promised to show me the poetry section."

But he couldn't tear his eyes from the way Elisha's face softened as she explained something to Thornton. He wished that gentle expression would be directed at him… then he remembered his duties. Protecting her reputation and his heart meant maintaining distance.

Thornton whispered something that induced a shy demeanor from Elisha, and Edgar's gloved hand balled into a fist.

"I had no idea old books could be so provoking," Lady Stanton said archly. "Though perhaps it's not the books you are reacting to."

"Victoria," he warned quietly, but his gaze remained fixed on the pair across the room. Elisha's gray wool dress should have looked plain among the silk and satin of the other attendees.

Instead, she outshone them all—her eyes bright with intelligence, her movements precise and graceful as she handled each volume.

When Thornton's hand moved to the small of her back, Edgar found himself stepping forward before he could think better of it. Lady Stanton's fingers dug into his arm, halting him.

"Now, now," she murmured. "What would Society say if you made a scene over a mere writer?"

The words hit their mark. He was a duke. She was… impossible. And he had no right to the jealousy burning in his chest.

Yet when the opportunity arose—when Lady Stanton's attention was occupied by a friend animatedly describing troubles with her modiste—Edgar seized it. He found Elisha standing alone by a window, and despite every rational thought in his head, he approached.

After their exchange about tea and Wordsworth, he watched her walk away, his heart hammering against his ribs. He had secured tomorrow's meeting, but at what cost? He was playing with fire, and both their reputations hung in the balance.

"Success?" Lady Stanton materialized beside him, her tone deceptively light.

"I have no idea what you mean," Edgar replied, though his eyes remained fixed on Elisha's retreating form.

"Of course not, darling. Of course not."

AFTERNOON OVER TEA AND SCONES

E LISHA SAT BENEATH the tea garden's white-painted pavilion, acutely aware of the Duke of Lancaster's gaze upon her. The afternoon sun filtered through latticed roses, yet she felt exposed despite the shelter. What madness had possessed her to accept his invitation? After witnessing his attention to those Society beauties at Lord Hardwick's gathering, she should guard her heart.

The duke cut an imposing figure across the table, his large hands making the delicate tea setting seem almost absurd. He watched her with an intensity that made her pulse quicken, though whether from attraction or unease, she couldn't quite determine.

"How wonderfully vibrant it is here," she remarked, desperate to break the charged silence. The gardens were indeed beautiful, a world away from her usual haunts—the crowded printing house, the modest schoolroom where she taught her students, the cramped office where she penned her reviews.

"I presume you've not had occasion to partake in a leisurely tea before?" His tone was gentle, curious rather than condescending.

"Indeed not, Your Grace. I've scarcely had the luxury of a sedate promenade through Hyde Park. My days are a constant flurry of activity, perpetually tardy for appointments." She kept her voice light, refusing to let him see how his casual reference to their different stations affected her.

"On that note," he said, leaning forward slightly, "I found your piece on Miss Charlotte Brontë most enlightening. How did you come by such intimate knowledge of her circumstances?"

The genuine interest in his voice sparked her enthusiasm despite her reservations. Elisha found herself explaining her meeting with the governess-turned-poet, her hands moving animatedly as she spoke. The duke watched her with such focused attention that she felt herself warming under his gaze, her cheeks flushing from more than just the afternoon heat.

"I simply had to make her acquaintance," she continued, forcing herself to focus on the conversation rather than the way his blue eyes seemed to drink her in. "I am certain she shall leave an indelible mark upon the literary world. Our conversation was utterly delightful. I had hoped my modest article might draw attention to her poetry."

Their conversation was interrupted by a flutter of excitement from a nearby group of young ladies who had spotted the duke. Elisha watched as they preened and posed, their expensive gowns and practiced gestures speaking of years of finishing school training she had never received.

"Are you acquainted with those ladies?" she asked, though she already knew the answer. She had seen him with their type at Lord Hardwick's gathering—had watched him charm and flirt with seemingly every eligible young woman in London.

"Not in the slightest," he replied, offering the ladies a polite nod that sent them into fresh paroxysms of excitement.

"You appear quite accustomed to their attention."

"I am, after all, a Mayfair Maverick," he declared with a touch of mockery that made her chuckle.

She studied him for a moment, seeing both versions of him at once—the notorious rake and the man who had seemed to truly see her.

"Do you ever get tired of the female attentions, Your Grace?"

"Yes, of course."

His quick response surprised her. "I find that surprising if I'm being honest."

"Is it because you believe the male ego to be a bottomless pit?"

"No," she replied carefully, "it's because I see you in scandal sheets every week. If you don't enjoy female attention, why are you seen so often with multiple women, different women?"

He fidgeted with his napkin, a surprisingly insecure gesture from such a commanding man. "I like being surrounded by beauty, Miss, and I like diversity."

The words confirmed her worst fears. She had been a fool to think she might be different, that their conversations about literature and social reform had meant anything more than a novel diversion for a jaded aristocrat.

She sat straighter, armor sliding into place. "May I ask why you asked me to meet you here, Your Grace?"

The question hung between them, heavy with all she couldn't say—Why pursue me when you have your pick of Society beauties? What game are you playing? How dare you make me feel special only to remind me that I'm just another face in your endless parade of conquests?

EDGAR MAINTAINED A thoughtful silence, watching as she withdrew into herself, her finger tracing the length of her silver fork in what he suspected was an unconscious gesture of anger or hurt. He had spoken carelessly, falling back on the rakish persona he wore like a comfortable coat, and in doing so had wounded her. The realization sat uncomfortably in his chest.

"You inquired regarding the assembly with Mr. Wordsworth," he said softly, attempting to recover their earlier warmth.

"Indeed," she replied, her tone carefully neutral. "I admire his literary prowess but find him equally evasive."

"You may not be aware that he has experienced quite a bit of personal loss, including the deaths of two of his children. He is also quite disillusioned about politics, especially radical reforms, which has pushed him toward a more conservative view. Your stance on the Poor Law and your literacy program may have caused him to shy away. He does not like to discuss politics, you see, as he has suffered from criticisms of his recent works."

Her expression softened slightly. "I had no idea. Thank you for enlightening me, Your Grace. It is interesting, is it not, how we all cope with tragedies and disappointments in our own way? Mr. Dickens has had a difficult childhood, what with his father's incarceration in the Marshalsea Debtors' Prison. Yet, he is the sunniest person one could meet, so generous with his time and thoughts."

"How intriguing," Edgar said, genuinely surprised. "One man shies away while another faces it head-on," Edgar observed, studying her with renewed interest. "Where do you fall on that spectrum, Miss Linde?"

She met his gaze steadily. "Somewhere in the middle, Your Grace. I was orphaned at five years of age, immediately beginning work at a workhouse until I secured a cleaning position at a boys' school at seventeen."

The simple statement, delivered without self-pity, humbled him. While he had been raised in luxury, taught by the finest tutors, this remarkable woman had taught herself to read by peering through schoolroom windows. His gaze dropped briefly to her décolletage, not in mere appreciation of her beauty now, but in wonder at the strength that lay beneath such a delicate exterior.

She flinched at his scrutiny, however, misinterpreting his intent. She quickly changed the subject. "How do you recommend we proceed with Mr. Wordsworth's assembly without overwhelming him?"

Edgar forced his attention back to the matter at hand, though his mind still reeled from her revelations. "Perhaps you could hold a reading for the students in your literacy program and a few ardent admirers. He might be persuaded to read to a group of students."

Her face brightened momentarily before doubt crept in. "That is perfect, Your Grace. The students will be thrilled. But…" She hesitated. "I'm afraid the *Metropolitan* lacks the means to host a grand function befitting someone of Mr. Wordsworth's stature and Mr. Thornton… Well, I don't know him very well."

The mention of Thornton sent an unexpected surge of jealousy through Edgar. The way that man looked at her, protected her, claimed her through his position at the *Metropolitan*…

"You needn't concern yourself with the expense," he said, perhaps too quickly. "I shall speak to Mr. Thornton. If he will not approve, I shall see to it. I am certain his pride will have him volunteering in no time."

"Thank you, Your Grace. Are you well acquainted with Mr. Thornton?"

"No, but we cross paths occasionally in Parliament when I am in attendance."

"Do you not take an active role in the House of Lords?"

The question caught him off guard. "In truth, I am not active in politics, nor do I feel strongly about any issues."

He watched disappointment cloud her features, and something inside him withered at the sight.

"How could you not feel strongly about issues as important as… the reform?" Her voice dropped, thick with frustration. "What do you have a strong conviction for, Your Grace? Do you believe in anything at all other than obtaining pleasure?"

The angry accusation hollowed him from within. "You are forgetting yourself, Miss Linde."

She paled slightly, looking away and biting her lower lip. "I beg your pardon, Your Grace. Thank you for a lovely afternoon."

She rose abruptly, forcing him to automatically do the same. For a moment, he was tempted to let her go—to retreat to his usual diversions and forget this maddening woman who dared to challenge him, to see through his carefully constructed facade. But as she strode toward the forested pathways with surprising speed, he found himself following, drawn by something stronger than pride or propriety.

He maintained a careful distance, noting with a mixture of concern and admiration that she didn't look back even once. When they entered a secluded area, her pace slowed, and she pressed her forehead against a tree, the gesture so vulnerable it made his chest ache.

The setting sun cast long shadows through the trees, wreathing her in twilight. Every instinct told him to turn back, to let her go, to avoid the complications that pursuing her would inevitably bring. But his heart, so long dormant beneath layers of guilt and cynicism, had other ideas.

"Elisha…" The name escaped him like a prayer.

She turned, startled perhaps by the intimacy of it, her lips parting but no words emerging. Her breathing was shallow, her chest rising and falling rapidly, and he found himself mesmerized by the trembling of her parted lips.

"I am sorry," he managed, his own breath unsteady.

He stepped closer, drawn by a force beyond his control, and cradled her face in his hands. Her eyes—a blend of forest green and summer sun—widened in surprise. Her lips, pink and full and slightly parted, beckoned him. Drawing in a deep breath that was full of her essence—ink and paper and something indefinably, uniquely her—he lowered his mouth to hers and kissed her.

The taste of sweet tea and scones hit his senses first, then the impossibly soft lips, as juicy as a ripe peach. He tasted her gently with the flick of his tongue, afraid she may burst. He ran his tongue along her smooth bottom lip contrasting to the ridges of her teeth. He nipped at her pouty bottom lip, the one he had been dreaming about. Edgar brought his hands down and wrapped his arms around her body. His hands took the liberty of a master, feeling every curve, every dip, and hovering over his favorite, softest parts.

He turned around to lean against the tree while wedging her between his thighs. She sucked in a breath over his mouth when he pressed her firmly against the evidence of his arousal. She was firm yet soft, timid yet eager.

"I have wanted you since the first day we met, Elisha," he rasped. "I need you. I want all of you."

He slipped his mouth over hers and left nothing unanswered in his kiss. He teased, coaxed, and took until she moaned and ground herself against his steely ridge. Her passion, coupled with her innocence, was intoxicating. She returned his kiss hesitantly at first then boldly.

"Come with me," he said, "allow me to love you wholly."

His request went unanswered, so he paused his mouth and waited, her hot breath tickling his cheek.

"I can't," she said, finally. "I won't."

Standing straight, he held her loosely and gazed down at her. His brow furrowed as he became aware of how miserable she appeared.

"Are you all right?"

"I'm fine," she said, stepping backward.

"My desire for you does not mean I do not respect you."

"I understand."

"Then why are you withdrawing yourself? Do you not feel the same way?"

"I do, but I shouldn't. This cannot end happily." With that, she fled.

MADNESS AND DESIRE

T HE IRON GATES of Bethlem Royal Hospital loomed before Edgar, their unyielding bars a stark reminder of the societal constraints he'd never before questioned. Until now. He found himself studying the imposing facade with an uncomfortable sense of kinship. Was he not, in his own way, confined within social restrictions?

The asylum's interior assaulted his senses—not merely with its cacophony of wails and mumbles, but with the disquieting notion that the line between sanity and madness might be far thinner than he'd once believed. After all, was it not a form of madness to contemplate throwing away generations of privilege and position for a woman who wrote literary reviews, one he'd seen only a handful of times?

A woman in a tattered gown twirled past him, her song a nonsensical tune about teacups and ravens. Yet there was something in her unfettered movements that spoke of freedom— the very freedom he found himself increasingly yearning for. In another corner, a man furiously scribbled equations on the wall with a piece of chalk, his eyes wild with perceived revelation. Edgar couldn't help but wonder if he looked similarly possessed when thoughts of Elisha consumed him in the dead of night.

His father's last words on his deathbed echoed in his mind: "Preserve our legacy, Edgar. The Lancaster name must remain untarnished." How bitter those words tasted now, as he searched the corridors for a familiar face.

He found Patrick Adams in a quieter wing, overseeing the transfer of a new patient—another soul deemed too dangerous to Society's careful order.

"Your Grace," Adams said, surprise evident in his voice. "I didn't expect to find you in such… colorful surroundings."

"Adams," Edgar nodded, fighting the urge to loosen his cravat. "Might we speak privately?"

Once sequestered in a small office, Adams' professional demeanor softened. The room was sparse but orderly, much like the carefully structured life Edgar had led before Elisha had upset everything.

"I must say, Lancaster, I'm curious why you sought me out here instead of at my home. This must be urgent."

Edgar ran a hand through his hair, a gesture that would have horrified his late father. "I confess, I find myself in a state of… unease regarding a certain matter."

Adams' eyebrow arched elegantly. "Unease? How extraordinary. This is most unlike you, Lancaster."

"Indeed…" Edgar moved to the window, watching as two orderlies escorted a patient across the courtyard. "My disquiet pertains to… a lady."

"A lady?" Adams echoed, and Edgar could hear the smile in his voice. "While you've had no shortage of dalliances with the fairer sex, I don't recall you ever expressing concern over a lady of quality."

Edgar's hand moved to massage the nape of his neck. "Miss Elisha Linde. I find myself curious about one Steven Thornton, the proprietor of the *Metropolitan Review*. He has recently taken a more active role in its operations."

"Ah, the lady who bested you so delightfully." A knowing smirk played at Adams' lips. "I see she's captured more than just your literary interest."

The heat that crept up Edgar's neck was mortifying. "I merely wish to ensure her safety and well-being," Edgar managed, though the words sounded hollow even to his own ears.

"Is that so?" Adams' smirk deepened as he settled into his chair. "Are you quite certain you're not simply gauging your competition? For I must say, Lancaster, I've never before witnessed you in such a state of... shall we say, heightened color?"

"I am not blushing!" The words escaped with such force that a passing orderly paused briefly outside the door. Edgar lowered his voice. "I simply wish to know more about the man's character. There are... rumors about his business practices that concern me."

"Nor have I ever seen you so quick to deny an accusation," Adams said, his amusement evident. "Or so invested in the business practices of London's publishing houses."

"Will you assist me in this matter or not?" Edgar barked, his patience wearing thin.

Adams chuckled softly. "Of course I shall aid my lovelorn friend in his hour of need."

Edgar opened his mouth to refute the assertion, then thought better of it. Looking out at the rain-slicked courtyard, he muttered, "I pray it is not so. I cannot possibly repeat history. The *ton* would never accept such a match. My own family would..."

Yet even as he spoke the words, he couldn't quite quell the traitorous flutter in his chest at the memory of their hungry kiss.

He turned to face his friend, his gaze sharpening with sudden intensity. "I implore you, tell me this is not the manifestation of love—this all-consuming preoccupation, these incessant thoughts of her. For if it is, I find myself in a most precarious predicament. The Lancaster name, my position in Society, everything I was raised to protect... not to mention Lucia's sacrifice..."

Adams' countenance softened, his usual teasing manner giving way to genuine sympathy. "I believe, my friend, that this has the potential to blossom into love. It is undoubtedly an infatuation, but is that not how all passionate love affairs commence? The question you must ask yourself is whether your name and position are worth the price of denying your heart."

Three days later, Edgar sat in his study, the morning paper spread before him but his attention entirely captured by Miss Lovelace's latest missive. His hands trembled slightly as he reread her words.

Metropolitan Review, *29 April 1840*

Dear Mr. Steele,

Your tea preferences are duly noted. I suggest you savor them while you can, for come January of next year, you may find yourself brewing your own. Your peculiar window requirements are understandable as it readily provides means of escape from debtors.

As for the matter of "sparring," I believe this was used as a euphemism for you certainly seem lonely, almost to the point of being desperate. Your lack of popularity with the ladies may be due to grand but meaningless gestures. I appreciate your concern for my well-being, but I assure you, I am fit enough to leave any man exhausted.

I suggest you focus your energies on squirreling away for the winter months as you shall depart with 1000 pounds sterling. Which brings me to the question, can you afford it? Or did you mean 1000 pounds of your pride? I certainly hope not.

Your amused rival,
E. Lovelace

Miss Lovelace's words burned in his mind like brandy—sharp, intoxicating, and dangerous. A knock at his door preceded Hereford's arrival.

"Ready for our ride?"

Minutes later, they cantered through Hyde Park's misty paths, the spring air heavy with the scent of wet earth and new grass. Edgar's attention kept drifting to the letter that seemed to burn against his breast pocket.

"You seem rather distracted this morning," Hereford observed. "Could it have something to do with a certain literary lady?"

Edgar's wry smile betrayed him. Wordlessly, he withdrew the paper and passed it to his friend, watching as Hereford's expression shifted from curiosity to barely contained mirth.

"Good God!" Hereford's eyes widened as he read. "'Fit enough to leave any man exhausted?' My word, Lancaster, she's practically throwing down the gauntlet!"

"Indeed." Edgar's voice was tight with mingled amusement and frustration. "But I cannot help wondering—are Miss Lovelace's barbs truly coming from a different lady than Miss Linde?"

Hereford's brow furrowed. "You suspect they're the same person?"

"Miss Linde and Miss Lovelace." Edgar's eyes fixed on the distant tree line. "Their wit, their challenge—they mirror each other so precisely it cannot be coincidence."

"And if they are one and the same?" Hereford's voice was careful, measured. "What then?"

Edgar's fingers tightened on the reins as he considered the implications. "It means I've fallen under the spell of a woman clever enough to craft two entirely different personas—one to critique my work, another to challenge me in person. And God help me, I find myself captivated by both versions of her."

"You've always been drawn to complexity," Hereford mused. "Though perhaps not quite this much of it."

Edgar's laugh held little humor. "No indeed. And yet..." He trailed off, remembering the taste of Elisha's kiss, the fire in her written words. "I find myself unable to stay away. These literary salons, the workhouse visits—I tell myself they're necessary for research, but in truth..."

"In truth, you're becoming as lovesick as any green boy." Hereford's tone was gentle. "Though I doubt any green boy ever faced quite such an intriguing dilemma."

They rode in silence for a moment before Hereford spoke

again. "What will you do?"

"What can I do?" Edgar's voice was soft. "She challenges everything I thought I knew about myself, about what I want. Every letter, every encounter leaves me more…" He cleared his throat. "More unsettled."

Later that evening, alone in his study, Edgar found himself rereading the letter for the hundredth time. The brandy in his glass caught the firelight as he traced her words with his finger. "Fit enough to leave any man exhausted." The boldness of it, the sheer audacity…

His body responded to the implicit challenge, imagination painting vivid pictures of Elisha—for surely it was her. In his mind's eye, he saw her as she'd been at their last meeting: the quick flash of her smile, the graceful curve of her neck, the way her teeth had caught her lower lip as she considered her next verbal thrust.

The brandy glass clinked against the side table as he set it down, his member swelling beneath his trousers. The propriety he'd spent a lifetime cultivating warred with the raw need her words and image sparked in him. His hand moved lower and held his hard length.

Her eyes, seductive smile, and cherry lips floated in his mind's eye. Her lips had glistened with moisture after a sip of champagne, her delicate hands wrapped around the stem of the flute, her pink tongue darting out to lick the dewy drop as her teeth bit her lower lip simultaneously. He imagined kissing those lips, tasting the champagne in her mouth and drawing the flavor into his own.

"Elisha," he breathed as he saw in his mind's eye the swell of her breasts, creamy and abundant… How he would have her lie on her back and bare her sex, pleasure herself while he watched. He could imagine her folds, pale pink with the prettiest dark pink in the center—her entrance, the coveted silken tunnel, that's where he belonged.

He imagined the moans she would make as she reached her

peak, and the sound alone would be enough to drive him over the edge. He would then bend over, kissing her sex, lapping up the creamy nectar.

Edgar stiffened and waited for the ecstasy to spill over in his practiced hand. As the hot liquid flowed, it brought not satisfaction but deeper hunger.

THE LITERARY SALON

T HE ATTIC ROOM above the *Metropolitan Review's* printing press hummed with anticipation. Elisha stood before the cracked mirror, trying to still her trembling hands as Thornton adjusted the drape of her new purple gown. His fingers lingered a moment too long at her shoulders.

"Perfect," he murmured, his dark eyes meeting hers in the mirror. "You look exactly as I imagined when I selected this gown."

"It's beautiful, Mr. Thornton. But surely it was too extravagant—"

"Nonsense." He turned her to face him, his expression earnest. "Tonight could change everything for us. William Wordsworth himself, here in our humble establishment. We must present ourselves as worthy of his patronage."

The press thundered below, its familiar rhythm steadying her nerves. Everything they'd worked for hung on this evening's success—the gazette's reputation, the literacy program, their dreams of expansion. Yet the proprietor's intensity, the way his gaze seemed to claim her, made her step back under the pretense of smoothing her skirts.

"Miss Thornton!" she called, perhaps a touch too brightly. "Might you help me with these pins? I fear they're coming loose."

Amelia appeared in the doorway, resplendent in burgundy silk. Her quick glance took in the scene—Thornton's proximity,

Elisha's careful distance—and she swept forward with a rustle of fabric.

"Brother dear, shouldn't you be attending to the final arrangements downstairs? I'll help Elisha finish preparing."

Thornton's jaw tightened almost imperceptibly, but his smile remained pleasant. "Of course. Though I trust you'll save me a dance later, Miss Linde?"

Only after his footsteps faded did Elisha release her held breath. Amelia's deft fingers worked at her hair, their eyes meeting in the mirror.

"He means well," Amelia said softly.

"I know." Elisha watched her friend secure a loose curl. "Your brother has been nothing but generous…"

"But?"

"But I cannot help feeling that his generosity comes with… expectations."

Amelia's hands stilled. "He admires you greatly. And truly, Elisha, would it be so terrible? My brother could offer you security, position, the means to expand our literacy program beyond our wildest dreams."

The press below missed a beat, its rhythm faltering, like Elisha's heart at the thought of another man's touch—broader hands, a deeper voice, eyes that sparked with challenge rather than possession.

"I cannot marry a man I do not love," she said quietly, "no matter how advantageous the match."

Before Amelia could respond, excited voices drifted up from below. The guests were beginning to arrive.

"Tonight isn't about Steven, or… or anyone else," she said firmly. "It's about proving that the *Metropolitan Review* deserves to be taken seriously. That our mission to bring education to those who need it most is worthy of support."

Amelia squeezed her shoulders. "Then let us go make history, my dear."

As they descended the creaking stairs, Elisha straightened her spine. She could do this—charm their distinguished guest, secure his patronage, advance their cause. And if her heart quickened at the thought of seeing a certain duke among tonight's guests, well… that was a weakness she would simply have to master.

Thornton waited at the bottom of the stairs, his hand extended. Behind him, the printing house had been transformed: mirrors caught and multiplied the gaslight, fresh garlands adorned the walls, and a display of their finest issues stood proudly near the refreshments.

"Shall we?" he asked, his smile warm with promise.

Elisha placed her hand in his, ignoring the voice in her heart that whispered it was the wrong hand, the wrong smile, the wrong man. Tonight wasn't about matters of the heart. Tonight was about securing their future—all of their futures.

The announcement of William Wordsworth's arrival sent a ripple through the assembled crowd. But it was the tall figure beside him that made Elisha's breath catch—the Duke of Lancaster, more handsome than ever in his perfectly tailored evening attire. The Marquess of Hereford flanked his other side, completing the impressive trio.

"Magnificent," Thornton murmured beside her, his hand finding the small of her back, propelling her forward. "Come, let us greet them."

Elisha forced herself to focus on the elderly poet rather than the duke whose blue eyes she could feel following her movement. "Mr. Wordsworth," she executed a perfect curtsy, "we are honored by your presence."

Wordsworth's face creased with genuine warmth. "The honor, my dear, is mutual. I must confess, your recent piece on the transformative power of poetry in education caught my attention. Most innovative thinking."

"You're too kind, sir." She felt Thornton's grip tighten slightly at her back—a reminder of his presence, his claim. "Though I believe much of the credit belongs to Mr. Thornton for providing a platform for such discussions."

"Ah, yes, Mr. Thornton." The duke's rich baritone sent an involuntary shiver down her spine. "You've taken... liberties since your personal involvement."

Elisha watched as the two men sized each other up with the careful politeness of natural rivals. Thornton's smile didn't quite reach his eyes. "Your Grace. I must thank you for facilitating this evening's gathering. The *Metropolitan Review* is always grateful for aristocratic patronage."

Something flashed in the duke's eyes, but his expression remained pleasantly neutral. "The Metropolitan's commitment to education deserves recognition. I believe Mr. Wordsworth agrees?"

"Indeed." Wordsworth nodded enthusiastically. "Most admirable work."

"Miss Linde has been instrumental in its development," the proprietor said. "Her passion for education is inspiring. Perhaps Miss Linde might show us these educational facilities? I'm sure Mr. Wordsworth would be fascinated by their practical implementation."

"An excellent suggestion," Amelia interjected smoothly, appearing at their side. "Brother, surely Mr. Wordsworth would benefit from your overview of our printing operations first? I believe you mentioned some innovative techniques you've implemented."

Thornton hesitated, clearly reluctant to release his hold on Elisha, but the opportunity to impress their guest proved too tempting. "Of course. Mr. Wordsworth, if you'd care to follow me..."

As the proprietor led the poet away, with Hereford and most of the crowd following, Amelia gave Elisha a meaningful look before hurrying after them. The duke remained behind, standing close enough that Elisha could hear his breathing.

"Your Grace," she managed, painfully aware of their near solitude.

"Miss Linde." His voice was low and intimate. "I find myself in need of assistance with those educational materials you mentioned. Might you show me?"

It was a terrible idea. She knew it even as she nodded, even as she allowed him to lead her outside toward his awaiting carriage. Every step seemed to echo with warning, yet she couldn't bring herself to stop.

The duke helped her into the carriage, his presence overwhelming in the confined space. Elisha sat in one corner, trying to keep some distance, but he sat beside her, his eyes somehow dark yet smoking like hot charcoal.

"Mr. Thornton seems quite protective of you," he said.

"He has been very generous," she said carefully, not daring to meet his eyes lest he scorch her. "The *Metropolitan Review* owes him a great deal."

"And you? What do you owe him?"

She turned to face him, finding him closer than expected. "Nothing."

"Then why does Thornton behave as though he owns you?"

"I don't know."

"If you don't have an understanding, do you hold any affections for him?"

"No. Not at all."

"Good. And do you hold any affections for me?"

"Edgar," she breathed. "I ought not to. We shouldn't be here at all." Yet she made no move to step away, her knees pressed against his, her heart thundering.

His hand came up to cradle her face, thumb brushing her cheek. "Tell me you feel nothing for me, and I'll walk away. Tell me you prefer his touch to mine."

"I—" The words died in her throat as his face lowered toward hers.

Time seemed to stop. His mouth was hot and soft. His embrace was at once gentle and fierce, tender yet demanding. Her senses swam as the walls of propriety crumbled around them. His hand caressed her thighs and buttocks, firm and possessive.

Before she knew it, he had her straddling his lap. His hand then unbuttoned her bodice, spreading the thin fabric apart, exposing her breasts.

"Edgar…"

When he drew back, the raw longing in his gaze made her heart clench. The world narrowed to just the two of them, everything else falling away in a rush of sensation and need.

Wordlessly, he claimed her mouth again and his hand squeezed her breasts. His mouth then drew in her nipple, pinching with his lips, brushing lightly with his teeth.

"Edgar, that's… Oh my…"

Her fingers clutched at his shoulders as waves of feeling crashed over her. His mouth knew exactly when to nip and when to suck. Each motion of his tongue pushed arousal toward her groin, her core aching, her thighs wrapping around his waist and writhing against him.

"Blast it, Elisha. You're sin itself."

Edgar pushed his aching hardness against her heat and continued his assault on her nipples.

"You're my undoing, Elisha," he breathed against her skin. "My sweetest torment."

Their breaths mingled, hearts racing in tandem. "When he stands near you, when he dares to touch you… remember this moment, remember my mouth on your flesh."

Edgar was careful not to ruin her coiffure or her dress but his need of her was evident. It wasn't long before she stiffened against him, her moan scraping against her throat, muffled by his hungry mouth. Her hips lifted to meet his hardness, to ease the hollow ache deep within.

Her breathing gradually steadied, but she felt the tension radiating from his body, heard the ragged edge in his voice as he whispered, "Be mine, Elisha."

The words she'd longed to hear, yet they pierced her heart like thorns. "To what end?"

"I cannot promise matrimony, but I can promise love and

devotion."

Pain bloomed in her chest, sharp and crushing. She forced herself to shake her head, though every fiber of her being screamed to accept whatever scraps of happiness he offered. "No. If you can't make me your wife, you shall not have me at all." Her voice quavered. "Please do not seek me out again. It will only make my heartache worse."

She felt his reluctance in the way his hands lingered as he released her, saw how he gathered his aristocratic mask around himself like armor. But beneath that careful composure, his temple pulsed with barely contained emotion, and her heart ached to smooth away the tension there.

Edgar studied her for a long moment before moving to help her alight. Elisha kept her eyes downcast, knowing that one look into those dark depths would shatter her resolve. Her hands pressed against her bodice, trying to still the wild beating of her heart that seemed to cry out his name with each thunderous beat.

Upon entering the building, she could hear Thornton's voice carrying from the printing room, explaining their operations to their distinguished guest. She climbed the stairs toward the classrooms to play her part in securing the *Metropolitan Review's* future. She would have to stand beside Thornton, accept his attentions, ignore the duke's presence.

But for now, she allowed herself one moment of weakness, one moment to remember the feel of Edgar's touch, one moment to mourn what could never be.

EDGAR REMAINED IN the carriage for several minutes after Elisha departed, his hands shaking as he attempted to restore order to his appearance. The scent of her lavender perfume lingered in the confined space, taunting him with what he could never truly possess.

I cannot promise matrimony. The words echoed in his mind like a death knell. How easily they had fallen from his lips, yet how they burned now in the aftermath. He could offer her his heart, his devotion, his fortune—everything except the one thing that would make her truly his.

The weight of centuries of Lancaster legacy pressed down upon him. His father's voice seemed to whisper from beyond the grave: "The family name, Edgar. Our bloodline. Our duty to the realm."

Yet as he made his way back into the building, following the sound of voices toward the makeshift classroom, all he could think of was the pain in Elisha's eyes when she'd pulled away from him. The way her voice had broken when she'd asked him not to seek her out again.

He found the assembled guests in the classroom, where Wordsworth had begun his reading. Edgar positioned himself against the far wall, his gaze immediately seeking Elisha. She stood near the doorway beside Thornton, who had placed his hand possessively at the small of her back—the same spot Edgar's own hands had caressed mere moments ago.

The sight sent a surge of jealousy through him so potent it nearly stole his breath. Thornton's touch was proprietary, claiming, everything Edgar's could never be in public. The man could court her openly, marry her respectably, give her the security and position she deserved.

Edgar's hands clenched into fists at his sides as he watched Thornton lean closer to whisper something in Elisha's ear. She shifted slightly, trying to create distance, but Thornton merely adjusted his position to maintain their proximity.

He doesn't even see her discomfort, Edgar thought with disgust. *He sees only what he wants to possess.*

"Who, doomed to go in company with Pain, And Fear, and Bloodshed, miserable train! Turns his necessity to glorious gain..."

Wordsworth's words seemed to mock Edgar's situation. How

could he turn this necessity—this impossible love—to any sort of gain? There was only loss here, only the slow torture of wanting what he could never have.

A small boy raised his hand, and Edgar found himself momentarily distracted by the child's earnest question about making soup from old vegetables. The boy's simple metaphor—finding sustenance where others might see waste—struck him with unexpected force.

Was that not what Elisha had done with her life? Taken the waste of her circumstances—orphaned, impoverished, discarded by society—and transformed it into something beautiful and meaningful? She had turned necessity into glorious gain, while he remained trapped by privilege and position.

His gaze found her again across the room. She had moved away from Thornton, edging toward the side of the classroom, and Edgar felt a moment of savage satisfaction when her fingers brushed against his as she passed. The brief contact sent fire through his veins, a reminder of what they had shared in the carriage.

But then Thornton was calling her name, asking for a private discussion about the program's future, and Edgar felt the walls of duty and expectation closing in around her just as they did around him.

"Miss Linde," Thornton's voice carried clearly in the small space. "Might we speak privately after the reading? There are matters I wish to discuss regarding the program's future."

Edgar's jaw clenched. He could read between the lines of that polite request. Thornton intended to propose—tonight, while the success of the evening was fresh in everyone's minds, while Elisha was flush with triumph and gratitude.

"Of course, Mr. Thornton," she replied steadily, though Edgar could hear the strain beneath her composure. "After all, the future of the program must be our primary concern."

The words were like daggers in his chest. She would accept Thornton. Of course she would. It was the sensible choice, the only choice that made sense for a woman in her position. Thornton could offer her everything Edgar could not—respectability, security, a future free from scandal.

Wordsworth's voice rose again, reciting another verse:

"Though nothing can bring back the hour Of splendor in the grass, of glory in the flower; We will grieve not, rather find Strength in what remains behind…"

Edgar felt something break inside him at those words. The hour of splendor—their stolen moments in the tea garden, in his carriage—was ending. Soon there would be nothing left but the memory of her taste, her touch, her surrender in his arms.

He watched as she lifted her chin and smiled at something one of the children said, the expression so false it made his heart ache. She was already preparing herself, already building the walls that would keep her heart safe from further damage.

This is for the best, he told himself. *She deserves better than a duke's castoff, better than a life lived in shadows and shame.*

But as the reading concluded and he watched Thornton approach her with that confident, possessive stride, Edgar found himself taking a step forward before catching himself. There was nothing he could do, nothing he could offer that would change the fundamental impossibility of their situation.

He was the Duke of Lancaster. She was from the workhouses. And no amount of desire, no depth of feeling, could bridge that chasm.

As the guests began to disperse and Edgar prepared to take his leave, he allowed himself one last look at Elisha. She was speaking with one of the children, her face animated with genuine warmth and affection. This was her world, her purpose, her calling.

Perhaps it was enough. Perhaps her work, her mission to educate and uplift others, would be sufficient compensation for the sacrifice of her heart. Perhaps she would find happiness with Thornton, or at least contentment.

Edgar turned away before he could do something foolish, like stride across the room and claim her as his own, damn the consequences. Some battles could not be won, no matter how desperately one might wish otherwise.

The carriage ride home passed in a blur of London streets and gaslight. It wasn't until he was safely behind the doors of his townhouse that Edgar allowed himself to truly feel the weight of what he had lost.

He had found the one woman who could see past his title to the man beneath, who challenged him to be better, who made him want to deserve her good opinion. And he would have to let her go.

But as he sat in his study with a glass of brandy, staring into the dying embers of the fire, Edgar made himself a promise. He would not forget her. He would not forget the way she had looked at him with such hope and longing, the way she had trembled in his arms, the way she had chosen her principles over her heart.

If she was to be Thornton's wife, then Edgar would ensure she never wanted for anything. The literacy program would have his support, his protection, his funding for as long as he drew breath. It was the only gift he could give her, the only way he could show his love without destroying them both.

It would have to be enough.

TEMPTATION'S PRICE

THE NEWSPAPER TREMBLED in Elisha's hands, its headline stark and damning: "Duke of Lancaster Observed Departing Infamous House of Ill Repute with Two Companions."

Elisha's quill lay forgotten, drops of ink staining the half-written article before her. She had been writing about the importance of moral leadership in society—the irony was not lost on her.

"I thought you should hear it from me rather than gossip," Amelia said softly, hovering by the desk. "Though perhaps I should have waited until—"

"No." Elisha's voice was steady, betraying none of the turmoil beneath. "Better to know now, before I made an even greater fool of myself." She forced her fingers to relax their grip on the paper. "Besides, did I not reject him? He owes me nothing."

"Elisha—"

"It simply proves I was right about him." The words tasted bitter. "A man of privilege playing at reform while indulging his basest appetites. I should be grateful for this confirmation of his character."

Amelia's silence spoke volumes.

"What?" Elisha demanded.

"You're angry."

"I'm disappointed. There's a difference."

"No," Amelia said gently. "You're angry because you care for him, despite your better judgment. And now you're trying to convince yourself you never did."

Before Elisha could formulate a denial, her eyes fell on the unopened letter from Mr. Steele. Here was a man who understood her, who challenged her intellectually without demanding she compromise her principles. Who had never presumed...

Her fingers broke the seal with more force than necessary.

As she read his philosophical musings on love, something shifted in her chest. His words spoke of yearning, of questioning, of the very struggle she herself faced. Was this not a safer harbor for her heart?

"He sounds like a man in love," Amelia observed, reading over her shoulder.

"Perhaps." Elisha traced the elegant script. "Or perhaps he simply understands that love, like any worthy pursuit, requires careful study and consideration rather than reckless abandonment to base instincts."

The printing press below thundered to life, its rhythm matching her pulse. She pulled a fresh sheet of paper toward her, dipping her quill with renewed purpose.

"What will you write?" Amelia asked.

"The truth, as I understand it." Elisha began to write, her script firm and clear. "That love without principles is merely appetite. That true partnership requires more than passion or position. That sometimes the hardest part of love is choosing not to pursue it."

Each word felt like both bandage and blade, healing even as it cut.

ACROSS LONDON, EDGAR stood at his window, a different newspaper crushed in his fist. The article about his supposed debauchery stared up at him, every word a deliberate knife twist.

"Quite the creative interpretation of events," Hereford drawled from his chair. "Though I must say, helping two intoxicated companions into their carriage lacks the scandal they're implying."

"She'll believe it," Edgar said quietly. "She'll see it as confirmation of everything she suspects about me."

"Then tell her the truth."

"To what end?" Edgar turned from the window. "She made her position clear. My title, my wealth, my way of life—they're all anathema to her principles. Perhaps it's better this way. Let her think the worst of me. It will make it easier for her to move on."

"And you? Will it make it easier for you?"

Edgar's laugh held no humor. "Nothing about this is easy, old friend." He moved to his desk, where a half-written manuscript lay waiting. "But I have my responsibilities, my duties. She was right about one thing. I've been living without purpose."

"And now?"

Edgar picked up his pen, studying the words he'd written as both Steele and himself. Words about love and pain, about the price of passion and the cost of denial.

"Now I write. I pour everything I cannot say to her into these pages. And perhaps, in time, that will be enough."

But as he bent to his work, the image of Elisha's face haunted him—not her beauty or her passion, but the fierce intelligence in her eyes when she spoke of making the world better. He had never wanted someone's good opinion so desperately nor felt its loss so keenly.

"There's something else you should know," his friend said carefully. "Thornton has been making inquiries about Miss Linde's background. Very… thorough inquiries."

Edgar's grip tightened on the pen. "What kind of inquiries?"

"The kind a man makes when he's considering a proposal." Hereford watched him closely. "He's been visiting her former places of employment, speaking with people who knew her in the workhouse."

The pen snapped in Edgar's hand, ink staining his fingers. "He means to offer for her."

"So it would seem." Hereford leaned forward. "The question is, what are you going to do about it?"

"Do?" Edgar laughed bitterly, wiping ink from his hands. "What can I do? She's made her opinion of me quite clear. And Thornton…" He stood, pacing to the window and back. "Thornton can offer her everything she wants—the printing house, the literacy program, the chance to make a real difference."

"Can he?" Hereford's voice was quiet. "Or can he only offer her the means to continue what she's already doing? You have the power to do so much more, if you choose to use it."

Edgar stopped pacing. "What do you mean?"

"You're a duke, man. You have influence in Parliament, connections throughout society. If you truly wanted to support her causes…" Hereford shrugged. "Well, I'd say that would be using your position for something worthwhile, wouldn't it?"

The words had Edgar sinking into his chair, mind racing. "She accused me of living without purpose, of failing to use my advantages for the betterment of society."

"And was she wrong?"

"No," Edgar admitted softly. "But to change now, to throw my support behind social reform… everyone would know why. They'd say I was trying to curry favor with a commoner."

"Let them talk." Hereford stood. "The question is, which matters more—their good opinion or hers?"

Edgar looked down at his ink-stained hands, then at the half-written letter to Miss Lovelace. Everything he'd been too cowardly to say to Elisha in person, he'd poured onto these pages under a false name.

"I need time," he said finally. "Time to prove I can be the kind of man she could respect before Thornton…"

"Then I suggest you start immediately." Hereford moved

toward the door. "Because from the looks of it, Thornton isn't planning to wait much longer."

After his friend left, Edgar pulled out a fresh sheet of paper. This time, he didn't write as Steele, but as himself—drafting letters to his solicitor, to his contacts in Parliament, to the various charitable organizations he'd ignored for so long.

If he was going to win Elisha's respect, he would have to earn it. Not with grand gestures or passionate declarations, but with genuine commitment to the causes she held dear.

And perhaps, in becoming the kind of man worthy of her love, he might find that purpose she accused him of lacking.

He only hoped he wasn't too late.

Metropolitan Review, *15 May 1840*

My Dear Miss Lovelace,

I trust you have not been pining for my correspondence during this prolonged silence. Pray, do not imagine that I have neglected our epistolary engagement. On the contrary, I have been most persistently occupied in pursuit of a more profound understanding of that most enigmatic of human experiences: love and romance.

I have taken it upon myself to consult with various luminaries in the fields of psychology, physiology, and neurology on this most intriguing subject. Furthermore, I have engaged in correspondence with authors of no small renown, seeking their insights on matters of the heart. Specifically, I had wished to know the answers to these questions:

Why is anything worthwhile so difficult to attain? How does a heart break when it cannot break? Why must pain precede healing?

I find myself most eager to learn your thoughts on these weighty matters, Miss Lovelace. Pray, do not keep me in sus-

pense regarding your own philosophies on this most captivating of subjects.

Yours in anticipation of your wise counsel,
Aengus Steele

Back at the *Metropolitan Review*, Elisha set aside her completed response to Mr. Steele, her thoughts still troubled. The printing press below had fallen silent, leaving an emptiness that seemed to echo her own.

"Elisha?" Thornton's voice made her start. He stood in the doorway, more formally dressed than usual. "Might I have a word?"

She looked up, noting the unusual tension in his bearing. "Of course."

He closed the door behind him, an action that made Elisha's pulse quicken with unease. He rarely sought such privacy in their discussions.

"I've been thinking," he began, moving to stand before her desk, "about the future of the *Metropolitan Review*."

"Oh?" She kept her voice neutral, though something in his tone made her want to retreat.

"Yes. About its potential, its growth…" He paused, studying her face. "About what it needs to truly flourish."

"We've made remarkable progress already," Elisha said carefully. "The Wordsworth evening alone has brought new subscriptions and—"

"I'm not speaking merely of business matters." His voice softened as he moved around the desk, too close for comfort. "I'm speaking of partnerships. Of joining forces in more… permanent ways."

Elisha's hands trembled slightly as she gathered her papers, trying to create some task to focus on. "Mr. Thornton—"

"Steven," he corrected gently. "Please. After all we've built together, surely we can dispense with formalities."

She forced herself to meet his gaze. His eyes held genuine

warmth, even affection, but something else lurked beneath—a certainty that made her nervous.

"I've made inquiries," he continued. "About your background, your circumstances. I wanted to be sure that any… offer I made would be appropriate and welcome."

Her stomach dropped. "Inquiries?"

"Nothing unseemly, I assure you. Merely ensuring that there were no impediments to what I hope to propose."

"And what exactly are you proposing?" The words came out sharper than she intended.

Steven actually smiled at her tone. "That directness—it's one of the things I admire most about you." He reached for her hand, but she managed to shift away under the pretense of straightening more papers.

"You're an extraordinary woman, Elisha. Your intelligence, your dedication to our cause, your beauty… you deserve more than the life of a mere employee."

"I am quite content with my position," she said firmly.

"But you could have so much more." His voice grew earnest. "Together, we could expand the *Review's* influence tenfold. The literacy program could reach every corner of London. Your dreams of education reform could become reality."

Each word was like a snare, making it harder to escape. He was offering everything she'd worked for, everything she believed in. The practical choice, the sensible choice, the choice that would secure her future and her causes.

So why did it feel like chains closing around her?

"You're very kind," she managed, "but I—"

"Don't answer now," he cut in smoothly. "Take time to consider. I know it's unexpected, though surely not entirely surprising. We work so well together, share so many goals…"

A knock at the door saved her from responding. Amelia entered, then stopped short at the scene before her.

"I apologize for interrupting," she said, her sharp eyes taking in Elisha's tension and her brother's proximity. "But Mr.

Wordsworth's letter has arrived. He wishes to contribute a regular article on education."

The news should have thrilled her. Instead, Elisha felt it like another brick in the wall being built around her future—a future tied inexorably to the *Metropolitan Review* and to Steven Thornton.

"Wonderful news," Steven beamed. "You see, Elisha? Everything is falling into place." He moved toward the door, pausing to add, "Think on what I've said. About our future together."

Only after he left did Elisha release her held breath. Amelia approached cautiously.

"Did he just…?"

"Not officially," Elisha said, her voice unsteady. "But the intent was clear enough."

Amelia sat beside her. "What will you do?"

Elisha looked down at her desk—at Steele's letter about love, at the newspaper with its tale of the duke's supposed indiscretions, at the fresh contracts that would secure the *Review's* future.

"I don't know," she whispered. "For the first time in my life, I truly don't know."

The printing press rumbled to life below, its steady rhythm usually so comforting. But today it felt like a countdown, marking the moments until she would have to choose between her heart's desires and her life's work.

And she wasn't sure, anymore, which was which.

SUFFERING AND COURTSHIP

THE RHYTHMIC THUD of gloved fists against leather resonated through the dimly lit pugilistic establishment. Edgar circled Patrick Adams in the ring, their bare torsos glistening with perspiration. The early morning hour afforded them privacy, the club bereft of patrons save for these two gentlemen, exorcising their frustrations through the noble art of fisticuffs.

Edgar's jab lacked its customary precision, his movements uncharacteristically languid. Adams deftly evaded the blow, concern evident in his expression as he landed a solid strike to Edgar's ribs.

"Your mind appears to be elsewhere today, Lancaster," Adams remarked. "Pray, what troubles you?"

Edgar shook his head, retreating a step to regain his breath. "It is of no consequence. Mere fatigue."

Adams snorted his disbelief. "Indeed. And I am a man of the cloth." He lowered his fists, signaling a cessation of their sparring. "I trust this has naught to do with Miss Linde and your recent sojourn to Madame Tansley's establishment?"

Edgar's head snapped up, his eyes narrowing. "To what do you refer?"

"Come now, do not feign ignorance," Adams chided, lightly tapping the duke's chest. "It is the talk of every scandal sheet in London. 'Duke of Lancaster Observed Departing Infamous House of Ill Repute.' What possessed you to act with such indiscretion when you have a lady's heart to win over?"

Edgar's brows furrowed. "I know nothing of this. I have not darkened Madame Tansley's door since February last."

Adams shook his head, his expression growing grave. "I wonder, then, who is spreading such falsehoods."

"I presume they are attempting to peddle more papers, or they were misinformed." Edgar's countenance darkened, concerned that the article may lower Miss Linde's opinion of him even further.

Adams nodded thoughtfully. "Perhaps. I may be overreacting."

Edgar turned away, his posture rigid. "What have you uncovered about Thornton?"

"He was the illegitimate son of a wealthy baron who lost everything when the nobleman died with a mountain of debt. No relative was willing to take him in, so he lived on the streets until he was accepted into a workhouse. He proved his intelligence, gaining promotion after promotion, and saved enough to purchase passage to India where he labored in mines until he came to own one. Then two. Then three. When he learned of his half sister from his father's mistress, he funded her publishing venture, placing himself as the proprietor. He sold his mines and returned to England only recently due to malaria. It seems that his constitution has improved."

Edgar's jaw clenched, his fingers curling into fists at his sides. "I see. And what of his character?"

Adams chose his words carefully. "By all accounts, he is a man of ambition and drive. With respect to female conquests, he seems quite selective. He has set his sights upon Miss Linde, doubling her wage and accompanying her to every literary and political salon of note."

Edgar flinched visibly. "I do not wish to hear of Miss Linde in the same sentence as that… man." He sank to the floor as if his bones had turned to lead.

"I confess I find great pleasure in witnessing your renewed

vitality after these many years of melancholy."

Edgar raised his head, startled. "Vitality? When have I demonstrated such exuberance?"

"Even in your moments of uncertainty regarding the lady, you were imbued with a vigor I had not witnessed in years! The last time your countenance bore such animation was when you believed you had unearthed a treasure chest in the cove. Do you recall the incident?"

"Aye. It was revealed to be a ruse perpetrated by your band of miscreants, the chest filled with naught but manure! I had labored to drag the accursed thing for a mile up the cliff face before I pried it open."

Adams erupted into peals of laughter at the recollection, barely able to articulate his words. "And you… you thought… to take an axe… the resultant spattering…"

Edgar glowered at his friend as Adams clutched his sides, overcome with mirth.

"I ought to have informed your father, that you might receive a sound thrashing," Edgar grumbled.

"Then your own sire would have administered a lashing for your lack of loyalty to a friend," Adams retorted, wiping tears of laughter from his eyes.

"You were no friend. Merely the son of an exiled nobleman."

"You speak true, we were no friends. We were brothers. You were well aware of the truth. It is why you never breathed a word of the incident to a soul."

"You were quite mad. What manner of person expends such effort on a mere prank? Had you applied such diligence to your studies, you might have become a productive member of society."

"More productive than safeguarding the Prince of Bavaria? Being awarded the Victoria Cross?"

"Certainly more productive than deriving amusement from my predicament."

Adams' laughter subsided, his expression growing more serious. "Come now, Lancaster. You know full well I take no pleasure in your distress. I merely wish to see you happy once more."

Edgar sighed heavily, running a hand through his disheveled hair. "And you believe Miss Linde to be the key to my happiness?"

"I believe she has awakened something in you that has long lain dormant," Adams replied carefully. "Whether she is the key to your happiness or merely the catalyst for change, I cannot say. But I implore you, do not dismiss these feelings so readily."

Edgar rose to his feet, pacing the room with restless energy. "And what would you have me do? Court a woman so far beneath my station? Invite the scorn and ridicule of the ton?"

Adams watched his friend's agitated movements, his voice gentle but firm. "I would have you follow your heart, for once in your life. The *ton* be damned. You are the Duke of Lancaster. If you cannot choose your own path, who can?"

Edgar paused, his hand resting on the mantelpiece. "It is not so simple, Adams. There are expectations, responsibilities…"

"And there is life, Lancaster," Adams interrupted. "A life that you have denied yourself for far too long. But before you decide if she is worth the risk, there is something you should know."

Edgar turned to face his friend, his expression grim.

"Mark Evans, he is the manager of the biggest textile factory in these parts. He is also possibly the leader of the Pioneers, although no one knows exactly."

Edgar's brows furrowed. "The group which has been in battles with the Widows?"

"That very one. Mark Evans was spotted by my men meeting with Miss Linde on two occasions in a dark alley past midnight."

The statement hung in the air between them, charged with possibility and fraught with uncertainty. Edgar felt his neck muscles tighten with tension.

"It seems Miss Linde is one of the authors of the reform pamphlets. If I had to guess, she stores the pamphlets at the

Metropolitan office, one of the reasons why she lodges there."

Edgar's face darkened like a thundercloud as a muscle in his jaw twitched. "Good Lord! Find out, will you? If the authorities discover her involvement, she could face sedition charges—transportation, or worse." His voice grew hard with barely controlled fury. "The foolish woman is risking her life for these causes."

He began pacing, his agitation evident. "And if she is storing them at the *Metropolitan*, bring them to my cave for storage. Meet with this Evans fellow and determine how else Miss Linde is involved. I shall step in to keep her safe whether she welcomes my protection or not."

Adams nodded then said, "I believe you have decided she is worth the risk."

Exhaling deeply, Edgar replied, "I would never forgive myself if something happened to her and I did nothing to prevent it. I did not comprehend the depth of my affliction until I strived to banish her from my thoughts. Alas, the more I struggle to forget, the more consuming my preoccupation becomes."

Adams stepped forward, placing a consoling hand on Edgar's shoulder. "Do you recall the tale your father recounted to us regarding the first Duke of Lancaster?"

Edgar nodded. "I remember he wed his commoner mistress, but the legitimacy of the marriage and their issue endured until his demise. It was not an easy existence for him and his family."

"But they remained wed and loved one another."

"Regarding that," Edgar said, tousling his hair. "Miss Linde has… refused my advances."

Adams regarded his friend pensively. "And how, precisely, did you advance?"

"Well… I informed her of my desire to bed her."

Adams snickered. "How have you earned the distinction of a rake when you are so woefully ignorant in the art of courting women?"

"I was overcome with panic. I knew not what to say when

she inquired if I would offer for her, but that was not the entirety of her statement. She refused me on the grounds that I am not putting my title and wealth to good use."

A rare smile graced Adams' visage. "I find myself admiring that lady, Miss Linde. You must court her properly before Thornton secures her affections."

Feeling a surge of possessiveness in his breast, Edgar rose to his feet, raising his hands to recommence their pugilistic exercise.

As he and Adams resumed their sparring, perspiration beaded on their brows, their breathing labored yet controlled. The rhythmic sound of fists meeting flesh and the occasional grunt of exertion filled the air.

"Tell me, Lancaster," Adams said between jabs, "what do you intend to do about your courtship?"

Edgar ducked a swift uppercut, countering with a hook to Adams' ribs. "Perhaps it's time to cultivate a new image. One that Miss Linde might find more appealing and believable."

As they continued their bout, Edgar's mind raced with possibilities.

"How can it be thus," Edgar said between jabs, his breath coming in short gasps. "I scarcely know her, not in any true sense. Can one truly succumb to the throes of love with such a dearth of knowledge about the object of one's affections?"

Adams grunted, dodging Edgar's next strike. "Love is a capricious thing," Adams said, intensifying his assault with a flurry of well-aimed blows. "It seldom awaits formal introductions or considers the niceties of courtship."

They continued their bout in silence for several moments, the only sounds their labored breathing and the dull thud of gloved fists meeting flesh.

"Your counsel, as always, is invaluable," Edgar said.

"Does this mean I have a free membership to your pleasure den?"

"This means you can own the pleasure den."

"Truly? Being in love does not mean you need to become old

and shackled."

"Yes, it does, my friend. Yes, it does."

THE METROPOLITAN'S OFFICE bustled with activity, the scratch of quills on parchment and the rustle of papers filling the air as Elisha and Amelia labored diligently, their heads bent over their respective tasks. Elisha had just finished reading Mr. Steele's latest letter, his philosophical questions about love weighing heavily on her mind.

Metropolitan Review, *20 May 1840*

Dear Mr. Steele,

A love worthy of the name should ignite a fire within the breast of man, while drawing forth the gentlest tears from the eyes of woman.

Similarly, a tale of love, when masterfully woven, ought to evoke these powerful responses from its readers.

I trust that your scholarly pursuits have not unduly diverted your attention from your literary endeavors. Pray, remember that but two months remain for the completion of your manuscript.

I remain, sir, your faithful correspondent, wishing you the very best of fortune in your authorial pursuits.

Your keen adversary,
E. Lovelace

She had just set aside her completed response when the tranquil atmosphere was shattered by a sharp rap upon the door, heralding the arrival of Steven Thornton.

Elisha observed how he cut a figure of unmistakable affluence and standing, attired in a perfectly tailored suit of the finest broadcloth, a gold watch chain draped elegantly across his waistcoat, and highly polished Hessian boots that gleamed in the daylight. Every aspect of his appearance seemed meticulously curated to project an image of success and authority.

"Ladies," he announced, inclining his head as he strode into the room. His gaze fixed pointedly upon Elisha. "I have been perusing your exchanges with this Steele fellow. What has become of the fire, the conflict? You are growing far too cordial for my liking."

Elisha straightened, her chin lifting in defiance. "Mr. Thornton, I assure you, my correspondence with Mr. Steele is—"

"Is imperiling the foundation of this journal's popularity," Steven interrupted. "I implore you to maintain a more... contentious tone. The public craves a battle of wits, not a friendly discourse over tea."

Elisha watched as Amelia rose to her feet, indignation flashing in her eyes. "Now see here, Steven. I am the editor, and it is my prerogative to determine the nature of the articles that grace our pages. What gives you the temerity to suddenly appear and begin dictating editorial policy?"

Steven nodded, and Elisha noticed a smile playing about his lips. "I am well aware of your position, dear sister. However, do I not have the right to voice my opinion for your consideration? Am I mistaken in requesting that Miss Linde adjust her style to maintain the satisfaction of our readership?" He turned back to Elisha. "I am not asking you to compromise your integrity as a writer. I merely entreat you to keep our readers in a state of breathless anticipation, to create more tension and suspense, as any accomplished novelist would."

Before Amelia could utter another word, Elisha smiled warmly. "Of course, Mr. Thornton. I comprehend your concern. The last two missives were mere exceptions. I assure you, we shall soon return to our customary verbal thrusts and parries."

She watched satisfaction spread across Steven's countenance. "I am most grateful, Miss Linde." Turning to Amelia, he said, "Now, that was not so dreadful, was it?"

Elisha observed Amelia cross her arms and fix her brother with a stern gaze.

"Miss Linde," Steven said, his voice as smooth as silk, "might I prevail upon you to accompany me to select furniture at this instant? I find myself clueless about color palettes."

Elisha blinked, momentarily nonplussed by the request. "Mr. Thornton, I fear that is quite impossible. Amelia—"

"I am fine. I can handle things from here, Elisha," Amelia said, and Elisha caught the delighted look on her friend's face. "Steven asked me to accompany him, but I suggested he take you instead. You are much better at that sort of thing."

Elisha hesitated, glaring at Amelia for her obvious matchmaking efforts.

"Very well, Mr. Thornton," Elisha acquiesced, reaching for her shawl. "A brief distraction might indeed prove beneficial."

She noticed Steven's smile widen with what appeared to be triumph. "Excellent. Shall we?" He proffered his arm with exaggerated gallantry.

"We shan't be long, Amelia," Elisha assured as she accepted his arm.

"See that you are," Amelia replied, her tone carrying a teasing note that was not lost on either of them.

As they perused the aisles of Mortimer's Fine Furnishings, the gaslit chandeliers casting a warm glow upon the polished mahogany and velvet upholstery, Elisha noticed Steven's demeanor soften perceptibly.

"Miss Linde," he began, his voice low and measured, "I am a self-made man. Nothing was ever bestowed upon me gratis, and I dwell in constant trepidation of returning to... to whence I originated."

"And where might that have been?" Elisha asked, her gloved hand tracing the curve of a Queen Anne chair.

She watched his jaw tighten visibly. "The workhouse. A veritable inferno on earth, Miss Linde..." He trailed off, evidently lost in painful reminiscences.

Elisha's heart squeezed beneath her corseted bodice. "I comprehend more than you might suppose, Mr. Thornton."

His eyes snapped to her countenance, and she could see dawning realization in his gaze. "Of course. You and Amelia… you were ensconced there together, were you not?"

Elisha nodded, her bonnet ribbons quivering. "We were. Different workhouse than you, I'm sure, but the same cruel world."

"I confess I am ignorant of the full extent of your and Amelia's sufferings," Steven said, his voice taut with what she perceived as suppressed emotion. "I remained unaware of her existence until after our parents… well, after their passing. I was dispatched to a workhouse in Manchester, commencing my labors in the textile mill. Fourteen hours daily, suffocating on cotton dust, my fingers rendered bloody by the unforgiving machines."

"For us, it was the arduous task of breaking stones and bones, shucking oysters," Elisha replied softly. "Our hands were raw and cut beyond recognition."

A weighty silence descended upon them, and Elisha felt the shared comprehension of past suffering forge an unexpected bond amidst the opulent surroundings.

Steven cleared his throat, straightening his cravat. "It is the impetus behind my relentless drive, my… protective stance toward all I have constructed. But I entreat you to understand, I genuinely desire what is best for Amelia, yourself, and our business ventures."

As they moved through the furniture emporium, Elisha scrutinized his countenance, contemplating the sincerity she perceived in his expression. "I am most appreciative of your sentiment, Mr. Thornton."

"However," he continued, his gaze intensifying as he ran a hand along the back of a Chippendale settee, "I meant what I articulated regarding your correspondence with Mr. Steele. It is of paramount importance to our business ventures that you perpetuate the conflict. Moreover, I find myself experiencing a tinge of… jealousy."

Elisha felt a rush of warmth suffuse her cheeks, her hand instinctively reaching for her fan. "Mr. Thornton, we are scarcely acquainted."

"That may be true," he conceded, adjusting the fit of his kid gloves, "but I certainly feel as though I know you intimately. Amelia has extolled your virtues on countless occasions, and upon our initial meeting a fortnight hence, I was utterly captivated by your beauty."

Elisha felt her breath catch in her throat, taken aback by the directness of his declaration. "Mr. Thornton, I… I am most flattered, but I must confess I find your words rather… unexpected."

Steven's gaze softened, and she observed a gentle smile playing about his lips as he gestured toward a display of fine china. "I apologize if I have discomposed you, Elisha. It was not my intention. I merely wished to express my admiration and… my hope that we might become better acquainted."

As they continued their perusal of the furnishings, Elisha found herself in a state of conflicted emotions. On one hand, Steven's shared history and apparent sincerity touched her deeply. On the other, his sudden declaration of interest left her feeling uneasy.

"Mr. Thornton," she began carefully, adjusting her shawl, "while I am touched by your words, I must remind you that my primary focus is on my work with our business ventures and our literacy program. Any… personal considerations must remain secondary to that purpose."

Steven nodded, and she observed a look of understanding cross his features as he examined an ornate Regency-style mirror. "Of course, Miss Linde. I would expect nothing less from a woman of your dedication and principles. Perhaps, in time, you might come to see that our goals are not so very different."

As they made their way toward the exit of Mortimer's Fine

Furnishings, Elisha tried to banish thoughts of the duke from her mind. She realized with a start that she had found genuine pleasure in her discourse with Steven and was begrudgingly developing a measure of respect for him. Despite his humble origins, he had clearly procured a substantial education, and his opinions on literature were surprisingly astute. She found herself chuckling at his wry observations regarding London Society.

"I am most grateful for this enlightening excursion, Mr. Thornton," she said as they paused by a display of Wedgwood china. "It has been… most illuminating."

He took her gloved hand, raising it to his lips in a gentlemanly salute. "The pleasure was entirely mine, Miss Linde. I do hope we might have the opportunity to engage in such discourse again in the near future."

As Elisha observed his figure approaching a shop staff member, she wondered about this enigmatic man who seemed at once charming and calculating, then vulnerable and guarded. She found herself quite at a loss as to how to regard him.

One thing, however, remained certain. He was not the Duke of Lancaster.

The comparison arose unbidden in her mind, and Elisha chided herself for allowing her thoughts to stray in such a direction. Yet she could not help but notice the stark differences between the two men. Where the duke exuded a natural, almost effortless charm, everything Mr. Thornton did felt studied and carefully crafted, though no less sincere for that calculation.

As she stepped into the carriage waiting outside, Elisha found herself feeling an inexplicable sense of loyalty to the duke—a man who, she reminded herself sternly, had no claim on her affections, especially given the recent scandal sheets.

"How was your outing?" Amelia asked when Elisha entered their shared office, her tone laced with barely suppressed curiosity.

Elisha paused, considering her response carefully. "It was… enlightening," she replied, echoing her words to Mr. Thornton.

"Your brother is a more complex man than I had initially supposed."

As she dipped her pen in ink, Elisha resolved to focus on her work, pushing thoughts of both men to the recesses of her mind. After all, she reminded herself, she had business ventures to manage and a literacy program to nurture. Matters of the heart would have to wait.

THE OFFER

THE GAZETTE'S OFFICE was thick with the scent of ink and oil, but the usual rhythmic clatter of the printing press had fallen silent. Elisha knelt beside the massive machine, her sleeves rolled up and her hands stained black with grease and ink as she helped two pressmen examine the seized gears.

"Elisha," Amelia called, weaving through the chaos with a stack of newspapers in her arms. "I've brought the latest editions from our competitors for your perusal."

Elisha nodded, not looking up from her work. "Thank you, Amelia. Just set them on my desk, if you would. I'll review them once we've got this beast running again."

Hours passed, the sun dipping low on the horizon before Elisha finally straightened, stretching her aching back. She made her way to her desk, eager to see what news the other papers deemed worthy of print.

As she leafed through the pages, a familiar name caught her eye. Her heart quickened as she read:

"Duke of Lancaster Spotted in Bath"

Frowning, Elisha read on. The article described Edgar dancing at a gentleman's club, "in the company of a striking blonde beauty." She shook her head, confusion warring with anger.

She reached for another paper, only to find another article:

"Lancaster's Latest Liaison? Duke Seen Dining in Bath"

This time, the duke was reportedly sharing an intimate dinner with a "vivacious redhead" at a fashionable restaurant.

Her hands trembling slightly, Elisha grabbed the last paper:

"Mayfair Maverick on the Move: Lancaster Charms Bristol"

The most recent sighting placed Edgar at a country house party, "his attentions devoted to the lovely brunette daughter of the host."

Elisha sat back, her mind whirling. Three sightings in three different locations, each with a different woman. She tried to reconcile these reports with the Edgar she knew, the man who had kissed her so passionately.

She closed her eyes, taking a deep breath to dispel the humiliation she felt. She would not be the first woman to be charmed by a rake only to be forgotten once she refused to give him her virtue.

What a fool she had been. Her skin still tingled where his lips had branded her, and her breasts ached with the memory of his mouth. She pressed her thighs together, fighting the persistent throb between them that refused to fade whenever she thought of him.

"Elisha?" Amelia's voice broke through her reverie. "Is everything all right? You look pale."

Elisha forced a smile, quickly folding the newspapers. "Yes, quite all right. Just... surprised by some of the news."

Amelia approached and slowly unfolded the papers, her expression growing concerned as she read.

"Oh, Elisha. I am sorry. How could he do this to you? I thought he was an honorable man."

Amelia placed an arm around her friend, squeezing gently for comfort.

"I thought he was too. I'm very glad to have refused him," Elisha said.

Amelia regarded her cautiously. "You refused his offer?"

Elisha shook her head. "No. I refused his request for... intimacy."

Elisha retreated to her desk, her fingers trembling slightly as she tried to focus on the tasks at hand. The familiar rhythm of their work routine offered a blessed distraction from her churning thoughts, though she couldn't help noticing how Amelia's usual chatter had given way to a weighted silence. Each time their eyes met across the room, she caught her friend's concerned glance. Amelia's loyalty meant everything to her, especially now.

The humming of the machine continued with frantic energy long after the usual closing hour. The breakdown of the machine had thrown their entire schedule into disarray, leaving a mountain of work to be completed before dawn. Elisha stood at the center of the chaos, her sleeves rolled up, hair escaping its pins, as she frantically reorganized the typeset for tomorrow's edition.

"Miss Linde," Steven Thornton's voice cut through the clatter, startling her. "How may I be of assistance?"

Elisha looked up, surprised to see him still present. She noticed his usual impeccable attire was slightly disheveled, his cravat loosened—a sign of the long day they'd all endured. "Mr. Thornton, I thought you'd gone home hours ago."

"No, I sent Amelia home just now. I couldn't possibly leave you to manage this crisis alone," he said as he removed his jacket. "Where shall I begin?"

For a moment, Elisha hesitated. Thornton had always been more of an overseer than a participant in the day-to-day operations of the gazette. Yet here he was, rolling up his sleeves, ready to dive into the mess of ink and paper.

"Well, if you're certain," she said, gesturing to a stack of jumbled type. "We need to sort these and reset the front page. The lead story has changed with the latest developments in Parliament."

Thornton nodded, immediately setting to work. For the next few hours, they labored side by side, their usual formalities falling away in the face of shared purpose. Elisha found herself appreciating Thornton's efficiency, his quiet competence a perfect complement to her meticulous attention to detail.

As the night wore on, Elisha noticed small acts of thoughtfulness from Thornton she'd never seen before. He anticipated her needs, fetching fresh ink before she could ask, steadying her hand when fatigue made it shake. In these moments, she glimpsed a side of him that intrigued her—less calculated, more genuine than his usual carefully controlled demeanor.

Finally, as the first light of dawn began to creep through the windows, the last page was set. Elisha sank into a chair, exhaustion etched on every line of her face. Thornton disappeared briefly, returning with a covered tray.

"I thought we might need some sustenance," he said, his voice gentle as he revealed a steaming pot of tea and a plate of delicate sandwiches.

Grateful beyond words, Elisha accepted a cup, the warmth seeping into her tired hands. As they ate in companionable silence, she found herself studying Thornton. The usual hard lines of his face were softened in the early morning light, and there was something in his eyes she'd never noticed before—a vulnerability that reminded her, unexpectedly, of her own struggles.

After a while, Thornton cleared his throat. "Miss Linde, there's a matter I wish to discuss with you, if you're not too fatigued."

Elisha looked up, curiosity overriding her exhaustion. "Of course, Mr. Thornton. What is it?"

He paused, and she watched him gather his thoughts. "We've both risen from humble beginnings," he began, his voice uncharacteristically soft. "We understand, in a way many of our peers cannot, the struggles of those less fortunate. The importance of hard work, of perseverance in the face of seemingly insurmountable odds."

Elisha nodded, memories of her own hardships rising unbidden. The long nights in the workhouse, the constant gnaw of hunger, the desperation to escape a life of poverty. She saw something in Thornton's eyes that suggested he carried similar memories.

"I've watched you these past months," Thornton continued. "Your dedication to the *Metropolitan Review*, your passion for giving voice to the voiceless. It's… admirable. More than that, it's inspired me to reconsider my own goals, my own potential to affect change."

He leaned forward, his gaze intense. "I believe that together, we could do so much more. Expand the publication's reach beyond London, push for meaningful reforms in Parliament, use our combined experiences and resources to make a real difference in the lives of those who've suffered as we once did."

Elisha felt her heart quicken at his words. This was a side of Thornton she'd never seen before, one that spoke to her deepest desires to create change in the world.

He paused, taking a deep breath. "Miss Linde—Elisha—it would be my honor to court you properly."

Elisha sat stunned, her mind whirling with the implications of his words. Thornton's proposal was pragmatic, yes, but it was also oddly romantic in its own way. He was offering her not just security, but a chance to fulfill her deepest ambitions.

"Mr. Thornton, I…" she began, her voice wavering with emotion. "I'm truly flattered. Your words and your vision speak to everything I've ever dreamed of achieving. But I'm not sure what to say."

She watched understanding fill his eyes. "Of course. This is not a decision to be made lightly. Perhaps you can give me your answer when you're ready."

Elisha nodded, grateful for the time given. "That is much appreciated, Mr. Thornton."

"Please, do me the honor of using my Christian name."

She smiled shyly. "Thank you, Steven."

"Whatever you decide, Elisha, know that my respect for you, my admiration for your work, remains unchanged."

With that, he bid her good morning, leaving Elisha alone with her thoughts and the heavy weight of his proposal.

As the sounds of London awakening filtered through the

windows, she considered her future. Steven offered stability, shared purpose, and the means to impact the world they lived in. It was everything she'd ever thought she wanted.

Yet unbidden, her thoughts drifted to Edgar, to stolen kisses, to the passion that had flared between them. Her heart ached with confusion and longing.

Later that evening, alone in her attic room, Elisha found herself holding another letter from Mr. Steele. The familiar script seemed different somehow, more hurried, less confident.

3 June 1840

My Esteemed Miss Lovelace,

Your eloquent words on love have left me in a state of profound contemplation. Your certainty has sparked within me a maelstrom of questions and doubts.

How does one truly identify love? Have you loved so wholly before, or are you falling in love now? Your conviction makes me question my own capacity for such emotion.

You write of courage in risking pain for joy. How does one summon such bravery? Are the physical manifestations you describe—the fire in the heart, the tears in the eyes—reliable indicators of love?

I feel adrift, Miss Lovelace, in an ocean of uncertainty. Your words have shown me the shoreline, but I find myself unable to navigate the treacherous waters between. Am I a coward for hesitating, for questioning, for seeking absolute certainty before acting?

Forgive this display of weakness. Your insights have stripped away my defenses, leaving me exposed. I await your response with equal eagerness and apprehension.

Your servant with deepest regard,
Aengus Steele

The flickering candlelight cast dancing shadows across the attic room as Elisha reclined in her narrow bed, the coarse linen of her shift a stark contrast to the fine paper of Steele's letter. Her brow furrowed as she read, her eyes widening with each vulnerable confession.

Elisha sat up, drawing her knees to her chest, the letter trembling slightly in her grasp. This was not the Steele she knew, or thought she knew. Gone was the bravado, the witty repartee, the confident assertions. In their place, she found a man laid bare, his doubts and fears spilled across the page like ink from an overturned bottle.

"How extraordinary," she murmured, her fingers tracing his name on paper.

Where was the man who had so confidently challenged her to a literary duel? Who had boasted of his understanding of romance and love? This letter revealed a different Steele altogether—one who questioned, who doubted, who feared.

As she re-read the letter, Elisha felt an odd sensation in her chest, a tightening that was both uncomfortable and strangely exhilarating. The questions Steele posed, the uncertainties he expressed—they echoed her own unspoken thoughts with an uncanny precision.

"How does one truly identify love?" she read aloud, the words hanging in the still night air.

Wasn't that the question that had kept her awake night after night, as thoughts of a certain duke plagued her mind? Could it be that Steele was romantically involved? Was this outpouring of vulnerability inspired by real, current experience rather than mere philosophical pondering?

Who was this mysterious Mr. Steele? She had always imagined him as a pompous, middle-aged author, set in his ways. But this letter painted a picture of a man grappling with deep emotions, perhaps even experiencing love for the first time.

Elisha shook her head, bemused by her own curiosity. "This is absurd," she chided herself. "He's your literary rival, nothing more. His personal life is none of your concern."

But as she folded the letter and placed it on her bedside table, she couldn't shake the feeling that something had shifted. The lines between rivalry and… something else… had blurred. Steele was no longer just a name on paper, a faceless opponent in their literary duel. He had become real, human, vulnerable.

As she blew out the candle and settled back into her bed, Elisha found herself wondering about the man behind the letters. Who was Aengus Steele, really? And why did his vulnerability touch her so deeply?

Sleep was long in coming that night, as every night for the past month or so, as Elisha's mind whirled with questions about Steele, about love, the Duke of Lancaster, and about her own heart's uncertain journey.

EDGAR SAT MOTIONLESS in his carriage, his eyes fixed on the attic room of the Metropolitan building across the narrow street. He had been appalled to find out from Adams that she resided there, alone. He had not been able to slumber comfortably in his room while Elisha Linde slept in this large building with no protection. So he came here and watched every night, finding comfort in their proximity.

As the light in Elisha's chamber flickered and died, he felt the now-familiar ache in his breast intensify, a pain as acute as any physical wound.

"Good night, Elisha," he whispered into the oppressive darkness. "I pray your dreams are kinder than my waking world."

He lingered, unable to tear himself away, his mind a flurry of thoughts centered on her loveliness, her strength. The quiet streets seemed to echo his profound loneliness, each distant footstep or muffled voice serving only to emphasize the vast emptiness that surrounded him.

Edgar's hand trembled as he reached for the decanter of brandy nestled in the carriage's compartment. He poured a generous measure, the amber liquid glinting in the dim lamplight. As he raised the glass to his lips, he caught sight of his reflection in the window—a man haunted by desires he dared not voice, tormented by a love he could not pursue.

"What a pitiful figure you cut, Lancaster," he muttered bitterly to his reflection. "A duke, reduced to lurking in the shadows like a common street urchin."

He drained the glass in one swift motion, welcoming the burn of the spirits as they coursed down his throat. It was a poor substitute for the warmth he truly craved—the warmth of Elisha's smile, the heat of her mouth when it met his own.

Edgar's mind wandered to the countless soirées and balls he had attended in recent weeks, each one a carefully orchestrated attempt to distract himself from thoughts of Elisha. Yet every debutante's laugh seemed shrill in comparison to her melodious tones, every witty remark fell flat against the memory of her razor-sharp mind.

He had danced, he had flirted, he had played the role of the charming duke to perfection. But each step, each smile, each empty compliment paid to vapid young ladies only served to underscore the vast gulf between the life Society expected him to lead and the life his heart truly desired.

"Damn it all," he growled, his fist clenching around the empty glass. "Damn propriety, damn expectations, damn the whole blasted Ton!"

His outburst was met with silence, the sleeping city indifferent to his anguish. Edgar slumped back in his seat, suddenly feeling every one of his years and the weight of his title pressing down upon him.

"What am I to do, Elisha?" he whispered, his eyes once again drawn to the darkened window across the street. "How am I to go on, knowing you are so near and yet forever beyond my reach?"

The question hung unanswered in the still night air. Edgar knew he should order his driver to return to his townhouse, to the cold comfort of his empty bed. Yet he remained, a silent sentinel in the night, clinging to the faint hope that perhaps, just perhaps, Elisha might spare a thought for him before she drifted off to sleep.

As the first hints of dawn began to lighten the eastern sky, Edgar finally stirred from his vigil. With a heavy heart, he rapped on the carriage roof, signaling his driver to depart. As the vehicle pulled away from the curb, he cast one last, lingering glance at the gazette building.

"Until tomorrow, my love," he murmured, the words a promise and a lament, "when I shall once again wage war against my own heart."

The carriage disappeared into the awakening streets of London, leaving behind only the fading echo of wheels on cobblestones and the lingering scent of brandy and longing.

THE FORBIDDEN FRUIT

THE MORNING LIGHT filtered through her attic window as Elisha carefully penned her response to Mr. Steele's vulnerable letter. His questions about love had stirred something deep within her, and she found herself being more honest than she'd ever been with a stranger.

4 June 1840

Dear Mr. Steele,

I confess to being lost in matters of love. While I've received gentlemen's attentions, my focus on my profession has precluded serious thoughts of matrimony. Perhaps I've yet to meet a man of inspiring character and intellect.

My educated yet humble origins place me in an ambiguous social position. Finding an educated man who accepts a wife more devoted to her vocation than domesticity proves challenging.

What of your circumstances, Mr. Steele? What keeps you unattached, if you are? If married, does your wife desire professional and financial autonomy?

Forgive this uncharacteristic vulnerability. I'm astonished to find my once-impenetrable heart affected by two fleeting encounters.

With the utmost regard,
E. Lovelace

As she sealed her response, Elisha couldn't help but wonder why she'd been so forthcoming. There was something about Steele's recent correspondence that made her feel safe to reveal her deepest thoughts—a quality she'd never experienced with any of her other literary correspondents.

On that balmy June evening, Elisha found herself in the affluent drawing room of Lady Gale's townhouse, feeling more keenly than ever the divide between her two worlds. Here she sat among London's literary elite, ostensibly to report on Mrs. Anna Maria Hall's reading, while her mind drifted to the erotic pamphlets being distributed in the East End—pamphlets she strongly suspected were connected to a certain duke.

Mrs. Hall's melodious voice filled the room, reading from *Marian; or, A Young Maid's Fortunes*—a tale of a common girl who dared to love above her station. The coincidence was not lost on Elisha.

It was then that she saw him.

Edgar stood against the far wall, a shadow of his usual resplendent self. His customarily immaculate appearance had given way to a carefully concealed dishevelment that only someone who knew him well would notice. But it was his eyes that caught and held her attention—hollow, haunted, rimmed with the darkness of sleepless nights. They didn't belong to a rake who had simply spent too many nights seducing women. There was something else there, something that made her chest tighten with concern.

Their gazes met across the crowded room, and for a moment, the rest of the world fell away. In that brief connection, she saw not just exhaustion or longing, but a bone-deep weariness that spoke of battles fought in darkness.

"...and so our Marian learned that true love knows no boundaries of class or circumstance." Mrs. Hall's voice penetrated Elisha's consciousness, followed by polite applause.

As the guests began to mingle, Elisha found herself torn between duty and desire. Mrs. Hall's story was exactly the kind of social commentary the Metropolitan needed—a bold challenge to Society's rigid hierarchies. Yet her eyes kept straying to where Edgar stood, noting how even the simple act of maintaining his posture seemed to require tremendous effort.

"Elisha," Amelia appeared at her elbow, eyes bright with excitement. "Mrs. Hall has agreed to speak with us. She specifically mentioned wanting to discuss her views on class barriers in romantic literature."

Elisha nodded and absentmindedly followed her friend, though her gaze drifted back to Edgar's corner. But he was gone, as though he'd never been there at all.

"Did you see His Grace?" Amelia whispered, following Elisha's line of sight. "He looked... unwell."

"He looked haunted," Elisha murmured.

Amelia studied her friend's face with knowing eyes. "I am sorry for your distress. I know you care deeply for him."

"I can't afford to," Elisha said firmly.

"And yet?"

Elisha sighed. "And yet I find myself wondering what keeps him sleepless at night. What shadows darken his door." She straightened her shoulders with visible effort. "But it doesn't matter. We have work to do."

As Amelia led her toward Mrs. Hall, Elisha couldn't shake the feeling that she was missing something vital—some piece of the puzzle that would explain Edgar's state, his mysterious activities in the East End, and the growing sense that greater forces were at work around them all.

But such mysteries would have to wait. She had a story to write, a reputation to protect, and a heart to guard. For now, that would have to be enough.

Several days later, Elisha received another letter from Steele that left her breathless with its emotional honesty.

8 June 1840

Miss Lovelace,

The anguish born of love is a torment unparalleled, a wound that deepens with each moment of reflection and regret, leaving naught but a scar to serve as a poignant reminder of the yearning once felt. Yet, amidst this anguish, one cannot help but feel most keenly alive, the pain a stark reminder of the precarious nature of inner tranquility, and how we ought to cherish those dear to us while they remain within our grasp.

I comprehend the depths of your suffering. It is a simple matter to safeguard one's heart when there exists no threat from which to protect it. In the face of true sentiment, however, such defenses prove nigh impossible to maintain. I do not believe any man or woman, regardless of their fortitude, possesses the strength to resist love's siren call.

As to my own circumstances, I remain unattached and unwed. Like yourself, I have grappled with the constraints imposed by the rigid stratification of our Society, finding myself enamored of women deemed unsuitable or, perhaps more cruelly, the right woman at an inopportune moment.

I confess to a propensity for falling in love with great ease and abandon, for I find myself irresistibly drawn to those rare inner qualities possessed by but a select few of the fairer sex. When I perceive these qualities in a lady, I find myself powerless to restrain the yearnings of my heart. Indeed, I freely admit to waging such a battle even as I pen these words, for I feel we have become confidants of a sort, and you have been most generous in sharing your own secrets.

Regarding your fleeting encounter, I assure you that even a single interaction possesses the power to move hearts and alter the fabric of one's soul, Miss Lovelace. There exists no warrior stalwart enough to reverse such a profound change. The fortunate gentleman who has succeeded in stirring your emotions may well be grappling with sentiments of his own, for you are, without doubt, a lady of singular quality. You embody all that an honorable man could desire in a companion.

With the utmost regard and deepest sympathy,
Aengus Steele

Elisha's hands trembled as she set the letter aside. The man's pain was palpable, his vulnerability so raw it made her own heart ache in sympathy. Who was this Aengus Steele who could write with such eloquence about love and loss? And why did his words resonate so deeply with her own confused feelings?

She found herself staring out her small window at the bustling streets below, wondering if somewhere in this vast city, a man was pouring his heart onto paper just as she did each night when sleep eluded her. The thought was both comforting and unsettling.

EDGAR SAT AT his desk, reading Elisha's latest letter for the hundredth time. To his valet's continued exasperation, his usually immaculate appearance had given way to a disheveled state—a thick beard obscured his jaw and his hair stood in complete disarray. But he couldn't bring himself to care about such trivial matters when he had wounded her so deeply.

Two encounters. Edgar's chest constricted. She must be referring to their kiss in the garden, their passionate moment in the carriage. She was affected by him, even as she corresponded with him unknowingly as Steele. The memories were almost too painful to bear.

He could still feel Elisha trembling beneath his touch, hear the soft catches in her breath, see the trust and desire in her eyes before reality had crashed back in. She'd offered him her forever, and he'd had to refuse it. The pain on her face had cut deeper than any blade.

"Cannot promise matrimony," he muttered, fury rising in his throat. The decanter of brandy beckoned from his desk, but he ignored it. He didn't deserve the numbing embrace of spirits. This pain was his penance.

A proper man would leave her alone, give her the chance to find happiness with someone who could offer her everything she deserved. Thornton was a good match, as much as Edgar loathed to admit it. She would have a comfortable life, respect in Society, children who would never know the shame of scandal.

But when Edgar closed his eyes, all he could see was the way she'd bloomed under his touch, how perfectly she fit in his arms. The thought of another man holding her, touching her, loving her… his fist clenched until his knuckles whitened.

"Damn it all to hell."

This wasn't mere lust—if it were, he could master it. No, what he felt for Elisha had taken root in his soul. Her quiet strength, the way her eyes danced when she challenged him intellectually… he loved every part of her.

A sharp knock at the door startled Edgar from his thoughts. Without waiting for a response, the Marquess of Hereford sauntered in, followed by the Earl of Carlisle and his wife, Charlotte, with Patrick Adams bringing up the rear.

"Good God, Lancaster!" Hereford exclaimed, handing him a letter while taking in Edgar's appearance with obvious shock. "Have you taken up residence in a bear's den?"

Edgar rose to his feet, a genuine smile breaking through his melancholy for the first time in weeks. "Carlisle, Charlotte! What a delightful surprise!" He moved to greet them, kissing Charlotte's hand and clapping Carlisle on the shoulder. "Welcome back to England. I trust your journey across the Atlantic was tolerable?"

Carlisle chuckled, his eyes twinkling with amusement at Edgar's unruly state. "More tolerable than whatever storm seems to have ravaged you, old friend. Or has your valet gone blind?"

Charlotte smiled warmly, though Edgar could see concern in her eyes. "It's wonderful to see you, Your Grace, though I expected you to be in somewhat better spirits."

"Ah, well," Edgar replied, attempting to smooth his rumpled

attire, "life can dampen even the most exuberant of souls. But tell me, what brings you to our shores?"

Carlisle's expression turned slightly more serious. "Business, I'm afraid. I've some matters to attend to in London that will keep us here for the summer. I hope you don't mind us pilfering through your liquor cabinet for such an extended period?"

"You're always welcome here. A whole summer, you say? Splendid!" Edgar exclaimed, genuinely pleased to have his friends near during this difficult time.

Adams laid a hand on his shoulder, concern etched on his face. "It's good to see your spirit lifted, Lancaster. What's been troubling you so deeply?"

Edgar sighed, running a hand through his unkempt hair. "It's... complicated."

"Let me guess," Hereford smirked with knowing familiarity. "It involves a certain Miss Linde? I believe another missive was delivered to you. Read it."

At the mention of Elisha's name, Edgar's carefully maintained composure cracked. He glanced at Carlisle and Charlotte, then back to his other friends. Her words were too precious, too private to share even with his dearest friends. He retreated to a corner by the window to read.

9 June 1840

Dear Mr. Steele,

Your letter has deeply moved me. Your understanding of love lost resonates profoundly, offering both comfort and disquiet. This pain, as you note, reminds me I'm alive and capable of deep feeling.

I'm humbled by love's power to undo my once-prized emotional fortitude. Your honesty about falling in love easily is refreshing, and I envy your open heart.

Your words about a single interaction's power to alter souls also comfort me. I've questioned my foolishness in being so affected by a brief encounter, and your assurance brings solace.

While I dare not hope the gentleman shares my sentiments, your kindness has become a light in these dark days.

Might I inquire further about your own heart's battle? I assure you of my discretion, as we've indeed become confidants.

With deepest gratitude,
E. Lovelace

He braced his hands against the study window, watching raindrops trace paths down the glass like the tears he refused to shed.

"I dare not hope the gentleman shares my sentiments…"

Her pain was palpable. He had allowed her to believe she was a passing fancy. That he wanted everything from her while giving little of himself. Her scent still seemed to cling to his coat from their last encounter—lavender and jasmine, innocence and temptation wound together. He should burn the damned thing.

"I cannot promise matrimony," he had told her. He could hardly contain the anger he felt with himself and their circumstances. He gripped the windowpane as if to shatter it.

"What happened? What's this about?"

Carlisle's voice startled him. Edgar turned around to face his friends whose expressions were etched with worry.

"Apologies," he said hoarsely, approaching the group. "I suppose you might as well hear it."

He proceeded to recount the entire story for Carlisle's and Charlotte's benefit—his dual identity as Steele, the wager, his growing feelings for Elisha, and the impossible situation he now found himself in. As he spoke, Edgar felt both relief at unburdening himself and apprehension at how Charlotte, who came from humble circumstances herself, might view his difficulty.

When he finished, Carlisle whistled low. "That's quite a predicament you've got yourself into, Lancaster."

"When you say Miss Linde, do you mean Miss Elisha Linde?" Charlotte asked, her eyes brightening with recognition.

Edgar leaned forward eagerly. "Why, yes. Are you acquainted

with her?"

"We are good friends, as I am with Miss Amelia Thornton. We bonded when we attended protests together a decade ago."

Edgar felt his heart lift. "How serendipitous!"

Carlisle grinned. "Surely there must be a way to resolve this situation? I'm an earl and I managed to wed my Charlotte without a hitch."

All the men stared at him in disbelief. Adams spoke dryly, "Your earldom was but one year old, and you were a stevedore before then. It hardly holds the same prestige as Lancaster's dukedom."

Edgar added, "And you had to move heaven and earth to marry your beloved. Do you not recall the misery you and your countess experienced?"

Carlisle's brows furrowed while Charlotte stared at her husband with obvious amusement.

"How convenient that you have no memory of the suffering you bestowed upon me," she said with fond exasperation.

"I recall what a scoundrel I was to you, darling. I suppose our issues were entirely different," Carlisle admitted sheepishly.

Just as Adams was about to respond, Charlotte's eyes lit up. "What if we were to make Miss Linde the most famous critic in London? Endear her to the *ton*? Make her the most desirable and celebrated person. If the *ton* wants to be seen with her, you will not face any backlash. They will support you politically and socially."

The group paused, each contemplating the suggestion. Edgar felt a glimmer of hope stir in his chest. "And how do you propose we do that?"

Hereford leaned forward, excitement building in his voice. "Start by writing to her again as Steele. Increase the stakes of your wager. Make it something the entire literary world will be watching."

Edgar nodded slowly, his mind beginning to race with possibilities. "What sort of stakes did you have in mind?"

Edgar listened intently as his friends spent the next hour crafting an elaborate plan. They decided on a special contest with a monetary award where readers across London would answer questions about Steele's and Lovelace's works. Whoever gave the most accurate and best responses would win. Readers would also vote for their favorite between the two tales. This would involve public readings by actors for those who couldn't afford to purchase the books.

"This is brilliant," Edgar said, feeling genuine excitement for the first time in days. Suddenly, his expression turned solemn. "Perhaps I should reveal my identity to Miss Linde? I cannot in good conscience carry on with this facade. I am ashamed every time she confides in me about Steele."

A chorus of protests erupted from his friends.

"Good God, man, have you taken leave of your senses?" Hereford's eyes widened with disbelief.

Carlisle shook his head vehemently. "Lancaster, that would be most unwise. Consider the implications."

Charlotte, ever the voice of reason, leaned forward. "Your Grace, I understand your desire for honesty, but revealing yourself as Steele could jeopardize everything we're trying to achieve."

Adams nodded in agreement. "Indeed. A wager against a duke may not be perceived as fair at all. It may upset those of lower stations. Not to mention Miss Linde feeling pressured to forfeit rather than risk humiliating a man of your station."

Edgar's brow furrowed. "Surely she wouldn't forfeit so easily."

Charlotte placed a gentle hand on Edgar's arm. "Perhaps not, but it would undermine our entire plan. If Elisha knows she's competing against you, how can she truly shine? The victory would always be tainted by the suspicion that you let her win."

Edgar sank into a nearby chair, the weight of their arguments settling upon him. "I see your points," he conceded reluctantly. "But keeping this secret… it feels like a betrayal of her trust."

"Sometimes," Adams said softly, "harmless deception is kinder. By maintaining this secret, you're giving Miss Linde the opportunity to prove herself on her own merits, without the shadow of your title looming over her." Adams then cleared his throat, his expression turning grave. "Speaking of deception, I took the liberty of investigating those unsavory rumors circulating about your supposed indiscretions."

Edgar's focus sharpened. "What did you discover?"

"The source appears to be none other than Steven Thornton." Adams' lips pressed into a thin line. "My investigation revealed he's been quite strategic about it. He drops carefully worded insinuations about your character to select individuals—particularly those known for their loose tongues."

"Thornton?" Edgar felt anger surge through him, though he couldn't say he was entirely surprised. "The bastard."

"I've exchanged some strong words with several newspaper editors," Adams continued. "I've received assurances they won't publish such unfounded allegations again."

Hereford clapped Edgar on the shoulder encouragingly. "That's one problem solved. Next, when Society is clamoring to be in Miss Linde's good graces, you shall step forward as her devoted suitor."

Edgar nodded, feeling his spirits lift considerably.

Carlisle spoke up with enthusiasm. "I suppose no grand victory party since you shall maintain your anonymity if you win, but you could have one for the public and fill the entire *Metropolitan* to this story to foster Miss Linde's popularity even more."

As the group settled back into planning the details of their scheme, Edgar felt a complex mix of emotions churning within him. Hope for the future, excitement at the prospect of elevating Elisha in Society's eyes, and a nagging discomfort at the continued deception warred in his chest.

As they finalized the details, Edgar cleared his throat. "Speaking of unconventional matches, how fare you, my lady? Still breaking new ground in the legal world?"

Carlisle beamed with obvious pride. "Indeed she is. Charlotte's just helped win a landmark case that's set tongues wagging from here to Washington."

"And how does society in America view such a contribution by a woman?" Adams asked with genuine curiosity.

"Some see it as progressive, others as scandalous. But we've found that popularity, rather than success, tends to silence even the loudest critics," Charlotte replied thoughtfully.

Edgar nodded, absorbing this wisdom. "I suppose there's a lesson in that for my own situation."

As his friends prepared to leave, Edgar felt genuinely buoyed by the possibilities they'd outlined. "Countess, gentlemen, I cannot thank you enough for your counsel… and for dragging me out of my misery."

Carlisle slapped him on the back with characteristic good humor. "That's what friends are for, old boy. Now, for the love of God, shave that monstrosity off your face. You look like a vagrant philosopher."

Laughter echoed through the study as Edgar's thoughts turned to Steele and Lovelace's feud. He needed to inject more heat and fire into his letters to keep the public hungry. No doubt she'd respond spectacularly. The thought made him smile.

THE DUCHESS OF LANCASTER

THE LANTERN LIGHTS fluttered softly in Edgar's study, casting dancing shadows across the dark paneled walls. Edgar was reviewing a ledger at his desk when his butler announced the arrival of Adams. His friend entered, his usual military bearing somewhat disheveled from what appeared to be a long night of surveillance.

"Lancaster, I have news regarding Miss Linde," Adams said without a greeting.

Edgar straightened, instantly alert. "Speak."

"My men followed her to the outskirts of town last night. She took considerable precaution against being followed. Quite skilled at it, actually." Adams' tone held a note of admiration. "She led us to a small print shop. The proprietor, Mr. Symon, seems a decent sort. Takes precautions, keeps no records." Adams cleared his throat. "However, others have begun asking questions. It may not remain secure much longer."

Edgar rose and leaned against the windowpane, his shoulders burdened by this news. The London night spread before him, a maze of shadows and gaslit streets where Elisha moved in secret, risking everything for her beliefs. "Buy the shop. Install someone trustworthy, someone who'll create identical plates with slight variations. If authorities seize them—"

"They'll believe they have the wrong press," Adams finished, nodding in approval. "Clever. And the real plates?"

"We'll find a new home here, alongside our other ventures." Edgar's lips curved slightly. "After all, who would suspect the duke of harboring radical literature alongside his collection of erotic tales?"

Adams studied his friend's face with obvious concern. "This is dangerous territory, Lancaster. If you're caught protecting reform writers..."

"Then I'll have excellent company in Newgate," Edgar replied dryly. "Set up the purchase. And Adams?" He caught his friend's eye. "Have your men keep watching her. Discreetly."

After Adams departed, Edgar returned to his desk, pulling out fresh paper. If he was to truly help her cause, he would need to expand his distribution network. He recalled a conversation he had overheard about the proprietor of the Royal Mail Coach Company retiring. Perhaps it was time the Mayfair Mavericks found a more meaningful pursuit than mere pleasure.

But first, he had a letter to write—one that would provoke Miss Lovelace into accepting his grand challenge.

Edgar winced as he composed the letter. Writing such harsh words to Elisha felt like driving daggers into his own heart, but it was necessary for their plan. She would be furious—and that fury would drive her to accept his challenge, setting their grand scheme in motion.

SEVERAL DAYS LATER, Edgar found himself in his carriage, heading to Lancaster Hall. The wheels crunched rhythmically against the gravel drive, each rotation bringing him closer to the ancestral seat of the Dukes of Lancaster. Through the carriage window, weak afternoon sunlight filtered through a veil of clouds, casting the imposing Georgian facade in shades of amber and shadow. Edgar leaned back against the plush leather seat, his fingers drumming an irregular pattern on his thigh as the familiar weight of expectation and guilt settled over him.

As the carriage drew to a halt before the grand entrance, Edgar caught sight of Simmons waiting at attention. The elderly butler had served the Lancaster family for three decades, his silver hair and lined face as much a part of Lancaster as its weathered stone walls.

"Your Grace, we had not expected you." Simmons' voice held carefully measured surprise. "Shall I inform the duchess of your arrival?"

"Yes, Simmons, thank you," Edgar replied, surrendering his hat and gloves. The familiar scent of beeswax and leather enveloped him as he stepped into the entrance hall. "I'll be in the blue drawing room."

The blue drawing room had always been his mother's favorite, its walls adorned with the accumulated treasures of generations of Lancasters. As Edgar paced the Turkish carpet, his gaze traced the familiar contours of antique vases and ornate picture frames. Each object seemed to whisper of past glories and long-held secrets, their presence both comforting and accusatory.

A delicate Chinese vase caught his attention—his father's gift to his mother on their twentieth wedding anniversary. The painted cranes seemed to watch him with ancient, knowing eyes as he touched the cool porcelain. The house felt alive with memories, each corner holding echoes of expectations he had failed to meet.

The soft click of the door opening announced his mother's arrival. The Duchess of Lancaster entered with the quiet authority that had always characterized her presence. Though her dark hair had begun to silver at the temples, Edgar noted that her eyes remained as sharp as ever as they assessed him.

"Edgar," she said, drawing him into a brief embrace that carried the subtle scent of rose. "This is an unexpected pleasure. I was not expecting you until Essie's birthday."

"Mother," he said warmly, noting his mother's subtle reminder of his sister's birthday. "I trust I find you well?"

The duchess settled herself on a chaise longue, her posture remaining as impeccable as it had been during his youth. "As well as can be expected for a woman whose son's exploits are the talk of London," she replied, her tone carrying gentle reproach. "Please tell me last week's article is not true. Surely you haven't been involved in a brawl at that notorious gaming hell on Jermyn Street?"

Edgar sighed heavily, sinking into a nearby armchair. The leather creaked softly beneath him. "I assure you, Mother, I have not set foot in that establishment in months. These reports are entirely fabricated."

Relief seemed to soften his mother's features. "I believe you, my boy. Still, these constant rumors are most distressing." She smoothed an invisible wrinkle from her silk skirts. "But then, what brings you home so unexpectedly?"

"Can a son not call upon his mother without an ulterior motive?"

Her knowing look, so familiar from his childhood escapades, told him she was not fooled. "Not when that son is you, my dear. You've hardly darkened my door these past weeks. Now, tell me truly, what brings you here?"

Edgar leaned forward, his elbows resting on his knees—a posture his mother would normally chide him for. The weight of his purpose pressed heavily upon him. "I've been reflecting. On my life, my choices." He paused, his voice dropping to barely above a whisper. "On Lucia."

The name hung in the air between them, heavy with unspoken sorrow. Afternoon light caught the crystal drops of the chandelier, casting rainbow prisms across the walls. Edgar watched his mother's face soften, maternal concern replacing her earlier assessment.

"Oh, my dear boy. It's been years since you've spoken of her."

"Five years," Edgar said softly.

His mother reached out, placing a comforting hand on his

arm. Her fingers, though delicate, carried surprising strength. "Edgar, you mustn't continue to blame yourself for what happened with Lucia."

"How can I not?" Edgar's voice cracked with emotion, the carefully maintained facade of the rakish duke crumbling. "I was supposed to protect her, marry her, defy convention and expectation. How naïve I was."

Edgar watched his mother's grip tighten on his arm. "Your father believed he was acting in your best interests, in the family's best interests."

"I trusted him at the time," Edgar said bitterly, rising to pace before the fireplace. "Now I know we were too concerned with scandal, with maintaining our precious position in Society."

Silence fell between them, broken only by the steady ticking of the ornate clock on the mantelpiece and Edgar's measured footsteps on the carpet. Finally, his mother spoke, her voice gentle but probing. "Is this why you've been so directionless these past years? Why you've neglected your duties in the House of Lords?"

Edgar nodded, unable to meet his mother's searching gaze. "Every time I considered taking my responsibilities seriously, I was reminded of the cost of those responsibilities. Of what I sacrificed—what Lucia sacrificed—so that the so-called social betters could enjoy their status quo."

"Oh, my dear," the duchess sighed, her voice thick with what Edgar recognized as understanding. "I had no idea you were still carrying such a burden." She leaned forward, her voice taking on a firmer tone. "Perhaps it's time to become the man she believed you to be. It's not too late, Edgar."

As the afternoon light began to fade, casting long shadows across the drawing room, Edgar felt a glimmer of hope stir in his chest for the first time in years. He straightened his posture as if a great weight had been lifted from his shoulders. "Indeed, it is high time I assumed my rightful place in the House of Lords, but not because of Lucia."

He met his mother's gaze, his nerves prickling with trepidation. "There is another who has captured my heart, a lady who is bereft of title or fortune. Orphaned in her tender years, she has risen above her circumstances with a grace that humbles and inspires me." His voice softened, taking on a worshipful quality. "Try as I might to banish her from my thoughts, to shield myself from repeating past mistakes, I find that life without her seems a pale and joyless affair."

Edgar watched his mother sit very still, her keen eyes never leaving his face as he continued, his voice dropping to barely above a whisper. "I implore you, Mother. Tell me I am at liberty to love her, that I need not sacrifice yet another woman to societal expectations. I beseech your counsel, for I find myself in dire need of her presence, and yet I am at a loss as to how to proceed."

The ticking of the mantel clock seemed to echo the rapid beating of Edgar's heart as he awaited his mother's response. Each second stretched like an eternity, pregnant with the weight of generations of tradition and expectation.

The duchess remained silent for a long moment, her eyes searching his face as if seeing him truly for the first time in years. When she spoke, her voice carried both gentleness and authority. "My dear boy, your words move me deeply. It gladdens my heart to see you so impassioned, so full of life once more." She paused, and Edgar could see her choosing her next words with care. "However, we must tread carefully in matters of the heart, especially when they intersect with matters of duty and station."

Edgar's face fell, but his mother held up a hand to forestall his despair. "I do not say no, Edgar. But neither can I give you my blessing without further consideration. Your marriage, should it come to pass, would impact not only you but our entire family. Your sisters' prospects, our standing in Society, our fortune—all could be affected."

She leaned forward, taking his hand in hers. The afternoon light caught the ancestral rings on her fingers, symbols of the very tradition they discussed. "We must meet this lady, Edgar. Your brothers, sisters, and I. We must assess her character, her suitability not just as your wife, but as a future Duchess of Lancaster. It is a heavy burden, and not one to be undertaken lightly."

Hope warred with apprehension in Edgar's chest as he nodded. "I understand, Mother. And I thank you for not dismissing the notion outright."

Edgar watched his mother's expression grow grave. "There is another matter we must consider, my dear. It pains me to speak of it, but you must be aware. There are those in Society who would seek to use such a match against us. In the most extreme cases, they might even attempt to have you declared..." she hesitated, the word clearly distasteful to her, "...insane."

Edgar recoiled, shock evident on his face. The word seemed to echo in the suddenly too-small room. "Insane? Surely not!"

His mother nodded solemnly, her face shadowed by the fading light. "It has happened before, to nobles who have made matches deemed too far beneath their station. While rare, it is not unheard of."

Edgar's jaw clenched, anger flashing in his eyes as he processed this new threat. He felt his mother pat his hand soothingly. "Do not do anything hasty until we have a plan. Our family must present a united front, and your chosen lady must be beyond reproach in her conduct and character."

She straightened, her voice taking on a more optimistic tone. "Now, tell me about this woman who has so thoroughly captured your heart. What is her name? How did you meet?"

As Edgar began to speak of Elisha, his heart lit with joy. He watched his mother dab at her eyes with her handkerchief, hope blooming clearly in their depths.

SUNLIGHT STREAMED THROUGH the tall windows of the London Fencing and Athletics Club, casting long shadows across the polished wooden floors. The air hummed with the distinctive song of steel meeting steel, punctuated by the measured footfalls of fencers advancing and retreating along the piste. The scents of leather and polish mingled with the subtle musk of exertion, creating an atmosphere both refined and vital.

Elisha stood at the edge of the practice area, the letter from Mr. Steele crumpling in her white-knuckled grip. Her usual composure had cracked, allowing a glimpse of the passion she typically kept carefully contained. The morning light caught the copper highlights in her carefully pinned hair, and she could feel the heat in her green eyes as she re-read the offensive missive.

Metropolitan Review, *10 June 1840*

My Esteemed Miss Lovelace,

I've read your critique of Zanoni in your so-called esteemed gazette. You praise the author's "masterful interweaving of mystical elements with human emotion," yet in the same breath, you decry the plot as "overly convenient." Make up your mind, madam! Or is consistency too much to ask of a critic who clearly prefers tearing down the works of better writers to creating anything of substance herself?

Your eloquent argument belies a heart as cold as a Siberian winter. Your clinical dissection of prose and laughable assertions on the human condition reveal your ivory tower isolation.

I humbly propose that we raise the stakes of our challenge to display our literary merits before Society. Let us arrange a grand literary salon at which our respective works shall be presented for discerning judgment. Select passages may be performed by the finest theatrical talents, ensuring accessibility to those of modest means. All participants would then engage in scholarly discourse regarding the relative merits of each tale, with a handsome prize purse to be awarded to the most eloquent of opinions. Such an event would not only elevate the literary arts but provide entertainment of the highest caliber for all of London Society.

I do wish you would put your money where your overactive quill is or admit defeat and spare us your highbrow pontificating. Prove you're more than a sharp tongue and bitter heart, or retreat to your shadowy perch like a coward.

Your exasperated servant,
Aengus Steele

Beside her, Amelia nearly bounced on her toes while watching the fencers, and Elisha noticed her friend's earlier pain seemed forgotten in her enthusiasm. Despite the physical reminder of her accident, Amelia moved with a grace born of determination, her pale blue morning dress swishing softly as she shifted her weight.

"Isn't it exhilarating?" Amelia gushed, turning to her friend. Elisha could see her eyes sparkling with barely contained delight as she watched a particularly skilled pair of fencers execute a complex series of attacks and parries. "I'm so glad you agreed to come with me. Just think of the practical applications, Elisha. We could learn to defend ourselves if ever accosted!"

But Elisha barely registered her friend's words, her attention wholly consumed by the letter. The paper trembled slightly in her hands, betraying the depth of her agitation. "'A heart as cold as a Siberian winter,'" she muttered, each word dripping with disdain. "The nerve of the man!"

"What's that?" Elisha noticed Amelia's enthusiasm dim as she registered her distress. Her friend moved closer, her limp more pronounced with the quick movement. "Another letter from Mr. Steele?"

"The very same," Elisha thrust the paper at her friend, her voice tight with controlled fury. "Just last week he was writing about the nature of love, and now this! Look how he accuses me of having a heart 'as cold as a Siberian winter'! The man is utterly baffling."

Elisha watched Amelia's expression shift from curiosity to

outrage while she scanned the letter. The delicate skin around her friend's eyes tightened with anger.

"These insults! Such ungentlemanly conduct. And after his recent letters were so different."

"He would likely argue I'm no gentlewoman," Elisha replied, a bitter laugh escaping her lips. The sound carried across the practice floor, and she noticed several fencers pause mid-bout.

"Is there a problem, ladies?"

The cultured voice cut through their conversation like a blade. Both women turned to find themselves face to face with the Marquess of Hereford. Elisha observed how he cut an imposing figure in his fencing attire, the white jacket emphasizing his broad shoulders and athletic build. Though he had removed his mask, his expression remained as guarded as if he still wore it.

"My Lord!" Amelia gasped, dropping into a hasty curtsy. Elisha watched her friend's cheeks flush pink with embarrassment as she slightly lost her balance, steadying herself against a nearby column. Elisha followed suit with a more controlled curtsy, though she kept her eyes defiant.

"We had no idea you were a member here, my lord," Elisha managed, straightening with practiced dignity.

Elisha felt Hereford's dark eyes regard them with measured gravity, lingering particularly on her. "Not just a member, Miss Linde. I'm the instructor today." His gaze flicked to the letter still clutched in Amelia's hand before returning to Elisha's face. "Now, I assume you ladies are the reporters I was warned about. You seem to be in distress. We could all hear you over the metal clanging. Is there something I can help you with?"

Elisha noticed Amelia step forward slightly, her earlier excitement about fencing completely forgotten. "I beg your pardon, my lord. We did not mean to be disruptive."

Elisha watched the marquess' eyebrows rise slightly, his mouth tightening at the corners. "Whether you meant to or not, Miss Thornton, the result is that you are distracting the students and putting their safety at risk. May I ask that you keep your voices to a minimum? Thank you."

With a curt nod that spoke volumes about his opinion of women in his fencing club, the marquess turned on his heel and strode back to his students, his boots clicking sharply against the wooden floor.

"What crawled up his backside and died?" Amelia muttered once he was out of earshot, and Elisha could see her earlier enthusiasm was thoroughly dampened.

Elisha didn't respond immediately. Her eyes followed the marquess' retreating form, her mind already formulating a plan. Finally, she straightened her shoulders, a determined glint in her eye. "I shall show him," she declared, tucking the offending letter into her reticule. "I shall show him and all of London that my cold Siberian heart burns with a passion for literature that his overheated prose could never match."

As Elisha's words rang with quiet conviction, the morning sun continued its journey across the practice floor, illuminating the dust motes that danced in its beam like so many scattered dreams. The rhythmic sound of steel on steel resumed, providing a martial counterpoint to the battle of words and wits that was about to unfold.

But more than that, Elisha felt something stirring within her—a fierce determination not just to respond to Steele's challenge, but to prove herself worthy of standing among London's literary elite. If he wanted a public battle, she would give him one he would never forget.

THE REFORM

Metropolitan Review, *17 June 1840*

Dear Mr. Steele,

Your latest missive, with its personal attacks and grandiose challenges, amuses me. How like a man cornered by superior intellect.

Your accusation of inconsistency merely reveals your lack of nuance. One can appreciate and critique different aspects of an author's work—a concept perhaps beyond your pulp romance sensibilities.

I accept your additional terms of the contest among our discerning readers, Mr. Steele. Prepare yourself. I shall expose the bankruptcy of your literary philosophy to London's scholars. Perhaps I should draft your concession speech, given your prose quality.

Grateful for your shortcomings,
E. Lovelace

Edgar sat at a desk in the otherwise empty room, stroking Elisha's name on parchment with his thumb. He found some reprieve since devising a stratagem with his friends, but waiting for his mother's blessing forced him to keep his distance a little longer.

He missed her. His heart seemed to tighten along with his lungs every time he thought of her. He wondered if she was suffering as he was. She seemed so sure, confident about her decision to avoid him, avoid a potential assault on her heart. She was right, of course. She had nothing, no protection, nothing to gain from an affair with no promise. But with the strength of hellfire, he missed her.

The knock on the door awoke him from the gloom he felt, introducing Hereford. His friend walked in with the confidence of a crane, then stopped abruptly.

"Did someone pass away overnight?"

Edgar waved away the remark. Hereford, noticing the letter on the desk, brightened. "I see the source of your sour expression. So, Miss Lovelace does it again."

Irked by Hereford's brightness, Edgar stood and walked to the tunnel door.

"Pay attention, Hereford," he said as he demonstrated the maneuvers necessary to open the hidden door.

"Brilliant! Who constructed this?"

"My steward. He's sworn to secrecy."

"Well, we know a place to bury him if he doesn't keep his mouth sealed," Hereford said jovially as he entered the passage.

The narrow tunnel was damp and musty, barely wide enough for a man to crawl through. Edgar led the way, his fine coat collecting dirt as he inched forward on his elbows. Behind him, Hereford suppressed a cough, the dust thick in the air.

"I say, Lancaster," Hereford whispered, his voice reverberating softly in the confined space, "we've done a remarkably fine job excavating this tunnel."

Edgar's response was muffled, his face close to the earthen floor. "Indeed, I have. You were nowhere near."

"And observe the precision of it all—right angles at every turn, as if carved by a master mason."

"You may direct your praises to my steward for that particular feat."

"I may have to entice him away to construct my own subterranean passage."

"And, pray tell, what purpose would that serve?"

"To sequester myself from my future bride, naturally."

"Ah, and who might the fortunate lady be?"

"That, my friend, remains a mystery even to me."

"Your nuptials seem doomed from the outset."

"Aye, I approach the altar with no small measure of trepidation."

"Patience, old friend. You may yet mature into the role of husband."

Edgar's progress halted as his outstretched hand met a wooden panel. With a soft click that seemed to echo their surreptitious purpose, it swung open, revealing a small chamber beyond. The two gentlemen extricated themselves from the narrow passage, straightening to their full height in the low-ceilinged space.

With practiced ease, Edgar located the matches and lantern positioned by the door. As the flame flickered to life, casting dancing shadows on the rough-hewn walls, he moved with barely contained excitement toward a set of shelves lining the far wall.

Hereford, brushing the dirt from his once-immaculate trousers, muttered, "Good God, Lancaster, I do hope this tunnel justifies the lamentable state of my attire."

"Oh, it does indeed," Edgar replied, his voice low with conspiratorial glee. "Cast your eyes upon this, my friend."

The shelves before them were laden with neatly stacked pamphlets and broadsheets, their titles barely visible in the flickering lamplight. As Hereford leaned in to examine them more closely, his eyes widened with shock.

"By Jove, Lancaster," he breathed, "you've been busy, haven't you? *The People's Charter: A Call for Universal Suffrage,*" he read. "*'Irish Repeal: The Case for Self-Governance.'* Lancaster, these are not the erotic tales we discussed. These are…"

"Highly controversial and potentially treasonable," Edgar finished, nodding. "Exactly. Which is why we must exercise the utmost discretion."

Hereford picked up another pamphlet, its cover adorned with a stark illustration of a workhouse. "*'The New Poor Law: A Treatise on Institutional Cruelty.'* My word, if these were discovered…"

"It would mean ruin," Edgar said grimly. "For us, and for the authors. Many of these writers are respected members of Society, secretly sympathetic to reform. If their identities were revealed…"

He left the sentence hanging, but Hereford nodded in understanding. In the charged political atmosphere, with Chartist uprisings and Irish unrest, such literature was dynamite.

"Now," Edgar said, pulling out Miss Lovelace's letter to lighten the mood, "What do you make of her response?"

Hereford scanned the letter, a smile tugging at his lips. "What do you know? She's accepted the challenge. A brave soul, she is."

"That she is, but…" Edgar sighed, running a hand through his hair. "I didn't anticipate how it would feel to wound her, even in my guise as Steele."

Hereford's expression softened. "It is adorable to witness you wearing your heart on your sleeve. I do not believe I have seen you thus, not even when…"

Edgar nodded, understanding his friend's intended words. "I loved Lucia but not with the urgency I feel now. Elisha, on the other hand… I care for her more than I should. More than is wise."

Hereford clapped him on the shoulder. "The heart wants what it wants, old friend. But for now, we must focus on the task at hand. This wager will make Miss Linde the talk of London's literary circles. It's a step toward making her acceptable in the eyes of Society."

Edgar nodded, squaring his shoulders. "You're right, of course. We must see this through."

Carefully replacing the pamphlets, Hereford paused. "Lancaster," he said softly, "are all these," he gestured at the controversial literature, "because of what Miss Linde said? This is dangerous."

Edgar's expression was somber as he nodded. "I know. Believe me, I know."

"I must ask. What exactly is your purpose with these pamphlets?"

Edgar turned to face Hereford, his expression resolute. "My only duty is to store them. The Pioneer's contacts will access them as needed."

"Can they be trusted?"

Edgar nodded. "Adams has obtained a signed letter from the leader, leverage I can use for protection should it be required."

"My next question is why are you showing me this?"

"These shall be hidden behind the erotic literature. I would not wish to disappoint any gentleman by giving them the wrong prohibited material. The letter from the leader is kept here." Edgar pulled out a small brick from behind the desk.

Hereford exhaled loudly. "I do not mean any offense, but I thought you did not believe in radical changes."

"That is true, but I am beginning to see that the reform is more urgently needed than I had believed. The Factory Act was a start, but it's not enough. We need comprehensive labor reform, Hereford. Shorter working hours, better conditions, a living wage."

"That's a radical position for a duke."

"It is, but I have a better chance of survival than all the others who are directly involved. These pamphlets are a way to spread the message but also to gauge the pulse of the reform movement. I must protect the authors who risk everything to speak out."

Hereford opened his mouth agape as realization dawned. "She is one of the authors! You are doing this to protect her!"

Edgar nodded. "Aye."

"Edgar, you're a noble fool. You are risking everything for a woman? What would your family say?"

"They are unaware."

Hereford puffed out air. "I must say, I did not realize how deeply you felt for Miss Linde. I cannot comprehend it."

"I pray you will one day," Edgar said. "Was it erroneous to involve you?"

Hereford shook his head. "No. The four of us have always helped each other in any way we could. You made the right decision by uniting as many powerful families as possible. It is about time my stuffy family did something good for others. I shall blame it on my least favorite uncle if I must."

"Ah, the one with a penchant for groping boys?"

"Aye, that one. And now, to the most important question… What is happening with our original venture of erotic literature?"

Edgar's eyes twinkled. "We continue as planned. We need a cover, more so now than before."

"Excellent. That's the spirit." Hereford gestured to the tunnel. "Shall we return to the world above? It is rather damp in here."

Metropolitan Review, *24 June 1840*

My Esteemed Miss Lovelace,

I must commend you on your ability to wield sarcasm as deftly as a fencer wields a foil. Bravo! It seems you are capable of passion after all, even if it is merely the passion of indignation.

Your ever-eager servant,
Aengus Steele

P.S. I've taken the liberty of reserving a front-row seat for your eventual public reading. I do hope you'll practice your enunciation. It would be a shame if my words were to lose their impact due to poor delivery.

The gentle clink of teacups and the soft murmur of conversation filled the cozy parlor of Hatchard's bookshop on Piccadilly. Elisha, Amelia, and Charlotte Carlisle sat ensconced in a quiet corner, their heads bent together in earnest discussion. The scene was a far cry from their first meeting seven years prior, when Charlotte, then a fledgling barrister, had represented Elisha and Amelia in their protest against the abhorrent conditions in London's workhouses. Through a clever combination of public sympathy and legal maneuvering, she had managed to prove their protest had actually prevented a deadly outbreak of typhus. The magistrate, though initially hostile, had been swayed by Charlotte's passionate argument that their actions had served the public good, particularly when several prominent philanthropists stepped forward to support their cause. *The Times* had even published a favorable account of the proceedings, turning what could have been a harsh sentence into a mere warning and cementing Charlotte's reputation as a defender of the downtrodden.

That fateful encounter had forged a bond between the three women, united in their pursuit of justice and social reform. Charlotte's impassioned arguments in the courtroom had not only secured better treatment for the workhouse inmates but had also kindled a fierce determination in Elisha and Amelia to affect change through the power of the written word.

As they partook of Earl Grey and nibbled upon delicate petit fours, Charlotte regaled Elisha and Amelia with a most fortuitous encounter involving the Duke of Lancaster, and the connections forged through her esteemed husband.

"What a remarkable coincidence!" Amelia exclaimed, her eyes alight with intrigue.

"Pray tell, is His Grace in good health? Does he remain in London?" Elisha inquired, her tone carefully measured.

Charlotte's gaze sharpened, a glimmer of curiosity in her eyes. "He appeared to be in fine fettle, as far as I could discern. Might I inquire as to your particular interest?"

"Elisha harbors tender feelings for the duke," Amelia said, her voice lowered conspiratorially. "Most ardent sentiments, indeed."

"I do not!" Elisha protested with haste, though her vehemence was met with skeptical glances from her companions.

"You shared an intimate moment," Amelia persisted, her tone gently chiding.

Charlotte's gloved hands flew to her mouth in astonishment. "Elisha! How utterly delightful! I trust the experience was agreeable?"

Elisha was certain her countenance had turned crimson as she shielded her face behind her hands. She offered a demure nod in response.

Her two friends emitted soft squeals of delight, embracing Elisha with unbridled enthusiasm, much to the curiosity of nearby patrons.

"I fear that fleeting moment shall remain singular in nature," Elisha confessed, her voice tinged with melancholy. "His Grace withdrew from my acquaintance following my rebuff of his proposition for a more... intimate association."

"Good heavens, how dreadfully unfortunate," Charlotte murmured, her tone laden with sympathy. "Are you quite certain that is the cause of his reserve?"

"What other explanation could there be? While he did not speak the words precisely, the implication was clear."

Charlotte regarded her friend with a measured gaze. "I might be inclined to concur with your assessment had I not made His Grace's acquaintance. However, having done so, I find myself less certain. The prospect of courting a lady beneath his station carries significant implications for every facet of his life, including his relations. Perhaps he endeavors to sway his family or seeks means to render your courtship feasible."

Elisha's lips curved in a wistful smile. "Believing he is a rake helps guard my heart." Elisha smiled brightly for her friends' sakes. "I appreciate your attempt to lift my spirits, my dear, but such efforts are unnecessary. I doubt a gentleman of his reputation would lose sleep over one such as myself. In any case, I have no desire to discuss or hear of him further. I have made my peace with the nature of men and the circumstances between us. I assure you, I'm quite well. Now, might we turn our attention to Mr. Steele's correspondence instead?"

"Speaking of Mr. Steele," Charlotte said, a mischievous glint in her eye, "I confess, I've read *Whispers of the Heart*."

"You haven't!" Elisha gasped. "Since when did you stop reading law periodicals?"

"Oh, I find myself with some leisure time when not fighting men alone," Charlotte grinned. "And so has Amelia, haven't you?"

Amelia blushed but nodded. "It was quite passionate, actually. Perhaps lacking in finesse when it came to certain, ahem, gestures, but the emotion was certainly abundant."

"I read it for the journal, but I can't believe you both read it by choice even after my review," Elisha said, shaking her head.

"The whole of London has, thanks to your feud," Amelia teased. "Aren't you the least bit curious about the man behind the words? I picture him as tall, blond, statuesque."

"Hardly," Elisha snorted. "I imagine he's of average height, pleasant enough to look at but rather portly, with thinning hair and a short beard to compensate."

Amelia and Charlotte exchanged amused glances. "You seem to have given this some thought," Amelia observed. "Have you seen him? Do you know his identity?"

"Of course not," Elisha lied. The truth was, she had imagined him just as Amelia had described except dark haired. She had forced herself to stop fantasizing about him, however, when her imaginary Mr. Steele merged with the image of the duke. It was too disturbing to contemplate. She might cope with losing one man, but two was too heartbreaking.

"Well, whoever he is, he's certainly good for business," Amelia said, lowering her voice. "Our subscription numbers have increased by ten percent each week since your correspondence began."

Charlotte's eyes widened. "Impressive."

As they continued to discuss the implications of Steele's challenge, Elisha found her mind wandering again to the Duke of Lancaster. She couldn't help but wonder what he would make of all this.

"Elisha?" Amelia's voice broke through her companion's reverie. "Where did your thoughts wander? You appeared leagues away."

"Oh, it was nothing of import," Elisha replied hastily, reaching for her teacup. "I was merely pondering whether Mr. Steele might occupy a prominent position in Society. If he possesses the means to donate 1000 pounds sterling, surely we might have heard of him."

"In truth, I have been endeavoring to uncover his identity, but to no avail," Amelia confessed. "It is most peculiar. None can offer any insight into Mr. Steele, even accounting for his nom de plume. I've been discussing the finer points with his solicitor, Mr. Beckett, but I dare not ask him to betray his client's confidence."

"When are the tomes to be published?" Charlotte asked, her legal mind ever attuned to the specifics.

"Let me see," Amelia said, consulting a small notebook. "The manuscript is to be submitted on the 15th of August, printed and distributed by October, with the final tally of orders to be completed on New Year's Eve."

"The final draft is due but one month hence," Elisha exclaimed, her palms pressed to her cheeks in dismay. "Between my articles and teaching duties, I have scarcely had a moment to write." She rubbed her temples, fatigue etched on her features.

"Have no fear on that account. I believe Steven has an idea."

"Truly? Such as?"

"I don't want to ruin the surprise for him. I will let him tell you, but it will help your literary endeavor."

"Whatever it is, I am deeply grateful, Amelia."

"Have you engaged an agent or a publishing house for your tale?" Charlotte asked, her posture straightening.

"I regret to say I have not had the opportunity to investigate the matter," Elisha replied, glancing uncertainly at Amelia, who shook her head in response.

"Splendid!" Charlotte exclaimed, her enthusiasm taking both women by surprise. "I confess I have been suffering from an excess languor since our arrival. Andrew is consumed by his business affairs, and while our social calendar overflows, it offers little in the way of intellectual stimulation. I am thankful to have found a purpose at last. I marvel that no one has approached you, given the veritable gold mine of publicity at your disposal. Once I secure an offer, I shall have it scrutinized by Andrew's solicitor, unless you have another in mind." Charlotte regarded them with keen eyes.

Both women shook their heads and murmured their gratitude.

Charlotte rose, gathering her parasol and reticule. "I shall take my leave to secure a publishing house and negotiate the most advantageous terms imaginable. My first call shall be to Chapman and Hall, the publishers of both Mr. Dickens and Mr. Steele. I intend to insist they match Mr. Steele's remuneration, given the profit they stand to gain from this literary wager. Should they prove recalcitrant, I shall not hesitate to approach Longman."

With a swift kiss upon each cheek, Charlotte hastened away. Elisha watched her departure, grateful for her advocacy yet somewhat unsettled by her precipitous exit.

THE MEETING

STEVEN THORNTON LEANED back in his plush leather chair, his eyes fixed on Elisha with an intensity that made her slightly uncomfortable. The office seemed to shrink under his scrutiny.

"Miss Linde," he began, his tone deceptively casual, "I find myself in need of your particular talents this evening."

Elisha raised an eyebrow. "Oh? And what talents might those be, Mr. Thornton?"

A smile appeared at the corners of his mouth. "Your journalistic acumen, of course. There's to be a function at the Reform Club. Several prominent members of Parliament will be in attendance."

"I see. And your interest in this gathering?"

Thornton leaned forward, his voice lowering conspiratorially. "You may not be aware, but I've been negotiating the purchase of the Royal Mail Coach Company. This event presents an opportunity to... shall we say, gauge the political climate surrounding the potential acquisition. I'd like you to accompany me," Thornton said smoothly.

Elisha hesitated, her mind racing. The thought of possibly seeing the Duke of Lancaster again made her pulse quicken both with excitement and dread. However, he had denied having strong feelings about the reform. Perhaps he wouldn't be in attendance.

Sensing her hesitation, Thornton pressed on. "There shall be opportunities to interview the Members of Parliament for the gazette, insider information on potential reforms. It is a chance to legitimize our paper as something more than a literary publication, for reform does not only apply to housing and working conditions, but education and literature as well."

Elisha became more alert at the mention of education. "Very well, Mr. Thornton. I shall accompany you to this function."

Thornton's smile widened, warmth spreading to his eyes. "Excellent. I'll have a carriage sent for you at seven o'clock this evening. And one more thing, Miss Linde. I've been considering your wager with Mr. Steele, and I believe I have a proposition that might interest you."

Elisha's eyebrows rose in curiosity. "Indeed, Mr. Thornton? Pray, do enlighten me."

"I wonder if you might benefit from a period of uninterrupted solitude to focus on your novel. Say, perhaps, a month away from the bustle of London?"

Elisha's eyes widened in surprise. "A month? That's a generous offer, Mr. Thornton. But I'm not certain I can afford to be away from my duties at the *Metropolitan* for so long."

Steven waved away her concern. "Consider it an investment in your talent, Miss Linde. Amelia tells me that she can manage in your absence, you shall continue to receive your wage, and I'm more than willing to fund this creative retreat."

"Mr. Thornton… I'm not sure what to say. Your generosity is overwhelming."

He smiled with a glint of satisfaction in his eyes. "Think nothing of it. However, I would suggest keeping this arrangement private. We wouldn't want you to be disturbed by well-meaning friends or colleagues. This is work, after all, not a leisure trip."

Elisha nodded, still somewhat dazed by the offer. "Of course, that makes perfect sense. But where would I go? I've no experience in seeking out suitable locations for such an endeavor."

"I've taken the liberty of making arrangements in Tunbridge Wells," Steven replied smoothly.

"Tunbridge Wells?" Elisha echoed, her brow furrowing slightly. "Why there, if I may ask?"

Steven's smile widened. "I have a property there that would suit your needs admirably. It's a tranquil locale, far removed from the clamor of London. The people there are discreet, accustomed to respecting the privacy of visitors. You'll find it the perfect environment for focusing on your work without distraction."

As he spoke, Elisha imagined writing by a window overlooking the tranquil countryside. It seemed like a dream.

"It sounds ideal." Excitement crept into her voice despite her effort to remain neutral. "But are you certain you can spare me for so long?"

"My dear Miss Linde," his tone was warm like melted butter, "I consider it my duty to nurture your considerable talents. The *Metropolitan* will benefit greatly from the fruits of your uninterrupted labor, I'm sure."

As she left his office, Elisha couldn't shake the feeling that she had just agreed to something far more complicated than a simple evening of interviews or writing a novel. The prospect of seeing the duke again, coupled with Thornton's ulterior motives, made her wary of potential pitfalls and unexpected revelations.

THE REFORM CLUB'S grand hall hummed with the carefully modulated voices of power. Crystal chandeliers cast their glow over mahogany panels and gilt-framed portraits of past Prime Ministers, their stern faces watching the evening's proceedings with painted gravity. The air was thick with tobacco smoke and ambition, each carefully orchestrated group below marking their territory like pieces on a chessboard. Elisha drew in a steadying breath as she entered on Steven's arm.

"The Factory Act supporters are gathered by the fireplace," Steven murmured, his breath warm against her ear as he nodded toward a cluster of Whig politicians. "Lord Melbourne seems particularly animated this evening. Perhaps the latest child labor reports have finally stirred his conscience."

Elisha followed his gaze, noting how the Home Secretary's usually languid demeanor had indeed given way to emphatic gestures as he addressed his circle. The Reform Club had arranged the hall with deliberate hierarchy—a raised dais at one end where the most influential Members of Parliament held court, while the rest of the gathering ebbed and flowed across the main floor like elaborate social currents.

Steven guided her through the crowd with practiced ease, his tailored evening wear and commanding presence drawing appreciative glances from the ladies they passed. There was something almost predatory in his grace, Elisha thought, watching him work the room. Each greeting, each perfectly timed laugh, served a purpose in his carefully constructed world.

"Miss Linde," he said, procuring two glasses of champagne from a passing footman, "I believe you'll find Lord Holland particularly interested in your latest article about the workhouse conditions in Manchester. His constituency has been… shall we say, restless since the Poor Law Amendment Act."

The subtle emphasis on "restless" spoke volumes. Elisha had heard whispers of riots in the northern manufacturing towns, of desperate workers and even more desperate measures. She accepted the champagne, using the moment to survey the room more carefully.

In one corner, Conservative Members of Parliament huddled like ravens, their black evening coats forming a barrier against unwelcome reform. She recognized Lord Wellington among them, his military bearing unchanged since his days commanding armies. Now he marshaled political forces instead, though with perhaps less success.

"The Chartists have them rattled," Steven commented, following her gaze. "Six demands for reform, each more radical than the last. Universal male suffrage?" He clicked his tongue softly.

"They fear it would upset the very foundations of Society."

"And would that be such a tragedy?" Elisha asked quietly, thinking of the faces she'd seen in the workhouses—men and women who had no voice in the laws that governed their lives. "Perhaps some foundations need shaking."

Steven's hand tightened slightly on her arm, though his pleasant expression never wavered. "Careful, Miss Linde. Such talk might be tolerated in our gazette, but here..." He let the warning hang unfinished as Lord Breckenridge approached.

It was then that she saw him.

The Duke of Lancaster stood in conversation with several Members of Parliament, his commanding presence drawing eyes even in this gathering of powerful men. His evening attire, impeccably tailored, emphasized the athletic build that spoke of regular fencing and riding rather than the soft indolence of many nobles. But it was his expression that caught and held her attention—intense, focused.

For a moment, their eyes met across the crowded room. The jolt of recognition, of connection, nearly caused her to stumble. The past weeks of silence stretched between them like an uncrossable chasm.

"Miss Linde?" Steven's voice brought her back to the present. He was watching her with concern but also calculation. "Shall we make our way to Lord Holland? I believe he's about to address the gathering about the latest reform proposals."

Elisha straightened her spine, grateful for the years of practice masking her emotions. "Of course, Mr. Thornton. Lead the way."

As they moved through the crowd, she could feel Edgar's gaze following their progress. The weight of it pressed against her shoulders like a physical touch, reminding her of all that remained unsaid between them. But there were more immediate concerns demanding her attention. The Reform Club might present itself as a genteel gathering place for politicians, but tonight it was a battlefield. And she had her own war to wage.

The gathered Members of Parliament arranged themselves in

a loose semicircle as Lord Holland took his position before the fireplace. The flames cast dramatic shadows across his aristocratic features as he cleared his throat. The rustle of silk and whisper of feet on carpet faded to expectant silence.

"Gentlemen—and ladies," he added with a perfunctory nod toward the feminine portion of his audience, "we gather at a crucial moment in our nation's history. The clamor for reform grows louder by the day. The Chartists march in our streets. The Factory Question divides our Parliament. Even now, children as young as nine labor in our mills."

Elisha's hand tightened on her notebook as she recorded his words. The careful political dance was beginning—acknowledge the problems, but heaven forbid they move too quickly to solve them. She noted how several of the Conservative Members of Parliament shifted uncomfortably at the mention of child labor. Many owned factories themselves.

"Lord Holland speaks eloquently of reform," Steven murmured beside her, his voice pitched for her ears alone, "yet his own textile mills in Lancashire are notorious for their conditions. Fascinating, is it not, how men can compartmentalize their consciences?"

Before she could respond, Lord Breckenridge's voice cut through the murmuring crowd. "And what would you have us do? Give in to every radical demand? Universal suffrage? Annual parliaments? The mob would have us tear down every institution that makes England great!"

"Is it not greatness we seek for all our citizens?" The Duke of Lancaster's voice rang out, clear and commanding. Elisha's heart leaped traitorously at the sound. "What glory is there in prosperity built on the broken backs of children?"

A charged silence fell over the gathering. Edgar had broken the careful choreography of political discourse. His words were too direct, too honest for these gilded halls.

"Your Grace," Lord Wellington interjected smoothly, "surely you understand the delicate balance we must maintain. Too rapid change could destabilize the very fabric of society."

"And too little change may tear that fabric apart," Elisha found herself saying. The words escaped before she could catch them back. Heads turned, some faces registering surprise, others disapproval at her intervention.

Edgar's eyes met hers across the room, a flash of pride and something deeper warming their depths. For a moment, the rest of the gathering seemed to fade away, leaving only their shared understanding of what was truly at stake.

Steven's hand at her elbow brought reality crashing back. "Miss Linde," he said, his tone carrying both warning and support, "perhaps you'd like to share your observations from your recent investigations into the factory conditions? I believe your firsthand account might illuminate our discussion."

She recognized his gambit for what it was—a masterful redirect that both legitimized her presence and served his own ends. The Reform Club might be a male domain, but Steven Thornton's protégée would be granted a hearing.

Drawing herself up, Elisha addressed the gathering. Her voice, though softer than the men's, carried clearly in the attentive silence. "Gentlemen, when we speak of reform, we speak not of abstract principles but of human lives. I have walked through the mills of Manchester and Bradford. I have seen children whose growth is stunted from long hours bent over machines, whose lungs are choked with cotton dust."

As she spoke, she was acutely aware of Edgar's presence, of how he had positioned himself to better hear her words. His support was almost physical, like a warm current in the otherwise cool political waters.

"Your Grace," she said, turning to address him directly, her heart thundering beneath her composed exterior. "In light of recent discussions on social reform, particularly regarding the accessibility of education for the lower classes, I wonder if you might comment on the importance of… shall we say, maintaining open channels of communication between different strata of society?"

The double meaning hung in the air between them. Around them, the gathered politicians might hear a discussion of class relations, but Edgar's slight stiffening told her he understood her true question.

His response, when it came, was equally layered. "Indeed, Miss Linde. Open communication is vital for any meaningful reform. However, one must also consider the complexities and potential consequences of bridging certain gaps in society. Sometimes, discretion and careful consideration of all parties involved is necessary before reopening certain channels."

"And how long," she pressed, her voice steady despite her racing pulse, "might such careful consideration take before action is deemed appropriate?"

The tension in the room was palpable now, though few understood its true source. Edgar's fingers tightened on his glass, his knuckles white with strain. Before he could respond, Steven smoothly intervened.

"An excellent point for further discussion," he said, his voice carrying just the right note of scholarly interest. "Perhaps we might explore these questions over refreshments? I believe the gentlemen would benefit from a moment to gather their thoughts on such weighty matters."

As the crowd began to disperse, breaking into smaller groups around the refreshment tables, Elisha found herself caught in Edgar's intense gaze. In his eyes, she read answers to questions she hadn't dared voice aloud. The political reform they discussed was vital, yes, but there were other barriers, other reforms that touched them more personally.

The evening air carried the first hints of summer as Steven led Elisha into the Reform Club's private gardens. Gas lamps cast pools of gentle light along the gravel paths, while the scent of night-blooming jasmine provided a sweet counterpoint to the tobacco-laden atmosphere they'd left behind. Above them, a quarter moon hung like a silent witness to their conversation.

"You exceeded all expectations this evening," Steven said, his voice carrying both pride and calculation. "Lord Melbourne himself commented on your eloquence. Even Wellington, old war horse that he is, seemed impressed."

Elisha walked beside him, acutely aware of the proper distance between them—close enough for a conversation, far enough to maintain decorum. The gravel crunched softly beneath their feet, a rhythmic accompaniment to their measured pace.

"They were merely being polite," she demurred, though her mind was still in the grand hall, still caught in Edgar's intense gaze. "I doubt my words will sway their votes when the Factory Bill comes before Parliament."

Steven stopped beneath a towering oak, its ancient branches casting dappled shadows in the lamplight. "You underestimate your influence, Miss Linde." His eyes, when they met hers, held an intensity that made her pulse quicken with unease. "But then, perhaps that is part of your charm."

He paused, seeming to choose his next words with care. "I feel compelled to speak frankly. Your exchange with the Duke of Lancaster did not go unnoticed."

Elisha's heart stuttered, but years of practicing composure kept her face serene. "His Grace seems to be a vocal supporter of reform. His opinion carries weight in the House of Lords."

"Indeed." Steven's voice took on a gentle, almost paternal tone that set her nerves on edge. "But I fear you may be misinterpreting his interest. The duke, while undoubtedly charming, has quite the reputation in certain circles. His frequent visits to establishments of questionable repute are well documented."

The words struck her core, each one carefully aimed. Elisha lifted her chin, grateful for the dim light that hid her expression. "I fail to see how His Grace's personal conduct relates to his political positions."

"Don't you?" Steven stepped closer, close enough that she could smell the expensive cologne he wore. "A man of his station… his dalliances with women of lower birth are legendary. But they never last, Elisha. They can't. The very society he claims to want to reform wouldn't allow it."

"Mr. Thornton—" she began, but he pressed on.

"I say this not to pain you, but to protect you. These past months, working together, I've come to…" he paused, emotion seeming to overcome him. "I've come to care deeply for your welfare."

The statement hung in the air between them, heavy with implication. Elisha's mind raced. Was this leading where she feared it might?

"Your concern is appreciated," she said carefully, "but I assure you, my interest in the duke is purely professional. His views on reform are relevant to our publication, nothing more."

Steven's smile held a touch of sadness. "If only that were true." He reached for her hand, his touch gentle but insistent. "Elisha, surely you must know how I—"

A sudden burst of laughter from nearby interrupted whatever he had been about to say. A group of gentlemen had spilled out into the garden, their voices carrying clearly in the night air. Among them, Elisha recognized Lord Breckenridge's distinctive drawl.

"Lancaster's gone soft," he was saying. "All this talk of reform… and did you see how he watched that reporter? Mark my words, she'll be his latest conquest, poor thing. Though I must say, Thornton's found himself quite a pretty pen-pusher…"

Steven's hand tightened on hers, whether in anger at the crude remarks or possessiveness, she couldn't tell. But the moment had shattered, leaving only the cool night air and the bitter taste of reality.

"We should return," she said, withdrawing her hand. "The evening grows late."

As they made their way back toward the club, Elisha's mind whirled with conflicting thoughts. Steven's warnings, the men's crude gossip, Edgar's intense gazes—all of it painted a picture she wasn't sure she wanted to see clearly. Was she being naive? Had she mistaken political passion for something more personal? And

Steven's almost-confession was another complication she wasn't prepared to face.

Yet through it all, one thought persisted. She had seen something in Edgar's eyes tonight, something that went beyond mere politics or passing fancy. The question was, did she dare trust it? Or was Steven right—were some gaps in society too wide to bridge, no matter how much the heart might wish otherwise?

The gas lamps seemed to flicker in sympathy with her uncertainty as they rejoined the gathering, each one a small beacon in the growing darkness. Tomorrow she would need to write about the evening's political discourse, to parse meaning from the careful dance of power and reform. But tonight, her heart and mind were engaged in a different kind of analysis altogether.

CRUSHING BONES

Metropolitan Review, *1 July 1840*

Dear Mr. Steele,

*Your latest missive provided a moment of levity amid my pro-
ductive writing. Your attempts at wit amuse me until pity
overtakes. Do continue trying, sir.*

*Your concern for my emotional recognition is misplaced. A
critic illuminates, not weeps. A surgeon doesn't cry over inci-
sions yet retains compassion. Don't strain your limited
imagination; take my word for it.*

*As for your comments on the complexities of the human
heart, it is precisely because I comprehend the intricacies of
human nature that I am able to discern the difference between
authentic emotion and overemotional sentimentality in prose.*

*From shucking oysters at the age of five, picking oakum,
crushing bones, to finally breaking stones when I was older, I
have encountered many emotions firsthand and witnessed the
suffering of many other downtrodden souls. I doubt you have
made your I-shall-donate-1000 pounds-sterling-for-my-
amusement wealth by crushing bones, have you, Mr. Steele?
Your temper tantrum over lukewarm tea does not suffice, sir.*

Your ever composed adversary,
E. Lovelace

Edgar sat at his desk, Elisha's letter in his hands. His eyes
scanned the words again and again, a mix of emotions playing
across his face.

At first, a smile tugged at his lips, appreciating Elisha's sharp wit and clever retorts. But as he read on, his expression grew more serious, even pained. He leaned back in his chair, closing his eyes as the weight of her words sank in. He had known of her humble beginnings, but to read her stark description of the trials she had faced… it shamed him deeply.

"Crushing bones," he murmured, shaking his head. The contrast between her experiences and his privileged upbringing had never been so apparent.

Edgar set the letter down on the desk, his brow furrowed in deep thought. He had started this correspondence for pride and monetary gain. But now, faced with the reality of Elisha's life and the depth of her character, he felt foolish and small.

"What have I done?" he whispered to the empty room. The dual identity he had created now felt like a trap of his own making. How could he continue goading and insulting her, knowing the pain and struggle she had endured?

Edgar stood, pacing the room as he grappled with his conflicting emotions. Pride in Elisha's strength and resilience warred with shame at his own actions. Admiration for her clashed with fear of losing her once the truth came to light.

Finally, he returned to the desk, pulling out a fresh sheet of paper. He had to respond as Steele and persist in his plan. Eventually, he would find a way to reveal the truth and hope that Elisha could forgive him.

With a heavy heart and a trembling hand, Edgar began to write:

Metropolitan Review, *3 July 1840*

My Esteemed Miss Lovelace,

Your account of childhood labor provides fascinating insight into your critical disposition. One might say you've gone from crushing bones to crushing spirits, though I confess your particular brand of brutality possesses a certain charm. How fortunate that your early experiences with oyster shucking prepared you so thoroughly for prizing open the shells of literary works to expose their true value.

I shall not bore you with tales of my own upbringing as you've already painted such a vivid picture of my supposedly pampered existence. I will point out that experiencing hardship is not the sole path to understanding human nature. Some of us achieve insight through observation and contemplation rather than manual labor.

Your assertion that a critic need not weep to illuminate rings hollow. Would you apply the same logic to authors? Must they remain emotionally detached to create work of merit? I suspect not. Yet you demand this curious double standard of critics.

As for my "temper tantrum over lukewarm tea", I assure you, madam, my complaints are reserved for matters of genuine substance. Such as critics who mistake cynicism for discernment.

Your reference to my charitable inclinations, while meant to wound, only reveals your own prejudices. Tell me, does the fact that I possess means to help others somehow diminish the value of doing so? Or perhaps you believe suffering alone grants one the right to speak on suffering?

Your ever intrigued opponent,
Mr. Steele

Edgar set down his pen, but the shame lingered. Each word he'd written as Steele felt like another betrayal, another layer of deception between them. He needed distance—from London, from the temptation to seek her out, from the constant reminder of his duplicity.

When Beckett arrived later that afternoon, Edgar barely looked up from his brooding.

"Your Grace," his solicitor began carefully, "forgive the intrusion, but I've been observing your… state of mind these past weeks. Perhaps what you need is time away from the complexities of London Society. A chance to gain perspective on matters of the heart."

Edgar's head snapped up. "What are you suggesting?"

"Your Kent estate, Your Grace. The railway negotiations require your eventual attention, though not urgently. But a retreat to the countryside might provide the clarity you seek."

The suggestion struck Edgar as both salvation and cowardice. "Perhaps you're right, Beckett. I shall depart immediately."

"Very good, Your Grace."

THE NEXT DAY, the grand dining room of Lancaster Hall echoed with the gentle clink of silverware and the low murmur of conversation. Despite the familiar comfort of his family estate, Edgar sat at the head of the table with his mind far away, barely registering the tender roast before him.

To his right, his mother presided over the meal with her usual grace. Edmund and Edwin sat opposite Essie and Eva, their youthful energy a stark contrast to Edgar's distracted demeanor.

"I say," Edwin suddenly announced, breaking through Edgar's reverie, "I've had the most amusing idea."

The table fell silent, all eyes turning to the second-born son.

"Do enlighten us," Essie said dryly.

Edwin leaned forward, his blue eyes sparkling and voice lowered conspiratorially. "I'm thinking of writing to Miss Lovelace as Mr. Steele."

Edgar's head snapped up, his attention fully engaged for the first time that evening.

"What nonsense is this?" Essie exclaimed, her brows furrowing.

Edwin grinned. "Just imagine it! I could have the letter printed in the papers, surprise the lady by confessing my undying love for her. Wouldn't that be a lark?"

Eva gasped, her hand flying to her mouth. "Edwin, you

couldn't! It would be terribly cruel to toy with her emotions so!"

"Oh, come now," Edwin said, leaning back in his chair, "it could be quite entertaining. The talk of the town, no doubt."

The duchess cleared her throat, her disapproval evident. "I hardly think such deception is becoming of a gentleman of four and twenty, Edwin."

All eyes turned to Edgar, awaiting his opinion on the matter. He sat with his countenance betraying nothing, though his heart raced with panic. "I believe it would be unwise to interfere in Miss Lovelace's professional affairs. Her correspondence with Mr. Steele is a matter of public interest, not a playground for our amusement. It seems to me you have too much time on your hands, Edwin. We shall discuss your future after dinner. It is not too late to consider the military as an option."

Edwin's face fell. As the conversation moved on, Edgar couldn't shake the unease that had settled over him. The thought of anyone else stepping into the role of Steele, even in jest, filled him with protective fury.

"I would like to discuss a matter of the heart," Essie began, her voice tinged with wistful longing. "I find myself longing for a sister-in-law, Edgar. A confidante to whom I might turn for counsel, one who would offer her shoulder in times of sorrow."

Edgar paused mid-bite, taken aback by this unexpected entreaty. His brothers, ever quick to seize an opportunity for mischief, affected exaggerated sobs and clasped their hands in mock plea.

"I, too, would welcome a sister-in-law," Edwin added. "Preferably before your hair begins to silver, Edgar."

The duchess cast a pointed glance at her taciturn son while deftly reducing her roast to more manageable morsels.

"Have you, perchance, a lady in mind who might prove a suitable addition to our family?" Edmund asked.

Edgar hesitated, then gestured toward his brothers. "Should you wish to enter into matrimony first, I would raise no objection."

Eva, the youngest of his siblings, placed a hand on her heart and regarded him knowingly.

"Nay, sister, I no longer mourn for Lucia," he assured her softly.

Eva and Essie both covered their mouths behind their hands, joyful tears pooling in their eyes.

"Edgar, whatever happened to that farmer's daughter? Do you remember? Lily, was it?" Edwin asked, followed by, "Ow! What?"

"Think, you imbecile!" Edmund barked.

"That will be pointless since there is nothing in that brain of his," Eva said.

"Someone tell me, or I shall make the same mistake again!" Edwin protested.

Just as Edmund was about to deal him an elbow to his side, Edgar said, "It's all right, Edmund." Directing his attention to Edwin, he continued, "You were away at school, so likely heard about her in bits and pieces. I do not fault you for not remembering. Her name was Lucia. She and I had an understanding, but it was not to be due to the vast differences in our stations."

Edwin frowned, the crease between his brows deepening as he sat pensively.

Essie snickered. "You snuck down to the village at every opportunity to steal moments with her."

Edgar sighed and leaned back in his chair, recalling the story which had lived in his mind for years. "For three glorious years, I believed we might defy the constraints of our stations. But Father..." He paused, his jaw tightening. "Father made it abundantly clear that such a union was not to be countenanced. He threatened to ruin her family if I persisted in my foolishness."

A hush fell over the table as he reached for his wine glass.

"I am so sorry, Edgar," Eva said gently.

"No, no, that is not whom I meant," Edwin said at last. "Perhaps she was a baker's daughter. She followed you everywhere when she was a child. Do you not recall, Edgar? She was only two or three years your junior. Then, one day, I chanced upon you two in a rather compromising embrace."

"Edwin!" The duchess' voice snapped like a whip. "Have you no sense of propriety in the presence of your sisters?"

"We are not entirely ignorant of such matters, Mama," Eva said.

"Speak for yourself," Essie retorted.

"Indeed, I shall. I witnessed you with—ouch!"

"Essie, you and I shall have words after dinner," the duchess said.

"Whatever became of her?" Edwin pressed, glancing around the table at the blank expressions. "The baker's daughter!"

"Her name was Lily. You were correct in that," Edgar said, clearing his throat. "We were young. It was mere youthful folly, nothing more."

"I encountered her just last year with her infant. She had married a physician in a neighboring parish. She appeared content," Essie offered.

Edgar smiled, grateful for the happy news. "I am relieved to hear it. In truth, I harbored guilt for causing her pain. I learned the harsh lesson that love, no matter how pure, often falters in the face of societal expectations."

"You seem to have a predilection for ladies of common birth, Ed—ow!" Edwin glared at Edmund while rubbing his side.

Edgar sighed inwardly. The pattern had not escaped his notice. Lucia. Lily. And now Elisha. Here he was, repeating history yet again. Or was he? This time he was maintaining his distance before misleading her, before they formed an attachment. All because he feared what his family stood to lose.

But his friends' voices echoed in his mind: *Elevate her to the most sought-after woman in London. Increase her popularity, and the* ton *shall accept her.*

A sudden, disquieting thought struck him—while he sat idly at his family's supper table, paralyzed by old fears and family patterns, he might be relinquishing Elisha to Thornton. The man had been positioning himself as her protector, her patron, her guide through London Society. Steven Thornton, with his wealth and influence, could offer her everything Edgar hesitated to provide.

The realization filled him with a sense of dread that cut through his comfortable retreat. Distance had indeed revealed what truly mattered—and what he stood to lose through his own cowardice.

Edgar set down his wine glass with trembling fingers. Perhaps it was time to stop repeating the mistakes of his past and start fighting for his future.

TENDER HEARTS

THE LIBRARY AT Lancaster Hall was bathed in the warm glow of the setting sun as Edgar and Edmund sat opposite each other, glasses of port in hand. The rich scent of leather-bound books and aged wood permeated the air, a fitting backdrop for their weighty conversation.

Edgar cleared his throat, fixing his brother with a steady gaze. "Edmund, I find myself pondering the future of our family and estate. Tell me, are you content managing our ancestral lands? Have you given any thought to marriage?"

Edmund's sapphire-blue eyes shone, a stark contrast to his dark hair. "I confess, I find great satisfaction in the work. As for marriage, I've no particular lady in mind at present. Why do you ask?"

"I've been reflecting on my duties," Edgar replied, his tone measured. "I've begun to take a more active role in the House of Lords and would like to do the same in the management of our estate. However, I'm cognizant of the fact that you've shouldered much of the burden in my absence."

Edmund nodded, a flicker of surprise crossing his features. "I see. And what does this mean for me?"

Edgar leaned forward, his expression earnest. "I propose this. We can work together as long as you'd like. When you decide you'd like more independence such as upon your marriage, I shall grant you a substantial portion of our properties and associated incomes. You'd be free to establish your own household, unless you prefer to remain here at Lancaster."

For a moment, Edmund sat in silence, clearly stunned by Edgar's proposal. When he spoke, his voice was thick with emotion. "Edgar, I… I'm deeply grateful for your generosity. I believe I would accept the offer. But tell me, what has brought about this change?"

Edgar's gaze drifted to the window, where the last rays of sunlight painted the gardens in hues of gold. "I've come to realize the weight of my responsibilities, both to our family and to society at large. It's time I assumed my proper place."

Edmund studied his brother's face, noting a newfound gravity in his demeanor. "Edgar, forgive my impertinence, but… is there a lady who has inspired this transformation?"

Edgar's chest felt heavy, but he quickly masked it with a wry smile. "Perceptive as ever, brother. There is someone. But the situation is… complex."

"Complex?" Edmund echoed delicately.

Edgar sighed, rubbing the stubble on his jaw. "She's not of our social circle. Brilliant, passionate, but a commoner. I find myself at a crossroads, torn between duty and desire."

Edmund's expression softened with understanding. "Ah, I see. And you fear the repercussions of such a match?"

"Indeed," Edgar nodded. "Yet I cannot shake the feeling that she might be worth any scandal, any societal backlash that may ensue."

A moment of silence stretched between them, thick with unspoken implications. Finally, Edmund spoke, his voice gentle but firm. "Edgar, I've watched you carry the weight of our title for years. If this woman brings you happiness, if she inspires you to embrace your responsibilities rather than flee from them… perhaps she's exactly what our family needs."

Edgar's eyes widened in surprise. "You would support such a match?"

"I would support your happiness, brother. I… I wish I had

stood up to Father, had supported you more with Lucia. I have regretted my cowardice ever since."

Edgar's heart filled with gratitude. "We were both too young and powerless for such courage. He was the law, he was God. Father could have broken us, and we both knew we stood no chance."

Edmund nodded. "I believe you are right. Well… Father is no longer with us. And it seems to me that this lady, whoever she may be, has already affected a positive change in you."

As the last light faded from the sky, the two brothers sat in companionable silence, each lost in thought. For Edgar, his brother's unexpected support was a beacon of hope in the tumultuous sea of his emotions.

The next morning brought an unexpected visitor. Adams arrived at Lancaster Hall, his usually composed demeanor betraying hints of urgency. Edgar received him in his study, noting the tension in his friend's shoulders.

"Adams," Edgar said, rising from his desk. "This is unexpected. What brings you to Kent?"

"I'm afraid I bring troubling news, Lancaster." Adams accepted the offered seat but remained on edge. "Miss Linde has been sent away from London."

Edgar's blood ran cold. "Sent away? By whom?"

"Steven Thornton. My contacts inform me she departed for Tunbridge Wells three days ago. Thornton claims it's to provide her uninterrupted time to complete her novel for the wager, but…" Adams paused, choosing his words carefully. "The circumstances seem suspiciously convenient."

Edgar's hands clenched into fists. "Convenient how?"

"The timing coincides perfectly with your absence. And Thornton has been making inquiries about your whereabouts." Adams leaned forward. "I believe he hopes to eliminate any competition for Miss Linde's affections."

Edgar realized with clarity that he'd been too impassive in the face of Thornton's machinations: the false reports about his activities, the timely railway matter, Thornton's possessive behavior at the Reform Club. The man had been maneuvering them like chess pieces.

"Where in Tunbridge Wells?" Edgar asked, his voice deadly quiet.

"I'm still gathering details, but I should have the exact location within the day." Adams studied his friend's face. "What do you intend to do?"

Edgar was already moving toward the door to summon his valet. "What I should have done from the beginning. Fight for her."

THE FLICKERING CANDLELIGHT cast dancing shadows across Elisha's spacious bedchamber in Steven Thornton's cottage in Tunbridge Wells. She sat at her small escritoire, a letter trembling slightly in her hands. The familiar script of Mr. Steele had arrived that morning, but this missive felt different—heavier somehow, weighted with emotion she hadn't expected.

15 July 1840

My Esteemed Miss Lovelace,

Your kind and empathetic words have touched me deeply. I find myself both heartened by your understanding and compelled to reciprocate your openness with a confession of my own. You inquired about the battle of the heart I alluded to in my previous letter, and I feel I owe you the truth, painful though it may be to recount.

Some years ago, I found myself irrevocably in love with a woman Society deemed far beneath my station. Lucia was her name—a name I did not utter aloud for years, yet one that echoes in the chambers of my heart with each beat. She was the daughter of a struggling farmer, possessing neither wealth nor noble lineage, but rich beyond measure in spirit, intellect, and grace.

Our love bloomed in secret, away from the prying eyes of Society and the disapproving glares of my family. For a time, I believed our affection strong enough to weather any storm, to overcome any obstacle. How naïve I was, how foolishly optimistic.

As rumors of our attachment began to circulate, the pressure from my family and peers became unbearable. I was reminded constantly of my duty to our name, to our legacy. The weight of generations of expectation bore down upon me, and to my eternal shame, I buckled beneath it.

In a moment of weakness, of cowardice I shall regret until my dying day, I severed our connection. I told Lucia we could no longer be together, that our worlds were too far apart, that I had responsibilities I could not ignore. The look in her eyes as I spoke those wretched words haunts me still—an assortment of disbelief, hurt, and a deep, abiding sorrow that seemed to dim the light in her heart. Two days later, her body was found in a nearby river.

The grief that followed was all-consuming, Miss Lovelace. It was a pain so profound, so shattering, that I feared I might never emerge from its shadow. In truth, I am not certain I ever have fully escaped its grasp.

If I could turn back the hands of time, if I could relive those fateful days, I would act differently. I would stand firm against the tide of disapproval, I would fight for Lucia with every fiber of my being. I would ensure she knew, beyond any doubt, that she was loved, cherished, and worthy.

This, Miss Lovelace, is the weight I carry, the regret that colors my every interaction, my every thought on matters of the heart. It is why I implore you not to give up hope, why I encourage you to fight for love if you believe it to be true. For the pain of loss, great as it may be, pales in comparison to the agony of regret.

I share this tale not to burden you, my dear friend, but to illustrate the depths of my conviction when I speak of love's power and importance. We live in a world bound by rigid rules and expectations, but I have learned, at great cost, that there are some things worth defying Society for.

I hope you can forgive the somber tone of this letter. Know that your friendship and understanding have been a balm to my long-wounded heart, and I am grateful for the confidence we share.

Your servant with deepest regard and utmost sincerity,
Aengus Steele

Elisha's throat felt tight with emotion as she read his words about Lucia for the third time. On her desk lay a well-worn copy of *Whispers of the Heart*, its pages marked with her critical annotations from months ago. With new eyes, she opened the novel to a passage she had once dismissed as overwrought:

"Each morning, he would position himself beneath her window, bearing a fresh bouquet of wildflowers gathered at dawn. Like a foolish boy, he counted the seconds until she appeared, just to see her smile as she discovered them. What matter if his boots were soaked with dew or his fingers pricked by thorns? Her joy was worth every discomfort."

Elisha had originally written in the margin: *"Unnecessarily dramatic. What gentleman of sense would engage in such theatrical displays?"*

Now, imagining a younger Steele—earnest and hopelessly in love—the scene touched her heart. She could picture him, probably feeling awkward and unsure, yet determined to show his affection in whatever way he could devise.

She turned to another marked passage:

"During a sudden summer storm, he draped his coat around her shoulders. The garment engulfed her slight frame, and she laughed at how the sleeves hung past her fingertips. That sound—her laughter— transformed the dreary day into something magical. He would have gladly stood there soaked to the skin, just to hear it again."

Her earlier note read: *"Maudlin sentimentality. Does the author believe readers will swoon over such obvious manipulation of emotions?"*

But now she understood—this wasn't calculated manipulation at all. It was simply truth, captured in all its raw, unpolished sincerity. He had written not to impress, but to remember.

Perhaps most revealing was the scene she had once considered the height of melodrama:

"When his father forbade their union, he vowed to build her a palace of books. Every evening, he would smuggle volumes into the hollow oak where they met—poetry, philosophy, adventures from distant lands. 'Your mind should know no bounds,' he told her, 'even if our circumstances do.' How naive he was, thinking love alone could triumph over the rigid constraints of their world."

Her original critique had been scathing: *"Absurd fantasy. The author assumes that a farmer's daughter would see beyond paper and ink, seeing poetry and adventure instead. Only persons with the luxury of time and wealth could make this conjecture. The author stretches credibility beyond repair."*

Tears sprang to her eyes as she realized he had done exactly that. It wasn't fantasy at all, but memory. A young man's desperate attempt to give his beloved the one thing he could—the freedom found in books, even as their own freedom to love was denied.

The scenes she had judged most harshly as a critic were, in fact, the most honest. What she had dismissed as clumsy attempts at romantic manipulation were actually moments of pure, unguarded truth. She thought of her own review, how she had torn apart his earnest expressions of love with clinical precision, and felt a deep shame.

Reaching for a fresh sheet of paper, she began to compose her reply. This time, she would write not as a critic, but as a friend who understood, at last, the courage it takes to bare one's heart, however imperfectly, to the world.

The candle burned low as she wrote, casting its gentle light over the letter and the book that had taken on such new meaning. Outside her window, the first hints of dawn began to paint the sky, but Elisha hardly noticed. She was lost in contemplation of how love—real, imperfect, human love—so often defies our attempts to judge it by literary standards.

20 July 1840

Dear Mr. Steele,

Your letter has moved me deeply. I confess I found myself reading it several times over, each time struck anew by the raw honesty with which you shared your pain. To bare one's deepest wounds requires tremendous courage, and I am both humbled and honored by the trust you have placed in me.

Lucia's story has touched my heart in ways I scarcely expected. Your description of her spirit, her grace, and the profound impact she had on your life speaks volumes about both her character and yours. That you loved her so completely, so purely, makes the tragedy of her loss all the more devastating.

I recognize in your words the weight of the regret you carry, the endless questioning of "what if" that must haunt your quieter moments. While I cannot ease that burden, I want you to know that your story has given me a deeper understanding of both love and loss. The remorse you express over not fighting harder for her shows a depth of self-reflection that few possess.

Your experience has taught me that some choices, once made, leave permanent marks upon our souls. Yet from these wounds can spring profound wisdom and compassion.

I must also confess something that shames me greatly. After reading your letter, I returned to your novel with fresh eyes. Passages I had once dismissed as overwrought sentimentality now reveal themselves as moments of genuine truth. I fear I allowed my critical eye to blind me to the authentic emotion you poured onto those pages. You were not manipulating your readers' feelings—you were sharing your own, raw and unguarded.

I realize now that the very scenes I criticized most harshly were likely the most difficult for you to write, drawn as they were from memory rather than imagination. For this misunderstanding, and for any pain my harsh critique may have caused, I am truly sorry.

I am grateful that you felt able to share this part of yourself with me. Know that your confidence will be held sacred. In our continued correspondence, I hope you will feel free to be entirely yourself, without fear of judgment or misunderstanding. True friendship, I believe, is built on such trust.

With deepest sympathy and warmest regards,
E. Lovelace

As she sealed the letter, Elisha felt something shift within her—not just her understanding of Mr. Steele, but her understanding of herself. She had spent so long protecting her heart with the armor of critical detachment that she had forgotten the beauty of vulnerability, the courage required to love openly despite the risk of loss.

Perhaps it was time to lower her defenses, at least a little. After all, even the most scholarly critic was, at heart, simply human.

EDGAR PACED HIS study at Lancaster Hall, Adams' letter clutched in his hand. His friend had been swift with the promised information—Elisha was staying at Rosemount Cottage on the outskirts of Tunbridge Wells, a property owned by Steven Thornton.

But it was the second piece of information that made Edgar's blood boil. Thornton had been spreading rumors in London's social circles, subtle insinuations about Edgar's "exploitation" and his "pattern" of involvement with women beneath his station. The man was systematically destroying Edgar's credibility while positioning himself as Elisha's protector.

Edgar set down the letter and moved to his desk, where Elisha's latest correspondence as E. Lovelace awaited his attention. Her words about Lucia, about understanding and forgiveness, had stirred something deep within him. For the first time in years, he felt truly seen—not as the Duke of Lancaster with all his titles and responsibilities, but simply as a man who had loved and lost.

But more than that, her willingness to reconsider her harsh critique of his novel showed a depth of character that humbled him. She could have easily maintained her critical stance, protecting her professional reputation. Instead, she chose empathy over pride, understanding over judgment.

He thought of their coded conversation at the Reform Club, the way her eyes had blazed with passion as she spoke of reform and justice. He remembered the moment their gazes had met across that crowded room, the electric connection that had made the rest of the world fade away.

Enough running. Enough hiding behind duty and social expectations. His conversation with Edmund had shown him that his family would support his happiness. Elisha's letters had shown him a woman worth fighting for. And Thornton's machinations had shown him what he stood to lose through inaction.

Edgar strode to the bellpull and summoned his valet. "We leave for Tunbridge Wells within the hour."

As he prepared for the journey that would determine his future, Edgar reflected on what he must do to bridge the gap between Edgar Lancaster and Aengus Steele, between the duke who admired Elisha Linde and the writer who had bared his soul to E. Lovelace. The path ahead was fraught with challenges, but for the first time since Lucia's death, Edgar felt ready to love.

TUNBRIDGE WELLS

THE BELL ABOVE Meryton's tinkled as Elisha stepped into the cramped bookshop, grateful for the familiar refuge of leather-bound volumes and musty paper. Three days in Tunbridge Wells had done little to ease the ache in her chest—Edgar's sudden disappearance from her life still felt like a physical wound.

She made her way toward the poetry section, seeking solace in Cowper's gentle verses. The shopkeeper's wife, Mrs. Phillips, nodded from behind her counter, and Elisha managed a polite smile in return. At least here, surrounded by books, she could pretend her world hadn't tilted off its axis.

"Mrs. Linde."

The voice, pitched low and carefully modulated, made her start. She turned to find a gentleman in plain dress approaching— brown coat, simple waistcoat, no ornamentation save a modest watch chain. His dark hair was combed differently, and he affected a slight slouch as though trying to appear less commanding, but something about his natural bearing…

"Indeed, sir." Her heart began an erratic rhythm as those impossibly blue eyes met hers. *Dear God, it's Edgar.* Unmistakably Edgar, despite the plain clothes and altered bearing. But here? Why?

"Allow me to introduce myself, madam. I am Jonathan Crook, at your service." He withdrew a calling card from his waistcoat and bowed slightly. "I am an author of modest renown, and I confess I've been most eager to discuss recent horticultural developments."

Elisha blinked. *Horticultural developments?* She glanced around the cramped bookshop, noting Mrs. Phillips pretending to dust nearby shelves while clearly listening. Understanding dawned.

"How… unexpected, Mr. Crook. Might we converse over there?" She gestured toward a small table tucked beside towering bookshelves. "The light is better for… botanical discussions."

As they seated themselves, Elisha studied his face, her fingers trembling as she arranged her skirts. The familiar scent of his cologne—washed over her in an intoxicating wave, making her heart stutter and her skin flush with recognition. This was Edgar, though she couldn't fathom why he was here, disguised, speaking of horticulture.

"I came here to warn you that some delicate blooms are at risk," he murmured, leaning forward just enough that his words wouldn't carry. "And I fear the head gardener has been… transplanting the prize specimen to a location where he might have complete control over its cultivation."

Head gardener. Elisha's mind raced. *Steven?* "I'm afraid I don't follow, Mr. Crook. Surely a head gardener wishes only the best growing conditions for his plants?"

"One would hope so. But sometimes a gardener's true interest lies not in the bloom's health, but in claiming exclusive rights to its beauty." His voice dropped lower. "Particularly when he fears another gardener might return to tend what was once his responsibility."

The pieces began clicking together. Steven had sent her away—not just for her writing, but to separate her from Edgar. "And this… other gardener? Where has he been while his bloom required tending?"

A shadow passed over his features as he looked away ruefully before meeting her eyes again. "Circumstances forced his departure. But he never stopped caring for the bloom's welfare, even from a distance."

"How convenient," she said coolly as the weeks of hurt resurfaced. "No correspondence, no word to acknowledge her existence. What manner of circumstances could be so pressing that he couldn't reassure her of his wellbeing?" She swallowed the lump forming in her throat. Her pride wouldn't allow her to display her heartache.

The accusation seemed to strike him into silence for a moment. When he spoke, the words came out cautiously.

"Perhaps the other gardener was endeavoring to improve his circumstances... his skills... to qualify for the bloom's tending."

"What is there to improve?" Her voice was cold and steely, full of restrained hurt. "He's a gardener. Don't all gardeners know how to sow their wild oats and coax seeds to sprout? In fact, I believe I saw several articles discussing his vast experience in sowing seeds in various gardens."

Edgar's face suddenly turned pink. He pulled on his neckcloth as if he were suffocating before clearing his throat. "Um... The head gardener spread rumors about the other gardener's... unsavory growing practices. Made it appear he was tending multiple gardens simultaneously, neglecting his most precious bloom.

The newspaper articles. Her breath caught. Steven had been behind those false reports. It shed light on why she'd been wary of him all along. "These rumors—were they true?"

"Completely fabricated. The displaced gardener spent his time watching over his bloom from afar, ensuring no harm came to her."

Air left her lungs and the weight seemed to lift from her ribs as understanding deepened. Edgar had been protecting her, even while absent. But still... the need to confirm his feelings for her was too great to ignore. "And why should this bloom trust a gardener who disappeared without explanation? Perhaps she's learned to flourish under the head gardener's care."

Edgar's knuckles turned white against the table. "Because the head gardener may not have the bloom's best interests at heart.

There are… delicate specimens in that garden that could be used against the bloom if discovered."

Delicate specimens… What could… Good heavens, surely not. The reform writing? Cold dread settled in her stomach. If Edgar had discovered her political activities… What could he be thinking of her? Is that why he'd kept his distance? *What if Steven had?*

"What sort of delicate specimens?" she asked as her guard reasserted itself once more.

"The kind that certain authorities consider… weeds. Dangerous to the established order of gardens."

Seditious material. There was no mistaking his meaning now. If that were the case, she could be arrested, transported, or worse. A chill settled over her. "And you believe the head gardener knows of these specimens?"

"I'm uncertain. But he's certainly positioned to discover them. And once discovered…" Edgar let the implication hang.

"He could use such knowledge to ensure the bloom's… complete cooperation," she finished, panic fluttering beneath her ribs.

A group of matrons entered the shop, discussing Lord Melbourne's latest scandal. Edgar and Elisha fell silent until the women moved toward the religious texts.

"There is another concern," Edgar continued, his voice low and wary. "The head gardener has been making himself indispensable to the bloom's livelihood. Should he choose to create circumstances that would compromise the bloom's reputation…"

Compromise. Marriage would be the only solution to salvage her honor. Elisha's fan fluttered against her chest as the full scope of Steven's potential manipulations became clear.

"And what does this displaced gardener propose to do about such machinations?"

"He's prepared a sanctuary. A place where the bloom could flourish safely while he deals with the head gardener's interference."

The sanctuary? Where… By Jove, he's not suggesting his own cottage? The impropriety should have shocked her, but her foolish heart only beat more eagerly.

"This sanctuary—it would be… properly supervised?"

Edgar's eyes held hers meaningfully. "The gardener would do his utmost to ensure the bloom's honor remained intact while protecting her from those who would exploit her."

Elisha studied his face, seeing both the man who had abandoned her and the one now offering her protection. "And after? What becomes of a bloom that requires such… unconventional protection?"

"The gardener hopes," he said softly, "that in time, he might prove worthy of tending such a precious specimen permanently."

Her heart stuttered at the implication, but she quickly chided herself for her gullibility. *He couldn't have meant he'd offer for her. No, he likely meant he'd protect her within his capacity as a duke.* "Pretty words, Mr. Crook. But this bloom has learned to be wary of promises from absent gardeners."

"Indeed." He leaned forward, intensity blazing in his eyes. "But sometimes a gardener must prove his devotion through actions rather than words. The question is—does the bloom trust him enough to accept his protection?"

The bell chimed again as more customers crowded the small shop. Edgar rose smoothly, every inch the polite stranger.

"It has been most illuminating discussing horticultural matters with you, Mrs. Linde. Should you wish to visit that garden sanctuary, it lies but a mile from your current location," he said as he handed her a card with *Rosemount Cottage* written on it.

"Indeed, Mr. Crook." Her voice scraped through her strained throat with a hint of tremor as she pondered spending the night in his company. "I shall… consider your advice about… transplanting."

Edgar tipped his hat and departed while Elisha remained seated, her mind spinning. Did she have the courage to trust Edgar again—or if two months of silence had taught her better than to place her faith in absent gardeners?

EDGAR PACED THE front parlor of the cottage he rented like a caged lion, his boots wearing a path in the Turkish carpet. Each tick of the clock on the mantel seemed to mock him. The afternoon sun slanted through the tall windows, painting golden stripes across the polished floor—how many more times would that light shift before she arrived? If she arrived at all.

Had she fully understood his coded message? More importantly, would she dare to come? The very impropriety of what he asked—an unwed woman arriving unchaperoned at a bachelor's residence—spoke volumes about his desperation. His grandfather would be turning in his grave at such a scandal, but after two months of separation, after watching her window darken night after night, propriety seemed a small price to pay for even a moment in her presence.

He replayed their conversation in the bookshop, analyzing each word, each glance. Had he made the danger clear enough? Had she understood when he'd mentioned Thornton's duplicity? The memory of her face—pale but resolute—haunted him. She'd looked thinner, the hollow of her cheeks more pronounced. Had she suffered as he had during their separation?

The sound of carriage wheels slowing outside the cottage sent his heart thundering against his ribs. A feminine figure in a pink muslin gown descended, a small trunk in her hands. Edgar's breath caught in his throat.

She had come.

The sound of the front door opening sent him striding toward the parlor entrance, propriety warring with desperation. Wallace, the butler, spoke in a measured tone. His voice drifted through the wood panels, followed by a softer, feminine murmur that made Edgar's heart stutter.

And then she was there, framed in the doorway like a vision from his fevered dreams. The afternoon sun caught the loose tendrils of hair escaping her bonnet, turning them to copper. Her small trunk—dear God, she'd actually brought it—looked heavy in her gloved hands. His heart clenched at the sight.

"Miss Linde," Wallace announced with pointed emphasis on her unmarried status, his disapproval radiating in waves. A young footman hurried forward to take her trunk, his eyes carefully averted but darting back to her face to steal glances.

Edgar found himself suddenly paralyzed. All his carefully prepared speeches evaporated like morning mist. Instead, he stepped forward and grasped her gloved hand, noting how it felt limp within his grip. Without a word, he drew her into the parlor, past the watchful eyes of the servants that came with the house.

"Do not disturb us unless summoned," he ordered, his voice rough with emotion. Wallace's face might have been carved from stone as he bowed and withdrew, closing the door with a quiet click that seemed to echo in the charged silence.

They stood there, barely breathing, listening to the retreating footsteps. When they faded entirely, Elisha swayed slightly, as if the strength that had carried her here was finally failing.

"Your Grace," she whispered, her voice catching. "I... I hope I understood your message correctly. About Mr. Thornton..."

Edgar moved closer, drawn by the vulnerability in her eyes. In the warm light filtering through the curtains, he could see every detail he'd missed in the dimness of the bookshop—the shadows beneath her eyes, the slight chapping of her lower lip where she'd worried it with her teeth, the way her hands clutched her reticule like a shield.

The sight of her standing in his parlor, brave and trembling and utterly perfect, undid him completely. Slowly, he reached for the ribbon of her bonnet. The satin was warm from her skin as he untied it with fingers that weren't quite steady. The bonnet—adorned with cheerful sunflowers that seemed to mock their forbidden situation—came away easily, revealing more of those escaped curls.

"It was most prudent of you to bring your trunk," he said

softly, placing the bonnet on a nearby table with exquisite care. What he didn't say was how the sight of it had sent hope blazing through his chest. She hadn't just come to hear his warning— she'd come prepared to stay.

"I was uncertain," she admitted, her eyes darting to the closed door, "if I might be in any peril, if Mr. Thornton had sent me here for a purpose other than writing." The words came out in a rush, as if she'd been holding them back since their meeting in the bookshop.

Edgar swallowed with effort as he fought to keep his voice steady. "I apologize for causing you alarm. I am uncertain if he meant any harm or merely sought to separate us."

"I don't understand." Elisha's voice betrayed her agitation. "Why would he when you have ignored me for these past two months?" The hurt in her voice was like a blade between his ribs.

"Perhaps he knew how strongly I felt about you and knew I would return for you." Edgar held her gaze, willing her to see the truth in his eyes. A tree branch swayed outside, sending shadows dancing across her face.

"Return for me?" Her voice caught. "Do you truly expect me to believe you had spared any thoughts for me while gallivanting with other women?"

Edgar frowned in confusion until he recalled the articles. "Are you referring to the rag sheets claiming I was seen with various women?"

Her eyes narrowed as she stiffened. "Pray, save us both the trouble. Tell me the truth. Tell me you lost your interest when I declined further advances." Her voice became thinner as her throat tightened. "That I only have myself to blame for believing a duke could see me as more than a passing fancy."

Edgar froze, her accusation fueling his rage like never before. So much so that he could not even raise his voice.

"You hold a rather low opinion of me." The words were soft, but she flinched as if he'd shouted. "If you believe me to be that kind of rascal, why are you here? Why did you come?"

She looked up at him then, vulnerability and hurt evident in her big bold eyes. "Because…" She buried her face in her hands as she shook her head. "Because I can't help myself. I'm a fool… risking my life, everything I've worked for, just to be closer to you."

Elisha turned her back to him then, her shoulders shaking. Edgar stared at the woman who stood in his parlor risking everything to be with him even for a moment, putting faith in him one more time that he may do right by her.

He moved closer until barely a breath separated them. "Elisha…" Her name was a prayer on his lips. "How I have missed you. I thought I would perish from needing you with every fiber of my being. I wished to converse with you, to see your smile, to stroke your hair…" His voice roughened. "Good heavens, I longed to hold you."

Her sobs stopped and her shoulders no longer quivered. With a kerchief over her mouth, she turned toward him slightly.

"I am sorry I have led you to believe I have been absent these past two months." The words tumbled out, raw and honest. "I have tried to steel my heart against you. To convince myself that my feelings were fleeting, that you deserved a man who lived with more conviction, who could offer for you without fear of consequences. And yet…" His voice faltered before strengthening with conviction. "And yet I find that my feelings for you have only grown stronger in our separation. They have taken root so deeply within me that I fear they have become a part of my being."

Tears spilled down her cheeks, but her eyes shone with joy as she gazed up at him. The sight undid him completely.

"I have been a prisoner of longing these past weeks. Every moment away from you has been an exquisite agony. You may believe I have been absent, but I was there, across from the *Metropolitan* building. Most nights, I watched the attic window darken and wished you sweet dreams."

He cupped her cheek, thumb brushing away her tears.

"I thought, in my folly, that by distancing myself from you, I could protect you from heartache. But in doing so, I realize I have only succeeded in bringing pain to us both."

She leaned into his touch, her eyes fluttering closed. When they opened again, they held such joy his breath caught. "And I thought…" her voice quavered, "I thought you didn't give me another thought… because I refused your bed…"

Unable to bear her pain for another moment, Edgar pulled her into his arms. She came willingly, her tears soaking his coat as he held her close. Each sob tore at his heart, revealing the depth of her hidden anguish. He pressed his lips to her hair, murmuring soft words of comfort and love.

As they stood there, wrapped in each other's arms while the afternoon light painted them in gold, the world beyond his parlor ceased to exist. They were no longer duke and commoner, no longer bound by Society's rigid rules. They were simply Edgar and Elisha, two hearts finally finding their way home.

And in that moment, Edgar knew with bone-deep certainty that he would move heaven and earth to keep her safe and to make her his in every way that mattered. Society's censure, his family's expectations, even his own fears—none of it could compare to the precious weight of her trust in his arms.

Her smile, when it came, was like sunrise breaking through storm clouds.

NEST

THE LATE AFTERNOON sun draped golden fingers through the oak leaves overhead, casting dappled shadows that danced across Elisha's muslin gown as she walked beside Edgar along a secluded path in the expansive gardens. Sweet-scented roses climbed ancient stone walls, their heavy blooms nodding in the gentle breeze that carried hints of lavender and freshly cut grass. The crunch of gravel beneath their feet mingled with the distant call of wood pigeons and the gentle splash of the fountain in the Italian garden beyond.

Edgar's hand, warm and sure against her own, sent delicious shivers up her arm. His thumb traced lazy circles on her palm. Here, sheltered by thick yew hedges and carefully tended topiaries, they might have been the only two souls in existence.

"Tell me, Elisha," Edgar began, his rich baritone carrying that particular tender note she had come to recognize as solely hers, "what occupies your pen these days? I find myself most curious about your current literary endeavors."

The gentle inquiry sent a flutter of unease through her breast. Elisha watched a pair of butterflies dance past, their wings catching the sunlight like scattered diamonds. She was loath to deceive him, yet revealing her identity as Miss Lovelace felt akin to handling a powder keg with trembling hands. The sharp-tongued critic who exchanged increasingly heated missives with a man had become the talk of every scandal sheet in London.

Despite the warmth of the day, a chill crept along her spine. Her reputation—no, more than that, Edgar's reputation by association—could be irreparably damaged. She stole a glance at his profile, noble and striking in the afternoon light. His dark hair gleamed with hints of chocolate where the sun touched it, and concern seemed to etch fine lines around his eyes that only heightened his appeal.

They paused beside a marble bench nestled among a bower of climbing roses. The sweet perfume of the flowers enveloped them as Edgar turned to face her, his expression so full of tender regard that her heart ached.

She drew a steadying breath, the stays of her corset suddenly feeling too tight. "Edgar," she began, her voice trembling slightly despite her efforts at composure, "there's something I must confess to you."

His eyes, their blue depths brightening in the golden light, fixed upon her face with unwavering attention. The intensity of his gaze made her pulse quicken, and she found herself gripping the delicate silk of her parasol too tightly.

"I… I am Miss Lovelace."

Something shifted in Edgar's expression—his eyes seemed to widen with what looked like surprise, understanding, and perhaps relief. He hesitated, and Elisha noticed his hand flex at his side, as though he, too, was wrestling with secrets of his own.

"You're Miss Lovelace?" His voice was soft but intent.

Elisha nodded, heat flooding her cheeks. The breeze picked up, carrying the distant toll of church bells across the garden. A curl escaped her carefully arranged coiffure, dancing against her cheek until Edgar, with exquisite gentleness, tucked it behind her ear. The brief contact left her skin tingling.

"Yes," she managed, fighting the urge to lean into his touch. "I've been writing under that pseudonym for some time now. I pray you're not too disappointed in me for keeping it from you."

"Disappointed?" Edgar's laugh was rich and warm as honey. "No, not at all." His hand lingered near her face, his thumb brushing her cheek with devastating tenderness. "I'm impressed, truly. Your writing is remarkable, Elisha. But why did you feel you needed to hide this from me?"

She lowered her eyes, watching the play of shadows across the gravel path. Her fingers worried the delicate lace of her gloves. "I feared it might change how you saw me. That you might not approve of my rather outspoken opinions." She glanced up through her lashes, finding his gaze still fixed upon her with an intensity that made her mouth go dry. "The colorful missives, drawing attention to myself in such a public manner… It was not my choice, if that helps. Amelia and I decided to publish the letters out of necessity, due to our difficulty attracting new readers."

Edgar gently lifted her chin with one finger, compelling her to meet his gaze fully. The touch, though slight, sent warmth coursing through her entire body. "Elisha, if I had any issues with your opinions and your ability to express them, I would have fled the first day we met."

A smile curved her lips at the memory, relief washing over her like a summer rain. Edgar opened his mouth to say something but hesitated. She waited patiently, her brows furrowed with questions when he said, "Thank you for trusting me with this, Elisha. It means more than you know."

His thumb traced the line of her jaw, and Elisha found herself swaying slightly toward him, drawn by an invisible force as inexorable as the tide.

LATER THAT EVENING, Elisha sat at her escritoire, the rich scent of leatherbound books mingling with the sharp tang of ink. Across the carpet, Edgar rustled through Parliamentary documents, his broad shoulders casting a looming shadow against the mahogany-paneled walls.

The flickering candlelight cast honeyed shadows across the study, reaching Elisha's corner where half of her was cast in shadow. She paused in her writing, the quill hovering above parchment as she watched a drop of ink fall, black as midnight, onto the creamy paper. Her copper curls, escaping their pins after hours of work, caught the golden light as she raised her eyes.

She found Edgar watching her, his sapphire eyes intent beneath the strong arch of his brow. A hint of a smile played about his lips—those aristocratic lips that had no business causing such a flutter in her breast. He held her gaze a moment longer than propriety dictated before returning to his papers, the signet ring on his finger glinting as he shifted the documents.

The mantel clock ticked away precious minutes as Elisha attempted to focus on her novel. The muslin of her day dress whispered against the chair as she adjusted her position, acutely aware of the tension building between them like storm clouds gathering on the horizon.

Edgar loosened his cravat, the silk rustling softly. The action exposed the strong column of his throat, and Elisha's fingers tightened around her quill. When she dared look up again, she found him watching her again, his eyes dark as a stormy sea. Heat bloomed in her cheeks, and she quickly lowered her gaze to her manuscript, where the words swam before her eyes like wayward fish.

The thunder struck. Elisha started, her hand jerking toward her inkwell. The delicate glass vessel wobbled precariously, and she steadied it with trembling fingers. A drop of ink stained her sleeve, blooming like a black rose against the pale fabric.

"Allow me," Edgar's deep voice broke the silence as he rose, withdrawing a pristine handkerchief from his coat pocket. He moved toward her, his steps muffled by the thick carpet.

"Pray, do not trouble yourself," Elisha protested. But he was already beside her, the heat of him warming her more surely than any fire could. His clean, masculine scent enveloped her as he bent to examine the stain.

"It is no trouble," he murmured, his breath stirring the loose curls near her ear. As he pressed the handkerchief to her sleeve, his fingers brushed against her arm through the thin muslin. The touch, though fleeting, sent a shiver racing down her spine.

Elisha's breath caught audibly in her throat. Edgar's hand stilled, and for a moment, neither moved. The air between them grew thick with unspoken words. She could hear his breathing, slightly uneven, matching the rapid flutter of her own heart.

"I fear the stain may set," she managed to say, though her voice emerged husky and strange to her own ears.

"Indeed." Edgar straightened slowly, his usual grace somewhat diminished. He ran a hand through his hair, disrupting its careful arrangement. The resulting dishevelment only served to heighten his appeal, much to Elisha's dismay.

When he returned to his desk, the room seemed larger and colder for the distance between them. Elisha rose on unsteady legs, smoothing her skirts with damp palms. She made her way to the bookshelf, feeling his gaze follow her movement like a physical caress. Her fingers trailed along the leather spines, unseeing, as she struggled to calm her racing pulse.

She reached for a volume at random, using the moment to gather her composure. As she turned, she caught Edgar's reflection in the darkened window. He appeared to have abandoned all pretense of work, his heated gaze fixed upon her with an intensity that made her fingers tremble on the book's spine.

Returning to her seat, Elisha tucked an errant curl behind her ear, the pins in her hair now hopelessly loose. The copper strands caught the candlelight, gleaming like newly minted pennies. Through lowered lashes, she observed Edgar's chest rise and fall with what seemed like quickened breaths, his right hand clenched upon the arm of his chair until his signet ring appeared to press white marks into his flesh.

The candles burned lower. Wax dripped like tears down their sides. Yet neither made a move to depart, caught in this delicious tension that crackled between them just like the lightning illuminating the room. Each glance exchanged added fuel to the fire building in Elisha's chest, propriety warring with desire as the night drew its dark velvet cloak around the study.

The grandfather clock in the hall struck ten, its sonorous chimes breaking the spell that held them bound. Elisha started, her book nearly slipping from nerveless fingers. She had not read a single word in the past quarter hour, her mind consumed by the overwhelming presence of the man across the room.

"I fear I have kept you overlong," Edgar said, his voice rough with what sounded like poorly concealed emotion. He stood, adjusting his waistcoat with hands that seemed less steady than usual. "The hour grows late."

"Indeed." Elisha rose as well, gathering her papers with careful movements that belied the chaos of her thoughts. A loose sheet escaped her grasp, floating to the carpet like a fallen leaf.

They both moved to retrieve it, their hands meeting over the errant page. Edgar's fingers were warm against hers, slightly calloused despite his noble birth—evidence of his fondness for riding. The touch lasted barely a heartbeat before propriety forced them apart, but it left Elisha's skin tingling as though branded.

"Edgar," she whispered, his name a forbidden pleasure on her tongue. The single word seemed to spark something within him. In two fluid strides, he closed the remaining distance between them.

"Tell me to stop," he breathed, his face mere inches from hers. The heat radiating from him made her head spin. "Tell me this is madness, and I shall leave this instant."

Instead, Elisha found her fingers curling into his coat lapel, the fabric warm from his body. Her heart thundered against her ribs like a wild creature seeking escape. "I cannot," she confessed, her voice trembling. "God help me, I cannot."

Time seemed to slow, then stopped entirely. Edgar's hand rose to cup her cheek, his touch featherlight, as though she were spun glass that might shatter at any moment. His thumb traced the curve of her cheekbone, leaving trails of fire in its wake. Elisha's eyes fluttered closed at the sensation, a soft gasp escaping her lips.

"Look at me," he commanded softly. When she did, the raw hunger in his gaze stole what little breath remained in her lungs.

"Edgar," she breathed again, and this time he moved like a man possessed.

His lips met hers with desperate intensity, months of restraint crumbling like ancient stone. One hand tangled in her hair, loosening what remained of her pinned curls, while the other pressed against the small of her back, drawing her closer until she could feel the rapid beat of his heart against her breast.

Elisha melted into him, her hands sliding up to his shoulders, feeling the coiled strength beneath fine fabric. His kiss was both gentle and fierce, reverent and demanding. He tasted of fine brandy and desire, and she found herself intoxicated by the combination.

When they finally broke apart, both breathing heavily, Edgar rested his forehead against hers. His usually immaculate hair was mussed where she had threaded her fingers through it.

"I must stop," he whispered hoarsely, though he made no move to release her from his embrace. "You—"

Elisha silenced him with another kiss, this one slower, deeper. She poured every unspoken word, every stolen glance, every midnight dream into it. His groan of surrender rumbled through his chest, and his arms tightened around her waist.

When they parted again, reality began to seep back in. She became acutely aware of their compromising position, the danger of this attraction. Yet she could not bring herself to regret it.

"We can never go back from this moment," she said softly, her fingers straightening his lapels with trembling care.

Edgar caught her hand in his, pressing a fervent kiss to her palm. "I do not wish to go back," he said, his voice carrying a conviction that sent warmth spiraling through her chest.

A noise in the corridor outside snapped them apart. They stood staring at each other, chests heaving, as footsteps passed by the study door. In the flickering candlelight, Edgar looked wild and dangerous and utterly irresistible.

"I should retire to bed," Elisha whispered, though every fiber of her being protested the very thought.

"Yes," Edgar agreed, his Adam's apple bopping as he swallowed. "Though it takes every ounce of my willpower to let you."

She gathered her papers with unsteady hands, acutely aware of his presence behind her. As she reached the study door, his voice stopped her.

"Elisha." She turned to find him watching her with an intensity that made her knees weak. "Dream of me tonight."

The intimacy of his request sent a shiver down her spine. "As if I could dream of anything else."

UNWELCOME VISITOR

THUNDER RUMBLED IN the distance as storm clouds gathered beyond the study windows, casting the room in an ominous half-light that made the candles flutter. Elisha sat at her small writing desk, surrounded by a sea of scattered papers and discarded drafts. The scratch of her quill against parchment had grown ragged after hours of work, matching the increasing wildness of her thoughts.

She leaned back, stretching her cramped fingers. The sharp ache in her joints seemed to pulse in time with the approaching storm. Rolling her shoulders to ease the tension, she caught a glimpse of her reflection in the window—hair escaping its pins, ink stains on her fingers, a fierce intensity in her eyes that would have scandalized Amelia.

The door opened with barely a whisper of sound. Edgar's reflection appeared behind hers in the darkened glass, and Elisha felt that familiar flutter in her chest—the one that never failed to accompany his presence. He moved with quiet grace, bearing two steaming cups of tea. The rich aroma of Earl Grey mingled with the petrichor drifting through the partially open window.

"How goes the writing?" he asked, setting one cup beside her carefully, mindful of her precious drafts. A drop of tea escaped, blooming like a copper rose on the saucer. The earthenware cup was from the servants' collection rather than his fine porcelain—a small detail that spoke volumes about his understanding of her preference for comfort over propriety when working.

Elisha turned to face him, unable to contain the excitement that brightened her features despite her exhaustion. "I think… I think I've finally cracked it," she said, her voice carrying that particular breathlessness that came with creative breakthrough. "The scene that's been giving me trouble for days—it's finally come together."

Edgar perched on the edge of the desk, his own cup cradled between his elegant hands. His eyes, sparkling blue in the candlelight, held genuine interest rather than the polite attention most men offered to a lady's literary pursuits.

"May I hear it?" he asked, his voice pitched low and intimate in the storm-darkened room.

Elisha hesitated, her fingers trailing over the pages. Sharing unfinished work always felt like exposing her soul to potential ridicule, yet he seemed to understand the vulnerable nature of a work in progress.

After a moment's consideration, she nodded, gathering the relevant pages with trembling fingers. The paper rustled like autumn leaves as she sorted through them, finally locating the passage in question. Her voice, when she began to read, started soft and uncertain, but grew stronger with each word, taking on the rhythmic cadence that emerged naturally when she was lost in her craft.

The approaching storm provided an oddly fitting accompaniment—distant thunder punctuating dramatic moments, wind stirring the curtains during quieter passages. As she read, she was acutely aware of Edgar's reactions: the slight intake of breath at a particularly poignant line, the way his fingers tightened on his cup during moments of tension.

As the last words left her lips, silence fell between them, heavy with possibility. Elisha kept her eyes on the manuscript, afraid to look up and see anything less than understanding in Edgar's expression. The grandfather clock in the corner marked each moment, its steady tick a counterpoint to her racing heart.

When she finally gathered the courage to meet his gaze, the intensity there stole her breath. He was watching her with an expression of wonder and fierce pride that made her chest tight with emotion.

"Elisha," he breathed, setting his cup aside with a soft clink of china against wood. "These chapters… they're extraordinary. The way you've developed these characters' inner conflicts…" He leaned closer, the desk creaking softly beneath his weight. "The tension throughout… it's masterful."

A flush crept up her neck, warming her cheeks. The praise from him meant more than all the literary accolades she'd received as Miss Lovelace. "You really think so?" she asked, hating the tremor of uncertainty in her voice.

"I know so," Edgar said with quiet conviction. He shifted, closing the distance between them until his knee brushed her skirts. The contact, though slight, sent awareness skittering along her nerves. "You have a gift, Elisha. This tale…" His hand covered hers where it rested on the manuscript, his thumb brushing over her ink-stained fingers. "It's going to change things for you. I can feel it."

Lightning flickered beyond the windows, briefly illuminating his features—the aristocratic planes of his face, the intensity in his dark brown eyes, the slight dishevelment of his cravat that spoke of hours spent bent over her manuscript, requesting chapter after chapter until the afternoon had slipped into evening.

Elisha's heart swelled with gratitude and something deeper, more dangerous. "Thank you, Edgar," she whispered, fighting the urge to turn her hand beneath his, to twine their fingers together. "Your faith in me means more than I can say."

He reached out with his free hand, gently tucking a stray strand of hair behind her ear. His fingers lingered against her temple, a touch so tender it made her eyes sting with unexpected tears. "You don't need my faith," he murmured, his voice rough with emotion. "You have talent, passion, and a voice that deserves to be heard." His thumb traced the curve of her cheek.

"The world is waiting for your words, Elisha. Don't keep them waiting too long."

The air between them grew thick with unspoken desires. Edgar's hand slid to cup her nape, his touch igniting sparks beneath her skin. Elisha found herself swaying toward him, drawn by that invisible force that always seemed to pull them together despite propriety, despite danger, despite—

A sharp knock at the door shattered the moment. They sprang apart like guilty children, Edgar straightening with practiced composure while Elisha busied herself gathering scattered papers with trembling hands.

"Enter," Edgar called, his voice betraying none of the tension Elisha could see in the rigid set of his shoulders.

The door opened with urgent haste, revealing Thompson, one of Edgar's most trusted men. His face was flushed from exertion, rain darkening his shoulders. The fact that he had entered through the main house rather than the servants' quarters spoke to the gravity of his news.

"Your Grace, Miss Linde," Thompson began, his voice carefully controlled despite his labored breathing. "I've just received word that Mr. Steven Thornton awaits the lady at her lodgings. Our man informed him that you had gone to the post office, Miss."

A chill that had nothing to do with the storm crept down Elisha's spine. Her eyes met Edgar's, finding her own concern mirrored there. "I had hoped he would not call," she said softly, fingers unconsciously crumpling the corner of her manuscript.

Edgar's jaw clenched visibly, a muscle ticking beneath the skin. The easy warmth of moments before had vanished, replaced by a cold fury that transformed his features into something almost predatory. "What business has he calling upon you unannounced?" The words emerged as a low growl.

Lightning flashed again, throwing harsh shadows across his face. Thunder followed almost immediately, rattling the windowpanes.

"It is his cottage, and I am his guest," Elisha reminded him, though the words tasted bitter. "It is not improper for him to inquire after his guest." Even as she spoke, her mind raced with the implications. Had Thornton discovered something? Was this seemingly innocent visit a trap?

Edgar pushed away from the desk with controlled violence, beginning to pace the small sitting room. His boots made no sound on the thick carpet, but tension radiated from every line of his body. The candlelight caught the signet ring on his finger as his hand clenched and unclenched at his side.

"Though I loathe the thought of you spending time in his company," he said finally, each word precise and careful, "it might be prudent for you to return to your house and politely send him on his way."

Elisha nodded, already rising to gather her things. The rustle of her skirts seemed unnaturally loud in the charged atmosphere. "I shall do so."

Edgar's frown deepened as he watched her movements. After a moment of tense silence, he said, "Exercise caution, Elisha. We know not what more Thornton is capable of." The warning in his voice made her pause in the act of collecting her papers.

She straightened, smoothing her skirts with palms that had grown damp with apprehension. "I assure you, I shall be the very picture of prudence."

Edgar crossed to her in two swift strides, close enough that she had to tilt her head back to meet his gaze. "Is it wrong of me," he asked, his voice dropping to an intimate murmur, "to feel possessive of you when I haven't made you any promises?"

Elisha's breath caught at his words, at the naked possession in his gaze. The storm pressed closer, making the air heavy and electric between them. "Of course not," she whispered, her hand rising to rest against his chest, feeling his heart thundering beneath her palm. "I felt similarly when I read about you and other women."

Edgar's expression shifted, confusion replacing the heat in his eyes. "What other women?"

"All those private meetings you had with ladies in Bath only recently." The words emerged more bitter than she'd intended. Lightning illuminated the room again, casting stark shadows across his suddenly rigid features.

"Elisha." Edgar caught her hand where it rested against his chest, pressing it harder against his heartbeat. His other hand rose to cup her cheek, thumb stroking along her jawline with careful tenderness that belied the intensity in his voice. "You must believe me. I have not engaged in any dalliances in Bath or elsewhere in recent months. Indeed, I have not been to Bath this year at all. According to my men's investigation, Thornton has been spreading rumors about me, likely to besmirch my name because he desires you for himself."

The implications of his words hung heavy in the air between them. Elisha's mind raced, pieces falling into place with horrible clarity. "I wondered…" she began, then fell silent.

"So you had suspected it yourself."

"I am uncertain of his motivation," she said carefully, studying Edgar's face in the flickering candlelight. "But it would not surprise me."

Elisha opened her mouth to speak, but Thompson's discreet cough from the doorway reminded them of the urgency of the situation.

Edgar's hands tightened briefly on hers before releasing her. "Go," he said softly. "But Elisha…" He caught her wrist as she turned to leave, his grip gentle but insistent. "Take Thompson with you. And the carriage. Trust your instincts."

The cryptic warning sent a shiver down her spine. "I shall be careful," she promised, resisting the urge to rise on her tiptoes and kiss him. Instead, she squeezed his hand once before stepping away.

The storm followed her progress down the corridor, thunder rumbling overhead like a warning. As she prepared to face Thornton, Elisha couldn't shake the feeling that she was walking into something dangerous.

The rain had begun in earnest by the time Elisha reached Thornton's cottage, fat drops hammering against the windows like nature's own warning. The familiar rooms felt different now—more confining than cozy, the shadows in the corners deeper and more threatening than she remembered.

As she stepped through the door, droplets still clinging to her cloak, she found Thornton rising from his seat. The polite smile on his face didn't quite reach his eyes, which studied her with an intensity that made her skin prickle.

"Elisha, how good of you to return so promptly," he said, executing a slight bow.

She forced herself to return his smile with practiced ease, though her heart beat a rapid tattoo against her ribs. "Steven, what a pleasant surprise. I do apologize for not being here to receive you properly." Her voice emerged steady, betraying none of the tension coiling in her stomach.

Movement caught her eye—Edgar's man, Thompson, positioned near the window with a ladder balanced carefully against his shoulder. The sight of him, this tangible connection to Edgar, steadied her nerves somewhat.

"Ah, Mr. Brown," she said brightly, "the lanterns in the front hall and the study need refilling. Do be careful on that ladder."

The man nodded silently before he made his way out, leaving the door ajar. The sound of the ladder being propped up in the corridor seemed unnaturally loud in the tense atmosphere.

"I could have had my servant complete the task," Thornton said. "You do not need to bother with hiring workers."

Lightning flashed, throwing his features into sharp relief for a moment. In that instant, Elisha caught a glimpse of something calculating in his expression that made her glad for the solid presence of Edgar's man outside.

"Thank you, that is very kind," she responded, carefully maintaining her facade of grateful guest. "But the man has had a string of bad luck recently and needs the work. It was no trouble at all."

A log shifted in the fireplace, sending sparks dancing upward. Thornton's smile widened slightly, though it still didn't warm his eyes. "That is very thoughtful of you, although I shouldn't be surprised by now."

He turned toward the door. "Sarah," he called to his maid, who had been hovering nervously in the shadows, "would you be so kind as to bring us some tea?"

The floorboards creaked beneath Sarah's retreating footsteps, each sound echoing in the charged silence. Elisha settled herself in the chair opposite Thornton, arranging her still-damp skirts with deliberate care. The fire's warmth failed to reach the chill that had settled in her bones.

Lightning flickered again, closer now, casting strange shadows across Thornton's face as he watched her with that unnervingly steady gaze. The storm pressed against the windows like a living thing, as if nature itself sought to warn her of danger.

"I cannot thank you enough, Steven, for this repast and the lodging," she began. "Your servants are just wonderful, and the townspeople are so very kind."

"It's my pleasure." His voice dropped lower, more intimate. "If, one day, I'm blessed enough to call you my wife, there isn't anything I would not bestow upon you."

Heat crept up Elisha's neck at the intensity of his stare and the boldness of his words. Through the doorway, she caught a glimpse of Thompson adjusting a lantern, the flame within casting a protective glow against the gathering dark.

"Um, thank you," she managed, her fingers twisting in her lap beneath the cover of her handkerchief. "I believe you will spoil your wife to no end."

"I sense you are leaning toward rejecting my offer of courtship." There was an edge to his voice now, like a blade wrapped in silk.

"Steven—"

"Please." He leaned forward, his earnest expression at odds

with the predatory stillness of his body. "Don't answer me now. Think on it some more."

Sarah's return with the tea tray provided a welcome interruption. The china rattled slightly in the maid's trembling hands as she set it down. Elisha noticed how the girl kept her eyes downcast, how she practically scurried from the room once she'd finished pouring.

The tea's fragrant steam rose between them as Thornton waited for Sarah's retreat before continuing. "I came to check on you… to ensure you are well cared for."

"How very thoughtful of you." Elisha lifted her cup, grateful for something to do with her hands. "I am well and want for nothing."

"I am glad to hear it." He paused, studying her over the rim of his cup. "There is one other thing. I couldn't help but notice that you and Mr. Steele have not corresponded for some time now. Is everything all right? I wanted to ensure all was well."

The seemingly innocent inquiry sent warning bells chiming in Elisha's mind. Perhaps she heard something in his tone she couldn't quite explain. She kept her features carefully neutral even as her pulse quickened. "I'm sorry to have given you reason to worry, but I assure you, everything is fine. The novel has been demanding much of my attention, and likely it is the same for Mr. Steele's, that's all."

Thunder crashed overhead, making the windows rattle in their frames. Thornton inclined his head, accepting her explanation with a smile.

"I am gratified to hear it." He set his cup down with precise care. "Now, as I've mentioned before, there is presently a tender process underway for the Royal Mail Coach Service contract." His eyes seemed to gleam with barely contained excitement. "It's a most advantageous opportunity, one that could vastly expand the business interests of the *Metropolitan Review*. Imagine our periodical being delivered to every corner in England."

Elisha's heart quickened, though not from Thornton's proximity. The memory of Edgar's touch, his passion, still lingered on her skin beneath her proper attire. It made Thornton's attentions feel even more unwelcome, like an intrusion upon something sacred.

She shifted in her chair, maintaining proper distance as Thornton elaborated on the Royal Mail contract. Her lips, still sweetly sore from Edgar's attentions, served as a constant reminder of where her heart truly belonged.

"I've submitted a tender," Thornton continued, unaware of her inner turmoil, "but the competition is formidable. You possess a singular talent for understanding people. You perceive that which others overlook. And forgive my bluntness, but as a lady, you may be privy to conversations and confidences that could prove advantageous."

Elisha's mind whirled with the implications. The Royal Mail Coach bidding was paramount to the Pioneers' cause. Was it a coincidence that Steven Thornton was bidding on it as well?

"It is certainly an intriguing proposition," she said carefully, her fingers absently touching her collar where Edgar's kisses had left invisible marks. "I would be pleased to render assistance, provided such an undertaking would not impinge upon my current obligations."

Thornton leaned forward, his voice dropping to an intimate tone that once might have flustered her. Now it only served to highlight how different it felt from Edgar's tender murmurs. "Should you accept my proposal, you stand to benefit considerably from the expansion of our business endeavors. Perhaps I might entrust one of the subsidiary enterprises to your capable management, while Amelia assumes proprietorship of the gazette."

The offer hung in the air between them. Once, it might have seemed like everything she'd ever wanted—independence, respect, the chance to make her mark on the world. Now it felt hollow, tainted by the knowledge that accepting would mean betraying her heart.

"Furthermore," Thornton pressed on, his gaze intense enough to make her want to shrink back, "I would be prepared to establish the business in your name, granting you full autonomy in its operation."

The magnitude of his offer struck her dumb for a moment. Even as her practical mind recognized the extraordinary nature of such an opportunity, her heart clenched with guilt. Not just for Edgar now, but for the intimacy they had shared, the whispered promises against heated skin.

A particularly violent gust of wind rattled the windows, making the lantern flames dance. In their flickering light, she caught her reflection in the darkened glass—cheeks still holding a hint of the flush Edgar had put there, lips that had been thoroughly kissed mere hours ago. The sight strengthened her resolve even as it complicated her position.

"Steven," she began, carefully modulating her voice to hide both her discomfort and the lingering effects of passion, "your offer is… most generous. I confess, I find myself quite overwhelmed by the scope of what you propose." Her hand unconsciously rose to her throat, where Edgar had gently raked with his teeth.

Thornton's expression softened. "I understand this is a weighty matter to consider. I do not expect an immediate response." He reached for her hand, and it took all her self-control not to flinch away. "Take the time you need to reflect upon it. I merely ask that you give it your most serious consideration."

His touch felt wrong—cold and impersonal. She withdrew her hand as gracefully as possible, pretending to adjust her shawl.

"Might I ask," she said, desperate to shift the conversation away from her, "if you intend to bestow the *Metropolitan* upon Amelia regardless of my response to your proposal?"

A shadow crossed his features before he smoothed them into a benign smile. "Indeed, I do. However…" That practiced bashfulness crept into his expression. "I had hoped to present it as a surprise upon the announcement of our... that is to say, if we were to announce our betrothal. I thought it a fitting wedding gift, considering Amelia's role in bringing us together."

"Oh, that is a most thoughtful gesture," she managed, her voice hoarse from suppressed unease.

She turned away to face the fireplace, using the moment to compose herself. The flames danced hypnotically, reminding her of candlelight on Edgar's skin, of the way his eyes had burned as he kissed her. The memory both strengthened her resolve and complicated her position enormously.

GUARDIAN ANGEL

THE LAST RAYS of sunset bled crimson across the sky as Elisha stepped through the door, the warmth of the lanterns doing little to ease the tension knotted between her shoulder blades. The library's familiar scents—leatherbound books, beeswax candles, the lingering trace of Edgar's sandalwood cologne—wrapped around her like a comforting embrace.

Edgar halted his restless pacing at her entrance, the floorboards creaking beneath his suddenly still feet. The dying light caught the dishevelment of his usually immaculate dark hair, evidence of fingers raked through it in agitation. His cravat hung loose, his waistcoat slightly askew—all signs of what appeared to be worry that had consumed him during her absence.

"Elisha." Her name emerged as half prayer, half breath. He crossed the room in those graceful, urgent strides, then hesitated. His hands lifted toward her, then faltered, as though unsure of his welcome after the weight of the day's revelations. "I've been beside myself with worry. Are you—" His sharp eyes searched her face, no doubt cataloging every nuance of her expression. "Are you all right? What did Thornton want?"

The careful distance he maintained, clearly trying to respect her space after such an emotionally charged day, nearly undid her. "Oh, Edgar," she sighed, closing the gap between them and pressing herself against the solid warmth of his chest. His arms came around her instantly, desperately, one hand cradling her head while the other spanned her waist.

She listened to the steady thrum of his heart beneath her ear, letting its rhythm calm her own racing pulse. The lingering chill from the evening air melted away in his embrace, though a different sort of shiver coursed through her as his lips pressed against her temple.

"Come," she murmured after several long moments. "We should sit. There is much to tell you."

They settled on the settee before the banked fire, its embers casting a gentle glow that softened the growing shadows. Their hands remained entwined, neither willing to relinquish that point of contact. Edgar's signet ring pressed against her fingers, a tangible reminder of the vast social gulf between them—a gulf that seemed simultaneously meaningless and insurmountable.

Elisha drew a steadying breath, the silk of her gown rustling softly with the movement. "First, I want you to know that my heart belongs to you, Edgar. Nothing that transpired today has changed that." She squeezed his hands, noting how the muscles in his shoulders seemed to remain taut despite her reassurance. A log shifted in the grate, sending up a shower of sparks that reflected in his dark blue eyes.

"But?" Edgar prompted gently, his voice carrying that particular strain she'd come to recognize—the careful control of a man accustomed to masking his emotions. The firelight caught the aristocratic planes of his face, highlighting the tight line of his jaw.

"But the meeting with Mr. Thornton was… unexpected, to say the least." Her fingers absently traced the lines on his palm. The touch seemed to ground them both as she began her tale.

She recounted her conversation with Thornton, watching emotions play across Edgar's features like shadows in candlelight that made her heart clench. When she reached the part about the Royal Mail contract, his hands tightened on hers.

"He asked for my help in securing the bid," she explained, her voice dropping to match the intimate hush of the room. "He believes my connections and insights could be valuable." A bitter laugh escaped her. "Though I suspect he seeks more than mere business intelligence."

Edgar's thumb traced soothing circles on her wrist, though she could feel the tension that seemed to thrum through him. "I see," he said carefully. "And did he say why he thought you'd be willing to assist him in this endeavor?"

Elisha hesitated, the weight of Thornton's proposition settling heavy in her chest. The memory of his calculating gaze made her appreciate anew the honest passion in Edgar's eyes. "He... he made me an offer, Edgar. A business proposition, of sorts."

As she detailed Thornton's proposal—the promise of partnership, financial independence, her own company—she watched Edgar's face with growing concern. The muscle in his jaw worked silently, and his posture took on that rigid quality she recognized from formal gatherings where he appeared forced to maintain his composure despite provocation.

"I see," he said when she finished, each word measured and precise. The careful control in his voice broke her heart more than any display of anger could have. "Thornton's offer is certainly... generous."

"Edgar," she said urgently, rising to her knees on the settee to cup his face between her palms. His skin was warm beneath her fingers, the slight roughness of evening stubble a reminder of their intimate familiarity. "You must understand, I have no intention of accepting his proposal. My heart—my body—belongs to you completely."

Edgar leaned into her touch, his eyes seeming to darken with what looked like a mixture of vulnerability and possession that made her breath catch. "But?" he prompted again as a gust of wind rattled the windowpanes.

Elisha sighed, sinking back onto the settee though she kept one hand against his cheek. "But I would be lying if I said the offer didn't affect me." She hurried on as what looked like pain flashed across his features, "Not because I'm tempted to accept it. Never that. But because it made me realize how deeply I've buried certain dreams—of recognition, of making my own path in the world of business and publishing."

The confession hung in the air between them, heavy as incense. Edgar captured her hand against his face, turning to press a kiss to her palm. The tender gesture, coming from a man whose every movement was usually calculated for propriety, made her heart ache.

"I understand, Elisha. Truly." His voice carried a rough edge that seemed to speak of barely contained emotion. "And I wish…" He broke off, jaw clenching. "God help me, I wish I could offer you the same opportunities."

"Oh, Edgar, no," Elisha breathed, shifting closer until their thighs pressed together. The heat of him through their clothing reminded her viscerally of their earlier passion, of promises sealed with more than just words. "That's not what I meant at all. What we have—" She pressed her free hand to his chest, feeling his heart thunder beneath her palm. "This is so much more important than any business venture."

Edgar covered her hand with his own. "Is it enough, though?" The vulnerability in his voice made her chest tight. "Am I enough?"

Tears pricked at her eyes. This proud, powerful man, who could command a room with a single glance, now looked at her with such uncertainty. "You are more than enough," she whispered fiercely, pressing closer until their foreheads touched. "Edgar, you must believe me. Yes, Thornton's offer stirred up old dreams. But they're nothing—nothing—compared to what I feel for you."

His eyes, when they met hers, seemed to shine with emotion in the firelight. "Oh, Elisha," he murmured, one hand rising to cradle her nape. "How am I so fortunate?"

They sat in silence for a moment, breathing each other's air, the crackle of the fire and distant roll of thunder their only accompaniment. Then Edgar pulled back slightly, though his hand remained warm on her neck. His expression had shifted, taking on that serious cast she recognized from their discussions of reform.

"As much as I wish I could offer you the same financial independence, the same business opportunities…" He paused, seeming to gather his thoughts. "I cannot. My family obligations are substantial."

Edgar rose and moved to the window where the last light was fading from the sky. His broad shoulders seemed to carry the weight of responsibility as visibly as any crown. "I have four siblings to see settled, not to mention my mother to care for," he said, his voice low and measured. "There are dowries to consider, estates to maintain, ensuring each of them has a proper start in life when they wed."

The firelight caught his profile, highlighting the aristocratic lines that spoke of generations of nobility.

"And even if I could offer you such independence," he continued, turning back to face her, "it would create expectations among my siblings and their future spouses. They would, quite rightly, expect the same treatment."

Elisha watched him from the settee, noting how his fingers seemed to flex at his sides—a subtle tell she'd learned meant he was steeling himself for something important. The air in the room seemed to thicken with anticipation.

"But, Elisha," he said, crossing back to her with purpose. "While I can't offer you what Thornton can in terms of business and financial independence, I can offer you something else. Something I believe to be far more valuable."

He knelt before her, taking her hands in his. The position, reminiscent of a proposal, made her heart flutter despite their already intimate connection. His hands were warm around hers, strong and sure, yet holding her as if she were something precious.

"I offer you partnership in a cause greater than ourselves," he said, his voice taking on that passionate tone that had first drawn her to him. "The work we do, the reforms we fight for—they have the power to change lives, to reshape society for the better."

His eyes seemed to blaze with conviction as he continued, "I know it's not the security Thornton offers. Our path will be fraught with danger, with uncertainty. But it will also be filled with purpose, with the knowledge that every day, we're working toward something truly meaningful."

"Reform?" she asked, her heart pounding against her ribs. "To what do you refer?"

"I am aware that you are one of the authors of the reform pamphlets, Elisha."

The words rendered her speechless. She tried to withdraw her hands, but Edgar held firm, his touch gentle but insistent. "How… How came you by this knowledge?"

Edgar leaned closer, his voice dropping to that intimate register that seemed to bypass her ears and speak directly to her heart. "My friend and private investigator, Patrick Adams, saw you meet with Mark Evans." The name of her childhood friend made her start, but Edgar's thumbs traced what felt like soothing circles on her wrists. "Further inquiries led us to a small print shop on the outskirts of London."

Elisha's breath hitched. The clandestine print shop had been her sanctuary, the place where her most dangerous words took physical form. The memory of ink-stained hands and the metallic scent of printing plates mingled with her rising fear.

"The proprietor, Mr. Symon, was initially reticent," Edgar continued, his eyes never leaving hers. In the deepening dusk, they seemed to glow with an inner fire. "However, upon learning of my intentions, he confided in me. He spoke of a lady, whose description matched yours precisely, who would visit in the dead of night to collect the freshly printed pamphlets."

A log shifted in the grate, sending up a shower of sparks that matched the panic sparking in Elisha's chest. But Edgar's expression seemed to hold nothing of condemnation—only what looked like fierce pride and something deeper, more tender.

"Fear not, my sweet," he murmured, releasing one of her

hands to cup her cheek. His palm was warm against her cool skin. "I took measures to ensure your safety. I purchased the print shop, installing a trusted associate as the new proprietor. The plates used for your pamphlets have been replaced with near-identical copies, each bearing a unique, barely perceptible mark."

Understanding dawned in Elisha's eyes as the implications of his words sank in. All this time, while she'd been terrified of discovery, he had been quietly protecting her, supporting her cause from the shadows.

"The true plates remain hidden, allowing your important work to continue unimpeded."

He brought their joined hands to his lips, pressing a fervent kiss to her knuckles. "I've also taken the liberty of establishing a network of trusted individuals to aid in the storage and distribution of your writings. They are unaware of your identity, of course, but are sympathetic to the cause."

Elisha listened, her heart a maelstrom of emotions. Fear at how close she had come to discovery warred with profound gratitude for his efforts. Admiration for his ingenuity and dedication to her cause swelled within her, mixing headily with the love that already consumed her.

"But why?" The question escaped her on a trembling breath. "What happened to having no real conviction?"

Edgar's expression seemed to soften, what looked like vulnerability crossing his features that made him appear younger. "Ah," he said quietly. His hand dropped from the mantel as he turned to face her fully. "The man I was then... he seems a stranger to me now."

He moved closer, moonlight and firelight playing across his aristocratic features. "I was raised to believe that maintaining the status quo was not just my right, but my duty. That change was dangerous, that reform threatened the very fabric of society." A self-deprecating smile touched his lips. "I was so certain of my convictions, or rather, my lack of them. And then..."

Elisha waited patiently, her heart thundering against her ribs.

"And then I met you." His voice roughened with emotion. "You challenged everything I thought I knew. Your passion, your intelligence, your unwavering belief in the possibility of a better world… It was like watching the sun rise after a lifetime of darkness."

He reached for her hand, his touch reverent. "Your words and your actions haunted me. I found myself lying awake at night, concerned about your well-being, wishing I could be there to protect you." His voice roughened with emotion. "Then I became angry that you found it necessary to take that kind of risk. Our duty as a society should be to protect all citizens. The more I observed, the more I read your writings, the more I couldn't ignore the truth in them."

"So you…" she whispered, hardly daring to believe. The firelight caught the unshed tears in her eyes, making them glimmer like stars.

"I decided I would like a society that values its every citizen, not just the wealthy or titled. It will not be easy, but I would like to try… with you." He shook his head with a quiet laugh. "Well, I discovered I had quite a talent for subversion."

Elisha's heart swelled with emotion, and she threw herself at him, entwining her arms around his neck as an overwhelming tide of emotion swept through her. Edgar held her tight, then took her mouth with his, all the frustrations of the past two months seeming to explode with impatience. He held a fistful of her hair with one hand while his mouth slanted to meet hers. Elisha's lips parted, her eyelids fluttering closed, and her body leaned against Edgar as if drawn by an invisible force. Her hands, which had been clutching her shawl tightly, slowly relaxed and reached for his shoulders.

She felt overwhelmed by the sensations of his heat, his essence molding to her, silken lips that seemed to melt beneath her own, the scent of soap mingling with the sweet taste of his mouth. She didn't feel capable of absorbing it all without… bursting.

The kiss was a revelation, sweet and intoxicating. Her heart felt as though it might explode with joy, every cell in her body alive with the sensation of Edgar in her arms.

He glided his lips lightly over her satiny lips, nipping them with his own. He then licked them with the tip of his tongue. His breath mingled with her heat and torched her insides, but despite his obvious hunger, he loosened his embrace. He reluctantly pulled away from her mouth and watched her long lashes flutter and open slowly. Elisha stood still, seemingly paralyzed.

"If you want more, you'll have to come for it," he rasped low.

Elisha's eyes shone in the candlelight, wide with shock. They were both breathless, their chests heaving. Edgar's thumbs traced gentle circles on her waist, the soft tickling of her breath teasing her senses.

"Elisha," he whispered tenderly.

She responded by pulling him down for another kiss, this one filled with all the passion and longing she had been holding back for so long. Her timid tongue darted out, copying his previous movements, brushing it across his lips, licking them ever so gently, and flicking the corners of his mouth, stoking her own fire.

"You drive me mad, woman," he groaned before taking possession of her mouth, wanting more of the sugary taste.

EDGAR'S FINGERS TRAVERSED the route of her form—brushing against the side of her breasts over coarse linen, the dip of her waist, then her round bottom. The swells of her tight bottom had him press his hard length against her stomach, eliciting a gasp that he swallowed with relish.

One hand kneaded her firm buttocks while his hips ground his steely length against her thighs.

"Bloody hell, you have the most tempting ass," he whispered

against her mouth.

He then released her mouth and held her gaze while pulling up the hem of her shift. Her eyes were half hooded, and her lashes tremored while her swollen lips glistened with moisture.

He closed his eyes and groaned upon feeling her bare flesh. When he opened them again, Elisha's had closed, her teeth biting down on her bottom lip, ripe and moist from his assault.

The look of pleasure on her expression unleashed his primal urges, all reason dissipating with blood pooling in his cock.

Holding her gaze, he took her hand and brought it to the hard ridge pushing against his trousers. He showed her how to use her palm and rub it the way he liked.

Releasing her hand, he dotted her neck with soft kisses, trying to control his breathing and the urge to free his member for her to grip.

"That's it," he cooed, feeling his member twitch under the delicious pressure.

"Am I doing it right?"

A smile curved his lips at the innocent question filled with desire to please. "Very well, darling. Perfect."

Then he moved his hand from her ass to her inner thighs, stroking with featherlight fingers, delighting in her moans and gasps.

"Bloody hell," he cursed under his breath when he felt the moisture dripping down her thighs. "Exquisite…" he murmured.

With a moan, she suddenly squeezed his cock, heightening his arousal.

"My God…" he groaned. He began to unfasten his fall, and Elisha watched with widened eyes. He slowly moved her hand to his member, gauging her reaction. With the curiosity of a cat, she explored his manhood with her delicate fingers, then gripped him firmly. He grunted with relief and pleasure when her fingers massaged his aching flesh.

"Like this," he said as he wrapped his fingers over hers and stroked his length. Elisha learned quickly, her observant mind catching the pressure and the friction he liked.

"Bloody hell, that's it. Just like that, Elisha," he rasped.

Then, when he worried her arm might be fatigued, he brushed away her hand and placed his member between her thighs, drenching it in her nectar. Back and forth, he rubbed, relishing her moans, ensuring he was stimulating her bud. She rewarded him by squeezing her thighs together.

"Elisha, release me. This is too… close… too… tempting," he rasped, fighting the urge to enter her, break her maidenhead and claim her.

Without a word, she tightened her hold on him, angling her body to heighten her own pleasure.

"Please," she whimpered.

Her pleading had his cock jerk with pleasure. He pulled the loose neckline of her shift and freed one breast while he glided his shaft between her thighs.

Sucking her tongue deep into his mouth, he fondled her breast, then took one coral nipple between his fingers, pinching it lightly. As she gasped, he pinched harder, her moans confirming her heightened pleasure. He resisted the surging need to release his seed, wanting to hear her scream first.

He increased the speed of his movements, relishing the feel of her slick quim and thighs enveloping him tightly. When Elisha began to thrust her hips to meet his shaft with her cunny, he had to still himself to control his urge to climax.

"Edgar… please…" Her breathing was ragged and he felt her slick moisture drench his cock.

"Christ, Elisha…"

He gripped her ass and lifted her off the settee. He rubbed his cock against her bud with urgent movements. With a sharp inhale, she became perfectly still, her open mouth unleashing silent screams. The sensual image of her face pushed him over the edge as he released his seed between her thighs, puffs of air leaving his lungs as they both arched their bodies before collapsing against each other.

Edgar's body shuddered head to toe from the aphrodisiac that was Elisha Linde. He leaned one hand against the arm of the settee while catching his breath. It was going to be impossible for him to stay away from her now. She possessed the beauty of Aphrodite and the sensual mind of Eros. If he taught her how to pleasure him, she would have the weapons of Hephaestus as well.

They lay there in comfortable silence, listening to the rain against the windows and the gentle crackle of the dying fire, finally home.

THE LANCASTERS

Elisha woke to the soft clink of china drifting from the sitting room below. Pale morning light filtered through the lace curtains, casting delicate patterns across the rumpled bedsheets that still held the faint scent of his cologne. Her body felt wonderfully languid, marked by the sweet ache of their passion the night before—a reminder that sent heat blooming across her cheeks.

She stretched beneath the coverlet, her skin still sensitive where his hands had mapped every curve, where his lips had branded her with kisses that seemed to burn even now in memory. The vulnerability of what they had shared lingered like morning mist, beautiful and fragile. Everything had changed between them in those firelit hours, and she could feel the shift as surely as she could feel the summer breeze through the partially open window.

Rising carefully, she wrapped her shawl around her shoulders and padded downstairs on bare feet, drawn by the domestic sounds of Edgar preparing their morning meal. She found him in the breakfast room, elegant even in his shirtsleeves, dark hair slightly mussed from sleep—or perhaps from her fingers threading through it in the darkness. The sight of him arranging delicate china cups with the same hands that had brought her such exquisite pleasure made her pulse quicken.

"Good morning," she said softly, suddenly shy in a way that

felt both new and ancient.

Edgar turned, and the warmth that flooded his eyes made her breath catch. "Good morning, my darling." He crossed to her in two strides, cupping her face with gentle reverence before pressing a tender kiss to her lips—soft, sweet, full of promise. "I trust you slept well?"

"Eventually," she murmured against his mouth, earning a low chuckle that vibrated through his chest where her palms rested.

"Minx," he whispered, then guided her to the small table he'd set by the window. Morning light caught the steam rising from fresh tea, and she noticed he'd arranged everything with careful attention—her favorite cup, toast cut precisely, even a small vase with roses from the garden.

"You needn't wait on me," she protested gently as he moved to pour her tea.

Edgar's eyes warmed. "I sent Thompson and Mrs. Davies to market this morning. I thought... after last night... you might appreciate the solitude." His voice dropped to that intimate register. "I wanted our first morning to be ours alone."

They settled into an intimate breakfast, knees occasionally brushing beneath the table, fingers lingering when he passed her the honey. The comfortable domesticity felt precious, like something stolen from a life she'd never dared dream possible. That Edgar had thought to dismiss his servants for the morning, giving them this private sanctuary, only deepened the intimacy of sharing this breakfast.

"Elisha," Edgar began after they'd shared several minutes of companionable silence, his voice carrying a particular note that made her look up from her tea. "There's something I wish to discuss with you."

The serious tone sent a flutter of unease through her chest. "Oh?"

Edgar reached across the small table to cover her hand with his. "I believe it's time for you to meet my family."

The words hit her like cold water, washing away the warm intimacy of the morning. Her teacup rattled against its saucer as she set it down with trembling fingers. "Your family? Edgar, surely it's too soon for such a step."

"Hm, do you think so?" His thumb traced soothing circles on her wrist, the same gentle touch that had worshipped her body in the darkness. "After last night, after everything we've shared, can you truly say it's too soon?"

Heat flooded her cheeks at the reference to their intimacy, but beneath the embarrassment lay a deeper fear. "But what if they disapprove? What if they see what I am—where I come from—and find me wanting?"

Edgar lifted their joined hands to his lips, pressing a fervent kiss to her knuckles. "Elisha, my sweet, brave girl. You have exceeded every expectation I've ever had. My family will see in you what I see—a woman of incomparable intelligence, grace, and passion."

She pulled her hand free to worry at the fabric of her shawl. "They'll see a workhouse foundling presuming to reach above her station."

"They'll see the woman I love," Edgar said firmly, rising to kneel beside her chair. His hands framed her face, forcing her to meet his earnest gaze. "The woman who has challenged my thinking, opened my heart, and changed the very course of my life. They'll see my choice, and they'll respect it because they love me."

The vulnerability in his voice, the absolute conviction, made her eyes sting with unshed tears.

"I propose we depart today and try the arrangement for a night or two. If you find it too disagreeable, we shall return at once and spend our time here in perfect contentment—just the two of us—until your novel is complete." His voice then dropped to that intimate register that seemed to bypass her ears and speak directly to her heart. "My estate in Kent awaits us, and with it, the chance to secure our future. Your identity as Miss Lovelace may soon become public knowledge with your wager coming to a close in a fortnight. We can speak to my family about using your notoriety to our advantage, ensuring you become the most sought-after dinner guest in London rather than a scandal to be whispered about."

The practical wisdom of his words couldn't quite overcome her terror, but she recognized the logic in them. Their secret world couldn't last forever. Eventually, they would have to step into the light and face society's judgment.

"Can we not have just a little longer?" she whispered, her fingers finding his where they rested against her cheek. "Just a few more days of this—of being simply Edgar and Elisha, without titles or expectations or the weight of centuries pressing down upon us?"

His expression softened with understanding and something that might have been regret. "I wish we could, my darling. Truly. But the longer we wait, the more difficult it becomes. I don't quite trust Thornton to accept his defeat quietly. I don't wish to give him a chance to sabotage our relationship. Better to face my family and the *ton* on our terms than to let circumstances force our hand."

She leaned into his touch, drawing strength from his certainty even as her heart hammered against her ribs.

"Very well," she whispered finally, the words catching in her throat. "I shall accompany you to Kent."

The smile that transformed his face was radiant as sunrise. He kissed her then, deep and thorough, tasting of tea and promises and the salt of her own tears. When they broke apart, both breathing unsteadily, he rested his forehead against hers.

"You won't regret this, Elisha. I swear it."

As they began to plan their departure, Edgar spoke of his siblings with obvious affection—Edmund's scholarly pursuits, Edwin's lack of aspirations, Eva's passionate advocacy for reform, young Essie's romantic dreams. For a woman who had grown up without family, his stories painted a picture of warmth and belonging that was both tantalizing and terrifying.

"They'll adore you," he assured her as they moved upstairs to pack. "Though I warn you, Eva in particular will likely interrogate you about your views on social reform. She's been following the reform pamphlets with great interest."

Elisha's step faltered on the stairs. "She's been reading them?"

"Avidly. Mother despairs of ever finding her a suitable husband when she insists on discussing workhouse conditions over tea." Edgar's chuckle held both pride and exasperation. "I believe you two will find much common ground."

The thought of finding an intellectual equal among Edgar's family both thrilled and terrified her. It would be wonderful to discuss her passion openly, but it also meant walking even closer to the edge of discovery.

HOURS LATER, THE carriage wheels crunched through frost-rimmed gravel, each turn bringing Elisha closer to the moment she'd both yearned for and dreaded. Through the window, Lancaster Hall emerged from the morning mist like something from a fairy tale—first its slate-gray turrets, then the weathered stone facade with its dozen gleaming windows that seemed to watch her approach with ancient eyes.

The closer they drew, the more her courage faltered. The estate was vast beyond anything she'd imagined, stretching across rolling parkland where deer grazed beneath ancient oaks. Gardeners moved like distant figures across manicured lawns, tending to dormant flower beds and clipped topiaries that spoke of centuries of careful cultivation.

"Breathe," Edgar murmured beside her, his gloved hand covering hers where it gripped the seat. "They're only people, after all."

People who could destroy everything with a single word of

disapproval, she thought, though she managed a tremulous smile. "People who happen to be your family, Your Grace. The most powerful family in Kent, if I'm not mistaken."

"Powerful, perhaps, but not heartless. They'll see what I see in you, Elisha. How could they not?"

The carriage rounded the final curve, and Elisha felt like she couldn't breathe. Up close, Lancaster Hall was even more magnificent—and intimidating. Ancient stones rose in Gothic splendor, ivy climbing the walls like grasping fingers, while carved griffins stood sentinel at the broad steps leading to massive oak doors. The morning sun had burned away the mist, revealing the full scope of wealth and history that surrounded them.

As the carriage halted, a liveried footman appeared to open the door. Edgar alighted first, his movements graceful and assured, every inch the duke on his own land. When he turned to offer his hand, Elisha grasped it perhaps too tightly, willing strength from his touch as she stepped down onto gravel that crunched beneath her boots with startling loudness.

She caught herself smoothing imaginary wrinkles from her best traveling dress, painfully aware of how the morning light would reveal every sign of careful mending, every place where skilled needlework had extended the garment's life.

On the steps stood three figures that could only be Edgar's family. The woman in the center commanded immediate attention—tall and elegant with silver-threaded dark hair and posture that spoke of generations of breeding. The Duchess of Lancaster, unmistakably, flanked by two younger women who shared Edgar's distinctive blue eyes. The sisters practically vibrated with barely contained excitement, but it was the duchess who held Elisha's attention, her face a masterpiece of careful neutrality while her sharp gaze cataloged every detail of their guest's appearance.

"Mother," Edgar said warmly, guiding Elisha forward with a gentle hand at the small of her back. "May I present Miss Elisha Linde."

Elisha sank into her deepest curtsy, grateful for years of careful observation that had taught her the proper forms.

"Miss Linde," the duchess said, her voice rich and cool as aged wine. "Welcome to Lancaster Hall." She extended her hand with regal grace, and Elisha rose to accept it, noting the weight of the rings adorning those elegant fingers—any one of which probably cost more than everything she had ever owned. "We have been most eager to make your acquaintance."

"Your Grace," Elisha managed, proud that her voice remained steady despite the thundering of her heart. "I am deeply honored by your welcome." She turned to the sisters, who had edged closer like eager children barely restrained by propriety. "Ladies, the pleasure is entirely mine."

"Oh, do say you'll tell us everything about London," the elder sister burst out, earning a swift, reproving glance from her mother. "We've been positively dying to hear about all the excitement. I'm Essie, and this is Eva."

"Essence," the duchess corrected with gentle firmness, using the girl's full name like a subtle rap across the knuckles. "Perhaps we might allow Miss Linde to step inside before beginning an interrogation?"

Eva, the younger sister, shot Elisha a sympathetic look that held surprising intelligence. "You must forgive us, Miss Linde. We've had nothing but Edgar's letters to sustain our curiosity, and he's been terribly stingy with details."

"There's nothing to forgive," Elisha said, finding herself beginning to relax fractionally at the sisters' obvious warmth. "I'm delighted to meet you both."

Then the great doors of Lancaster Hall groaned open with the weight of centuries, revealing a soaring entrance hall where portraits of long-dead Lancasters gazed down from gilded frames. Elisha's throat constricted as she stepped inside, feeling the weight of those painted eyes upon her. These were Edgar's ancestors, their noble faces watching as she—the nameless workhouse child—dared to enter their hallowed domain.

The click of the duchess' heels on polished marble echoed through the vast space as she led them toward what she called "the morning room"—though its proportions rivaled those of entire houses Elisha had known. Footmen materialized to open doors and relieve them of outer garments, their trained gazes carefully averted yet somehow taking in every detail.

"I trust you had a pleasant journey?" the duchess inquired as they settled around an elegant table positioned near tall windows that overlooked frost-touched gardens stretching to distant hills.

"Very pleasant, Your Grace," Elisha replied, accepting a cup of tea served on china so fine she could see the shadow of her fingers through it when she lifted it to her lips. "The countryside is quite beautiful at this time of year."

"Indeed," the duchess agreed, studying Elisha over the rim of her own cup with the practiced assessment of a woman accustomed to evaluating potential threats to her family's well-being. "Though I imagine it's quite different from London."

Different as a hovel from a palace, Elisha thought, but she smiled politely. "Refreshingly so. The air alone is enough to make one feel quite transformed."

Eva leaned forward, her eyes bright with intelligence that reminded Elisha startlingly of Edgar. "Speaking of transformation, Miss Linde, I've been reading the most fascinating articles about conditions in London's workhouses. They've been appearing in several papers, and the author's perspective seems... unusually well-informed."

Elisha's teacup rattled against its saucer before she could steady her trembling hand. From the corner of her eye, she saw Edgar stiffen almost imperceptibly, though his expression remained pleasantly neutral. The duchess' eyebrow arched a fraction, and Elisha realized with sinking dread that nothing—absolutely nothing—escaped this woman's notice.

"Eva, my dear," the duchess said with deceptive mildness, "perhaps we might save such weighty topics for a more appropriate time?"

But Eva, with all the passionate determination of an intelligent young woman testing the boundaries of acceptable discourse, pressed on. "But Mother, didn't you yourself say that these articles showed remarkable insight? That they demonstrated an understanding of social conditions that could only come from—"

"More tea, Miss Linde?" Edgar interrupted smoothly, reaching for the delicate pot with steady hands.

Elisha met his eyes briefly, drawing courage from the warmth and confidence she found there. "Thank you, Your Grace," she said, then turned to Eva with what she hoped was a composed smile. "I would be very interested in hearing your thoughts on those articles, Miss Eva. Perhaps during our visit, we might discuss them in greater detail?"

It wasn't quite a confession, nor quite a denial, but something carefully balanced between the two. The duchess' sharp glance was not lost on her, and she felt rather than saw the older woman's mental calculations. This was dangerous ground indeed, but Eva's obvious passion for social reform offered an unexpected bridge.

"I should like that very much," Eva said, her face lighting with genuine pleasure. "It's so rare to find someone willing to discuss such matters seriously."

"Eva reads everything she can find on the subject," Essie added with fond exasperation. "Mother despairs of ever finding her a husband when she insists on lecturing gentlemen about working conditions over dinner."

"Knowledge is never wasted," Elisha said quietly, "regardless of one's station or prospects. The ability to think clearly about the world's problems is a gift that should be cultivated, not discouraged."

Something shifted in the duchess' expression—a subtle softening that might have been approval. "An interesting perspective, Miss Linde. I confess myself curious about your own background. Edgar has been rather… economical… with details."

Here it was—the moment Elisha had dreaded. The truth would damn her, but lies would be worse if discovered. She chose her words with infinite care.

"I was fortunate to receive an education despite humble beginnings, Your Grace. Perhaps that perspective allows me to see certain social issues with… clarity."

It was truth, carefully pruned of its most damaging branches. The duchess inclined her head slightly, accepting the response while clearly filing it away for future consideration.

The conversation moved to safer topics—the weather, local news, plans for the estate's winter months. Elisha found herself gradually relaxing as the sisters' warmth and Edgar's steady presence surrounded her like armor against her fears.

THAT EVENING, AFTER an elaborate dinner that showcased the full magnificence of Lancaster hospitality, the family gathered in a drawing room that could have housed a dozen families in comfort. Elisha, her nerves finally beginning to settle after successfully navigating the formal meal, found herself drawn into the easy banter of Edgar's siblings.

"I propose a game," Edmund announced, appearing suddenly with the mischievous grin that marked him unmistakably as Edgar's brother despite his scholarly appearance. "Something to truly test our wit and mettle."

Eva clapped her hands in delight. "Charades! It will be perfectly entertaining with fresh participants. I cannot recall the last time Edgar condescended to play parlor games with mere mortals."

"He has always claimed to be either too dignified or too occupied with ducal responsibilities," Edwin added with the particular relish younger brothers reserved for embarrassing their elders.

"Shall we divide into teams?" the duchess suggested, her earlier reserve giving way to maternal fondness as she watched her children's enthusiasm.

"Perhaps," Edgar proposed with exaggerated gallantry, "we might pair the ladies with us gentlemen. Elisha, would you do me the honor of being my partner?"

"I should be delighted, Your Grace," Elisha replied with delight.

As the game commenced, Elisha found herself pleasantly surprised by how easily she fell into the rhythm of aristocratic entertainment. Years of careful observation had taught her to read subtle cues and social signals, skills that translated beautifully to charades. She and Edgar worked together with an intuitive understanding that drew admiring comments from his siblings, their success built on the deep knowledge of each other gained through their intimate conversations.

During Edmund's turn, he struggled valiantly to convey his assigned word, his gestures growing increasingly frustrated and desperate. Elisha watched with growing sympathy as the scholarly young man windmilled his arms with growing exasperation.

"Lord Edmund," she said at last, her tone light, "if your intention is to recreate the great windmill battle of Don Quixote, I must say you've succeeded admirably."

The room erupted in laughter, Edmund included, his face flushing with good-natured embarrassment. "Am I truly so obvious in my theatrical incompetence?"

"Only to those of us who share your affliction," Elisha replied warmly, and caught the duchess observing their exchange with what looked suspiciously like approval.

As the evening progressed, Elisha felt herself relaxing fully for the first time since their arrival. These people—Edgar's people— were welcoming her not just with politeness but with genuine warmth. Eva engaged her in passionate discussions about social reform that left them both breathless with excitement. Essie shared confidences about the local young men with delicious scandal. Even the duchess unbent enough to share amusing anecdotes about the children's younger years that had Edgar groaning in theatrical mortification.

When the clock chimed eleven, signaling the end of a proper evening's entertainment, the duchess rose with regal grace. "Miss Linde," she said, her voice carrying a warmth that had been notably absent earlier, "I must thank you for a most delightful evening. It has been… illuminating."

Elisha curtsied deeply, her cheeks flushed with pleasure and the lingering effects of several glasses of excellent wine. "The delight has been entirely mine, Your Grace. I count myself fortunate to have been welcomed so graciously into your family circle."

Something passed across the duchess' face at the word "family"—surprise, perhaps, or calculation. But her smile remained genuine as she inclined her head in acknowledgment.

Later, as Edgar escorted Elisha through the lamplit corridors to her guest chamber, his pride was evident in every line of his bearing. "You were magnificent," he murmured, his hand warm and possessive at the small of her back. "I do believe you've charmed them all completely."

Elisha glanced up at him, her heart swelling with a dangerous combination of love and hope. "Even your mother?"

"Especially my mother," Edgar chuckled, pausing outside her door to frame her face with gentle hands. "Though she would never admit to being charmed by anyone, of course. It would quite ruin her reputation for impeccable judgment if she were to express an opinion."

As they lingered in the intimate circle of lamplight, Elisha felt a surge of hope so intense it was almost painful. The evening had been a revelation—not just of her ability to navigate Edgar's world, but of the possibility that she might actually belong in it. These people could become her family, this grand house could become her home, this life of intellectual discourse and warm affection could become her reality.

"Thank you," she whispered, rising on her toes to press a soft kiss to his lips. "For believing in me. For bringing me here. For showing me what might be possible."

Edgar's arms came around her, holding her close as if she were something infinitely precious. "This is only the beginning, my darling," he murmured against her hair. "Tomorrow you'll meet the staff properly, and Mother will undoubtedly find excuses to assess your household management skills and your facility with French. But tonight... tonight you've taken the first step toward becoming the Duchess of Lancaster."

The title sent a shiver through her—half terror, half exhilaration. It seemed impossible that the workhouse foundling could aspire to such heights, yet here she stood in the halls of Lancaster House, wrapped in the arms of its master, accepted by his family.

Perhaps fairy tales could come true after all.

INTIMACY

THE CARRIAGE WHEELS crunched over the familiar gravel drive as Edgar's cottage in Tunbridge Wells came into view, its windows glowing warmly in the gathering dusk. Elisha felt her shoulders finally relax for the first time in days as they approached the sanctuary that had become their private haven.

"Home at last," Edgar murmured beside her, his voice carrying the same relief she felt. The past three days at Lancaster Hall had been a triumph, but an exhausting one. Every conversation had been carefully navigated, every glance scrutinized by his family's watchful eyes.

As the carriage drew to a halt, Edgar stepped down first and turned to offer his hand. The simple gesture now carried new weight after his mother's blessing and his siblings' enthusiastic acceptance.

"How does it feel to have conquered the Lancaster family?" he asked with a smile as they approached the front door.

"Rather like surviving a very elegant battlefield," Elisha replied, earning his warm chuckle. "Though I confess, I'm still somewhat stunned by their acceptance."

Edgar paused at the threshold, his expression growing tender. "They saw what I see—an extraordinary woman worthy of their respect and affection." He lifted her gloved hand to his lips for a gentle kiss. "My mother hasn't warmed to anyone so quickly in years."

As they entered the cottage, the familiar scents of beeswax and lavender enveloped them. The house felt different some-how—no longer a secret refuge but a proper home where their future was taking shape.

"I've given the staff the evening off," Edgar said as he helped her remove her traveling cloak. "I thought we might appreciate some privacy after being so thoroughly observed these past days."

Elisha felt a deep sense of gratitude. The constant performance of being the perfect potential daughter-in-law had been more draining than she'd realized.

"That was thoughtful of you," she said softly. "I feel as though I've been holding my breath for three days straight."

Edgar's hands came to rest gently on her shoulders, his thumbs tracing small circles through the fabric of her traveling dress. "Then let me help you breathe again."

THE PRIVATE SITTING room felt impossibly intimate with just the two of them, a fire crackling in the grate and candles casting dancing shadows on the walls. Edgar had poured them each a glass of wine, but Elisha found herself more intoxicated by the freedom to simply be herself again.

"Eva's knowledge of reform quite took me by surprise," she said, settling into the familiar armchair while Edgar took his place on the nearby settee. "I hadn't expected to find such a passionate ally within your family."

Edgar's expression grew thoughtful, then slightly troubled. "About that…" He set down his wine glass and leaned forward, his blue eyes growing serious. "Elisha, I must ask directly—how deeply are you involved with the Pioneers?"

The question she'd been dreading throughout their visit had finally come. Elisha felt her stomach tighten as she set down her own glass with careful precision.

"I once worked alongside a boy named Mark Evans at the workhouse," she began, choosing her words carefully. "He was different from the others—literate, passionate about poetry and politics. He often spoke of our power to affect change if we united."

Edgar nodded with recognition. "The same Mark Evans who now leads the Pioneers in London?"

"Yes." She drew a steadying breath. "We'd lost contact after we'd been moved to different workhouses. Then a year ago, he recognized my name after reading one of my articles in the *Metropolitan Review*. Mark approached me about contributing to their cause—writing pamphlets that could reach a broader audience."

She watched Edgar's expression grow more serious, concern replacing his earlier contentment. "He also suggested I could weave some of our findings into my newspaper articles, disguised as general social commentary."

Edgar held her gaze steadily. "Elisha, surely you understand how dangerous that is. If anyone were to make the connection—"

"I know the risks," she interrupted, placing her hand on his. "But Edgar, I cannot ignore the opportunity to make a real difference. These aren't abstract political theories—they're about people still suffering in conditions I know intimately."

He sighed wearily. "And this Mark Evans," he said with careful neutrality that didn't quite mask the jealousy beneath, "was he merely a fellow resident, or was there something more between you?"

Heat crept up Elisha's neck. "We were... fond of each other once. But that was long ago, Edgar. I was young, and those feelings have long since faded."

"Are you certain?" Edgar's voice carried an edge she'd rarely heard. "It seems you're willing to risk a great deal for his cause."

"It's not his cause," she said firmly, taking his hands firmly. "And it's not about Mark. It's about all those still trapped in workhouses, laboring in dangerous factories, sleeping rough in

London's streets. I have a voice now, a platform. How can I remain silent when I could help them?"

Edgar squeezed her hands, his expression torn between admiration and fear. "I understand your passion—it's one of the things I love most about you. But I worry about your safety, your reputation…" He paused, pain flickering across his features. "My family's position."

The words stung, even though she understood. "Some things are worth the risk," she said softly.

They sat in contemplative silence before Edgar spoke again, his voice heavy with emotion. "If I've had suspicions about your activities, others surely have as well. Thornton has likely been documenting everything, waiting for the right moment to use it against you."

The weight of his words settled over her like a shroud. She could see the genuine terror in his eyes.

"This transformation won't happen overnight," he continued urgently. "Please, consider the long-term consequences. Consider us."

Elisha met his gaze steadily. "I shall consider it," she said softly, though she couldn't mask the reluctance. "Grant me time to reflect on the matter properly."

AN HOUR LATER, steam rose from the copper tub in Edgar's private chambers, scented with lavender oil that perfumed the air with its soothing fragrance. Elisha watched in fascination as Edgar tested the water temperature with his wrist, adjusting it with the care of an experienced servant.

"You needn't wait on me," she protested softly, though warmth flooded her chest at his tender attention.

Edgar glanced up with a smile that made her pulse flutter. "After the performance you gave these past days, it's the least I can do. You were magnificent, but I could see the strain it cost you."

He straightened, his eyes growing serious. "Let me take care of you, Elisha. Tonight, there are no watching eyes, no expectations to fulfill. Just us."

The simple words carried such weight of love and promise that tears pricked her eyes. How had she lived so long without this—without someone who saw her exhaustion and sought to ease it?

"The water's perfect," Edgar said, then moved toward the door. "I'll leave you to—"

"Stay." The word escaped before conscious thought could stop it. Edgar froze, his hand on the door handle, surprise evident in every line of his body.

"Stay," she repeated more softly, heat flooding her cheeks even as longing filled her voice. "Please. After these days of careful distance, of stolen glances and proper behavior… I don't want to be alone."

Edgar turned slowly, his blue eyes dark with something that made her breath catch. Instead of another word, Elisha reached for the fastenings of her traveling dress, her fingers working the buttons with deliberate slowness. Edgar's sharp intake of breath was audible in the quiet room.

"Let me," he said roughly, crossing to her in three quick strides. His hands replaced hers, fingers trembling slightly as he worked the buttons free. "I've dreamed of this…"

The dress pooled at her feet, followed by her stays and chemise, until she stood before him in nothing but the flickering candlelight. Edgar's eyes roamed her form with reverent hunger, his hands hovering near her skin without quite touching.

"Beautiful," he breathed. "So beautiful it takes my breath away."

With infinite care, he helped her into the warm water, his touch gentle and respectful even as desire blazed in his eyes. Elisha sank into the lavender-scented bath with a sigh of pure pleasure, feeling the tension of the past days begin to melt away.

"Better?" Edgar asked, settling on a stool beside the tub, his sleeves rolled up and coat discarded.

"Much." She leaned back against the copper rim, studying his face in the golden light. "You look as though you need this more than I do."

Edgar chuckled, some of the strain around his eyes easing. "Watching you navigate my family's expectations while hiding my own feelings proved more challenging than I'd anticipated."

"Your feelings?" she asked softly.

His hand found hers where it rested on the edge of the tub, fingers intertwining with infinite tenderness. "The urge to claim you publicly, to show everyone that you belong with me. The frustration of maintaining proper distance when all I wanted was to touch you, to reassure myself you were mine."

Warmth spread through her chest. "I'm yours," she whispered.

"Yes," he agreed, bringing her wet hand to his lips for a kiss. "You're real, and you're mine."

As the water began to cool, Edgar retrieved soft towels warmed by the fire. His movements were careful, respectful, yet charged with an intimacy that made Elisha's skin tingle with awareness.

"Turn around," he said softly. "Let me wash your hair."

The simple request sent shivers down her spine. She complied, gathering her copper curls and lifting them as Edgar's gentle hands worked sweet-scented soap through the strands. His touch was hypnotic, fingers massaging her scalp with tender care.

"You have the most beautiful hair," he murmured, his voice rough with something deeper than mere appreciation. "Like copper wire touched with flame."

When he began rinsing the soap away, warm water cascading down her back, Elisha felt herself melting under his ministrations. This was intimacy beyond anything she'd imagined—not rushed passion but patient devotion, the kind of care that spoke of a future filled with such tender moments.

"Your turn," she said when he'd finished, turning to face him with water droplets clinging to her lashes.

Edgar's eyes widened. "Elisha, you needn't—"

"Fair is fair," she interrupted with a smile that felt more confident than she felt. "Besides, I want to."

Carefully, she rose from the tub, accepting the towel Edgar wrapped around her. The sight of her standing before him, hair damp and skin glowing from the warm water, seemed to steal his ability to protest further.

"The water's still warm," she said softly, her newfound boldness surprising them both. "Let me tend to you now."

Her fingers worked at his cravat with deliberate slowness, then moved to the buttons of his waistcoat. Each piece of clothing was removed with the same reverent care he'd shown her, until he stood before her magnificently bare in the flickering candlelight.

When his chest was revealed, she couldn't help but trace the strong lines of muscle with wondering fingertips. "My turn to say beautiful," she whispered, and felt him shudder under her touch.

"Elisha," he breathed, her name coming out rough with desire.

"Into the tub," she commanded gently, and watched with fascination as this powerful duke obeyed her soft-spoken direction. The water displaced around his larger frame as he settled into the copper basin, his knees drawn up in the confined space.

She knelt beside the tub as he had done for her, reaching for the soap with eager hands. "Let me tend to you," she murmured, beginning to wash his broad shoulders with tender care.

Edgar's eyes fell closed as her soapy hands explored the planes of his chest, following the path of dark hair that arrowed downward. When her fingers grew bolder, tracing lower, his sharp intake of breath made her pulse race with newfound power.

"You're going to be the death of me," he groaned as her

touch grew more deliberate.

"I certainly hope not," she replied slyly, "when I've only just begun to explore you properly."

His response was a mix of grunt and chuckle, soon swallowed by her searching mouth. With a groan, his large hand cupped the back of her head as he devoured her mouth. Elisha consumed his every gasp, every groan, as her soapy hand roamed his body. She learned what made him pant, what made his muscles tense with pleasure as she teased him with gentle caresses on his abdomen, then between his thighs. When she stroked his balls under water and felt them draw tight while he exhaled sharply, she felt a heady rush of feminine triumph.

"Elisha," Edgar's voice was strained as her curious exploration grew more purposeful. "What are you—oh, Christ—"

"Showing you how thoroughly you've corrupted your proper young lady," she whispered against his ear before gripping his hard length. With her soapy hand, she stroked him firmly from the root to the tip, reveling in his hardness and thickness. The combination of warm water, slippery soap, and her increasingly bold ministrations soon had Edgar gripping the edges of the tub, his control hanging by the thinnest of threads.

"I need…" he started, then seemed to lose the ability to form coherent words.

"Tell me," she coaxed, intoxicated by this reversal of power. "Tell me what you need."

Instead of words, Edgar's hands found her waist, lifting her with surprising ease. "You," he said simply. "Always you."

To her shock, Edgar reclined fully in the copper basin, the warm water lapping at his chest, while Elisha's knees bracketed his face.

"My beautiful, my love," he breathed against her heat, his words vibrating through her core. "So perfect, so sweet…"

"Edgar—oh!"

The sensations were overwhelming—his warm mouth on her quim, the steam-filled air, his strong grip on her bottom while she gripped the edge of the tub… The sensation of his tongue swirling her quim while his mouth tasted her most intimate flesh… his moans reverberating through her core… only to realize he was pleasuring himself while driving her toward her peak… It wasn't long before pleasure overwhelmed her and they crested toward their climax together. When release finally claimed them both, it was with cries that echoed off the chamber walls, unchecked and unashamed.

Afterward, they remained entwined in the cooling water, hearts racing and bodies trembling with the magnitude of what they'd shared. Edgar's arms held her securely against his chest as aftershocks of pleasure continued to ripple through them both.

"We'll need to refill the tub," Elisha murmured eventually, earning his rich chuckle.

"Worth every drop," he replied, pressing reverent kisses to her damp temple.

She lifted her head to meet his gaze. "You're a bad influence, Duke."

Edgar's smile was radiant as he drew her down for another kiss. "My revolutionary," he murmured against her lips. "In every possible way."

As they finally emerged from the tub, helping each other with towels and gentle touches, Elisha marveled at her transformation. She was no longer the cautious and uncertain woman who had entered this chamber. She was Edgar's equal in passion, his partner in pleasure, his match in every way that mattered.

THE DUCHESS'S PLANS

EDGAR STARED AT the letter in his hands, his mother's familiar script bringing both affection and dread in equal measure. The afternoon light streaming through the study windows of their Tunbridge Wells cottage seemed to mock the darkness of his thoughts as he read the duchess' latest scheme.

Across from him, Elisha sat with her own unopened correspondence from Thornton, her green eyes fixed on his face with growing concern. How beautiful she looked in the golden light, and how completely unaware she was of the deception that was about to entangle them both further.

"It seems my mother has taken matters into her own hands," he said, forcing lightness into his voice while his stomach churned with guilt. "She's planning a house party to celebrate the completion of your novel and Mr. Steele's."

The irony was suffocating. His mother wanted to invite Mr. Steele—him—to celebrate a competition with Miss Lovelace. The web of lies he'd woven was becoming a noose, and he could feel it tightening around his throat.

Elisha's eyebrows rose in surprise. "A house party? But I've hardly finished the first drafts."

Edgar managed a chuckle, though it felt hollow. "That has never deterred my mother from seizing an opportunity for social orchestration." His voice grew more strained as he continued to the truly problematic part. "There's more. She's asked me to extend an invitation to Mr. Steele directly, as apparently no one seems to know how to contact him."

The words tasted bitter on his tongue. Of course no one could contact Steele—he existed only in Edgar's imagination and carefully crafted letters. How was he supposed to navigate this latest complication? He couldn't have Steele decline the invitation without disappointing his mother, but accepting would create an impossible situation.

"And what does your mother hope to accomplish through this gathering?" Elisha asked, her fingers fidgeting with her shawl in that way that told him she was nervous.

Edgar consulted the letter again, though he'd already memorized every damning word. "She's quite explicit about her intentions." He read aloud, hearing his mother's imperious tone in every syllable: "'This is not to be misconstrued as my blessing, Edgar. Rather, it's an opportunity to assess the girl's potential while she engages with the *ton*. Moreover, it will allow us to gauge Society's response to her presence. The main purpose of the gathering, however, is to celebrate the two most talked about authors in London.'"

Watching Elisha's face pale at the clinical assessment made his chest tight with protective fury. Yet beneath his indignation lurked the uncomfortable knowledge that his own deception was far worse than his mother's calculated schemes.

"I shall feel like a prized mare at auction," Elisha said quietly, wrapping her arms around herself.

Edgar was beside her in an instant, taking her cold hands in his. "Elisha, this represents another step forward for us. This will bring us closer to a formal courtship announcement."

If only it were that simple. If only he could tell her the truth without destroying everything they'd built together.

"Do you think Mr. Steele will accept the invitation?" she asked, and Edgar felt his heart stop.

The question he'd been dreading. How could he answer honestly when the truth would shatter everything between them?

He rubbed his chin, buying time while his mind raced through possibilities. "I don't know him," he said carefully, hating himself for the continued deception, "but given his public rivalry with Miss Lovelace, he may find it rather trying to be surrounded by her acquaintances and admirers."

The words felt like glass in his throat. How had what started as an impulsive defense of his ego evolved into this labyrinth of lies?

Elisha was quiet for a moment, and Edgar watched emotions play across her face—resignation, determination, something that might have been relief. "I suppose it is inevitable that we shall cross paths in Society eventually. Perhaps it is best to face that reality with you at my side. Might I extend invitations to Amelia and Steven as well?"

The mention of Thornton's name sent jealousy surging through Edgar's veins like poison. Steven. When had she begun using his given name? "Steven, is it?" he said, unable to keep the edge from his voice. "I had presumed you held little regard for the gentleman, yet it seems you consider him a friend."

Elisha's expression shifted, taking on that patient look she got when she thought he was being unreasonable. "We are neither friends nor foes, Edgar. He is my superior at the *Metropolitan*, but also my best friend's brother. He has been kind to me, whatever his other motivations might be."

Kind to her. The words rankled more than they should. "He attempted to separate us," Edgar said, his voice carrying more heat than he intended. "And not out of concern for your wellbeing."

"Perhaps," she said, then lifted her chin with growing confidence that somehow made his jealousy worse. "But it's equally possible that he was attempting to protect me from what he perceived as a notorious rake—namely, you. Your reputation does leave rather a lot to be desired, after all."

The accusation stung because it was true. Before Elisha, he had been exactly what she described. But the next words hit like a well-timed jab to the face.

"His only true transgression in your eyes is that he has actually proposed to me—which is more than I can say for yourself."

Edgar felt the blood drain from his face. The words hung in the air between them, a challenge and an accusation wrapped in simple truth. Thornton had done what Edgar hadn't—made an honest offer, laid his cards on the table, treated Elisha with the respect of a straightforward proposal.

While Edgar continued to deceive her.

The guilt was overwhelming. She deserved better—deserved honesty, deserved a man who could offer marriage without the shadow of the *ton's* ostracization hanging over their relationship.

"You are right," he said quietly, the admission feeling like acid on his tongue. "You may invite him, though I shan't pretend enthusiasm at the prospect of watching you navigate waters filled with Mr. Thornton and other gentlemen who might seek your attention."

"The waters shall not only teem with potential suitors," Elisha said with a small smile, "but with eligible ladies as well."

Edgar frowned, genuinely confused despite his internal turmoil. "Surely that cannot be Mother's objective when she knows perfectly well where my heart lies."

He watched Elisha lean back against the settee cushions. "Your mother is a shrewd woman, Edgar. If I were in her position with a son of my own, I might employ the very same strategy. She may wish to ensure you are certain about your choice by tempting you with more eligible ladies."

"Indeed…" he said, recognizing his mother's strategic mind but also impressed by her cold logic. "That does sound possibly like something she would orchestrate." He studied Elisha's face, dreading how this might be hurting her feelings. "Does this prospect trouble you?"

"Not exactly," she said, and Edgar felt warm affection flow through him. "After all, you are not the one issuing these invitations. Had you been the one to surround yourself with beautiful debutantes, I might feel quite differently about the matter."

"That is remarkably rational of you, my darling," he said, leaning closer.

Laying a gentle kiss on her throat, he said in a low voice, "Now, perhaps you should read your correspondence from Thornton."

Edgar sat up as Elisha reached for the letter. Her expression changed as she read, concern replacing curiosity. "What is amiss?" Edgar asked with alarm.

"'My dearest Miss Linde,'" she read aloud, "'I trust this missive finds you in good health and spirits. I cannot help but observe the conspicuous absence of correspondence between yourself and Mr. Steele. As the proprietor of *Metropolitan Review*, I feel duty-bound to intervene in this matter.'"

Edgar stiffened. "Intervene?" he managed to say. "What the devil does he mean by that?"

But even as he spoke, Edgar's mind was racing ahead to the implications. If Thornton was monitoring Steele's communications, if he was planning to take action…

"'I have taken it upon myself to arrange a public revelation of the victor, to transpire on the eve of the New Year,'" Elisha continued reading. "'Despite my earnest efforts, I have been unable to locate Mr. Steele or his representative, but I have dispatched a communiqué to his publisher to this effect.'"

The world seemed to tilt on its axis. A public revelation. On New Year's Eve. Edgar felt panic rise in his throat. How was he supposed to appear as both Steele and himself? How could he maintain the deception when Thornton was forcing a public confrontation?

"While I can understand his eagerness for a dramatic conclusion," Edgar said, fighting to keep his voice steady, "the timing is most inconvenient."

Inconvenient. The understatement of the century. This was a disaster of epic proportions, and Edgar had no idea how to navigate it without destroying everything. Not only would he be ridiculed for penning a romance novel, but Elisha would be humiliated. If not publicly, then at least personally. No, Steele could not appear in person. He'd send a representative on his behalf.

"Indeed," Elisha agreed, setting the letter aside. "I shall be obliged to reveal myself as Miss Lovelace, lest he intends to declare a winner without my presence."

"You will likely be compelled to reveal your identity regardless, should my mother proceed with her plans," he said gently. "She's far too cunning not to see the advantage in your notoriety."

"Do you mean to imply that your mother would deliberately exploit my fame to gain my approval by the *ton*?"

"Without question. If maintaining your anonymity is of paramount importance to you, I could speak with her about it."

Elisha sat in contemplative silence, her expression changing from one of indecision to one of determination.

"Please, do not trouble yourself," she said finally. "My primary motivation for maintaining anonymity was to avoid unwanted attention from authors and publishers. If revealing my identity will facilitate our courtship and future together, then I am prepared to do so."

Edgar pulled her into his arms. When he kissed her, it was with desperate tenderness, trying to pour all his love and regret and fear into the connection of their lips. She was so precious, so brave, so completely deserving of a happy future.

"My brave, brilliant love," he murmured against her lips when they finally broke apart. "I am in awe of your courage."

They spent the remaining afternoon discussing the house party, the guest list, the strategies they might employ. But beneath Edgar's careful responses and practical observations, his mind was spinning with increasingly desperate scenarios.

How could he handle Thornton's forced revelation on New Year's Eve? How could he explain Steele's absence from the house party and the revelation? Should he confess to her now? Every day he delayed telling her the truth made the eventual revelation more devastating. But, no. His friends' pleas rang in his ear. Could not a loving deception be forgiven when the alternative meant destroying the single opportunity granted to one who had suffered so much? This was Elisha's moment to shine. He was certain of it.

As evening shadows lengthened across the study, Edgar held Elisha close, caressing her hand.

"Are you frightened?" he asked softly.

"Terrified," she admitted honestly. "But also… excited. For the first time, I feel ready to claim my place in your world. Not as an imposter or interloper, but as your equal."

The words were like daggers to his heart: that this extraordinary woman should feel inferior in his world. "You have always been my equal, Elisha," he said, and meant it with every fiber of his being. "Soon, the rest of the world will know it too."

As darkness fell beyond the windows and candles flickered to life around them, Edgar sat with Elisha in his arms and strengthened his resolve. He would do everything in his power to protect her from anyone who would see her as less than the future Duchess of Lancaster.

THE BALL

ELISHA HAD BEEN back in London for two weeks, and the glorious time she spent with Edgar at Lancaster Hall seemed almost like a dream. Their parting had been tender, full of whispered promises and stolen kisses, yet his subsequent letters were frustratingly formal—brief reports about estate business and family matters, lacking the warmth she craved. When she'd questioned him about it, he'd explained apologetically that his sisters had taken to holding his correspondence up to windows before his secretary could dispatch them, searching for romantic declarations to tease him about.

She smiled at the memory as she sorted through the morning papers in her office at the *Metropolitan Review* when a headline in the *Financial Times* caught her eye:

LANCASTER HOLDINGS EXPANDS: SIGNIFICANT INVEST-MENT IN TRANSPORTATION SECTOR

Her heart began to race as she read the details: "His Grace, the Duke of Lancaster, has emerged as a significant investor in Hargrove & Sons Transportation Company, with an estimated investment of thirty thousand pounds over the past month. This strategic acquisition has fueled speculation about a potential merger between Lancaster Holdings and the Hargrove empire. Sources close to both families suggest this business alliance may herald a more permanent connection…"

"Fascinating reading, isn't it?"

Elisha started at Steven Thornton's voice, her hands trembling as she set down the paper. She hadn't heard him enter her office.

"The financial section isn't usually your preferred morning literature," he observed, settling himself in the chair opposite her desk with the satisfied air of a cat who'd cornered a mouse.

"I was merely checking our competition's coverage," she managed, though her voice sounded strained even to her own ears.

"Indeed?" Thornton reached over and smoothly retrieved the paper, his sharp eyes missing nothing. "Though I suppose this particular piece holds a more personal interest."

"I don't see how," she said stiffly, though her stomach was churning with dread.

"No?" He raised an eyebrow, his expression one of practiced sympathy that somehow felt more threatening than comforting. "My dear Elisha, surely you understand how these arrangements typically unfold among the nobility. Business alliances paving the way for marriage alliances—it's practically a sacred tradition."

"I fail to see how you're privy to His Grace's private business matters," Elisha said, trying desperately to maintain her composure while her world tilted on its axis.

Thornton's smile held a hint of superiority that made her temper flare. "When one moves in financial circles, such information flows as freely as wine at a gentleman's club. Just yesterday at my club, Mr. Hargrove's banker was discussing another substantial investment from Lancaster Holdings. Five thousand pounds, I believe was the sum mentioned." He leaned forward slightly, lowering his voice to a conspiratorial whisper. "These are not mere business transactions, Miss Linde. The pattern is quite clear to those of us who understand how these arrangements work."

"And you understand them well, do you?" There was ice in her voice now.

"Better than most, I'm afraid." His tone softened with what seemed like genuine sympathy, though something in his eyes remained calculating. "One must secure the business interests before securing the personal ones. And why shouldn't he?" Thornton continued, spreading his hands as if the logic were inescapable. "One can hardly blame His Grace when he has ambitions for expanding into railways. Miss Hargrove is acknowledged to be one of the Season's beauties, and the merger of their families' business interests would increase their combined wealth exponentially."

Elisha sat very still, her mind reeling. She thought of their last intimate encounter in the garden, how genuine his declarations of love had seemed, how tenderly he'd held her afterward. She had believed his protestations that he wasn't wealthy enough to offer her what Steven had. Yet here was evidence, if Thornton's words could be believed, that while Edgar was professing his devotion to her, apologizing for his limitations, he was quietly orchestrating a very different future.

"I imagine we'll be seeing less of him at the gazette now," Thornton mused, his voice carrying just the right note of regret. "Though his brief association with us has certainly elevated our standing in certain circles." He stood, adjusting his cuffs with meticulous care. "Miss Linde, should you ever need a friend who understands the bitter taste of aristocratic duplicity, my door is always open."

She was still staring at the newspaper when Steven reached the door, the words blurring before her eyes. Before he could exit, Amelia burst in, waving an envelope with barely contained excitement.

"Elisha! Oh, Steven, you'll never guess what's just arrived," she exclaimed, her cheeks flushed.

Elisha looked up, blinking away the tears that had begun to gather. "What is it?"

Amelia thrust the elegant envelope toward her. "An invitation! To the Duke of Lancaster's estate in Kent. And it's for all of us!"

Elisha took the invitation, remembering the duchess' letter to Edgar as she read. "This is for a house party, Amelia. For an entire week."

"Is it? That's even better!" Amelia practically bounced on her toes. "A week-long house party at a duke's estate! We simply must attend!"

"I don't know," Elisha said weakly, the paper feeling heavy as lead in her hands. "It will be costly. There's work to be done, and I have nothing appropriate to wear to such an event."

"Does it matter? We shall wear our best frocks and hold our heads high. Come now, Elisha, when will we ever get another chance like this? Think of the connections we could make for the gazette!"

Before Elisha could formulate a response, Thornton clapped his hands together decisively. "Excellent! I shall be delighted to escort you both," he announced, his tone brooking no argument. "Now, you'll need proper attire for such an occasion. I suggest you visit Madame Delacoure's establishment on Bond Street. Ballgowns, shoes, accessories—spare no expense. I shall cover all costs."

"Oh, that's not neces—" Elisha began, but he held up a hand.

"Consider it an investment in the gazette's future," he said smoothly. "After all, we can't have our most talented writers looking anything less than spectacular at such an important social event."

With that declaration, he strode from the office, leaving both women staring after him in stunned silence. Amelia turned to Elisha, her eyes sparkling with excitement, but Elisha felt only a growing sense of dread. The duchess' scrutiny, the performance she'd have to give before Society, Edgar's potential betrayal, and now Thornton's suspicious generosity—it all felt like pieces of a puzzle she couldn't quite solve but knew would form a picture she wouldn't like.

THAT AFTERNOON, DESPITE her inner turmoil, Elisha found herself drawn to Edgar's London townhouse. She hadn't planned the visit, but the newspaper article and Thornton's insinuations gnawed at her thoughts until she could bear the uncertainty no longer. She needed to see Edgar, to hear him deny these rumors himself, to look into his eyes and find the truth.

As she approached the impressive Georgian residence, however, the front door opened. Elisha quickly stepped back into the shadow of a neighboring building, her heart stopping as Miss Hargrove emerged. The young woman's usually impeccable appearance was notably disheveled—her fashionable bonnet sat askew, her golden curls had escaped their pins, and her cheeks were flushed a becoming pink. Most tellingly, she was adjusting her gloves with hurried, almost furtive, movements as she descended the steps.

Behind her came Edgar's butler, Simmons, his usually impassive demeanor betraying clear discomfort as he escorted her to the waiting carriage. His shoulders were rigid with disapproval, and he avoided looking directly at his charge.

"Please extend my deepest gratitude to His Grace," Miss Hargrove's clear voice carried in the quiet street, accompanied by a laugh that sounded both breathless and satisfied. "The afternoon has been most… illuminating."

"Of course, my lady," Simmons replied with wooden politeness.

She paused at the carriage door, and Elisha caught a glimpse of a secret smile playing about her perfect lips—the expression of a woman well-pleased with herself. "I do so look forward to our next… business discussion."

Elisha pressed herself harder against the cold stone wall, willing herself to disappear as Miss Hargrove's carriage rolled past mere feet away. Her mind raced with painful possibilities, each more devastating than the last. Miss Hargrove had clearly spent an intimate afternoon in Edgar's home, emerging in such a state of disarray…

The implications were unmistakable, weren't they? And yet, somehow, her heart refused to accept what her eyes had witnessed. This was Edgar—the man who had held her so tenderly, who had whispered words of love against her skin, who had promised her a future together. Surely there had to be another explanation.

But what other explanation could there be?

She remained hidden until the butler had returned inside and the street was empty again. For a long moment, she considered marching up to that imposing front door and demanding to see Edgar, demanding an explanation. But pride and heartbreak held her back. If he was indeed courting Miss Hargrove, if their relationship had been nothing more than a pleasant diversion before he fulfilled his ducal obligations, she would not give him the satisfaction of seeing her pain.

By the time she reached her own modest lodgings, tears were flowing freely down her cheeks. How could she have been such a fool? To think that a duke would choose a common-born writer over a lady of impeccable breeding and fortune? She had let his tender caresses and passionate declarations blind her to the harsh realities of their different worlds.

Yet even as her heart broke, a part of her remained defiant. She would attend his house party. She would hold her head high and face whatever truth awaited her there. She owed herself that much, at least.

THREE DAYS LATER, Elisha stood before the mirror in Madame Delacoure's exclusive fitting room, hardly recognizing the elegant woman who stared back at her. The crimson silk gown transformed her completely—its rich color brought out the warmth in her complexion, while the expert tailoring emphasized curves she hadn't known she possessed.

"Magnifique!" Madame Delacoure declared, adjusting the fall of the skirt with practiced hands. "You shall be the belle of any ball, mademoiselle."

Beside her, Amelia practically glowed in her own creation—a confection of pale blue silk that made her eyes sparkle. "Oh, Elisha, you look absolutely stunning. Surely no gentleman could resist such elegance."

As they admired their reflections, voices from the adjacent fitting room drifted through the thin walls, and both women fell silent, unconsciously straining to hear.

"Did you hear about the Duke of Lancaster?" a woman's voice asked, pitched low but carrying clearly in the quiet shop.

"Oh yes," another replied with obvious relish. "They say he's finally bowing to family pressure to secure the succession."

Elisha felt her blood turn to ice, though she forced herself to remain motionless as Madame Delacoure continued her adjustments.

"About time, I should say," the first voice continued. "And what a match it will be—the daughter of that transportation magnate. What was his name again?"

"Hargrove," the second voice supplied helpfully. "Olivia Hargrove. They say she's an absolute beauty, and her father's company would complement the duke's holdings perfectly."

"I heard from Lady Binbrook that the duchess is positively beside herself with joy," the first voice added with obvious satisfaction in sharing such choice gossip. "Apparently, she's already begun planning the wedding breakfast. Talk about counting one's chickens!"

A tinkle of laughter followed. "Well, when you're the mother of England's most eligible bachelor, I suppose confidence comes naturally. Oh, to be a guest at that announcement!"

Elisha caught Amelia's concerned gaze in the mirror, seeing

her own distress reflected there. The gossip confirmed everything Steven had suggested, and everything she'd feared since witnessing Miss Hargrove's departure from Edgar's townhouse. Her chest felt tight, as if the elegant corset had suddenly become a vise.

"Elisha?" Amelia's soft voice broke through her spiraling thoughts. "You look rather pale. Would you like to sit down?"

She forced a bright smile, though it felt like it might crack her face. "I'm perfectly fine. Just... surprised by the latest gossip, I suppose."

"It's only gossip," Amelia said gently, but her eyes remained worried. "We mustn't put too much credence in drawing room chatter."

Before Elisha could respond, Madame Delacoure stepped back with a satisfied nod. "Voilà! You are both transformed into goddesses. Such gowns deserve to be seen at the finest gatherings."

As Elisha allowed herself to be helped from the elaborate gown, her mind kept returning to the overheard conversation. The pieces seemed to fit together with devastating clarity—Edgar's distance since London, the business investments, Miss Hargrove's intimate visit, and now Society's expectation of an imminent announcement.

She had been naive to think their passionate interludes could overcome the immense barriers they faced. He was a duke, after all, with responsibilities to his family name and holdings. What was one besotted writer compared to a strategically advantageous marriage?

A WEEK LATER, Elisha stood in the receiving line at Lancaster Hall, her crimson silk gown rustling softly as guests moved past in a glittering procession. The ballroom beyond sparkled with the light of a thousand candles reflected in crystal chandeliers, and the air hummed with music and refined conversation.

Edgar stood at the head of the line with his family arrayed beside him in order of precedence. Lady Hargrove hovered nearby with obvious satisfaction, while her daughter Olivia's golden head was bent intimately close to the Duchess of Lancaster's as they whispered together like old friends. The sight made Elisha's stomach clench painfully as she remembered the morning's gossip sheets: "Duke of Lancaster Expected to Announce Engagement at Autumn Ball."

"Ready?" Steven asked quietly beside her, his steady presence providing the only anchor in what felt like a storm-tossed sea.

She managed a serene smile that she prayed concealed her inner turmoil. "Of course."

They joined the queue, and Elisha tried to ignore how the bold crimson of her gown suddenly felt too presumptuous, too attention-seeking. What had possessed her to choose such a striking color? She wasn't here to compete for a duke's attention. Was she?

As they drew closer, she watched Edgar greeting his guests with practiced charm, looking every inch the aristocrat in elegant evening black that emphasized his tall frame and broad shoulders. When his gaze found her in the line, something flickered in those blue depths that made her treacherous heart skip a beat.

"Miss Thornton," he greeted Amelia first, his manners impeccable.

"Your Grace," Elisha managed when her turn came, sinking into a curtsy that she prayed disguised her trembling limbs.

"Miss Linde." He took her gloved hand, and she tried desperately not to notice how his touch lingered a moment longer than propriety dictated. "I'm delighted you could attend this evening."

The warmth in his voice seemed genuine, but Elisha forced herself to remember Miss Hargrove's disheveled appearance, the whispered speculations about wedding plans.

"I must say, Your Grace," Steven interjected smoothly, his

hand coming to rest protectively at the small of her back, "Miss Linde looks particularly enchanting this evening. I daresay she'll be the belle of the ball."

Elisha watched something dark and dangerous flash in Edgar's eyes before his expression returned to diplomatic neutrality. "Indeed," he replied with careful politeness. "Though I'm certain all the ladies present will shine tonight."

His gaze drifted meaningfully toward where Miss Hargrove stood in her cloud of pale silk, and Elisha felt her chest tighten with fresh pain.

"Mr. Thornton flatters me beyond my merit," she said quickly, grateful for Steven's steadying presence. At least one gentleman in her acquaintance could be counted upon to lend her support when needed.

"If you'll excuse me," Edgar said with a slight bow, "I must continue greeting my guests."

As Steven guided her into the magnificent ballroom, Elisha refused to look back, though she could feel Edgar's gaze burning between her shoulder blades. She had her own concerns to focus on—her career, her reputation, her heart's preservation. Let Edgar Lancaster announce his engagement to Miss Hargrove. She had a literary feud to engage and books to publish, and no time for dukes who played with women's hearts.

But her treacherous pulse still quickened when she turned to glimpse at him, his expression unreadable as he watched her retreat on Steven's arm.

The ballroom was a vision of opulence that took her breath away. Crystal chandeliers cast dancing light across polished marble floors, while the walls were lined with gilt-framed mirrors that multiplied the brilliance thousandfold. The air thrummed with the gentle strains of a string quartet and the cultured murmur of England's finest families.

"Quite the spectacle," Steven remarked, guiding her toward the refreshment tables with practiced ease. "I daresay the duke has spared no expense for this particular gathering."

"Indeed," Amelia murmured, her eyes wide as she took in the seemingly endless parade of silk, jewels, and inherited wealth surrounding them.

"I suppose when one is planning to announce an engagement..." Steven let the implication hang in the air like smoke.

As the evening progressed, Elisha found herself grateful for her companions' unwavering support. They formed a protective triangle among the swirling dancers and scheming socialites, taking turns fetching glasses of champagne and offering wry commentary on the various dramas unfolding around them. Steven proved surprisingly observant, his dry wit making Amelia giggle behind her fan as he noted Lady Worthington's increasingly desperate attempts to secure an introduction to the Foreign Secretary.

Despite her heartache, Elisha couldn't help but be drawn into several fascinating conversations. Lord Gower proved eager to discuss her latest article on working conditions, while Lady Whitmore shared pointed observations about the government's response to recent labor unrest. She spoke at length with several gentlemen about reform movements, carefully sidestepping any mention of her own involvement while gathering useful intelligence for her future writings.

The hours slipped by in a blur of music and movement, couples whirling past in brilliant displays of skill and fashion. Through it all, Elisha remained acutely aware of Edgar's presence, though she carefully avoided looking in his direction as he performed his duties as host. She noticed, however, that he remained notably distant from Miss Hargrove, speaking with her only when absolutely necessary and dancing with her only once despite several obvious openings.

"Your feet must be aching," Amelia observed sympathetically as midnight approached, noticing how Elisha shifted her weight. "Perhaps we should find somewhere to rest?"

"Just a little longer," Elisha heard herself saying, though she couldn't explain the compulsion to remain. The announcement everyone expected hadn't yet materialized, and something stubborn in her refused to leave until it did—whether from hope or the need for final confirmation of her worst fears, she wasn't entirely certain.

Steven turned to her then, offering his hand with an elegant bow. "Miss Linde, would you honor me with a dance?"

Heat crept up her neck as embarrassment washed over her. "I'm afraid I must decline. I… I don't know how."

His eyebrows rose in genuine surprise, but he recovered smoothly. "Ah, what a pity. Perhaps we might remedy that situation another evening." He turned to his sister with renewed purpose. "Amelia, shall we take a turn? I've been hoping for an opportunity to approach Mr. Hargrove about certain business matters."

As Steven led Amelia onto the dance floor, Elisha found herself alone for the first time all evening, feeling more isolated than ever among the glittering crowd. She took refuge near the refreshment table, her back to the wall as she watched the elegant couples spin past.

"Miss Linde!"

She turned to find Ladies Essie and Eva approaching with barely contained excitement, Edgar following in their wake. The young women bestowed quick kisses on her cheeks before immediately fluttering away toward a group of young gentlemen, leaving her unexpectedly alone with their brother.

He cut a devastating figure in his evening clothes, and she forced herself to remember that he would soon belong to another woman entirely. This was likely nothing more than a duke's final taste of freedom before his official engagement announcement.

"Your Grace," she managed, executing a careful curtsy.

"Miss Linde." He bowed with exquisite formality before extending his hand. "Would you care to dance?"

The irony was almost too much to bear. "I must decline, Your Grace. My dancing skills are wholly inadequate for public display." And she had no desire to become tomorrow's gossip—

the naive writer who allowed herself to be toyed with by a duke.

His smile turned unexpectedly boyish, transforming his features in a way that made her heart clench painfully. "Then perhaps you'd allow me to remedy that deficiency? There's a small music room just off the ballroom where we might practice without an audience. My sisters would be happy to provide proper chaperonage."

Elisha's eyes widened in alarm. Had he taken complete leave of his senses? "I'm not certain that would be entirely appropriate, Your Grace." Especially not with Miss Hargrove somewhere in the ballroom, probably watching their every interaction with those calculating eyes.

"I assure you, Miss Linde, my intentions are completely honorable," he said with a gleam in his eyes that suggested otherwise. "It would be a great shame for you to attend such a magnificent ball and never experience the pleasure of dancing."

Against every instinct of self-preservation, Elisha found herself placing her gloved hand on his proffered arm. One brief lesson couldn't cause any real harm, could it? And perhaps it would help her finally purge these foolish romantic feelings from her foolish heart once and for all.

"Very well," she said with as much dignity as she could muster. "I place myself in your capable hands, Your Grace."

Edgar led her through a side door into an elegant music room appointed with comfortable chairs and a small pianoforte. The space was intimate without being improper, lit by several branches of candles that cast everything in warm, golden light. She expected to see his sisters following, but when she turned around, they were entirely alone.

The soft click of the lock engaging made her spine stiffen with alarm. "Your Grace, I would prefer the door remain unlocked," she said with icy formality, though her heart hammered against her ribs.

His eyes narrowed slightly at her tone before his lips curved in that familiar smile—the one that had once made her knees weak but now only fueled her resentment. "And I prefer it secured against interruption." His casual dismissal of her wishes only confirmed her worst suspicions about his character.

How dare he compromise her reputation this way while planning to announce his engagement to another woman?

"Let us begin with the basic waltz steps," he said, apparently oblivious to her inner turmoil.

Elisha lifted her chin with newfound resolve. If he thought he could toy with her while courting Miss Hargrove, he would soon discover she possessed more backbone than that.

He approached with practiced grace, taking her right hand in his left while placing his other at her waist. The contact sent an unwelcome shiver of awareness through her, and she silently cursed her body's continued betrayal. These were the same hands that would soon lead his bride down the aisle, she reminded herself fiercely.

"Place your left hand on my shoulder," he instructed softly, as if gentling a nervous mare.

She complied with rigid formality, fighting the urge to step away from the heat radiating from his body. The familiar scent of his cologne—sandalwood and something uniquely masculine— threatened to undermine her carefully constructed defenses. Did Miss Hargrove find his presence equally intoxicating? Had she, too, been seduced by his practiced charm?

"Excellent," he murmured, maintaining that insufferable composure while she struggled with the impropriety of their situation. "Now, follow my lead. Step back with your right foot as I step forward with my left…"

As he guided her through the basic patterns, Elisha found her treacherous body responding despite her emotional turmoil. His touch was confident yet gentle, his instructions clear and patient. She hated herself for noticing how perfectly they fit together, how naturally her smaller frame aligned with his larger one.

"You're a remarkably quick study," Edgar observed, and she could hear genuine admiration in his voice.

Elisha looked up, meeting his gaze with carefully constructed indifference. She would not let him see how much this masquerade wounded her. "I have an excellent instructor, Your Grace."

The opening strains of a waltz drifted in from the ballroom beyond, and Edgar's grip on her hand tightened almost imperceptibly. "Shall we try it with musical accompaniment?"

She nodded, not trusting herself to speak as they began to move in earnest. Despite the emotional shield she erected, she found herself caught up in the magic of the moment—the swirl of her crimson skirts, the play of candlelight across the room's elegant furnishings, the intensity of Edgar's gaze as he guided her through the steps.

"You're trembling," he said softly.

"I'm concentrating," she replied, though they both knew it was a lie.

As the music swelled around them, Edgar drew her slightly closer, close enough that she could see the flecks of silver in his blue eyes, close enough to count the dark lashes that framed them. "Elisha," he murmured, her name like a caress on his lips.

She forced herself to maintain eye contact, to project an image of cool sophistication even as her heart shattered anew. "Yes, Your Grace?"

Something flickered across his features—confusion, perhaps, or concern. "You seem… different tonight. Distant."

"Do I?" She managed a brittle smile as they continued their elegant circuit of the small room. "I cannot imagine why you would say such a thing."

He studied her face intently, and she saw the exact moment understanding began to dawn. His steps faltered slightly before he recovered, never missing a beat of the music.

"Whatever you think you know—" he began, but she cut him off with a laugh that held no warmth.

"I think I know nothing at all, Your Grace. Which is precisely as it should be, is it not?"

The final notes of the waltz faded into silence, and Elisha

gracefully disengaged herself from his embrace. She executed a perfect curtsy, grateful for all those etiquette lessons she'd observed from the servants' corridors of various grand houses during her impoverished youth.

"I am most grateful for your instruction, Your Grace," she said with brittle politeness. "Though I confess surprise that you could spare the time from your other... obligations."

Edgar's hand shot out to capture hers before she could withdraw completely. "Don't," he said urgently, all pretense of casual flirtation abandoned. "Whatever you think you know about my situation, you're wrong."

"Am I?" She met his gaze steadily, proud that her voice remained level. "I understand congratulations are in order. Miss Hargrove will make a most suitable duchess."

"What?" His confusion appeared genuine, but Elisha had learned not to trust appearances where Edgar Lancaster was concerned.

"She looked quite... satisfied when I saw her leaving your townhouse," she continued, each word carefully chosen to inflict maximum damage. "Adjusting her gloves, her bonnet thoroughly askew. Your butler appeared most uncomfortable escorting her out. Tell me, Your Grace, do all your business negotiations conclude in such a manner?"

Understanding crashed across Edgar's features, followed immediately by something that looked like panic. "Elisha, it isn't what you imagine."

"Isn't it?" She pulled her hand free of his grasp, stepping back until several feet separated them. "The substantial investments in Hargrove's transportation company, the private meetings, the intimate afternoon visits... Should I continue?"

"No," Edgar said fiercely, moving closer despite her retreat. "You're painting a picture that bears no resemblance to reality."

He crowded her against the silk-papered wall, his hands braced on either side of her head as he stared down into her face with desperate intensity. "You're right about one thing. I have been deceiving you. But not in the way you think."

She turned her face away, unable to bear the seeming sincerity in his voice. If this was another performance, it was his finest yet.

"Look at me," he commanded softly, and when she didn't comply, he gently turned her face back toward his with one finger beneath her chin. "The business dealings with Hargrove are part of something much larger. Something I've been trying to protect you from."

Despite her best efforts to remain unmoved, she found herself searching his face for signs of deception. "What are you talking about?"

"The pamphlets," he said quietly, and her breath caught. "The Pioneers. The Royal Mail contract."

Understanding began to dawn, though she hardly dared hope. "The Royal Mail contract?"

"It's crucial to everything we've been working toward," Edgar said urgently. "With control of the postal system, we could expand our distribution network across all of England. Every town, every village—we could reach them all with our message of reform."

"And Miss Hargrove?" Her voice was barely above a whisper.

A rueful smile tugged at one corner of his mouth. "Has been conducting a rather passionate affair with my secretary. When you saw her leaving the house in such disarray, she'd been meeting with him in my absence. Poor Simmons was appalled by the impropriety but felt obligated to escort her out properly."

Hope fluttered tentatively in Elisha's chest, though she tried to suppress it. "You've been so distant since we returned to London…"

"To protect the mission," he said with fierce conviction. "If anyone connected you to me during these delicate negotiations, it could expose both our reform activities and compromise the Royal Mail contract. Thornton may already suspect our involvement with the Pioneers. I couldn't risk everything we've worked for, no matter how much I wanted to see you."

The explanation made terrible sense but doubt lingered. "Why did you not inform me of this?"

Edgar's expression darkened. "I sent several messages to your lodgings, each one marked for your personal receipt only. None reached you?"

She shook her head, and his jaw clenched with suppressed fury.

"Thornton," he ground out. "He must have intercepted them."

Before she could respond, Edgar's hands framed her face with exquisite gentleness. "I've spent this entire evening watching you, not anyone else. The way you touched your throat when you were listening to Lady Camperdown's story about her travels. How Thornton's hand deliberately lingered at your glove when his sister spoke of her garden. The way you unconsciously swayed to the music even while claiming you couldn't dance."

"You noticed all that?" Elisha whispered, her carefully constructed walls beginning to crumble.

"I noticed everything," he said with quiet intensity. "How you kept to the edges of the room, observing everyone with those keen eyes of yours. How you bit your lower lip exactly seventeen times—yes, I counted—while pretending not to look in my direction."

She felt heat rise to her face at the embarrassing detail.

"I have to continue this charade a little longer," he continued, his thumb tracing the curve of her cheekbone. "I have to smile and make pleasant conversation while dying inside every time Thornton makes you laugh. I have to pretend I don't want to call him out every time he stands too close." His voice grew rough with emotion. "But don't for one moment think my heart isn't entirely, irrevocably yours."

"Edgar," she breathed, and suddenly the fight went out of her completely.

"I love you," he said simply, the words carrying the weight of absolute truth. "Only you. Always you."

Unable to resist any longer, she reached up to touch his face, marveling at the way he leaned into her palm as if starved for her touch. "I thought I'd lost you."

"Never," he said fiercely, covering her hand with his own. "You couldn't lose me if you tried."

When he kissed her, it was with desperate tenderness, as if he could pour all his love and regret and longing into the connection of their lips. She melted against him, her arms circling his neck as months of separation and misunderstanding dissolved in the heat of renewed passion.

"We should return," she murmured against his mouth when they finally broke apart, though she made no move to step away.

"Yes," he agreed, though his arms tightened around her waist. "Though it will take every ounce of my self-control to watch you dance with other men for the rest of the evening."

"Then perhaps," she said with a smile that felt like sunshine after rain, "you should claim the next waltz before anyone else has the chance."

His answering grin was pure happiness. "My lady, it would be my very great honor."

As they prepared to return to the ballroom, Edgar caught her hand one final time. "There's something else you should know," he said seriously. "About Thornton's manipulations tonight, about his interference with our correspondence—this cannot continue. After tonight, we move forward together, openly. No more shadows, no more deceptions."

Elisha squeezed his fingers, her heart soaring with renewed hope. "Together," she agreed.

MOTHER'S APPROVAL

THE DUCHESS' PRIVATE parlor, where the Lancaster family had assembled, was full of vigor and animated voices. Edgar occupied a plush armchair, his siblings arrayed about him in various positions of repose, while the duchess held court nearest the hearth. The servants attended to their duties, proffering tea as the siblings, still attired in their riding habits, regarded Edgar with barely concealed concern.

"Well, brother," Edmund commenced, his usual mischievous tone replaced with something more serious, "how go your business negotiations with Mr. Hargrove? There's a rumor you're courting the man's daughter rather than pursuing a coaching contract."

Eva's eyes sparkled with knowing mischief. "Indeed, Edgar. Your frequent meetings with the Hargroves, combined with your rather obvious avoidance of Miss Hargrove at the ball, has some speculating you're trying too hard to keep your courtship a secret."

The duchess set aside her china teacup with a delicate clink, her piercing gaze fixed on her eldest son. Though her features remained composed, there was curiosity rather than disapproval in her voice. "I must confess, your strategy perplexes me, Edgar. If business is your sole objective with the Hargroves, why risk encouraging speculation about romantic entanglements?"

Edgar exhaled deeply, realizing he could no longer evade the conversation. "The Hargrove negotiations are more delicate than they appear. Mr. Hargrove has certain expectations about potential family connections that I've been carefully neither encouraging nor discouraging."

"You mean he's hoping you'll offer for his daughter," Eva said with characteristic bluntness.

"Precisely. And while I have no intention of doing so, maintaining his hope serves our business interests. The coaching contract could be worth fifty thousand pounds annually."

A heavy silence descended upon the chamber as the family absorbed the implications. The duchess broke it with a thoughtful observation.

"And yet at the ball, you barely acknowledged the young lady. Surely such obvious disinterest sends its own message?"

"That was unintentional," Edgar admitted, running a hand through his hair in frustration. "I found it impossible to feign interest at the risk of hurting Miss Linde."

His sisters exchanged knowing looks, their earlier concern transforming into something closer to sympathy and understanding.

"Ah," Eva said with dawning comprehension. "You're caught between business necessity and personal inclination."

"Meanwhile," Edwin observed with a growing grin, "you did a sufficient job of appearing content during your single, perfunctory dance with Miss Hargrove."

"I'm pleased I managed that much," Edgar said, his voice strained with evident discomfort. "I felt immensely guilty toward Miss Linde, but the Hargrove contract is crucial to our other interests."

The duchess' eyes sharpened with curiosity. "Other interests?"

Edgar nodded grimly. "Something I need to discuss with you separately. But I confess, maintaining this pretense grows more difficult by the day."

Edmund leaned forward with genuine concern. "But what of

the aftermath, brother? Mr. Hargrove may be expecting a declaration that will never come. Such disappointed expectations could prove costly."

"What course of action do you intend to pursue?" Essie asked cautiously. "You cannot indefinitely maintain this charade without either offering for the lady or severely damaging business relations."

Edgar thought about what Elisha had witnessed—Miss Hargrove exiting his townhouse, disheveled. He was glad the lady wouldn't be too heartbroken when he ended their association, though he wasn't at liberty to divulge this information. "I am cognizant of the risks. My hope is to secure the contract soon, after which I can gracefully withdraw from any personal entanglements. But the negotiations have proven more protracted than anticipated."

"And what of Miss Linde in all this?" the duchess asked, her voice laden with maternal concern. "The poor dear must be wondering at your behavior, regardless of your true intentions."

"Does she understand the situation?" Essie asked with genuine worry. "It would be cruel indeed to leave her in ignorance of your business machinations."

"Most importantly," Eva added thoughtfully, "I did notice her in Mr. Thornton's company rather more than strictly necessary at the ball. Perhaps she's taking precautions of her own."

Edgar's jaw tightened at the mention of Thornton, but he forced himself to answer calmly. "Miss Linde is fully apprised of my situation. I explained the business necessity during our private conversation."

"And she acquiesced to this arrangement?" Edmund asked, clearly impressed.

"Indeed, she did. Though I suspect the deception pains her as much as it does me. While I am grateful for your intentions regarding this gathering, Mother, I confess I shall be relieved when tonight's performance concludes and I may return to Tunbridge Wells where Elisha and I need not maintain this tiresome pretense."

"I must confess, I find myself rather impressed," the duchess remarked, her stern countenance softening considerably. "It is no small feat for a young woman to comprehend such intricate business maneuvering from her intended, regardless of its necessity. Many would succumb to insecurity and jealousy."

Edgar regarded his mother with cautious optimism. "Am I to infer that you approve of Miss Linde as my future bride?"

The duchess chuckled softly, shaking her head with what might have been admiration. "Impressive indeed… and cleverly done," she murmured under her breath. Meeting her eldest son's eager gaze, she declared, "You have my blessing, provided your affections for her are sincere and unwavering and your siblings offer their approval as well."

Overcome with emotion and relief, Edgar rushed forward to embrace his mother. As he released her, she raised her chin, her voice gentle yet firm. "You must seek your brothers' and sisters' consent. If we cannot elevate Miss Linde's popularity, their prospects may be adversely affected."

Edgar turned to face his family, meeting each of their gazes in turn. Edmund and Edwin nodded their assent readily, while Essie declared with conviction, "Your happiness is worth any sacrifice, dear brother."

Eva, in a display of unbridled enthusiasm, clapped her hands and flung herself into Edgar's arms. "You have endured such prolonged suffering for the past five years. I yearn to see you content at last." Edgar stroked her hair tenderly, swallowing the lump that had formed in his throat.

"When did you all mature so gracefully?" he asked, a twinge of guilt rising in his heart at having been so absorbed in his own affairs that he'd failed to notice his siblings' growth.

"It appears we are unanimous in our approval," the duchess observed with satisfaction. "Now, we must devise our strategy. We shall disseminate careful rumors regarding Edgar's true intentions toward Miss Linde, thereby sowing confusion about the Hargrove situation from the outset. In this manner, Miss Hargrove shall not be caught entirely unawares when Edgar withdraws from consideration."

THE GENTLE RAP upon her chamber door startled Elisha from her contemplation. She had been lost in thought, pondering the previous evening's events—Edgar's obvious discomfort during his brief dance with Miss Hargrove and their private conversation that had explained so much while raising new concerns about the precarious nature of his business negotiations.

"Pray, enter," she called, smoothing her skirts as she rose from her perch by the window.

To her astonishment, it was not Amelia nor a maidservant who entered, but the Duchess of Lancaster herself. The elder woman's regal bearing commanded the room, her silver-streaked tresses elegantly coiffed and her gown a masterpiece of understated opulence.

"Miss Linde," the duchess said, her voice warm yet tinged with unmistakable authority. "Might I prevail upon you to join me for a private discourse before we prepare for dinner?"

Elisha executed a deep curtsy, her heart racing with uncertainty about this unexpected summons. "Certainly, Your Grace. I am most honored."

The duchess conducted her to a small, exquisitely appointed sitting room within the guest quarters. Once they were seated in chairs positioned to encourage intimate conversation, the elder woman's penetrating gaze settled upon Elisha with the intensity of a master strategist evaluating a potential ally.

"Miss Linde, Edgar has spoken of you with great fondness and respect. You are but the second lady he has presented to his family." The duchess' eyes met Elisha's, studying her with the keen perception of someone accustomed to reading character.

"His heart is not easily won, and I harbor no desire to witness my son endure further heartache. His position carries tremendous responsibility and even greater scrutiny. Any union he enters must be capable of withstanding the considerable pressures inherent in his station."

Elisha nodded slowly, her hopes and fears warring within her. "I comprehend your concerns, Your Grace. You question whether I possess the fortitude to endure such demands."

"It is not merely a question of endurance, my dear," the duchess said with surprising gentleness. "It concerns tact, the ability to deflect criticism with grace, to discern the true nature of others, to maintain one's standing in Society while supporting your husband's political endeavors. These skills are paramount for a duchess—and you shall undoubtedly make enemies by virtue of your humble origins. The ceaseless gossip, the potential damage to Edgar's influence in the House of Lords, the impact upon his siblings' marriage prospects... I expound on these matters to illuminate the gravity of Edgar's decision to present you to his family."

Elisha felt her throat constrict with the weight of responsibility being laid before her. While she had understood the challenges would be significant, she had not fully grasped their far-reaching implications. "I beg your pardon for bringing such potential tribulation to His Grace and to your family, Your Grace. I confess I may have been naive about the consequences."

The duchess reached out, patting Elisha's hand with unexpected warmth. "I believe your intentions to be entirely honorable, but in our world, pure intentions are not always sufficient protection. I implore you to consider with utmost care what a union with Edgar would truly entail. Can you withstand the constant scrutiny, the unfair criticisms, the false accusations that will inevitably come?"

Elisha drew upon her inner reserves, thinking of the trials she had already survived. "I believe I possess the requisite strength, Your Grace. Competition was fierce in every sphere I inhabited during my formative years. I fought for every necessity—clothing, shelter, sustenance, employment. I was compelled to develop resilience, to anticipate others' motivations, to never indulge in self-pity, and to rise again after each setback. I learned true peace only when I established my career as a writer."

The duchess nodded approvingly, her eyes brimming with what might have been compassion. "The duty of a duchess also encompasses loving her duke unreservedly, providing him with domestic tranquility amidst the storms of public life. Are you capable of such selfless devotion when your upbringing necessarily taught you to prioritize your own survival? I observe the manner in which my son regards you, Miss Linde. Should his heart be shattered again, I fear he may not recover."

Elisha considered the question carefully before responding. "With respect, Your Grace, I could never have survived in complete isolation. Without the support of my companions and our small community watching over one another, it would have been impossible to emerge unscathed. I learned early the vital importance of nurturing one's community, of mutual support and loyalty. These lessons would serve me well as Edgar's wife."

The duchess' expression transformed, satisfaction spreading across her refined features. "I am most grateful for the joy you bring to my son. It has been years since I have witnessed such light in his eyes, such purpose in his bearing. I am inclined to lend my assistance to you both—if you are amenable to participating in a small deception."

Elisha's eyes widened in surprise and not a little alarm. "Deception, Your Grace?"

The duchess leaned forward conspiratorially, her voice dropping to an intimate whisper. "We shall craft a new narrative for you, my dear. One that might render you more palatable to the *ton's* sensibilities. Pray tell, have you any knowledge of foreign ancestry in your lineage?"

Elisha shook her head, bewildered by this unexpected turn. "Not to my knowledge, Your Grace. Though I must confess my understanding of my family history is exceedingly limited. I was raised in an orphanage from a very young age and retain no real memories of my life before that time."

The duchess regarded her thoughtfully, without a trace of pity in her calculating gaze. "That actually affords us considerable latitude for creativity. Now, let me consider…" She studied Elisha intently, taking in her bone structure, coloring, and bearing. "Your features and complexion… yes, I believe we could quite convincingly present you as having Prussian ancestry. Tell me, child, how proficient are you in languages?"

"I have some command of French and German, Your Grace," Elisha replied, still struggling to comprehend this sudden development.

The duchess clapped her hands together with evident delight. "Splendid! Now, attend most carefully to what I tell you. Henceforth, you are Elisha von Linde, granddaughter of a Prussian baron. Your late father was a minor nobleman who married an English lady of good family. You were reared primarily in England but spent your childhood summers at your grandfather's estate near Berlin, which accounts for your linguistic abilities."

Elisha's head whirled with the elaborate fabrication being constructed around her. "But surely, Your Grace, people will investigate such claims—"

"Leave that concern entirely to me, my dear," the duchess interrupted with a dismissive wave of her hand. "I shall initiate the whispers myself through carefully chosen confidantes. A few well-placed remarks about your aristocratic bearing, your instinctive knowledge of proper etiquette… Before the Season concludes, the *ton* will be competing to claim they always recognized the nobility in your demeanor."

She fixed Elisha with a stern but encouraging gaze. "Regardless of my son's deep affection for you, it would significantly benefit your literary career to gain acceptance among the *ton*, would it not?"

Elisha nodded slowly, beginning to see the wisdom in the duchess' strategy. "Indeed, Your Grace. Such acceptance would afford me entry to the most prestigious literary salons and gatherings."

"Precisely my thinking. However, remember that this deception will demand the utmost discretion and unwavering commitment from you. Are you prepared to undertake such a challenging role?"

Elisha drew a deep breath, weighing the moral implications against the practical benefits. Any lingering doubts about Edgar's feelings for her had been dispelled by his family's obvious preparation to welcome her, and perhaps, with time and the duchess' guidance, she could prove her worth to Society through her own merits rather than fabricated lineage.

"I am, Your Grace. I shall do whatever proves necessary to secure our future."

The duchess squeezed her hand with genuine affection. "Excellent. We shall commence our campaign this very evening at dinner. Remember, you are now Elisha von Linde, and you must comport yourself with the quiet confidence of one born to privilege while maintaining the modesty appropriate to your station. Can you manage such a performance?"

Elisha straightened her posture and tilted her chin at precisely the angle she had observed among countless aristocratic ladies. "I believe I can, Your Grace."

"Outstanding. Now, I shall provide you with one of Essie's finest gowns—you are fortunately of similar proportions. Come along, my personal maid possesses quite magical abilities when it comes to transforming a lady's appearance."

EDGAR STOOD AT the threshold of the grand dining hall, observing the steady procession of guests making their entrance. The chamber had been transformed to accommodate the considerable number of attendees, with several smaller circular tables arranged throughout the space rather than the customary single long table. Each was elegantly appointed with the finest china, crystal, and gleaming silverware, while liveried footmen stood ready to guide guests to their designated seats.

His attention was immediately captured when his mother made her appearance. To his utter astonishment, Elisha was at her side, the two women engaged in what appeared to be animated and comfortable discourse. Edgar felt his breath catch at the sight of her, resplendent in an evening gown of deep purple silk that accentuated her graceful figure and brought out the emerald depths in her eyes.

As they approached his position, Edgar could not help but notice a subtle but unmistakable transformation in Elisha's demeanor. She carried herself with a newfound air of quiet assurance, her chin tilted at an angle that suggested innate confidence rather than acquired boldness. It was a bearing he had witnessed countless times among the aristocracy, but on Elisha, it seemed both surprisingly natural and faintly troubling.

"Edgar, my dear," his mother said as they reached him, her voice carrying a note of satisfaction that immediately put him on alert, "I've had the most delightful and illuminating conversation with Miss von Linde. Were you aware that her grandfather was a Prussian baron?"

Edgar's eyebrows rose sharply in genuine surprise. This was certainly news to him, and he found himself studying Elisha's face for any sign of discomfort or deception. Instead, he found only a serene smile and steady gaze.

"Indeed?" he managed, striving to maintain a neutral tone while his mind raced with questions. "How fascinating. I do not believe you have mentioned such distinguished lineage before, Miss von Linde."

"Oh, I seldom speak of family history," Elisha replied with perfect poise and just the right note of modest reticence. "It seemed rather impolite to call attention to such matters, particularly given the current political tensions on the Continent."

The duchess laughed with what sounded like genuine delight. "Nonsense, my dear child. You should take appropriate pride in your heritage. Come, allow me to introduce you to some of our other guests. I'm certain they would be most intrigued to hear about your childhood summers near Berlin."

As his mother smoothly guided Elisha away toward a group of influential peers, Edgar felt a deep furrow creasing his brow. This unexpected development sat most uneasily with him. He had always held Elisha's forthright nature and complete lack of pretension among her most admirable qualities. This sudden revelation of aristocratic connections seemed not only entirely out of character but potentially dangerous.

His growing misgivings only intensified as the formal dinner commenced. To his further astonishment, he discovered that Elisha had been seated at the high table—his own table at the head of the room—a position traditionally reserved for only the most distinguished guests. She was strategically placed between his mother and Lord Williams, one of the most influential and well-connected peers in attendance.

Throughout the elaborate meal, Edgar found his attention repeatedly drawn to Elisha's end of the table. She appeared to be acquitting herself admirably in conversation with both Lord and Lady Williams, her melodious laughter occasionally rising above the general murmur in response to some witticism. In stark contrast to her apparent ease and growing confidence, Edgar remained tense and increasingly troubled.

As the first course was presented, Edgar leaned discreetly toward his mother. "Tell me, Mother, what inspired Miss von Linde's prominent seating arrangement? It represents quite an aggressive introduction to Society."

The duchess merely smiled with satisfaction. "I thought it would be refreshing to alter our usual social hierarchy somewhat. Moreover, Miss von Linde has such fascinating stories to share about Continental Society. Were you aware she is fluent in German?"

Edgar's frown deepened. If she possessed such linguistic skills, why had she shown no interest in Mr. Christian Heine's recent literary soirée? Deciding to test this new narrative directly, he caught Elisha's eye across the table and inquired in perfectly pronounced German, "Meine Mutter hat mir erzählt, dass Sie fließend Deutsch sprechen, Fräulein von Linde."

Without missing a beat, Elisha smiled with becoming modesty and replied, "Die Herzogin schmeichelt mir, Euer Gnaden. Ich kann einfache Gespräche führen, spreche aber nicht fließend."

Surprised and somewhat relieved that she was not engaging in complete fabrication, Edgar nodded approvingly before switching to French. "Et en français?"

"J'ai appris d'une française rencontrée en échange de cours d'anglais," she responded smoothly.

Edgar addressed Elisha directly when other guests at his table were occupied in discourse. "Miss von Linde, I confess myself rather surprised not to have encountered you at Mr. Christian Heine's exclusive literary gathering last week. Given your apparent linguistic abilities and obvious interest in Continental literature, I should have thought such an event would prove irresistible."

Elisha's serene smile remained perfectly composed. "Ah, indeed. I had harbored considerable hopes of attending, but my application for invitation was politely declined. It appears that my publication and I were not deemed sufficiently prestigious for such an exclusive gathering."

Edgar's expression shifted to one of genuine surprise and indignation. "Insufficiently prestigious? That seems utterly preposterous. Miss Lovelace and Mr. Steele have become the subject of intense discussion throughout London's literary circles. Surely your professional reputation should have secured your welcome."

"You are most gracious to say so, Your Grace," Elisha replied with perfect grace. "I fear not everyone shares your generous assessment of our modest efforts. I confess to considerable curiosity about the gathering, however… Was Mr. Steele himself in attendance?"

Edgar inclined his head in confirmation, noting with growing unease the sudden brightness in her eyes. "Indeed, his presence caused quite a sensation among the assembled literati."

Elisha's entire demeanor seemed to sparkle with barely contained interest. "How fascinating! Pray tell, what manner of man is he? I have often found myself pondering the character of the individual behind such compelling prose."

Edgar studied her expression carefully, noting the eager curiosity that seemed to transcend mere professional interest. "Well, he proved younger than many had anticipated—I should estimate no more than thirty years. Tall in stature, with dark brown hair, and quite handsome if the ladies' reactions provided any indication. He possesses considerable personal magnetism—charming yet intellectually formidable, with a sharp wit that kept even the most accomplished conversationalists alert."

As he spoke, Edgar observed with growing dismay the faint but unmistakable blush that suffused Elisha's cheeks. Her eyes seemed to sparkle with an emotion he could not precisely identify but knew instinctively he disliked.

"Miss von Linde," he said with careful casualness, "I hope you are not developing a romantic attachment to Miss Lovelace's literary rival?"

Elisha's blush deepened noticeably, and she quickly averted her gaze. "Certainly not, Your Grace. I am merely curious about my professional competition."

"Of course," Edgar replied, though his tone suggested skepticism. "I must say, such a development would provide material for quite the romantic novel. It possesses all the elements of popular fiction, does it not?"

Elisha smiled without meeting his eyes, and Edgar found himself torn between admiration for the becoming color in her cheeks and inexplicable jealousy toward his own alter ego.

For the remainder of the dinner, Edgar studiously avoided extended eye contact with Elisha, finding himself increasingly disturbed by the evening's revelations. Her easy adoption of this fabricated identity, her transformed bearing, her apparent romantic interest in his literary persona—it all created a complex web of deception that sat most uncomfortably with his understanding of their relationship.

As the elaborate meal drew toward its conclusion, Edgar found himself torn between admiration for Elisha's remarkable adaptability and growing unease about the path they were all embarking upon. She was performing her role brilliantly, but at what ultimate cost? And what would happen when the inevitable investigations began and the truth of her origins surfaced?

The questions haunted him as he prepared to fulfill his duties as host, casting shadows over what should have been a triumphant evening. Change was indeed coming—he could feel its approach like a gathering storm—and he was no longer entirely certain whether it would bring salvation or catastrophe to all their carefully laid plans.

THE GARDEN

AS THE LAST of the dinner guests retired for the evening, Edgar made his way to his mother's private sitting room. His mind was awhirl with questions and suspicions, all centered upon Elisha and the evening's peculiar events. He rapped upon the ornate door, entering at his mother's soft, "Come in."

The duchess was seated in her favored chair, a tome resting in her lap. She looked up as Edgar entered, a knowing smile playing upon her lips. "I had anticipated your visit, my dear."

Edgar dispensed with pleasantries. "Mother, what machination are you orchestrating with Miss Linde?"

The duchess closed her book, setting it aside. "Whatever can you mean?"

"Pray, do not affect ignorance," he said, pacing the chamber. "This sudden revelation of her aristocratic lineage, her placement at dinner... It is all rather excessive, is it not? Surely, a diligent reporter could easily uncover the truth of her birth with a few well-aimed inquiries."

His mother's smile did not waver. "While that may be true, I am relying upon the *ton*'s inclination to believe what they wish to believe."

Edgar ceased his pacing, turning to face her. "Is the fabrication of a false heritage truly necessary? We are deceiving our guests."

"We are affording her an opportunity that was denied her due to misfortune. Who is to say that she is not of noble birth? She comports herself with remarkable grace. You care for her, Edgar. I perceive it in your eyes and know the truth of it from your words. This is not the moment to suddenly embrace righteousness. We both know you harbored no scruples about deception where your pleasure was concerned."

Edgar ran a hand over his jaw, suppressing his frustration. "The consequences of my deceptions were trifling. What shall transpire if the truth about her is discovered? She would be crucified, tenfold worse than had we been forthright."

The duchess rose, approaching her son. "It need not come to light, Edgar. Who would dare to accuse a duke and his duchess? And if they do, we deny it with enough fortitude to create doubt in their minds. With time, people shall accept her as one of their own."

"Elisha is a woman of principle. Does she concur with your scheme?"

"At times, my dear, we must compromise our ideals for the sake of love." The duchess' voice was soft, tinged with an ancient melancholy. "And Miss von Linde, while principled, is not without wisdom. She comprehends which aspects of our Society she may hope to alter and which she must accept."

"I pray you are correct, Mother. I fear only for her well-being. I dread losing her to the cruelty of the *ton*."

"You shall be at her side to shield her from some of the pain. Love is not always sufficient, Edgar, but Elisha possesses the resilience to thrive regardless of circumstance. It was this quality I sought to ascertain before bestowing my blessing, and she has not disappointed. She possesses all the requisite skills to navigate the treacherous waters of high Society. She demonstrated as much to me this day."

Edgar sank into a nearby chair, the gravity of the situation weighing heavily upon him. "And should she wish to discontinue this charade?"

The duchess' expression softened. "Then she will have proven herself worthy of you in a manner no title could ever hope to match. But the choice must be hers and yours, Edgar. I can but provide the opportunity while I still draw breath."

"I am most profoundly grateful, Mother."

The duchess nodded. "Then go to her, my dear. And remember that oftentimes the kindest truths are those which open doors rather than close them."

As Edgar rose to take his leave, the duchess reached for a small, ornate box resting upon the nearby escritoire. With delicate fingers, she opened it, revealing a ring of exquisite craftsmanship nestled within.

"Edgar, my dear," she said, her voice imbued with emotion, "this ring has been in our family for generations. Your father presented it to me upon our betrothal, and now I entrust it to you."

She removed the ring from its velvet cushion, holding it up to the soft candlelight. The large emerald at its center sparkled brilliantly, surrounded by a halo of diamonds set in intricate gold filigree.

"When you are prepared to announce your engagement to Miss von Linde, I should be most gratified to see this adorning her finger," the duchess continued, placing the ring in Edgar's palm.

Edgar gazed at the precious heirloom, his eyes widening with profound gratitude. The weight of tradition and family legacy in his hand filled him with an overwhelming sense of joy and purpose.

"Mother," he breathed, his voice thick with emotion, "I... I am utterly overcome. This gesture means more to me than words can express."

In a display of unbridled enthusiasm, Edgar enveloped his mother in a warm embrace, then lifted her. The duchess, momentarily startled, yelped and laughed.

"My boy," she murmured, her voice suffused with laughter. "Go and claim the happiness that has eluded you for so long."

EDGAR, WITH ALL haste and purpose, made his way to Eva's bedchamber, his footsteps echoing through the quiet corridors. Upon reaching her door, he rapped firmly, his urgency palpable in the late evening hour. The door creaked open, revealing Eva's startled lady's maid, who bade His Grace wait in the hall. Edgar acquiesced, though his demeanor betrayed the restlessness of a man with momentous news to share.

Moments later, his sister emerged, swathed in a frilled dressing gown, her hair neatly tucked beneath a lace-trimmed nightcap. Her countenance bore the unmistakable mark of sisterly vexation.

"What urgent matter compels you to disturb me at this unseemly hour?" she asked, her tone sharp with irritation.

Edgar, undeterred, pressed forward. "I must know which guest chamber houses Miss Linde. It is a matter of utmost importance."

Eva's visage transformed from annoyance to astonishment, her eyebrows arching in a manner that might have amused Edgar had the situation been less momentous.

"And for what purpose do you seek this knowledge? I'll not be party to any impropriety that might besmirch a lady's reputation," she declared, her voice tinged with righteous indignation.

"Eva! You wound me with such base assumptions," Edgar protested. "I assure you, my intentions are nothing short of honorable."

His sister's arms crossed, her expression hardening into one of skepticism that made Edgar feel as though he were once again a callow youth under her scrutiny.

"If your purpose is merely conversation, surely it can wait until a more appropriate hour."

"You must understand, I have Mother's blessing in this endeavor," Edgar countered, his patience wearing thin.

Eva's face contorted in distaste. "Good heavens, Edgar! Do you seek maternal approval for all your intimate pursuits? How utterly unseemly!"

Edgar heaved a weary sigh, his eyes rolling skyward in exasperation. "Nay, sister. Mother has given her blessing for me to court Miss Linde properly. I have made her wait long enough. I can tarry no longer in expressing my intentions."

As he spoke, Eva's countenance underwent a remarkable transformation. The angelic features that belied her oftentimes devilish nature emerged, delight evident in her eyes.

Eva clasped her hands together, her eyes alight with excitement. "Oh, Edgar! Are we to anticipate nuptial festivities in the near future? Heavens, a sister-in-law at last!"

"I implore you, lower your voice," Edgar admonished, casting a wary glance toward the lady's maid's quarters. He drew Eva closer and whispered, "Which chamber?"

"The Hydrangea Room," she replied, a knowing smile on her lips.

"You have my deepest gratitude," Edgar said, though something in Eva's expression gave him pause.

Eva's smile turned distinctly smug. "I must say," she whispered conspiratorially, "Mr. Steele and Miss Lovelace's feud bears a striking resemblance to your and Miss Linde's arguments during our game night."

Edgar started, his hand flying instinctively toward her mouth before catching himself. "You are entirely mistaken. I am a duke with weighty responsibilities to the estate. I hardly possess the leisure time to engage in literary dalliances."

"Oh, Edgar," Eva's eyes twinkled with mischief. "Your solicitor, I'm afraid, harbors a particular weakness where I'm concerned. Poor Mr. Beckett stood no chance against my considerable charms."

Edgar erupted. "Your charms? How dare he trifle with a woman so many years his junior! I'll kill him!"

She bristled with indignation. "He's done nothing improper, to my chagrin. Besides, I am twenty years of age! He is merely a decade my senior. And might I add, far more interesting than the simpering boys Mother parades before me at every social gathering."

"I shall have stern words with Beckett on the morrow," Edgar growled, his protective instincts flaring.

"Oh, do show mercy," Eva pleaded, her hand resting upon his arm. "The poor man was quite overwhelmed by my persistent inquiries. Besides, who else should know of your secret identity if not your devoted sister?"

Edgar's expression grew grave as the implications settled upon him. "Tell me truly, does anyone else share in this knowledge?"

"Certainly not. I would not relinquish such a delectable secret without due compensation. I intend to leverage it to my considerable advantage in due course."

"Eva, I implore you," Edgar said urgently, "breathe not a word of this to any living soul, regardless of whatever temptation might be offered."

"But surely the Mayfair Mavericks are privy to this information," she said with a pout. "It seems most unjust that your own flesh and blood should be kept in ignorance while your gambling companions know all."

"I beseech you, Eva. Not a whisper to anyone—especially not to Miss Linde herself," he pleaded, understanding the precarious nature of his position.

A sly smile curved her lips as she recognized her advantage. "Ah, but what price are you willing to pay for my continued discretion, dear brother?"

Edgar sighed, recognizing the shrewd negotiator his sister had become. It behooved him to dictate terms rather than allow Eva time to formulate increasingly expensive demands.

"I shall host a grand soirée for you and your particular circle of friends," he offered.

"In a townhouse of my very own in London?" Eva's eyes shone with barely contained glee.

He narrowed his eyes. "Your own entertainments in the London house—a weekly salon with full household support and guest privileges."

"How about a small cottage instead?" she countered with a glint in her eyes.

Edgar regarded her sternly. "How about your own wing of the London house with separate entertaining privileges?"

Eva crossed her arms with a pout. "With my choice of chaperone rather than Mother's."

Edgar held up both hands. "Now, you know I cannot go against Mother."

Eva spun on her heels. "Very well. I shall speak to Miss Linde—"

"All right, you sly fox," Edgar exclaimed. Once Eva turned around slowly to face him, he extended his hand with resignation. "Should you breathe so much as a syllable to anyone about my... extracurricular activities, you shall forfeit both the entertainment and chaperone privileges posthaste."

Eva grasped his hand with enthusiasm, sealing their accord with a vigorous shake before emitting a most unladylike squeal of delight. "Oh, Edgar! You have made me the happiest of sisters!"

"When did you become such an accomplished negotiator?" he asked with grudging admiration.

"I learned from watching Mother, naturally," Eva replied with an impish grin. "Now go, claim your happiness before dawn breaks and propriety reasserts itself."

THE SOFT GLOW of candlelight illuminated Elisha's chamber as she pored over the latest literary offering she was tasked to review. Her quill scratched softly against parchment as she made notations, her brow furrowed in concentration. The evening's events played through her mind—the duchess' startling proposal, the dinner performance, Edgar's probing questions about her supposed heritage.

Although the deception sat uneasily with her, she understood that love sometimes required compromises, even ones that challenged her principles.

Suddenly, a gentle thud against her windowpane startled her from her thoughts. Elisha paused, quill suspended mid-air, listening intently. Another soft impact followed, then another. Curiosity piqued, she rose from her seat and approached the window, her cotton wrapper rustling softly as she moved.

Peering into the moonlit garden below, Elisha's eyes widened as she beheld Edgar standing beneath an ancient oak, a handful of pebbles poised to launch at her window once more. Their eyes met across the distance, and Edgar gestured urgently for her to join him in the garden.

She shook her head and waved her refusal, mindful of propriety and the risk of discovery. But when Edgar dropped to one knee on the dewy grass, his hands clasped at his heart in a gesture of supplication, her resolve crumbled.

With her heart hammering against her ribs, Elisha hurried from her chamber and down the servants' stairs, her bare feet silent on the cold stone. Stepping into the cool night air, she spotted Edgar's tall figure beckoning from the shadows behind the rose hedges. She approached cautiously, acutely aware of her scandalous attire—nothing but her thin cotton nightgown and wrapper.

As she drew near, he stood waiting by a marble-topped garden table, his expression carrying such earnest intensity that she forgot to breathe.

"Why are we meeting here?" she whispered, glancing nervously toward the house. "What if someone sees us?"

Edgar reached for her hand, drawing her deeper into the alcove where climbing roses provided a natural curtain of privacy.

"The walls in your chamber are notoriously thin—thin enough for whispers to carry to neighboring rooms."

"Truly?" she asked, startled by this revelation.

"Indeed. Eva made quite certain of it when arranging your accommodations." At her shocked expression, he chuckled softly. "We are well hidden here, love. This particular corner is concealed from all the windows save a broom closet."

In the dim moonlight, Elisha glared at him with indignation, which only seemed to make his quiet laughter deepen.

"You did not expect me to be entirely without experience in such matters, did you?" he asked, still chuckling at her expression.

"No, but I did not expect you to possess intimate knowledge of every prospect from the hundred windows on this side of the house alone."

"Perhaps it stems from childhood games of hide and seek," he suggested with feigned innocence, "though I confess I prefer your more scandalous interpretation."

"Oh…" Heat crept up her neck as understanding dawned.

"Always assuming the worst about me, Miss von Linde," he teased gently.

She bristled and quickly changed the subject. "What matter is so pressing that it could not wait until morning?"

Edgar drew a deep breath, his gaze fixed on Elisha with an intensity that seemed to pierce the very depths of her soul. The moonlight caught the sharp planes of his face, highlighting the sincerity in his expression.

"Elisha," he began, his voice impossibly tender. "Mother has given her consent. I would be honored beyond all measure if you would grant me leave to court you properly."

Her hand flew to her breast, as if to steady the tumultuous beating of her heart. "What… what does that mean?" she asked softly, her voice catching in her throat.

His eyes met hers, brimming with such joy and love that it left her quite breathless. "It means that as soon as the Royal Mail negotiation concludes, I shall declare to all who will listen that I am courting you, Miss Elisha von Linde—granddaughter of a most conveniently distant Prussian baron," he said with a knowing smile.

Edgar stepped closer, bringing them deeper into the rose-scented alcove. His hand found the small of her back, the heat of his palm burning through the thin fabric of her wrapper. "It means I shall call upon you openly, be seen with you at every social gathering, and declare to the world that you belong to me."

His other hand settled possessively on her waist, and Elisha felt her knees weaken at the claiming touch.

Elisha's heart thundered against her ribs. "Edgar," she breathed, her voice trembling with emotion, "I can't believe it…"

"Neither can I," he said softly. "I wish we didn't have to wait, but alas, we must for a cause greater than ourselves."

Her body swayed toward his as if drawn by an irresistible force.

"I have something for you," Edgar murmured, his voice rough with emotion. From his waistcoat pocket, he withdrew a ring that caught the moonlight and scattered it in brilliant facets. "This belonged to my mother, and her mother before her. It has graced the hand of every Duchess of Lancaster for three generations."

Elisha's breath caught as she stared at the exquisite emerald surrounded by diamonds. "Edgar, it's beautiful, but I cannot—"

"You can," he interrupted gently, taking her left hand in his. "Because I am asking you to be my wife, Elisha. To be my duchess, my partner, my beloved companion for all the days of my life."

Tears sprang to her eyes as the magnitude of his words settled over her. "Are you… are you certain?"

"I am," he said simply, his thumb tracing gentle circles on her palm. "I am asking you to marry me, to face whatever challenges Society may present together, to build a life founded on love and shared purpose."

"Yes," she whispered, the word emerging before conscious

thought could intervene. "Yes, Edgar, with all my heart."

The smile that transformed his features was radiant as star-light. With infinite care, he slipped the ring onto her finger, where it settled as if it had always belonged there. "My love," he murmured, raising her hand to press fervent kisses to her knuckles. "My future duchess."

Unable to contain her joy any longer, Elisha stood on her toes and pulled his mouth down for a kiss that spoke of promises and passion, of a future that belonged to them both. Edgar pulled her closer, his arms tightening around her waist. Elisha melted into his embrace, her arms winding around his neck as longing and uncertainty dissolved in the heat of their connection.

When they finally broke apart, both were breathing unsteadily. Edgar's gaze peered into hers, his pupils dark with desire.

"We should return," Elisha murmured, though her body betrayed her words by pressing closer to his warmth.

"Should we?" Edgar's voice was rough. His hands roamed her back, then squeezed her bottom, eliciting a gasp from her lips. "God, Elisha… I've thought of nothing but you since the moment we parted in Tunbridge Wells. I've dreamed of you…"

The low rumble of his words sent liquid heat pooling in her belly. "Edgar…"

"Say my name again," he commanded softly, his lips finding the sensitive spot beneath her ear. "I love the way it sounds on your lips."

"Edgar," she gasped as his teeth grazed her throat. Her fingers threaded through his thick hair, holding him closer even as rational thought urged her to pull away.

"My love," he murmured against her throat. "Do you know what you do to me? How you've changed everything I thought I knew about desire, about love?"

His confession undid her completely. With a soft cry, she pulled his mouth back to hers, kissing him with all the passion and love she'd been forced to hide. Edgar responded with equal fervor, his tongue sweeping into her mouth to taste and claim.

The marble table pressed against her back as Edgar's body crowded closer, his arousal evident through the layers of their clothing. The hard proof of his desire sent answering heat spiraling through her core.

"What if I told you I've dreamed of holding you like this? What if I confessed that I've thought of nothing but being inside you?"

"Then do," she whispered.

WITH REVERENT CARE, he lifted her onto the smooth marble surface, his hands gentle despite the urgency of his need. The cold stone made her gasp, but Edgar's mouth quickly claimed the sound.

"Are you certain?" he asked, pulling back to search her face in the moonlight. "Once we cross this threshold, you'll be mine in every way that matters."

"I've never been more certain of anything," she replied, her hands working at his waistcoat buttons. "I want to belong to you completely."

Edgar captured her hands, stilling their movement, over-whelmed by the magnitude of what was about to happen. "And I want to belong to you," he said, his voice thick with emotion. "My heart, my body, my future—all of it yours."

As clothing fell away and moonlight painted their skin silver, Edgar's hands trembled with anticipation. Her wrapper pooled like moonbeams around her, revealing curves that took his breath away. The sight of her naked before him—trusting, willing, exquisite—sent blood rushing to his already aching cock.

"My beautiful bride," he breathed, his voice rough with need as he positioned himself between her thighs. His member, thick and heavy with desire, pressed against her folds. A groan escaped his throat at the contact—so wet and silky. Soon she would be his wife in truth, but tonight, she would become his in the most primal way possible.

He traced the slopes of her breasts with reverent fingers, then bent over to take her nipple in his mouth. Elisha tilted her head back with a soft moan as he began to suck and nip at her peak. Soon, he couldn't wait any longer. His cock ached to be buried inside her.

"Look at me," he commanded softly, his own breathing unsteady. "I want to see your eyes when I claim you."

With exquisite care, Edgar began to enter her, his cockhead breaching her entrance. The sensation was overwhelming—her tight heat enveloping him inch by inch, her body yielding to his invasion with such sweet resistance that he nearly lost control immediately. She gasped at the unfamiliar intrusion, her nails digging into his arms, and Edgar stilled, every muscle in his body coiled with the effort of restraint.

"Breathe for me," he rasped before he began to suck on her nipple while his body screamed for completion. The feel of her— so incredibly tight, so wet and warm around him—threatened to undo all of his control. "You're so small, so perfect."

His hands roamed her body as she adjusted, one cupping her breast while the other found that sensitive pearl nestled in her folds. When he began to stroke her there, she melted around him, her body opening like a flower accepting rain.

"That's it," he groaned as she gradually took more of him. "Christ, you feel incredible. Like silk and fire." His voice broke on the words as sensation overwhelmed him. Every nerve ending felt alive, every touch magnified. The scent of lavender mixed with her arousal, the feel of her skin like satin beneath his hands, the sight of his cock disappearing into her body—it was almost too much to bear.

When she finally accepted him completely, Edgar thought he might die from the pleasure. She surrounded him like a velvet glove, her inner muscles fluttering around his length in ways that made him see stars.

"So deep," she whispered, wonder in her voice, and Edgar felt his heart swell with possessive pride.

"Mine," he breathed against her throat, beginning to move with slow, deliberate strokes. "Every inch of you belongs to me now." The sensation of withdrawing and then sliding back into her welcoming heat was indescribable—like coming home and claiming heaven all at once.

As they found their rhythm together, Edgar lost himself in the symphony of sensations. The slick friction as he moved within her, the way her breath hitched with each thrust, the crescendo of her soft moans that went straight to his bollocks. Her hands roamed his back, her nails leaving crescents in his skin.

"My duchess," he rasped, his pace increasing as she began to move with him. "My heart, my everything." Each endearment was punctuated by a thrust that had her crying out beneath him.

Edgar wrapped his arms around her back and bottom to protect her from the hard surface, absorbing the cold, but he barely noticed anything beyond the exquisite torture of her body accepting his. When she wrapped her legs around his waist, taking him even deeper, he nearly came undone.

"Please," she gasped, and Edgar could feel her body tightening around him, her release building. "Edgar, I need—"

"I know what you need," he growled, his hand finding her pearl again. "Come for me, my love. Let me feel you around me."

When she shattered beneath him, her body convulsing around his cock in waves of pleasure, Edgar's vision went white. The sensation of her climax gripping him, milking him, pushed him over the edge with devastating force. With a groan that seemed torn from his very soul, he followed her into bliss, his seed spilling hot and deep inside her as her name fell from his lips.

The aftershocks seemed to go on forever, their bodies locked together in the most intimate of embraces. Edgar felt fundamentally changed, marked by this woman who had given herself to him so completely. She was his now—branded by his touch, claimed by his body, bound to him in ways that went far beyond any legal ceremony.

Afterward, as they lay entwined on the marble surface with his coat draped over them, Edgar felt fundamentally changed. And he couldn't remember when he'd ever been this happy.

"No regrets?" he asked softly, pressing a kiss to her temple.

"None," she replied, her hand finding the ring that now graced her finger. "How could I?"

Edgar smiled, full of contentment and possessive satisfaction. Tomorrow, he would conclude his business with Hargrove. Soon after, he would announce their engagement to the world.

"This is not goodbye," he reminded her as they prepared to return separately to avoid discovery. "This is the beginning of our future."

"Our future," Elisha repeated, the words sounding sweet. "I like the sound of that."

As they parted ways under the benevolent gaze of moon and stars, Edgar watched her disappear into the house and vowed he would move heaven and earth to protect her and the life they would build together.

TROUBLE

THE CRISP MORNING air was heavy with the scent of damp earth and gunpowder as Edgar, Mr. Hargrove, and a select group of gentlemen made their way across the misty fields of the Lancaster estate. Among the party was Miss Hargrove who had insisted on joining the shooting expedition despite the raised eyebrows of some of the more traditional guests.

As they paused to allow the beaters to flush out a covey of pheasants, Edgar seized the opportunity to broach the subject that had been weighing on his mind.

"I say, Hargrove," he began, keeping his tone casual, "I've been giving some thought to the Royal Mail Company contract. I don't suppose you might shed some light on how the bidding process is progressing?"

Mr. Hargrove, a portly man with a ruddy complexion who had built his transportation empire from nothing, chuckled. "Ah, Your Grace, business in the midst of sport? Well, if you must know, your group and Thornton's associates are the frontrunners at present."

Edgar's interest was piqued. "Is that so? And who exactly comprises Thornton's group, if I may ask?"

Hargrove lowered his voice, glancing around to ensure they weren't overheard. "Well, there's Lord Bentley, Sir Richard Lamb, and Mr. Simon Kelly, to name a few."

Edgar's brow furrowed as he contemplated this intelligence.

These gentlemen were all staunch Conservatives, and all rather vocal in their opposition to reform movements.

"However," Hargrove said with a meaningful look, "Thornton assures me that his associates will share… compatible interests for the sake of this contract, if you take my meaning."

Edgar nodded carefully. As a self-made man, Hargrove would naturally be wary of aristocrats who looked down upon those of humble origins.

"Indeed, I comprehend you perfectly," Edgar replied. "What, in your estimation, is the wellspring of Thornton's associates' interest in the Royal Mail contract? With the exception of Mr. Thornton himself, none of these gentlemen are wont to involve themselves in commercial ventures."

Before Mr. Hargrove could respond, his daughter interjected, her keen ears having caught the latter part of their exchange. "Your Grace, surely you do not mean to insinuate that Mr. Thornton's group harbors ulterior motives?"

Edgar smiled tightly at the woman's lack of tact, transforming his carefully worded inquiry into a blatant accusation. With practiced ease, he schooled his features into a mask of polite interest.

"My dear Miss Hargrove," he said smoothly, "I would not presume to impugn the motives of such esteemed gentlemen. I merely seek to understand the landscape of this particular venture more thoroughly."

Mr. Hargrove cleared his throat, casting a reproving glance at his daughter. "Quite right, Your Grace. In matters of business, one must always consider who one's partners truly are."

As they readied their firearms, Edgar's thoughts remained fixed on the curious alliance between Thornton and those Conservative members of Parliament. The potential ramifications for the reform movement, should Thornton and his associates gain control of the Royal Mail, were deeply troubling.

THE GRAND BALLROOM of Lancaster Hall buzzed with the gentle murmur of conversation and the soft clink of crystal as Edgar oversaw the final preparations for the evening's entertainment. The house party had been in full swing for several days, and tonight's card games promised to be a highlight of the gathering.

As he surveyed the room, his eyes were drawn to the entrance, where he saw a sight that made his blood run cold. Steven Thornton was entering the ballroom, and on his arm was none other than Elisha. Edgar felt a surge of fury course through him as he watched her lean against Thornton's arm, laughing at something he'd said, her hand resting familiarly on his sleeve.

What the devil was she playing at? After their intimate encounter in the garden, after accepting his proposal, how could she be so familiar with another man?

"Edgar, darling," his mother's voice cut through his rage, "do try not to look as though you're about to challenge Mr. Thornton to a duel."

The duchess had appeared at his side, her keen eyes taking in the scene before them. Edgar forced himself to relax his posture, though his voice remained tight. "Mother, I assure you, I have no such intentions."

"I should hope not," she said with a wry smile. "It would be terribly inconvenient to have to explain bloodstains on the new Turkish carpet."

As Thornton and Elisha approached, Edgar schooled his features into a mask of polite indifference, though his jaw ached from clenching. "Mr. Thornton, Miss von Linde," he greeted them, his tone carefully neutral despite the jealousy burning in his chest.

"Indeed we are, Your Grace," Thornton replied smoothly, his possessive hand at Elisha's waist making Edgar's vision darken. "Miss von Linde has been regaling me with the most fascinating tales of her recent interviews."

Elisha, her cheeks slightly flushed and her movements just a touch unsteady, spoke with more animation than Edgar had ever seen from her. "Oh, yes! I was just telling Mr. Thornton about my meeting with Lord Kelly. You know, the one who's so vehemently opposed to reform?"

Edgar felt his heart sink. Was she about to reveal more than she ought? But as Elisha continued, he began to detect something deliberate in her manner—the way her voice carried just far enough, the calculated stumble over a word.

"It was the most extraordinary thing," she said, her voice pitched slightly louder than usual, as though she'd had perhaps one glass of champagne too many. "There I was, expecting to encounter this fearsome opponent of progress, and instead I found the most charming gentleman! He made me quite rethink my position on several matters."

Edgar watched, fascination replacing jealousy, as Elisha continued her performance. She was brilliant—playing the slightly inebriated Society lady to perfection while subtly guiding the conversation. To what end, he couldn't tell.

The duchess raised an eyebrow, clearly intrigued. "Did he indeed, my dear? How fascinating. Perhaps you'd care to elaborate as we make our way to the card tables?"

As they moved across the room, Elisha maintained her act, punctuating her tale with little laughs and theatrical gestures that gave the impression of a woman whose tongue had been loosened by wine. She continued to lean against Thornton, touching his arm frequently, and Edgar could see how the man preened under her apparent attention.

"You see," she continued, swaying slightly as they walked, "Lord Kelly had the most compelling arguments about the potential consequences of hasty reform. Did you know, he once had a footman who taught himself to read, and the poor man became so disillusioned with his station that he ran off to America?"

Edgar, listening intently, began to admire the subtlety of Elisha's maneuvering. She was drawing out the opposition's arguments while appearing to be swayed by them.

"Of course," she added with a conspiratorial wink at Thornton that made Edgar's hands clench despite understanding her strategy, "I'm sure Mr. Thornton and his associates have much more practical concerns when it comes to matters of business and politics. After all, one can hardly run a successful enterprise if one's workforce is constantly agitating for change, can one?"

As they reached the card tables, Edgar found himself torn between admiration for Elisha's clever performance and the primitive urge to tear her away from Thornton's side.

"Well then," the duchess said, settling into her chair with a rustle of silk, "shall we begin? I, for one, am most eager to see how the cards fall this evening."

As the evening progressed and the cards were dealt, Edgar watched Elisha carefully guide the conversation, drawing information from her fellow players with seemingly innocent questions and observations. She made sure to keep Thornton's glass filled, laughing at his stories, touching his arm in apparent admiration. Edgar had to admit her performance was masterful, even as it made his blood boil to watch.

It was during a lull in the game, as Mr. Hargrove reshuffled the deck, that Edgar noticed Thornton's guard beginning to slip. Elisha had just finished recounting an amusing anecdote about a reformist pamphleteer she'd supposedly interviewed, when Thornton's expression darkened.

"You know," Thornton began, his words slightly slurred, his voice low and bitter, "there was a time when my family understood the importance of maintaining the natural order of things."

Edgar felt the tension at the table shift as all eyes turned to Thornton. Even his mother seemed taken aback by the sudden change in tone.

Elisha leaned closer to Thornton with apparent curiosity.

"Oh, do tell us more, Steven. Your family sounds fascinating."

Thornton took a long sip of his brandy before continuing, the alcohol having clearly loosened his tongue. "My father was a baron, did you know? He had estates, influence, everything a family could want."

"What happened?" Mr. Hargrove asked, his voice gentle.

Thornton's laugh was bitter, his usual polished demeanor cracking before Edgar's eyes. "What always happens when men of breeding forget their place and start entertaining dangerous ideas. He fell in love with reform, with the notion that commoners could better themselves, that birth shouldn't determine one's station in life."

Edgar felt a chill as he watched the man's true nature emerge. He caught Elisha's eye briefly, seeing a flash of understanding pass between them.

"Before long," Thornton continued, oblivious to the effect his words were having around the table, "he was using our family's resources to fund radical causes. Supporting the very people who should have been grateful for their station rather than grasping for more."

Edgar observed Mr. Hargrove's expression growing increasingly cold, though Thornton, deep in his cups and lost in his bitterness, failed to notice the change.

"Within a decade, he'd lost everything," Thornton said, his voice thick with resentment. "His estates, his place in Society, his title. All because he couldn't see that some barriers exist for a reason. The common classes need to understand their place—they're not capable of the responsibilities that come with true power."

An uncomfortable silence fell over the table. Edgar watched Elisha maintain her act, reaching out to pat Thornton's hand with apparent sympathy.

"How dreadfully unfair," she murmured. "No wonder you're so passionate about preserving the proper order of things."

"Precisely," Thornton nodded, seemingly grateful for her

understanding. "These so-called reformers, these pamphlet writers stirring up discontent—they don't understand the chaos they're unleashing. Common people getting ideas above their station, thinking they deserve the same considerations as their betters…" He gestured dismissively. "It's unnatural. Dangerous."

Edgar felt his own tension mount, but Elisha pressed on flawlessly. "And I suppose that's why you're so invested in securing the Royal Mail contract? To prevent such dangerous ideas from spreading?"

"Among other things," Thornton said with a satisfied smile. "Control the flow of information, control the masses. Keep them content in their proper places."

Edgar watched Mr. Hargrove's face darken further at these words. The man who had built his transportation empire from nothing was clearly appalled.

Rising from his chair with deliberate slowness, Hargrove fixed Thornton with a steely gaze that Edgar had rarely seen from the usually genial businessman. "Mr. Thornton, I believe I've heard quite enough for one evening."

Thornton looked up, confusion clouding his wine-flushed features. "I beg your pardon?"

"You speak of the common classes as though they're beneath consideration," Hargrove said, his voice trembling with rage. "As though hard work and merit mean nothing compared to the accident of birth."

Edgar watched realization begin to dawn on Thornton's face, but it was clearly too late.

"I am a common man, Mr. Thornton," Hargrove continued, his voice growing colder. "I built my business with these hands, earned every penny through determination and honest labor. And you sit at my table, speaking of people like me as though we're cattle to be managed."

Edgar felt triumph surge through him as he watched Thornton's panic mount.

"Mr. Hargrove," Thornton began, desperation creeping into

his voice as sobriety returned with alarming speed, "I assure you, I meant no offense—"

"No offense?" Hargrove's voice was dangerous now. "You've just told me that people of my class are incapable of responsibility, that we need to be kept in our proper place. That the very ideas of advancement and merit that built this country are 'dangerous.'"

Edgar held his breath as Hargrove turned to him, the man's decision clearly made. "Your Grace, I've made my choice regarding the Royal Mail contract. A man who holds such contempt for the working people who would use our services has no business controlling them."

Edgar kept his expression carefully neutral despite the elation coursing through him. "I'm honored by your confidence, Mr. Hargrove."

"The contract is yours, Your Grace. We'll sign the papers tomorrow morning."

Edgar watched Thornton's face go ashen. "Mr. Hargrove, surely we can discuss—"

"There's nothing to discuss," Hargrove said firmly. "I've seen your true character tonight, sir, and I want no part of it."

As the evening broke up in awkward silence, Edgar caught Elisha's eye. The pleased gleam in her gaze confirmed what he'd suspected. His brilliant, clever future wife had just secured them a crucial victory through nothing more than wine and well-placed sympathy.

THE CRISP MORNING air carried the scent of triumph as Edgar stood in his study, the signed Royal Mail contract spread before him on his mahogany desk. Mr. Hargrove had arrived at dawn, as promised, his determination to distance himself from Thornton's group evident in every brisk movement. The papers had been signed within the hour, sealing not just a business arrangement but a crucial victory for the reform movement.

Edgar allowed himself a moment of satisfaction as he reviewed the terms. Elisha's brilliant performance the night before had made it all possible.

The sound of heavy, unsteady footsteps in the corridor alerted him to an approaching presence. The door to his study burst open without ceremony, revealing Steven Thornton in a state Edgar had never witnessed before. The man's usual immaculate appearance was disheveled and his eyes were bloodshot. But it was the expression on his face that gave Edgar pause: raw desperation mixed with fury, making his features appear haggard and almost haunted.

"You bastard," Thornton said, his voice hoarse but lacking its usual control. "You've ruined everything."

Edgar remained seated behind his desk, projecting calm authority despite the volatile energy radiating from his uninvited guest. "Mr. Thornton. You seem somewhat... worse for wear."

Thornton's face crumpled slightly at the subtle mockery before hardening again. "Don't play games with me, Lancaster. I know what you did last night. You and Elisha—she played me perfectly."

Edgar noted the man's impudence in addressing him, the way Thornton's voice softened when he spoke her name even in anger.

"She was magnificent, wasn't she?" Thornton continued, beginning to pace the room with jerky, agitated movements. "Hanging on my every word, making me believe she was finally seeing sense. Making me hope..." His voice broke slightly on the last word.

Edgar said nothing, watching the man's composure fracture before his eyes.

"Do you know what it's like," Thornton said suddenly, stopping his pacing to face Edgar, "to have someone look at you the way she looked at me last night? Of course you do. Even if it was an act, for a few hours I felt like… like I mattered to her."

The raw pain in his voice was unmistakable, and Edgar felt an unexpected stab of pity despite everything.

"I suppose you think you've won," Thornton continued, his voice growing steadier as he fought for control. "The contract is yours, but you've made a fatal error, Your Grace."

"Have I indeed?"

Thornton moved closer to the desk, his usual predatory confidence replaced by something more desperate. "You see, while you and Elisha were congratulating yourselves on your clever victory, I've been gathering information of my own. Information that could destroy both of you."

Edgar felt ice flood his veins but kept his expression neutral. "I'm afraid I don't follow."

"Oh, I think you do," Thornton said, his voice taking on a pleading quality that Edgar found more unsettling than threats. "I know about your involvement with the Pioneers. I know about the printing press, the distribution networks, the funding you've been funneling to revolutionary causes. And I know you're Mr. Steele."

Edgar's blood turned to ice, but he forced himself to remain still.

"Yes, I know about that too," Thornton continued, and Edgar was surprised to see tears gathering in the man's bloodshot eyes. "The great literary rivalry—how romantic that lovers should compete with words. But here's what I don't understand, Lancaster." His voice dropped to a whisper. "You have everything. Title, wealth, position, respect. You could have any woman in England. Why her?"

The question seemed torn from somewhere deep inside him, and Edgar found himself genuinely considering it.

"She's brilliant, yes," Thornton continued, his words tumbling out faster now. "Beautiful, passionate, brave. But I could give her things too. I've built something real. My media empire, my connections—I've dragged myself up from nothing, and I could take her with me to the very top."

Edgar opened his mouth, but the man held up a shaking hand.

"Let me finish. Please." His words came out cracked and desperate. "I know she loves you. I see it in her eyes when she looks at you, the way she never looks at me. But I could love her more. I could love her in a way that transforms both our lives."

Edgar stared at the broken man before him, seeing clearly now that this wasn't just about business or social climbing—this was about a man who had convinced himself that love alone could redeem a lifetime of rejection and struggle.

"You don't understand what it's like," Thornton continued, his voice becoming increasingly frantic. "To have nothing, to be nothing. My father discarded my mother like she was rubbish, left us to starve while he played at being a philanthropist. I've spent my entire life fighting for scraps while men like you have everything handed to them. Elisha—she could change everything for me. She could make me legitimate in ways money never could."

"Steven," Edgar said gently, using his first name deliberately, "she's not a prize to be won. She's a person with her own desires, her own choices."

"But I could make her happy!" Thornton exploded. "I know her mind, her work, her passions. I've supported her career, believed in her talent. Doesn't that count for something?"

"Perhaps it's not enough."

Thornton's face crumpled, and for a moment he looked like the abandoned child he had once been. But then something hardened in his expression, desperation crystallizing into dangerous resolve.

"Then I'll make you a deal," he said, wiping his face roughly with his sleeve. "Work with me instead of against me. I'll give you a full partnership in my media empire—controlling interest, if you want it. Together we could shape public opinion, control the narrative. You'd have more influence than any reform pamphlet could ever achieve."

Edgar raised an eyebrow. "And in return?"

"Step aside. Let me court her properly. Maybe if I had a real chance, without your shadow over everything…" He trailed off, the futility of his request evident even to him.

"And if I refuse?"

Thornton's expression shifted, desperation giving way to something darker. "Then I'll expose everything. Your identity as Steele, your funding of seditious activities. The King will brand you a traitor."

The threat made Edgar's vision darken with rage, but Thornton pressed on, his voice breaking again.

"I don't want to harm you. Lord knows I'm not this person. But if I can't have her, if I lose the only thing that could give my life meaning…" He met Edgar's eyes, and the anguish there was unmistakable. "What else do I have left?"

Edgar studied the man before him—broken, desperate, clinging to a love that was slowly destroying him. "You're asking me to abandon the woman I love so you can pursue someone who will never return your feelings."

"She might," Thornton whispered. "Given time, given a real chance…"

"No," Edgar said firmly but not unkindly. "She won't. Not especially after you send me to hang. And deep down, you know that."

Thornton stood frozen for a moment. Then his face contorted with renewed fury and desperation.

"Then you've made your choice," he said, his voice hollow. "I'll give you until tomorrow evening to reconsider. End your relationship with Elisha. Do not communicate with her in any form from this point onward. Do this, and I'll keep your secrets."

Thornton moved toward the door, then paused and looked back, his expression a mixture of hatred and desperation. "It doesn't have to be this way, Lancaster. We could both have what we want."

"We cannot both have the same woman," Edgar said quietly. "And what of what Elisha wants?"

Thornton's face crumpled one final time before he straightened his shoulders and walked to the door. "Choose wisely, Your Grace. Everything you love hangs in the balance."

Edgar remained at the window long after Thornton's footsteps faded down the corridor, his mind racing through the implications. The man's threats were not idle. The fact that he knew about the printing press proved it.

The choices before him were stark: submit to Thornton's demands and lose Elisha forever, or face exposure that would see him branded a traitor. Neither was acceptable.

But perhaps there was a third option. If he could disappear for a time—remove himself from London while finding a way to neutralize Thornton's evidence—he might yet protect both himself and the cause. It would mean leaving her without explanation, letting her believe he had abandoned her. The thought twisted in his chest like a blade.

Yet what choice did he have? Better she think him a faithless coward temporarily than him facing the gallows and leaving her—and potentially their child—for good.

HOLLOW

THE SUN CAST a warm glow over the manicured gardens of Vauxhall Pleasure Gardens, where London's elite had gathered for an afternoon of refined entertainment. Elisha found herself in the midst of this glittering assemblage, feeling every bit the outsider despite her carefully chosen gown of pale blue silk and the emerald ring that caught the light on her finger.

At her side stood the Duchess of Lancaster, her silver-streaked hair elegantly coiffed beneath a fashionable bonnet. Flanking them were Edgar's sisters, Lady Essie and Lady Eva, their youthful exuberance barely contained by the constraints of proper Society.

Three weeks. It had been three weeks since Edgar's sudden departure on "urgent business," and Elisha was beginning to wonder if this elaborate social debut was merely an elaborate distraction from his continued absence. She'd received exactly two letters—brief, formal affairs that read more like business correspondence than notes from her beloved fiancé.

"Now, my dear," the duchess said, her voice low and measured, "remember to keep your chin up and your back straight. You mustn't let them see any hint of uncertainty."

Elisha nodded, trying to quell the butterflies in her stomach—and the hollow ache that had taken residence there since Edgar's departure. "Yes, Your Grace. I'll do my best."

Eva leaned in, her eyes sparkling with mischief. "And if anyone dares to snub you, just mention that you're writing a novel. That'll set their tongues wagging faster than Lady Romney's pug chasing a fox!"

"Eva!" Essie admonished, though her lips twitched with amusement. "We're supposed to be helping Elisha fit in, not cause a scandal."

The duchess sighed, though there was fondness in her exasperation. "Girls, please. This is important for Elisha and for your brother." Her tone carried a weight that made Elisha wonder if the duchess, too, was concerned about Edgar's prolonged absence.

As they made their way through the gardens, Elisha couldn't help but marvel at the spectacle around her, even as part of her wished Edgar were here to share it. Ladies in elaborate gowns twirled delicate parasols, while gentlemen with carved ivory canes and top hats engaged in animated conversation. The air was filled with the sweet scent of roses and the gentle strains of a string quartet—all of it beautiful, yet somehow incomplete without Edgar's warm presence beside her.

"Lady Gale," the duchess called out, waving gracefully to a stern-looking woman in purple silk who appeared to have swallowed something particularly unpleasant. "How lovely to see you. May I introduce Miss Elisha von Linde?"

Lady Gale's eyes narrowed as she took in Elisha's appearance with the intensity of a hawk examining a mouse. "Von Linde? I don't believe I'm familiar with that family name."

Before Elisha could respond, Eva stepped in smoothly with the confidence of someone who'd clearly been practicing. "Miss von Linde is a dear friend of ours, Lady Gale. She's quite the literary talent. In fact, she's been corresponding with Mr. Dickens about his latest work."

Lady Gale's eyebrows rose with interest, transforming her expression from suspicious to merely curious. "Is that so? Well, Miss von Linde, you must tell me all about it. I find Mr. Dickens' stories quite diverting."

As Elisha launched into a discussion of Dickens' use of social commentary in his novels, she caught the duchess giving her an approving nod. Perhaps she could do this after all—even without Edgar here to anchor her courage.

The afternoon wore on in a whirlwind of introductions and carefully navigated conversations. Elisha found herself discussing poetry with a viscount who quoted Byron with more enthusiasm than accuracy, debating the merits of landscape painting with a baroness who had strong opinions about the proper use of clouds, and even sharing a laugh with a group of debutantes over the latest fashion faux pas at court—apparently, Lady Worthington had worn the same shade of pink as Princess Alexandra, causing what Eva dramatically termed "a crisis of unprecedented proportions."

Yet through each interaction, Elisha felt Edgar's absence like a phantom limb. She found herself turning to share a witty observation with him, only to remember he wasn't there. When Lord Lichfield made a particularly pompous pronouncement about the intellectual capacity of lady writers, she ached for Edgar's supportive smile and the way his eyes would flash with protective indignation on her behalf.

As the sun began to set, casting a golden glow over the gardens, the duchess drew Elisha aside to a secluded grove where the sounds of the gathering faded to a gentle murmur.

"You've done wonderfully, my dear," she said, her voice warm with genuine pride. "I do believe you've won over quite a few of our harshest critics."

Elisha felt a flush of pleasure at the praise, though it was tinged with melancholy. "Thank you, Your Grace. I couldn't have done it without your guidance and support. I only wish…" She trailed off, not wanting to voice her disappointment.

"You wish Edgar were here," the duchess finished gently.

Elisha's composure wavered slightly. "I understand his obligations, truly I do. But I confess I don't understand why this particular business required such… discretion. Or such an extended absence."

The duchess' expression grew troubled, and for a moment, Elisha saw past the composed facade to the worried mother beneath. "Edgar's affairs are often more complex than they appear on the surface, my dear. Sometimes the very people we seek to help must be protected from the knowledge of our assistance."

Before Elisha could ask what she meant, Essie and Eva appeared, their faces alight with excitement.

"Oh, Elisha, you were marvelous!" Essie exclaimed. "Did you see Lady Reedshaw's face when you quoted Byron? I thought she might faint from shock—or perhaps jealousy that someone under thirty actually understands poetry!"

Eva nodded enthusiastically. "And the way you handled Lord Jefferey's interrogation about your background was masterful! When you mentioned spending summers 'on the Continent,' he looked positively green with envy."

The duchess smiled indulgently at her daughters before turning back to Elisha and guiding them further from prying eyes and ears. "You've taken your first steps into our world, my dear. It won't always be easy but remember this: You have a strength and intelligence that many of these people can only dream of. Never let them make you doubt your worth."

As they reached a secluded corner of the gardens, away from the gentle surveillance of Society matrons, Elisha gathered her courage. "Your Grace, I cannot express my gratitude sufficiently. For your guidance, your acceptance, for giving Edgar and me a chance at happiness." Her voice dropped to barely above a whisper. "Though I confess, I sometimes wonder if I'm holding him back from a more suitable match."

The duchess' expression softened with something that looked remarkably like maternal affection. "My dear child, you are exactly what Edgar needs. You've returned laughter to his voice, purpose to his stride. He carries himself taller because of you, fights for things that matter because you've shown him what's worth fighting for."

As the duchess' words touched her deeply and her eyes began to glisten with unshed tears, the older woman glanced around to ensure their privacy before leaning closer and lowering her voice dramatically.

"Speaking of fighting for things that matter," she said with a mysterious smile, "the meeting location has changed."

Elisha's brows furrowed in confusion. "Meeting, Your Grace?"

The duchess nodded, her eyes twinkling with mischief. "After all, the eagle soars when chains are broken, does it not?"

Elisha froze as recognition dawned, her mind struggling to process what she was hearing. The phrase was a code used by the Pioneers—one she'd helped develop herself. Finally, her eyes widened with shock that was equal parts amazement and alarm.

The duchess smiled patiently, as if watching a particularly bright student solve a complex equation. "I am so delighted to discover that great minds think alike, Miss von Linde."

"You…" Elisha stammered, glancing around frantically to ensure they weren't overheard. "You are one of us?"

The duchess chuckled softly, clearly enjoying Elisha's astonishment. "Of course, my dear. When Edgar discussed his newfound passion for social reform, did you truly think I would simply sit in my drawing room, embroidering cushions while my son risked his neck for justice?"

Elisha's mouth fell open. "But… how? When? Does Edgar know?"

"He knows I support his efforts, though I suspect he has no idea of the extent of my involvement," the duchess replied with evident satisfaction. "You see, my dear, a woman of my position has access to drawing rooms where men speak freely, assuming we're too busy planning dinner parties to understand matters of import. The intelligence I've gathered has proven quite valuable to our mutual acquaintances."

"But the risk—"

"Is far less for me than for Edgar, or indeed for you," the duchess said firmly. "Should I be discovered, I'm merely an eccentric widow with radical sympathies. But you and Edgar..." She shook her head gravely. "The consequences would be far more severe."

Elisha felt a rush of emotions—admiration, fear, and a deep gratitude for this remarkable woman who had welcomed her not just as a future daughter-in-law, but as a fellow conspirator in the fight for justice.

"Your Grace," she said softly, "I'm honored by your trust. And your courage."

The duchess squeezed her hand warmly. "The honor is mine, dear child. Edgar has found not just a wife, but a true partner. Someone who shares his burdens and his purpose. That gives this old woman considerable peace."

As they began walking back toward the main gathering, Elisha felt a newfound respect for the woman beside her. "When is the next meeting?"

"Tomorrow evening, at the print shop. There are developments Edgar will want to know about upon his return." The duchess' tone carried a hint of concern that made Elisha's stomach tighten with fresh worry.

"Developments?"

"Nothing that can't wait until after we've finished charming these insufferable aristocrats," the duchess said with renewed lightness. "Now, shall we go demonstrate how thoroughly a reformed orphan and a radical duchess can conquer high Society?"

With shared smiles of conspiracy and determination, they stepped back into the swirl of afternoon Society, their secret safely guarded behind pleasant conversation and perfect etiquette.

ELISHA RETURNED TO Lancaster Hall with the duchess and her daughters, her heart light with the afternoon's success yet heavy with Edgar's continued absence. However, hope flickered when she spotted familiar luggage in the entrance hall—surely Edgar had returned at last.

But as the minutes stretched into an hour, and an hour into the evening, her excitement curdled into disappointment. The luggage, she learned from an apologetic footman, belonged to Lord Edwin, who had arrived for a brief visit before departing for Scotland.

Shortly after dinner, her heart sank completely when the duchess approached her in the drawing room, her expression carefully neutral in that way that signaled bad news delivered with maximum diplomacy.

"My dear," the duchess began gently, "I'm afraid Edgar has sent word that his business in the north will require more time than anticipated. Something about a particularly complex situation with some tenants."

Elisha felt her chest tighten, though she managed to keep her voice steady. "I see. I do hope all is well."

"Oh, quite," the duchess assured her, though her eyes held a flicker of something that might have been worry—or guilt. "These matters can be so unpredictable. However, before you return to London tomorrow, I absolutely insist we fit you for some new autumn gowns. We cannot have the duke's fiancée attending the Season's events in last year's fashions, can we?"

Before Elisha could protest, she found herself whisked away to the duchess' private chambers. The room had been transformed into a whirlwind of activity, with seamstresses, bolts of fabric, and what appeared to be enough silk to outfit a small army.

"Goodness," Elisha breathed, taking in the chaos. "This seems rather… extensive for a few gowns."

"Nonsense," the duchess declared, directing her to stand upon a small platform in the center of the room. "You'll need walking dresses, carriage dresses, evening gowns, and at least three ball gowns. And that's just to start."

"Three ball gowns?" Elisha's voice rose an octave. "Your Grace, surely that's excessive—"

"Ow!" she yelped as a pin found its mark.

"Oh, do stand still, dear," the duchess chided gently, though her eyes twinkled with amusement. "Beauty requires patience, as they say."

"I'm beginning to think it requires more courage than patience," Elisha muttered, earning a poorly concealed giggle from one of the younger seamstresses.

"Arms up, miss," instructed the head seamstress, a formidable woman who wielded pins like weapons and measured Elisha with the precision of a military strategist.

As they worked, the Lancaster siblings filtered in and out of the room like a parade of helpful chaos. Edmund offered color commentary on various fabric choices ("The burgundy makes you look consumptive, Miss von Linde") while Edwin contributed by reading aloud from a gothic novel in dramatically inappropriate voices. Essie provided practical advice about which styles were most comfortable for dancing, and Eva offered increasingly creative suggestions for hiding weapons in formal wear.

"Eva," the duchess said sharply as her youngest daughter demonstrated how a fan could double as a defensive weapon, "we are dressing a lady for Society events, not equipping her for a siege."

"One never knows when such skills might prove useful," Eva replied with suspicious innocence. "Besides, Elisha should be prepared for anything, especially with Edgar gallivanting about the countryside indefinitely."

The comment hung in the air with uncomfortable weight. Elisha caught the duchess' sharp glance at Eva, who suddenly became very interested in examining a bolt of green silk.

"Edgar's absence is temporary," the duchess said firmly,

though something in her tone suggested she was trying to convince herself as much as Elisha. "These... tenant issues can be remarkably complex."

"What sort of tenant issues require such secrecy?" Edwin asked with the blunt curiosity of a young man. "And why couldn't Edgar simply send his land agent to handle matters?"

"Edwin," Edmund warned quietly, but their brother pressed on.

"It's been nearly a month, Mother. That's hardly a typical estate matter."

The room fell uncomfortably silent except for the soft whisper of fabric and the careful snip of scissors. Elisha felt her heart sink further as the implication became clear—Edgar's family was as puzzled by his extended absence as she was.

"Perhaps," she said carefully, "His Grace has simply found it necessary to be... thorough."

"Thoroughly absent," Eva muttered, earning another sharp look from her mother.

"Eva, that's quite enough," the duchess said with finality. "Edgar's affairs are his own to manage, and we must trust his judgment."

But as the evening wore on and Elisha submitted to endless fittings, measurements, and fabric selections, she couldn't shake the growing certainty that something was terribly wrong. Edgar wouldn't simply disappear without explanation.

Unless, perhaps, he had secrets that had finally caught up with him.

THE NEXT MORNING brought crisp autumn air and the bustle of departure preparations. Elisha stood in the entrance hall of Lancaster Hall, feeling rather like a fraud, as she stood surrounded by an almost ridiculous number of boxes containing carefully selected gowns from the duchess' and Essie's own collections which were altered overnight to fit her smaller frame.

The duchess approached with a folded paper in her hands, her expression mixing maternal warmth with something that looked suspiciously like determination.

"Your schedule for the remainder of the Season," she announced, pressing the paper into Elisha's hands. "And before you protest, remember that when Edgar returns, you'll need to be established in Society as his proper fiancée."

Elisha unfolded the note and felt her mouth fall open. Invitations to Almack's Assembly Rooms—the holy grail of social acceptance—sat alongside requests for private viewings at the Royal Academy of Arts, the Thames Regatta at Henley, and at least a dozen other events that would have been impossibly beyond her reach mere months ago.

"Your Grace, this is… overwhelming," she managed.

"It's necessary," the duchess replied firmly. "And you won't be facing these events alone. Essie and Eva will accompany you to the appropriate gatherings, and I'll be there for the more formal occasions."

"But Edgar—"

"Will return to find you thoroughly established as the most sought-after young woman in London," the duchess finished with conviction that seemed to convince everyone but herself.

As the carriage rolled toward London, Elisha stared out the window at the countryside and tried to silence the growing whisper of doubt in her mind. Edgar's absence might be perfectly innocent—urgent business that required discretion and time. But combined with Thornton's recent strange behavior, the upcoming literary contest, and her own involvement with the Pioneers, she couldn't escape the feeling that forces were gathering beyond her understanding.

The hollow ache in her chest, which had started as simple longing for Edgar's presence, was slowly transforming into something much more troubling: the fear that when Edgar finally returned—if he returned—everything between them might have changed irrevocably.

She touched the emerald ring on her finger, Edgar's promise made tangible, and tried to hold onto the memory of his voice declaring his love. Whatever was keeping him away, whatever dangers he might be facing, she would be ready. The duchess had armed her with more than just gowns and social invitations— she'd given her weapons for surviving the treacherous waters of high Society.

And if Edgar needed saving from whatever shadows had claimed him, Elisha von Linde—soon to be revealed as the infamous Miss Lovelace—would be prepared for that battle too.

The Season ahead promised to be a test of everything she'd learned about courage, deception, and the price of love. She only hoped that when the final curtain fell, Edgar would still be there to share whatever victory or defeat awaited them both.

THE CONTEST REVEAL

T HE *METROPOLITAN REVIEW* building hummed with excitement on this most auspicious New Year's Eve, its normally staid offices transformed into something resembling a literary salon crossed with a theatrical venue. In the front rows, aristocrats in silk and jewels sat beside working men in their Sunday best, shop clerks who had saved to attend this literary event, and servants who had been granted the evening off. The *Metropolitan Review's* celebration had drawn from all levels of society, and now they were all witnessing this unprecedented moment together.

Elisha stood near the makeshift stage, her hands trembling slightly as she smoothed the sapphire blue silk of her gown—one of the duchess' many contributions to her wardrobe over the past three months.

Three months. The number echoed in her mind like a funeral bell. Three months since Edgar had vanished on his mysterious "urgent business," leaving behind only scattered, formal letters that read more like reports from a distant acquaintance than correspondence from her beloved fiancé.

The cream of London's literary Society had gathered for this momentous occasion, their anticipation crackling through the air like electricity before a storm. Elisha's eyes swept the assembled crowd for what felt like the hundredth time, searching desperately for Edgar's familiar tall frame among the sea of silk and satin. Her heart performed its now-familiar dance of hope and disappointment when she confirmed, once again, that he was nowhere to be seen.

"Miss von Linde," a warm voice interrupted her melancholy survey. She turned to find Charlotte Brontë approaching, her eyes bright with interest. "How exciting this must be for you. I confess, I'm quite envious of the clever mind behind Miss Lovelace's sharp wit."

Elisha managed a smile, though it felt brittle on her lips. "You're very kind, Miss Brontë. Though I fear tonight may prove that wit alone isn't sufficient for victory."

"Nonsense," came another voice as Elizabeth Barrett Browning joined them, supported by her husband Robert. "I've read every piece Miss Lovelace has published. The woman has a gift for combining passion with precision that rivals any writer in London."

If only they knew they were speaking to Miss Lovelace herself. The irony would have amused Elisha more if her stomach weren't tied in knots of anxiety—not just about the contest results, but about Edgar's continued absence and what it might mean.

Near the front of the assembly, the Duchess of Lancaster sat with regal grace, flanked by her children. Edgar's siblings had become Elisha's lifeline during these lonely months, their warm friendship a reminder that she wasn't entirely alone in the world. Essie caught her eye and offered an encouraging smile while Eva made a subtle gesture that looked suspiciously like she was miming throttling someone—presumably Mr. Steele, should he prove victorious.

The sight of Edgar's empty chair beside his family sent another pang through Elisha's chest. Even for this momentous occasion, he couldn't be bothered to appear. What urgent business could possibly be keeping him away from this?

Steven Thornton moved through the crowd with practiced ease, playing the perfect host while his eyes held an intensity that made Elisha's skin crawl. He'd been different these past months—

more pointed in his comments about Edgar, but his charm was more forced and strangely distant. He behaved as if he was awaiting a judgment of sort, perhaps even the Grim Reaper.

"Miss von Linde," Thornton appeared at her elbow as if summoned by her thoughts, his voice pitched low and intimate. "You look radiant this evening. Though I confess, I detect a touch of melancholy."

"I'm perfectly well, Mr. Thornton," Elisha replied, stepping back slightly to put distance between them. "Simply nervous about the evening's proceedings."

"Ah, yes, the great revelation," he said with a smile that didn't reach his eyes. "I do hope Mr. Steele has the courtesy to appear for his moment of triumph or defeat," Thornton said, not exactly meeting her gaze. "It would be rather disappointing if our mysterious author proved too... unreliable to face the consequences of his literary challenge."

The subtle barb could have been directed at anyone, but something in his tone made Elisha bristle on behalf of the absent author. "I'm certain Mr. Steele will conduct himself with proper dignity, whatever the outcome."

"Of course," Thornton murmured.

Before he could say anything else, Amelia appeared with perfect timing. Her dearest friend had an uncanny ability to rescue her from her brother's increasingly uncomfortable attentions.

"Elisha, there you are! The duchess specifically requested we sit with her during the announcement."

Grateful for the rescue, Elisha allowed herself to be guided toward the front rows, though she couldn't shake the feeling of Thornton's eyes following her progress.

"Are you quite all right?" Amelia whispered as they took their seats. "You look rather pale."

"Just nerves," Elisha lied, though the truth was far more complicated. Tonight would bring at least some answers—even if they weren't the ones she most desperately wanted.

As the clock struck the quarter hour, a hush fell over the assembled crowd. Thornton ascended the stage with measured steps, his bearing composed and theatrical. He surveyed the expectant faces before him, a slight smile playing at the corners of his mouth.

"Distinguished guests," he began, his voice carrying clearly, "we are gathered here on this auspicious evening to witness the culmination of a most extraordinary literary duel. The feud between Mr. Steele and Miss Lovelace has captivated our fair city for many months, their verbal sparring a source of great entertainment and intellectual stimulation."

Elisha felt her heart hammering against her ribs as all eyes in the room seemed to turn toward her.

"As you are all aware," Thornton continued, "both parties agreed to pen a romantic novel, published this past October. It is my great pleasure to announce the titles of these works. Mr. Steele's offering is entitled *My Heart's True North* while Miss Lovelace has presented us with *The Duke's Folly*."

A murmur of interest rippled through the crowd. Elisha's throat went dry as she waited for the summaries that would lay bare the contents of both novels.

"*My Heart's True North*," Thornton announced, "tells the tale of a shipping merchant's son who discovers his life's passion in a brilliant young woman working as a governess. Through her expertise in astronomy and mathematics, she opens his eyes to new ways of viewing both the stars above and the Society around them. Yet when her revolutionary theories about celestial navigation promise to transform the shipping industry—his family's livelihood—he must choose between protecting his inheritance and supporting the woman who has charted a new course for his heart."

Elisha found herself genuinely intrigued by the story. Mr. Steele had crafted something that sounded both romantic and intellectually compelling.

Thornton's gaze swept the crowd before he continued. "*The*

Duke's Folly presents a compelling narrative of love, pride, and regret. It chronicles the tale of a duke who, pressured by societal expectations, forsakes his true love—a woman of common birth—and announces his betrothal to a more 'suitable' match. Only after months of increasing misery does he realize his grave error and break his engagement. However, when he returns to claim his true love, he finds she has already promised herself to another—a man who recognized her worth from the start. The story explores the price of pride, the weight of duty, and the bittersweet reality that sometimes love's timing can be as crucial as love itself."

A hushed silence fell over the room as both summaries concluded. Around her, Elisha heard polite murmurs of interest, though she doubted anyone could see the deeper significance in her story.

"Both sound thoroughly engaging," murmured Lady Pemberton to her companion.

"Indeed," came the reply. "Such imagination these authors possess."

"But before we announce our victor," Thornton said, his voice cutting through the murmurs, "we have another prize to award. The recipient of our literacy contest—a prize of five hundred pounds sterling for demonstrating the greatest understanding of both novels—is…" He paused dramatically, clearly savoring the moment. "Master Jonathan Rochford!"

The crowd turned as one to see not the expected scion of nobility, but a thin boy of perhaps sixteen years. His clothes were clean but threadbare, his shock of unruly hair and wide eyes speaking of poverty and hope in equal measure. He made his way to the stage with hesitant steps, clearly overwhelmed by the attention.

"Congratulations, Master Rochford," Thornton said warmly as the boy accepted his prize envelope with trembling hands. "Your answers to our questions about the novels were truly exceptional. Pray tell, how did you prepare for this contest?"

Jonathan's voice shook as he replied, "If it please you, sir, I… I couldn't afford the books. But I listened to the actors reading them aloud in Hyde Park every day. I memorized as much as I could, sir."

Elisha felt tears spring to her eyes at the boy's simple dignity and obvious intelligence. Around her, the assembled crowd had fallen silent, struck by the stark reminder that literature, and perhaps literacy, were not a privilege enjoyed by all.

"Your dedication is truly commendable, young man," Thornton said, and his emotion seemed genuine. With sudden decisiveness, he offered the two handsomely bound volumes in his hands to the boy. "In addition to your well-earned prize money, I should like you to have these—the very novels you studied so diligently. May they be the first of many in what I hope will be a lifelong love of literature."

As Jonathan's eyes filled with gratitude, scattered applause began. It swelled quickly, filling the hall with thunderous approval. Elisha found herself clapping enthusiastically, moved by both the boy's determination and Thornton's unexpected kindness. Thornton then said something to Jonathan Rochford, and the boy bowed repeatedly to him before he left the stage.

When the applause finally died down, Thornton cleared his throat and withdrew a ledger from his coat pocket. "And now, esteemed guests, we come to the moment you have all been waiting for. The revelation of the winner of this unprecedented literary wager."

Elisha's mouth went dry. In mere moments, she would learn whether Miss Lovelace or Mr. Steele had emerged victorious. She looked around the audience, wondering if Mr. Steele was among them, but was quickly distracted by Thornton's voice.

"I shall now reveal the monthly sales figures for both works," Thornton announced, adjusting his spectacles with theatrical precision. "Commencing from their publication in October."

The room fell silent save for the rustle of silk and the distant sounds of New Year's revelry from the streets beyond.

"For the month of October: *My Heart's True North* by Mr. Steele sold 2,332 copies, while *The Duke's Folly* by Miss Lovelace sold 2,592 copies."

A murmur rippled through the crowd. Elisha felt a flutter of hope despite her anxiety. She was ahead, if only slightly.

"In November," Thornton continued with deliberate pacing, "Mr. Steele achieved 3,405 copies sold, while Miss Lovelace reached 3,234."

Gasps and whispers filled the air as the lead changed hands. The numbers were remarkably close—closer than anyone could have predicted.

"And finally, in December—Mr. Steele sold 4,234 copies while Miss Lovelace sold 4,312."

The tension in the room was almost unbearable. Elisha watched as several audience members began calculating frantically, their lips moving silently as they worked out the totals. Her own mind raced through the arithmetic, scarcely daring to hope.

"The final totals, ladies and gentlemen," Thornton announced, his voice ringing with authority, "are as follows: Mr. Steele's *My Heart's True North* has sold a total of 9,971 copies while Miss Lovelace's *The Duke's Folly* has sold… 10,138 copies."

For a heartbeat, silence reigned. Then the room erupted in a cacophony of gasps, exclamations, and applause. Elisha felt the world tilt around her as the reality sank in—she had won. Miss Lovelace had defeated Mr. Steele by the narrowest of margins.

"Therefore," Thornton's voice rose above the growing tumult, "by a margin of merely one hundred and sixty-seven copies—the victor of this unprecedented literary duel is Miss Lovelace!"

The applause was thunderous, but Elisha barely heard it over the roaring in her ears. She had won—but Edgar wasn't here to see it. Neither was Mr. Steele as far as she was aware. After months of anticipation, after all their literary sparring and passionate exchanges of letters, he was absent for the moment of truth.

"Ladies and gentlemen," Thornton called out, gesturing toward where she sat frozen in disbelief, "may I present our victor, the incomparable Miss Lovelace!"

The moment had come. Three months of maintaining her secret identity, three months of social climbing and careful performance, had led to this instant. As the crowd's attention focused on her with laser intensity, Elisha rose from her seat on trembling legs.

Then chaos erupted. Gasps of astonishment mingled with exclamations of "Miss von Linde!" and "Can it be?" Some faces showed delighted surprise, others shock, and a few—those who had been privy to the duchess' careful campaign—wore knowing smiles of satisfaction.

Elisha ascended the stage with as much dignity as she could muster, her cheeks burning under the scrutiny of London's literary establishment. This was her moment of triumph, the vindication of everything she had worked for.

As she reached Thornton's side on the stage, he leaned slightly toward her, his voice pitched for her ears alone.

"My heartiest congratulations," he murmured, maintaining proper distance. "I had always been certain of your triumph."

"Thank you, Mr. Thornton," she replied, acutely aware of the hundreds of eyes upon them. "I'm grateful for your support."

As they turned to face the assembled crowd, Elisha felt the weight of hundreds of eyes upon her. The thunderous applause seemed to fade into the background as her gaze swept the room, still desperately hoping against hope that Edgar might have arrived at the last moment to witness her triumph.

And then, in the far corner of the chamber, she saw a familiar figure.

Edgar stood half-hidden in shadow, his tall frame unmistakable despite his altered appearance. His dark hair was longer than she remembered, and he was dressed in the simple clothes of a working man rather than his usual aristocratic finery. Their eyes met across the crowded room, and she saw him offer her a warm, proud smile.

He was here. He had come to see her moment of victory.

Relief flooded through her so powerfully that she felt her knees weaken. Whatever urgent business had kept him away for three months, he had managed to return for this moment. The hollow ache in her chest began to ease for the first time in months.

But something in Thornton's sudden stillness beside her made her glance at him. His face had gone pale, his eyes fixed on Edgar's location with what looked like shock and something approaching panic. His composed demeanor cracked for just an instant before he recovered himself.

"Mr. Thornton?" she whispered. "Are you quite well?"

"Perfectly," he replied, though his voice sounded strained. "Simply… surprised by an unexpected guest."

Why would Edgar's presence surprise Thornton so much? And why did the man look almost… frightened?

The questions sent a chill down her spine, but before she could analyze them further, the crowd's continued applause demanded her attention. Whatever was happening between Edgar and Thornton, she sensed it was far more significant than a simple social awkwardness.

THE TRUTH

THE APPLAUSE GRADUALLY subsided as the assembled crowd settled into expectant silence, waiting to see what would happen next. Elisha remained on the stage beside Thornton, her heart still racing from the joy of seeing Edgar after three long months of absence. Whatever had kept him away, at least he was safe and had returned to her. To his family.

But Thornton's continued pallor and the rigid set of his shoulders suggested something was terribly wrong. His eyes remained fixed on Edgar's corner of the room with an intensity that made Elisha's skin crawl.

"Ladies and gentlemen," Thornton began, his voice carrying clearly despite a slight tremor that only someone standing close could detect, "before we conclude this evening's festivities, I believe there is one more revelation that London's literary society deserves to witness."

A murmur of curiosity rippled through the crowd. Elisha turned to look at him, confusion evident on her face. This wasn't part of the program they had discussed.

"Mr. Thornton?" she whispered, but he held up a hand to forestall her question.

"You see," Thornton continued, his composure returning as he seemed to draw strength from some internal resolve, "we have spent these many months entertained by the rivalry between Miss Lovelace and the mysterious Mr. Steele. Their exchanges of wit, their verbal sparring, their passionate defenses of opposing viewpoints—all of it has captivated our fair city."

Elisha felt a growing sense of unease. Something in Thornton's tone suggested this was building toward something she wasn't prepared for.

"But I believe," Thornton said, his voice rising with theatrical authority, "that the time for mystery has passed. Ladies and gentlemen, I give you the man behind the nom de plume that has so enthralled London's literary circles—Mr. Steele is none other than His Grace, the Duke of Lancaster!" Thornton dramatically pointed to Edgar who remained standing, motionless.

The words rang out across the stunned assembly, but instead of the gasps of recognition Thornton clearly expected, a murmur of confusion rippled through the crowd. Heads turned toward Edgar's corner, where several people squinted in the dim light, trying to make out his features beneath the long hair and working man's clothes.

"I beg your pardon, Mr. Thornton," called out Lord Whitworth from the front row, "but that gentleman hardly resembles the Duke of Lancaster. Are you quite certain of this identification?"

"Indeed," added Lady Worthington, raising her lorgnette to peer more closely. "The hair, the attire... surely you are mistaken?"

Thornton's confident smile faltered slightly. "I assure you, that is indeed His Grace. Perhaps if he would join us on the stage, the resemblance will become clearer."

"Come forward, Your Grace!" Thornton called out, though his voice now carried a note of uncertainty. "Surely you won't let doubt linger about your identity?"

The crowd's attention focused on the corner where Edgar stood, though many still looked skeptical. Murmurs of "Could it be?" and "Impossible!" drifted through the room as Edgar began making his way through the assembly.

As Edgar reached the stage and ascended to the platform,

Thornton seemed to regain his confidence.

"Your Grace," Thornton said with forced joviality, "I trust you're not too disappointed by your narrow loss to the incomparable Miss Lovelace? A mere hundred and sixty-seven copies—so close to victory!"

Edgar turned to face the assembled crowd, and when he spoke, his cultured, aristocratic voice rang out clearly across the silent room. "I congratulate Miss Lovelace on her well-deserved victory. Her talent has always been extraordinary."

The effect was immediate and electric. The crowd erupted in gasps of recognition as Edgar's unmistakable voice confirmed his identity. Ladies grabbed their fans, gentlemen straightened in their chairs, and a buzz of shocked conversation filled the air.

"Good heavens, it truly is the duke!" exclaimed Lady Binbrook.

"The Duke of Lancaster, writing novels under a pseudonym!" whispered Lord Holland to his companion. "What is the world coming to?"

The words finally struck Elisha like thunder as the crowd's recognition confirmed what she could barely comprehend. Mr. Steele—her literary rival, her intellectual equal, the man whose letters had challenged and inspired her for months—was Edgar.

Edgar. Her beloved Edgar had been deceiving her all along.

Pieces began falling into place with horrible clarity. How Mr. Steele's confessions of heartbreak corresponded with her own heartache, the timing of Steele's letters that matched Edgar's presence in her life.

How could he have let her pour her heart out in letters to him while maintaining such an elaborate deception? How many times had she confided her feelings about Edgar to Mr. Steele, not knowing they were the same person?

Thornton seemed to relish the shock rippling through the assembly before continuing with renewed confidence. "But I'm afraid circumstances have changed somewhat, Your Grace. You see, your literary endeavors have proven to be merely the tip of a much larger iceberg."

Edgar's expression grew guarded, but he said nothing.

"Ladies and gentlemen," Thornton addressed the crowd, "the Duke of Lancaster is a man of many talents and many secrets. But perhaps his most interesting secret is his involvement with certain… reform movements that some might consider rather seditious in nature."

The room fell silent as the implications of this accusation sank in. Elisha felt her heart stop beating as she realized what was happening. This wasn't just about literary deception—Thornton was about to expose everything.

"Mr. Thornton," Edgar's voice carried a warning note that would have made lesser men step back.

But Thornton seemed energized by the danger, his eyes bright with malicious triumph. "You see, His Grace has been using his considerable wealth and influence to support radical causes, to undermine the very social order that elevated him to his position."

Gasps and murmurs of shock rippled through the audience. Several lords near the front looked scandalized, while others seemed confused by this sudden turn from literary entertainment to political accusation.

"These are serious allegations," Edgar said, his voice deadly quiet. "I hope you have evidence to support such claims."

"Oh, I have evidence," Thornton replied, clearly savoring his moment of power. "But more than that, I have witnesses. After all, Miss Lovelace here has been working alongside you, hasn't she?"

Elisha felt the world tilt around her as every eye in the room turned to her. The secret she had guarded so carefully, the work that could see her imprisoned or worse, was being laid bare before London's most influential people.

"That's enough," Edgar said sharply, stepping protectively in front of Elisha. "Miss von Linde has no involvement in any political activities. Your quarrel is with me alone."

"How gallant," Thornton sneered. "But I'm afraid the evidence suggests otherwise. Who do you think has been writing those detailed exposés of working conditions?"

The accusation hung in the air like poison. Elisha felt paralyzed by shock and fear, unable to speak or move as her carefully constructed world crumbled around her.

Then, from somewhere in the crowd, a clear voice rang out: "If you mean to prosecute His Grace or Miss Linde for his commitment to reform, then you must be prepared to do so against me as well."

Charles Dickens stepped forward, his face set with determination. "For I, too, have penned such works. I, too, have used my pen to shine light on injustice and suffering."

Before the crowd could fully process this declaration, William Wordsworth rose from his seat. "And I, gentlemen. My hand has crafted many a reform pamphlet."

One by one, prominent authors began standing throughout the room. Elizabeth Barrett Browning and her husband Robert, declared, "We both stand guilty of such charges, if charges they be."

Charlotte Brontë's quiet voice carried clearly: "As do I."

Alfred, Lord Tennyson joined them, his beard quivering with emotion. "Count me among their number."

Within moments, the most celebrated literary minds in England were rising from their seats and making their way toward the stage. The sight was extraordinary—authors who had shaped the very soul of English literature, standing together in defiance of those who would silence them.

Elisha felt tears spring to her eyes as she watched these giants of literature risk everything for Edgar—and for her. And for what is right. The courage and solidarity of their gesture moved her beyond words.

Dickens stepped forward to address the crowd, his voice carrying the moral authority that had made him the conscience of a generation. "If you wish to bring charges against His Grace for his commitment to justice, then you must be prepared to charge us all. For we are united in our belief that literature has the power to illuminate truth and inspire change."

Charlotte Brontë's quiet voice added, "We stand together not as rebels, but as witnesses to truth. If that makes us criminals, then let history judge who truly served justice."

The room erupted into chaos, but this time, for a different reason. The focus was no longer on the scandal but the solidarity. Voices rose in defense rather than condemnation.

"Shame on those who would silence our greatest minds!" called out someone from the back.

"These authors have brought honor to England!" shouted another.

As Elisha watched the literary community rally around them, she felt a profound sense of gratitude and humility. Whatever anger she felt toward Edgar's deception paled beside the magnitude of their sacrifice.

THE PROPOSAL

THE ROOM STILL buzzed with heated discussions between supporters and critics of the assembled authors when Edgar stepped forward from the group of literary giants surrounding him. The sight of him moving toward the front of the stage made conversations falter and heads turn. Even in his working man's clothes, his bearing commanded attention.

Elisha watched him approach with her heart hammering against her ribs. The man she loved—the man who had deceived her for months—was about to speak, and she had no idea what words could possibly bridge the chasm that had opened between them.

Edgar's eyes found hers across the few feet that separated them, and in them she saw a vulnerability she had never witnessed before. Not the confident duke, not the mysterious Mr. Steele, but simply a man who may lose everything.

Around them, the crowd had fallen completely silent, sensing they were about to witness something unprecedented.

"Miss von Linde," Edgar said, taking a step closer to her. "I stand before you not as the Duke of Lancaster, not as Mr. Steele, but as Edgar—simply Edgar—a man who has made grievous errors and wishes to make amends."

The formality of his address wasn't lost on her. He was acknowledging that he had forfeited the right to intimacy, that he was starting from the beginning.

Tears began to gather in Elisha's eyes despite her efforts to maintain composure.

His voice grew rough with emotion. "My greatest sin was perhaps not the deception itself, but the arrogance that led me to believe I had the right to make such choices for you. You deserved the truth, deserved the chance to decide for yourself whether a man capable of such duplicity was worthy of your affection."

Elisha's tears were flowing freely now, though she couldn't tell if they were born of heartbreak or hope.

Edgar slowly lowered himself to one knee in front of her, and gasps rippled through the assembled crowd. The sight was extraordinary—a duke kneeling before anyone in public was shocking enough, but the mixed assembly made it even more remarkable.

"Your Grace," someone whispered, "surely this is highly irregular!"

But others—particularly the working-class attendees who understood the value of love over station—called out encouragement. "Good on you, sir!" shouted a voice from the back.

"Elisha," he said, and the use of her given name felt like a caress after the formal distance of moments before. "When I first put pen to paper, it was to ease the suffering of a heart torn asunder by loss. With each letter we exchanged, each verbal sparring match, I felt the ice around my heart begin to thaw. As Miss Lovelace and yourself, you challenged me, inspired me, and ultimately, made me believe in the possibility of love once more. You taught me that true nobility lies not in birth, but in character."

His voice softened, becoming almost reverent. "With you, I am not just a better man. I am whole. I stand before you now, stripped of all pretenses, offering you my heart, my soul, my very being. For in loving you, I have found my true self. And if you'll have me, I vow to spend every day of my life striving to be worthy of the love you've awakened in me."

The silence in the room was absolute. Even the sounds from the street beyond seemed muted as London's elite and common folk alike held their collective breath.

Elisha stared down at him, her mind reeling. Everything she had believed about their relationship had been built on lies, yet the man kneeling before her was offering something she had never expected: complete honesty, vulnerability, and a chance to begin again.

From the corner of her eye, she caught sight of Steven Thornton. He stood frozen at the edge of the stage, his face a canvas of conflicting emotions. The rage and desperation that had driven him to expose Edgar's secrets had transformed into something else entirely. As he watched Edgar's vulnerable declaration, watched the raw honesty passing between the two people he had tried to tear apart, understanding seemed to dawn in his eyes.

His shoulders sagged slightly, the fight draining out of him as he witnessed something he had never truly comprehended before.

Thornton's hands, which had been clenched into fists, slowly uncurled. His face, which had been twisted with bitter triumph only moments before, softened with what looked remarkably like resignation—and perhaps, grudging respect.

In the distance, the sounds of the New Year's celebration continued, oblivious to the drama unfolding within these walls. Soon, midnight would strike and a new year would begin.

Elisha's eyes filled with tears as she looked down at Edgar—truly looked at him for the first time without the veils of deception between them.

This was all too much to comprehend. She needed more time.

Without a word, she stepped back from Edgar's kneeling form. The crowd murmured in confusion as she turned away, and to her eternal gratitude, Amelia appeared at her side.

"Come," her dearest friend whispered, taking Elisha's arm

with gentle firmness. "Let's get you away from here."

Elisha allowed herself to be guided toward the side exit, her mind spinning with Edgar's words and the impossible choice that lay before her. Behind them, Edgar remained on one knee, staring after the woman he loved disappear into the night without giving him an answer.

In the distance, church bells began to chime, marking the arrival of a new year.

BETWEEN HOPE AND DESPAIR

THE MORNING LIGHT filtered weakly through the heavy curtains of Edgar's London townhouse as Hawkins moved about the master's bedchamber with his usual quiet efficiency. Three days had passed since New Year's Eve—three days since Edgar had knelt before half of London's literary society only to watch the woman he loved walk away without a word.

Edgar sat motionless in the chair before his dressing table, staring at his reflection with something approaching horror. His hair hung past his collar in unkempt waves, while his beard had grown wild and unruly during his months of exile. He looked like a man who had wrestled with demons and lost.

"Well," Hawkins observed dryly as he laid out his implements with surgical precision, "I see the romantic poet aesthetic has reached its natural conclusion. Shall I assume Your Grace wishes to maintain this... Robinson Crusoe appearance for your morning constitutional?"

Edgar's laugh was hollow. "Does it matter? She's probably already decided I'm beyond redemption."

"Undoubtedly," Hawkins agreed with cheerful brutality, running his fingers through Edgar's tangled locks. "Though one might argue that looking like a vagrant could work in your favor. Nothing says 'tortured by love' quite like appearing as though you've been living in a cave."

"Your sympathy is overwhelming," Edgar muttered.

Hawkins began working a comb through the worst of the tangles, his movements gentle despite his sharp tongue. "Might I inquire what has been occupying Your Grace's time these past three months, if not basic grooming?"

Edgar winced as the comb hit a particularly stubborn knot. "I've been… thinking."

"Ah, thinking," Hawkins repeated with mock enlightenment. "How very productive. And did this extensive contemplation yield any insights?"

"I needed time to process everything," Edgar said defensively. "The deception, Thornton's accusations…"

"Quite right," Hawkins agreed, continuing his work patiently. "Nothing says 'I am engaging in important reflection' quite like neglecting one's toilet."

Edgar sat blankly while Hawkins worked his magic.

"They saved us both," Edgar said quietly, watching hair fall to the floor around his chair. "I still can't believe Dickens stood up like that. And Charlotte Brontë—she barely knows me or Elisha, yet she was willing to risk everything."

"Writers," Hawkins observed with philosophical detachment, "are peculiar creatures. They spend their lives crafting stories of justice triumphing over villainy. When presented with a real-life opportunity to play the hero, they can hardly resist the temptation."

Edgar felt some of the tension in his shoulders ease as Hawkins worked. "Thornton looked… broken at the end. Almost pitiful."

"Yes, well, there's nothing quite like watching one's carefully laid plans crumble in spectacular fashion to deflate the ego." Hawkins moved to examine Edgar's wild beard with professional assessment. "In front of London's literary elite, no less. It's almost as if he wanted to fail dramatically."

"I think he was past caring about strategy," Edgar said, remembering the desperation in Thornton's eyes. "He was a man with nothing left to lose."

"Unlike yourself, of course," Hawkins noted, beginning to trim the beard with careful precision, "who merely risks losing the love of his life, his reputation, and quite possibly his life."

Edgar met his valet's eyes in the mirror. "She walked away, Hawkins. Without a word. I knelt before half of London and laid my heart bare, and she just… left."

Hawkins paused in his trimming, his expression softening almost imperceptibly. "Your Grace, if I may venture an observation? The lady in question has spent months believing herself in love with two different men, only to discover they were the same person. I imagine the poor woman feels rather like Viola in Twelfth Night—caught in a web of mistaken identities not of her own making."

"You think she might forgive me?" Edgar's voice carried a hope he was afraid to acknowledge.

"I think," Hawkins said carefully, returning to his work, "that a woman of Miss Linde's caliber is not likely to abandon such a connection over wounded pride."

Edgar felt his heart lift slightly for the first time in days. "So you believe she'll give me another chance?"

"I believe," Hawkins replied with a slight smile, "that she's probably sitting in her office at this very moment, wondering if you're brave enough to come to her. The question is: Are you?"

As Hawkins put the finishing touches on Edgar's transformation, Edgar studied his reflection. He looked like himself again—polished but not overly formal, respectable but approachable.

"There," Hawkins announced with satisfaction. "No longer resembling a castaway, though I've maintained just enough dishevelment to suggest sleepless nights and tormented passion. One must strike the proper balance between respectability and romantic suffering."

Edgar rose from the chair, feeling lighter than he had since New Year's Eve.

Hawkins began tidying his implements with meticulous care

while talking almost to himself. "If the lady rejects Your Grace after everything you've been through together, I shall personally pack your bags for an extended tour of the Continent. Sometimes strategic retreat is the only option left to a gentleman."

Edgar paused at the door to his dressing room. "And if she forgives me?"

A genuine smile crossed Hawkins' weathered features. "Then I shall begin preparing for a wedding, Your Grace. Though I do hope you'll give me adequate notice—orchestrating a ducal wedding requires significantly more effort than trimming an overgrown beard."

As Edgar allowed Hawkins to complete his transformation as a duke, he felt something he hadn't experienced in months: hope. Whether Elisha would accept his apology, whether she could forgive his deceptions, remained to be seen. But for the first time since New Year's Eve, he believed it might be possible.

An hour later, the morning sun was crisp and bright over London's rooftops when Edgar presented himself at the *Metropolitan Review*, his appearance once again befitting a duke in love.

As he approached the imposing building, he noticed a slim figure huddled near the entrance. He recognized young Jonathan from the literacy contest, his clothes showing signs of a night spent outdoors. The boy's eyes widened in recognition.

"Your Grace," Jonathan whispered, ducking his head in deference.

Edgar paused, studying the young man's worn appearance. "You're the book wizard from the contest, are you not? What brings you here at such an early hour?"

"Mr. Thornton offered me a job at the gazette but didn't specify when he expected me."

After a brief exchange about Mr. Thornton's promise and Jonathan's daily vigil since, Edgar's heart softened. "Come, let us make our inquiries together."

Taking a deep breath, he raised the brass knocker and announced their arrival. The young man's wide-eyed anticipation seemed to equal his own.

"Your Grace! What a pleasant surprise!" Amelia said with a bright smile. "And I remember you. You are Jonathan, the famous book wizard."

Jonathan smiled shyly at the compliment, shifting from right foot to left.

As Amelia Thornton ushered them into the office she shared with Elisha, Edgar's eyes took in every detail of the room. He developed a new appreciation for the small space, though he'd seen it before, likely because he wasn't certain if he'd see it ever again after today. The office bore the unmistakable touches of care and refinement. He noted the simple paintings of vases of wildflowers, their simple beauty an indication of the inhabitants' sensibilities.

Settling onto the worn settee, Edgar felt an unfamiliar flutter of nervousness in his chest. He had faced down lords and ladies in the most intimidating of social situations, yet here, in this unpretentious setting, he found himself battling thousands of butterflies in his gut. Jonathan mirrored his own apprehension, remaining standing while shifting his weight.

When Elisha entered the room, Edgar's breath caught in his throat. Her simple day dress and hastily pinned up hair only served to enhance her natural beauty in his eyes. He rose to his feet, summoning every ounce of his ducal composure.

"Miss von Linde," he began, allowing a hint of playfulness to color his tone, "I come to report for duty as your personal assistant, as per the terms of our wager. I am a man of my word, after all."

Edgar cleared his throat, his eyes moving between Elisha and Jonathan. "I happened upon young Jonathan quite by chance. As I approached the *Metropolitan's* offices, I observed him standing near the entrance."

He turned to Jonathan with a gentle smile. "I recognized him from the literacy contest, of course. Upon inquiry, he shared his daily vigil, awaiting Mr. Thornton's promised opportunity."

Elisha's brow furrowed as she processed this information. "Mr. Thornton hasn't been in since the contest. I am sorry you waited all this time. Why did you not ask someone for help?"

Jonathan looked at Edgar as if to ask for permission to speak. Upon his nod, the boy said, "I asked a man fixing the machine, Miss, but he chased me away."

After a moment of contemplation, Elisha addressed Edgar, her tone businesslike yet tinged with warmth. "Very well, Your Grace. Since you've volunteered your services, I believe we should put them to good use."

She glanced at Jonathan, taking in his filthy appearance with compassion. "Our first order of business shall be to attend to the young man's immediate needs. Your Grace, I task you with assisting Jonathan in refreshing himself. The washroom is just down the hall."

Edgar's eyebrows rose slightly, uncertain how to go about washing away weeks, if not months, of grime using a wash basin, but he nodded in acquiescence.

Elisha continued, "Once he's bathed, I believe some clean attire would be in order. Your Grace, might I impose upon you to procure some suitable clothing? Perhaps from your own wardrobe as I doubt any shops are open at this hour."

The boy began to protest, his eyes wide with the suggestion of donning a duke's shirt.

For a moment, Edgar was taken aback by her instructions. Then he smiled with admiration. "As you wish, Miss von Linde. I shall dispatch a messenger to my residence forthwith."

Turning to Jonathan, he said with warmth, "Come, young man. Let's get you sorted."

THE SOUND OF water splashing and muffled conversation drifted from the washroom as Elisha stood frozen in the center of her office, her hands slowly coming to rest on her hips. For the first time in months, Edgar was here—not as a memory or a longing, but flesh and blood mere steps away. The careful composure she had maintained since his arrival began to crack like ice under spring sun.

A whirlwind of emotions swept through her with startling intensity. Relief flooded her first—he was alive, he was safe, he had returned to her. But close behind came a surge of anger so fierce it took her breath away. Three months. Three months of wondering, worrying, crafting careful letters that revealed nothing of her growing desperation. Three months of his family's pitying glances and carefully neutral responses to her inquiries about his welfare.

He looked well, perhaps a bit thinner, but now cleanly shaven and neatly attired compared to New Year's Eve. She pressed her palms more firmly against her sides, trying to contain the trembling that threatened to betray her inner chaos. How dare he appear so casually, as if nothing had happened?

But beneath the anger lurked something far more dangerous—the treacherous hope that his presence rekindled. The way he had looked at her when she entered the room, the familiar warmth in his voice when he spoke her name, the gentle way he guided young Jonathan—all of it reminded her of why she had fallen in love with him in the first place.

And then there were the secrets. Mr. Steele. Her literary rival, her intellectual equal, the man whose letters had become the highlight of her days, was Edgar. The revelation should have felt like betrayal, and part of it did. But another part—a part she was afraid to examine too closely—felt like the final piece of a puzzle clicking into place. All those moments when Mr. Steele seemed to understand her thoughts, when his letters seemed to mirror her dilemma with Edgar. Of course it had been him. How had she not seen it?

The knowledge left her feeling exposed, vulnerable in a way that made her want to flee. Every confession about Edgar himself, every moment of emotional intimacy—he had witnessed all of it while wearing a mask.

Elisha wrapped her arms around herself, suddenly cold. The careful emotional walls she had built during his absence—the ones that had allowed her to function, to work, to carry on as if her heart hadn't been carved out of her chest—were crumbling with alarming speed. She had told herself she was fine, that she could manage without him, that perhaps his absence was for the best.

How wrong she had been.

The sound of Edgar's laughter from the washroom sent a sharp pang through her chest. She closed her eyes, fighting against the tears that threatened. This was neither the time nor the place for such vulnerability. They were not alone, and she would not give him the satisfaction of seeing how deeply his absence had affected her. Not yet. Not until she understood what game they were playing now.

But as she stood there, listening to the mundane sounds of Edgar helping Jonathan prepare for the day ahead, Elisha realized that all her careful emotional distance had been an illusion. One look from those familiar blue eyes, one sound of his voice speaking her name, and she was as lost as ever.

ONCE THE BOY was dressed in new clothes and smelled like soap, he and Edgar stood in front of Elisha's desk, waiting for further instructions. Elisha looked up from a book she had been pretending to read. "I'd like both of you to inventory our writing supplies. We'll need to ensure we have sufficient stock for the upcoming edition."

"As you wish, Miss von Linde," Edgar said, and Elisha felt her cheeks warm at the sound of his voice. She shook her head, trying to dispel the confusing assortment of emotions his presence evoked.

As the day progressed, Elisha found herself constantly aware of Edgar's presence. She assigned him various tasks—sorting correspondence, organizing files, even fetching tea—all the while stealing glances at him when she thought he wasn't looking. The gentle way he guided Jonathan, the diligence with which he approached his assigned tasks, the occasional warm glance he cast in her direction—all served to deepen her conflicted feelings.

When she learned that Jonathan was literate, she gave the task of transcribing some handwritten notes, noticing with approval how the boy threw himself into the work with earnest dedication.

As evening approached, Elisha felt emotionally drained. The day had been a constant battle between her professional demeanor and her tumultuous inner thoughts. She had opened her heart to 'Mr. Steele,' and now Edgar stood before her, embodying both the man she had considered a confidant and the duke who had swept into her life so unexpectedly.

"I believe that concludes our tasks for today," she announced, her voice betraying a hint of fatigue. "Thank you both for your diligent work. Your Grace, you need not return. I shall consider your debt paid. Jonathan, do you have a place to stay?"

The young man dropped his head. "Yes, Miss."

"Poverty is not a crime nor is it shameful. I would have been on the streets if it wasn't for finding a spot in the workhouse," Elisha said to the boy whose eyes were widening.

"I'll ask again. Do you have a safe and clean place to stay?"

Jonathan shook his head.

Elisha's heart went out to the boy, and without hesitation, she said, "You may stay here, then. There is no bed, but we shall make do with what we have until I can purchase something tomorrow. What do you say?"

Edgar stepped forward gently, his expression kind but firm. "Miss von Linde, your generous heart does you credit, but I must respectfully suggest an alternative." He turned to Jonathan with a warm smile. "Young man, I have a household with many empty rooms going to waste. You would have proper quarters, regular meals, and access to an extensive library. Moreover, I could arrange for tutoring to supplement your obvious intelligence."

Jonathan's eyes darted between Edgar and Elisha, clearly overwhelmed by the sudden abundance of options.

"I understand your desire to help," Edgar continued, addressing Elisha, "but a young man needs structure and guidance that I am better positioned to provide. I can ensure he arrives here each morning for work, should he choose to continue with the *Metropolitan*, or we might explore other opportunities that suit his talents."

Elisha dared not meet Edgar's gaze, fearing the current of emotions it could provoke. Instead, she studied the boy's face for a moment before she nodded slowly. "The choice is yours, young man. You're welcome here, but His Grace offers advantages I cannot match."

Jonathan looked between them both, then spoke with quiet dignity. "Begging your pardon, Miss, but His Grace speaks sense. I'd be grateful for the opportunity, if it means I can still help you here every week."

"Of course," she assured him. "We shall discuss arrangements that provide you with the most comprehensive education."

With a bow in Elisha's direction, Edgar and Jonathan departed, leaving her laden with unspoken emotions and unanswered questions.

Elisha remained in her office long after the building had grown quiet, reviewing manuscripts by lamplight and trying to quiet the tumult in her mind. The revelation of Edgar's dual identity still felt surreal, like stepping into one of the novels she helped publish.

A gentle knock at the street entrance startled her from her thoughts. Frowning, she made her way downstairs, wondering who would call at such a late hour. Opening the door revealed Edgar standing in the lamplight, his breath visible in the cool night air, a bouquet of winter blooms in one hand and a leatherbound book in the other.

"Your Grace," Elisha said, surprise evident in her voice. "What brings you here at this hour?"

Edgar's eyes, usually so confident, now held a hint of uncertainty. "Miss von Linde, I hope I'm not intruding. Might I have a moment of your time? There are things that must be said, and I find I cannot wait until morning."

Elisha hesitated, acutely aware of the impropriety of receiving a gentleman caller alone at such an hour. Yet something in his expression—vulnerable, almost pleading—made her step aside. "Please, come in from the cold."

Instead of leading him to the more intimate setting of her private quarters, Elisha guided him to her office, now shadowy and cold in the absence of fire. She lit several lanterns, their warm glow pushing back the darkness, and positioned her chair facing the settee where she gestured for Edgar to sit.

Without taking the seat, Edgar offered the bouquet with hands that trembled slightly. "These are for you," he said, still holding the carefully arranged assortment of white hellebores, deep red winter roses, and sprigs of holly—a composition both festive and elegant.

"They're beautiful," Elisha murmured, accepting the flowers, careful not to touch his hands. "Though I confess surprise at finding such blooms in winter."

"I may have imposed upon my gardener's considerable skills," Edgar admitted with a ghost of his usual humor. "But beautiful things require effort, particularly in the darkest seasons."

Elisha brought the bouquet closer to her face to avoid his gaze, inhaling their delicate fragrance. Edgar was watching her with an intensity that seemed to burn her skin. Without warning, he reached toward her, but Elisha stepped back sharply.

"Elisha," he breathed, his voice breaking on her name. His face crumpled at her rejection, confusion and anguish warring in his eyes as his hand fell uselessly to his side.

"God, how I've missed you. Every day, every moment—"

"Why?" The word escaped her throat as barely more than a whisper as she clutched the flowers to her chest like armor against the pain that still lived there. "Why did you stay away? All these months without a word, without even a letter. I thought…" She couldn't finish the sentence, couldn't voice the fear that he had simply grown tired of her.

Edgar's throat worked as he struggled to find words. "There were threats," he began, his voice hoarse. "But that's not—that's not what matters. What matters is that I've been dying without you. Every morning, I woke wanting nothing more than to come to you, to explain everything, to hold you again."

She watched him run both hands through his hair, the gesture betraying months of sleepless nights. "Steven Thornton discovered my identity as Mr. Steele. He knew about my involvement with the Pioneers, the funding I'd been providing to their cause. He gave me an ultimatum—end our relationship permanently, never contact you again, or he would expose everything to the authorities."

Elisha felt her eyes widen in shock, her grip instinctively tightening on the book.

"But do you know what tormented me most?" Edgar's voice cracked with emotion. "It wasn't the threat of the gallows. It was the thought that you believed I had chosen to leave you. Every night I lay awake knowing you were suffering, thinking I had abandoned you without cause."

His eyes were bright with unshed tears. "I couldn't risk involving you. If Thornton suspected you knew anything, if he thought you were complicit… But Christ, Elisha, the agony of staying away from you nearly killed me. I wrote you dozens of letters I could never send. I stood outside your building in the rain just to see your shadow in the window."

"You could have told me," she whispered, though even as the words left her lips, she understood the impossible position he had faced.

"I wanted to," he said desperately. "Every fiber of my being screamed to run to you, to confess everything, to beg you to wait for me. But I couldn't risk your safety."

Elisha watched the raw pain play across his features as he continued. "I spent months working to neutralize his threats—gathering evidence of his illegal activities, building a case that would destroy him if he moved against me. But every day without you felt like dying slowly."

Her analytical mind began piecing together the implications, but her heart was focused on the naked anguish in his voice, the way his hands shook as he spoke of missing her.

"I feared by the time I was free to come to you, it would be too late," he whispered. "That you would have moved on, found someone worthy of your love—someone who wouldn't put you through such hell."

Elisha stood in contemplative silence, understanding dawning alongside a complex mix of emotions. The anger she had nursed began to shift, not disappearing but evolving as she saw the sacrifice he had made, the torment he had endured. But her heart still bore deep scars from those silent months.

"I see," she said finally, but she made no move to close the distance between them.

Confusion flickered across Edgar's face as he searched her expression desperately. Then understanding dawned.

"I never intended to deceive you," Edgar said, his voice low and earnest. "What began as a simple response grew into something I could never have anticipated. Our correspondence touched something deep within me, revealing parts of myself I had kept hidden, sharing pieces of my soul I had never shown anyone. And when you began to open your heart to me, our letters became something sacred. I was terrified that if you learned my true identity, I would lose this precious connection we had built, or that the wager would be unfair given my advantage as a duke."

He paused, his gaze meeting hers with a passion that spoke volumes. "The thought that I may have betrayed your trust fills me with shame. I understand completely if you cannot forgive me, but I dare to hope you might give me the chance to earn back your regard."

Elisha stood in contemplative silence, her fingers tracing the soft petal of a rose. When she finally spoke, her voice was soft and trembling. "The letters I wrote to Mr. Steele came from my heart. I thought they were going to a dear friend. To discover the recipient was not who I believed… it feels like betrayal. And yet I cannot find anger in learning that my confidant has been the man I love all along, and that the man I love now stands before me as my dearest friend."

Edgar reached for the nearest wall and leaned against it as if his legs had weakened. They remained silent for a while until he looked up at her motionless form. "Then why do you still pull away? If you're not angry with me and understand why I had to leave—"

"Because understanding doesn't erase the pain," she said, her voice steady but fragile. "And because…" Her breath caught as months of suppressed agony rose to the surface. "When you wrote to me as Mr. Steele about Lucia, when you told me her name was one that 'echoes in the chambers of your heart with each beat'—I knew then that I was reading about a love so profound it had shaped your very soul."

She watched Edgar go very still, recognition and horror dawning in his eyes as he realized the true cause of her pain.

"You want to know why I pull away?" The words came faster now, her composure beginning to crack. "Because you wrote to me about how you would 'fight for Lucia with every fiber of your being' if you could turn back time. You said she was 'loved, cherished, and worthy' in a way that made my heart ache with longing. Then I read *Whispers of the Heart* and saw how she gave you wings, how colors seemed brighter and the air itself more alive because of her love."

Tears began streaming down her cheeks, but she pressed on, her voice growing stronger even as it broke. "When you learned of her death, I felt every moment of your anguish. You wrote that you wanted to follow her into the grave, that food lost all taste, that music became noise, that you stopped truly living. And when you finally chose to breathe again—when you dragged yourself back from that abyss—you swore that part of your soul would always belong to her."

She was sobbing now, months of insecurity pouring out. "How am I supposed to compete with that? I am flawed and mortal and utterly, hopelessly ordinary compared to her memory. How am I supposed to fight for your heart against a love so perfect, so pure, so complete that it survived death?"

Edgar started toward her, but she held up a trembling hand to stop him.

"I am flesh and blood," she continued, her voice raw with pain. "I cannot possibly measure against a ghost."

She wiped at her streaming eyes with the back of her hand, abandoning all pretense of composure. "I love you with everything I am, but I cannot bear to spend my life wondering if I'm enough, if you're settling for second-best because she's beyond your reach. I cannot marry you knowing that when you hold me, you might be wishing I were her."

The words hung in the vast chasm between them. Edgar stared at her in stunned silence, finally understanding the depth of her pain, the true reason for her distance. His own tears began falling freely as he saw what his grief had cost them both.

"Oh, my darling," he whispered, his voice broken. "You don't understand—you couldn't possibly understand what you mean to me."

But Elisha turned away from him, unable to bear the pity she saw in his eyes.

As if he suddenly remembered, Edgar held out the book he'd been carrying—a first edition of *My Heart's True North* by Edmund C. A. "I want you to have this. It's... it's the story I wrote, inspired by you."

Elisha's fingers trembled as she accepted the book, her heart racing. She found comfort in the weight of the volume in her hands.

Edgar's voice grew stronger, more desperate. "I bared my heart for you in *My Heart's True North*. Please, read it. You'll see—you'll understand that what I feel for you… it's not an echo of what I felt for her. It's something entirely different, entirely new."

When she didn't respond, he moved to the settee and sank into it heavily. "I'll stay here until you've finished reading, whether that's tonight or any other time you need. I won't leave you alone with this pain."

Elisha looked at him through her tears, seeing the exhaustion and anguish etched in every line of his face. "What are you saying?"

"I'm saying I've lived without you for months, and it nearly destroyed me. I won't walk away again, not when you're hurting, not when there's still hope that you might understand." His voice was tender but resolute. "I'll sleep here, I'll wait as long as it takes for you to see that you're not competing with anyone. You're not second choice or a consolation prize. You're everything, Elisha."

The tenderness in his voice, the way he spoke her name, began to crack the protective walls around her heart. After a long moment, she nodded slowly, too emotionally spent to argue.

"I'll get you a blanket," she whispered.

She moved toward the stairs to her room above the office on unsteady legs, feeling as though her heart had been turned inside out. Behind her, she heard Edgar settling into the furniture with a soft sigh that spoke of months of exhaustion finally catching up with him.

ELISHA APPROACHED THE book with trembling hands, her heart hammering against her ribs. Part of her was terrified to read his words—what if they confirmed her worst fears? What if she discovered that their love wasn't enough to overcome what she might find within these pages? The possibility that she might close this book unable to accept him, unable to move past the shadow of his perfect love for Lucia, made her stomach clench with dread.

She opened to the first page with trepidation, her breathing shallow as she began to read. But as the night wore on, her initial terror began to give way to wonder. Edgar wrote of Lucia with reverence and fondness, acknowledging the profound impact she had made on his life. But when he wrote about Elisha, something entirely different emerged—not an echo of old love, but something blazing and new and transformative.

"She came into my life like dawn after the longest night, illuminating my very soul with her radiance. But this is not the gentle restoration of what was lost—this is rebirth. Where I once believed my heart would remain forever shrouded in darkness, she revealed that true love doesn't merely heal old wounds. It creates something magnificent and unprecedented from the ashes of what came before."

Her hands shook as she continued reading.

"What I felt for Alice was the tender love of youth— beautiful and pure but incomplete, like a song half-written. What I feel for Clara is the symphony of a man's full heart— complex, layered, deeper than I ever imagined possible. She doesn't fill the space Alice left behind because she occupies an entirely different realm of my soul, one that didn't exist until she created it simply by being herself."

Her heart thundered against her ribs as she recognized herself in his words, not as a replacement for Lucia, but as something entirely new and profound. She pressed her palm to her mouth to stifle the sob of joy threatening to escape.

As dawn approached, she reached the final page. There, in Edgar's elegant handwriting, was a personal inscription:

"Elisha, my love, my heart's true north. You are my guiding star, my transformation, my everything. I love you not despite my history, but because you've made me capable of a love I never knew existed."

The words blurred through her tears as months of doubt and fear dissolved like morning mist.

She understood now.

Dabbing her eyes with her handkerchief, Elisha crept quietly down the stairs to the office. There he lay sleeping, his long frame draped awkwardly across the small settee, one hand still reaching toward where she had been sitting.

Moving with infinite care, she settled herself beside him, curling against his chest and pulling the blanket over both of them. The steady rhythm of his heartbeat beneath her ear felt like coming home after a long journey through darkness.

Edgar stirred at her touch, lifting his head in momentary confusion. When he realized it was Elisha in his arms, she felt his sharp intake of breath, felt the moment when desperate hope bloomed in his chest.

"Did you read it?" he whispered against her hair, his voice thick with sleep and emotion.

"Every word," she murmured against his chest.

His arms tightened around her as though he feared she may fly away from him. "Then you know," he whispered into her hair.

"I know," she whispered, and for the first time in months, she truly did.

They lay together in the growing light of dawn, listening to their hearts beat in perfect synchronization, each pulse a testament to a love that had survived doubt, fear, and separation to emerge stronger and more certain than before.

EPILOGUE

ON A RESPLENDENT July morning, the grand cathedral of St. Paul's stood adorned with cascades of white roses, delicate baby's breath, and sprigs of lavender. The air was thick with anticipation as London's elite, literary luminaries, and cherished friends gathered to witness the union of Edgar, the Duke of Lancaster, and Miss Elisha von Linde.

As the first notes of Handel's *Arrival of the Queen of Sheba* filled the vast nave, the assembled guests turned to behold the bride. Elisha, a vision in ivory silk and Honiton lace, glided down the aisle on the arm of Mr. Charles Dickens, her mentor and friend. Her gown, a masterpiece of elegance, boasted a fitted bodice adorned with seed pearls and a voluminous skirt that whispered against the marble floor. Atop her carefully coiffed locks sat a delicate tiara, from which cascaded a gossamer veil.

At the altar, Edgar stood tall and regal in his formal attire, his eyes never leaving Elisha as she approached. Beside him, the Marquess of Hereford, his best man, smiled broadly, his own joy evident. To the side, Amelia Carlisle, resplendent in lavender silk as maid of honor, held Elisha's bouquet and beamed with tears of joy for her dearest friend.

The front pews were a gathering of notables. Edgar's family sat proudly, his mother dabbing at her eyes with a lace handkerchief. Amelia Thornton, who had risked her own position and defied her brother's wishes to support Elisha's happiness, beamed at her dearest friend. Nearby, Charlotte sat with the Earl of Carlisle and Patrick Adams, her face aglow with happiness.

Among the guests, one could spot the crème de la crème of London's literary circle. William Wordsworth and Lord Tennyson engaged in whispered commentary. Elizabeth Gaskell and the Brontë sisters added their own air of romantic sensibility to the proceedings.

Near the back of the cathedral, Steven Thornton stood quietly, his bearing markedly different from the desperate man who had tried to destroy them mere months before. When Edgar had approached him about the railway investment, Thornton had initially been suspicious, but the duke's straightforward business proposition had gradually dissolved his skepticism. Now, watching Elisha approach Edgar, Thornton's countenance betrayed something resembling resignation and serenity.

As Elisha reached the altar, Edgar took her hand, his touch gentle yet sure. The Archbishop of Canterbury began the ceremony, his sonorous voice echoing through the cathedral.

"Dearly beloved, we are gathered here in the sight of God and this congregation, to join together this man and this woman in holy matrimony…"

The vows were exchanged with clear voices and unwavering gazes. Edgar's deep baritone resonated with emotion as he pledged his life and love to Elisha. In turn, her melodious tones carried to the farthest reaches of the cathedral as she promised herself to him.

As the newlyweds turned to face their guests, a figure near the side caught Elisha's eye. Jonathan Rochford, the boy whose life had been changed by their literary contest, stood tall and proud in a fine new suit, his transformation from street orphan to promising young scholar evident in his confident bearing.

The Archbishop's voice rose in proclamation: "I now pronounce you man and wife. Your Grace, you may kiss your bride."

As Edgar drew Elisha into a tender embrace, the cathedral erupted in joyous applause. The peals of bells rang out across

London, heralding not just a union of two hearts, but the dawn of a new era—one where love could bridge the divide between classes and literature had the power to transform lives.

"To which estate are we headed?" Elisha asked once their carriage pulled away from the church.

"Patience, my dear wife," Edgar said, his voice warm with amusement.

"I'm not getting any younger," she complained playfully.

Edgar pulled his bride close to his side, pressing a tender kiss below her ear. "You look as beautiful as a summer garden in full bloom."

"Such poetry from my literary husband," she teased, settling into his embrace.

As the carriage drew to a halt before the bustling train station, Edgar's eyes twinkled with anticipation. He stepped out first, then turned to extend his hand to Elisha with a gentlemanly flourish.

"My dear wife," he said, his voice low and warm, "allow me to assist you."

Elisha placed her gloved hand in his, her brow furrowing in curiosity. As she alighted from the carriage, her gaze swept across the station, taking in the steam and clamor of the railway platform.

"Edgar," she whispered, surprise evident in her voice, "I had thought we were bound for your country estate. What brings us to the railway?"

Edgar's lips curved into a mysterious smile as he offered her his arm. "All shall be revealed presently, my love."

He guided her through the throng of travelers, past the usual passenger cars and toward a gleaming private carriage at the rear of the train. As they approached, a liveried attendant bowed deeply and opened the door.

Elisha's eyes widened as she stepped inside. The interior was a marvel of luxury—rich mahogany paneling and plush velvet upholstery created an elegant sitting room, while beyond, she caught a glimpse of a beautifully appointed sleeping chamber.

"Edgar," she gasped, turning to him in wonder, "what is this?"

He chuckled softly, helping her remove her traveling cloak. "This, my sweet, is our conveyance to the country estate. A more expeditious and comfortable mode of travel than a lengthy carriage ride."

As they settled into the sumptuous armchairs, the locomotive released a gentle hiss and the train began to move. Edgar leaned forward, his eyes bright with satisfaction.

"You see, this railway line is a joint venture between myself, Carlisle, Hereford, and our former adversary, Steven Thornton."

"Steven Thornton?" She looked at him in astonishment.

"Indeed. After our New Year's Eve revelations, I approached him about this investment. Personal feelings aside, I respected his business acumen and knew he possessed both the funds and connections we needed."

"But Edgar, that man tried to ruin you, risked your life for his own selfish purposes."

Edgar reached for her hand, his expression thoughtful. "I would rather have our former enemy as a close ally than a distant threat. Besides, I cannot entirely blame him for his temporary madness—I, too, might have acted desperately if I thought I was losing you forever."

"That's hardly the same thing."

"Perhaps not, but he has proven himself an excellent partner thus far. His connections from his time in India, combined with the earl's influence and my own resources, have created opportunities we never imagined possible." Edgar's voice carried genuine respect. "Steven has established a legitimate distribution company using the railways, and his strategic mind has been invaluable."

Elisha's quick intelligence grasped the implications immediately. "The pamphlets," she whispered, understanding dawning in her eyes. "This is how you've been distributing them so effectively."

Edgar nodded, bringing her hand to his lips for a gentle kiss. "Among other enterprises, yes. Steven's business provides perfect cover for discreet communications, and the railway's telegraph system allows for coordination across great distances."

"My brilliant husband," she said softly, leaning in to place a tender kiss on his cheek. "You've managed to turn an enemy into an asset."

"Sometimes the best partnerships are forged from former conflicts," Edgar replied, drawing her closer. "Steven understands the value of what we've built together, and he's chosen to be part of something larger than his own ambitions."

"Even literary criticism?" she teased, tilting her head to look at him.

"Especially literary criticism," he confirmed with mock solemnity. "Though I reserve the right to thoroughly debate any negative reviews of your work."

"And I reserve the right to challenge any critic who dares impugn your prose."

Their laughter mingled in the gentle darkness as the train continued its journey through the night. As evening painted the sky in shades of rose and gold, Edgar led Elisha to the sleeping chamber. There, in the privacy of their mobile sanctuary, they came together not with desperate passion but with the deep, abiding love of two souls who had found their perfect match.

Later, as Elisha lay nestled against Edgar's chest, she traced lazy patterns on his skin while he played with the golden strands of her hair.

"Do you ever regret the deception?" she asked softly. "The months we lost to misunderstanding?"

Edgar was quiet for a moment, considering. "I regret the pain it caused you—caused us both. But I cannot regret the journey that brought us here. Every trial, every doubt, every moment of anguish led us to this perfect understanding. We know now that our love can survive anything."

In the distance, church bells chimed midnight, marking not just the end of their wedding day but the beginning of their shared mission. As sleep finally claimed them, Edgar and Elisha dreamed of the stories yet to be written, the minds yet to be changed, and the love that would sustain them through whatever challenges lay ahead.

Their greatest adventure was just beginning.

The End

Thank you for reading. Please consider leaving a review on Amazon and Goodreads.

Please follow me on www.dragonbladepublishing.com/team/ mihwa-lee for my Dragonblade Publishing releases.

For updates, promos, and ARC opportunities, please sign up for my newsletter at www.mihwawrites.com

Join Mihwa's Den of TMI on FB for fun discussions, prizes, and ARC: www.facebook.com/groups/2110002726016346

About the Author

Mihwa Lee is NOT a New York Times, USA Today, or Amazon Best Selling Author. But what she is not, she makes up for with her sense of humour, unusual life experiences, and imagination. The combination of these qualities can yield entertaining stories and parties. As a result, she is a sought-after guest at all parties and karaoke except those that have banned her.

Mihwa became a writer after retiring as a medical expert witness in brain injury (like Law & Order but boring) because she hates disposable income and thought it would be fun to piss off her teenagers. She has bookmarked her favourite steamy scenes in her books for her children in case they need her advice once she's gone. Her children are mortified but tolerate her legacy because of the potential for a passive income.

Mihwa is passionate about equalising the world population through education. She has set up a scholarship in Costa Rica (where she used to live) to send underprivileged Latin American youths to university and/or fund their entrepreneurial ventures.

Mihwa believes in living life to the fullest. Therefore, she writes steamy historical romance like a woman possessed.

linktr.ee/mihwawrites
FB reader group: Mihwa's Den of TMI
TikTok: @mihwa.lee
IG: mihwawrites
YouTube: @DesireDialogue

www.ingramcontent.com/pod-product-compliance
Lightning Source LLC
Chambersburg PA
CBHW062113290726
48975CB00001B/213